M000196076

Sydney's Passion

Sandy
Thank You for
your support!
Susie Wright

SUSIE WRIGHT

Copyright © 2022 Susie Wright
All rights reserved
First Edition

Fulton Books
Meadville, PA

Published by Fulton Books 2022

ISBN 978-1-63985-341-0 (paperback)
ISBN 978-1-63985-503-2 (hardcover)
ISBN 978-1-63985-342-7 (digital)

Printed in the United States of America

Contents

CHAPTER 1

Race Day

"Ladies and gentlemen, this is your announcer, Hudson Hammond! I would like to personally welcome everyone to Keeneland Racetrack on this gorgeous Saturday afternoon! But not nearly as gorgeous as many of our equines that are in house today! Many of you have traveled from across the world to get a look at these fine equines, and with all the new faces I see, many of you may not know that we have our very own auction house on-site. So please be sure to stop by the auction house to see if we may have any new additions for your ranch or farm," Hudson states in an eager but deep voice. "We have been in the business of equestrians right here in the horse capital of the world, Lexington, Kentucky, since the mid-1930s. Only the best of the best look to race here!"

"Today we have a special for all you beautiful ladies out there in the audience with those amazing bonnets. Do you think you have what it takes to win a contest for the most creative? Most formal? Most beautiful? Or best takes the show? Well, then, don't forget to sign up! Head to the registration booth just behind the stands, but hurry before it's too late!" Hudson proudly reports as he takes a sip of water, then adds, "Judging starts just after the race finishes, at the same location."

"And now, the moment you have *all* been waiting for, would you please stand as we prepare for our national anthem? Today it will be sung by none other than local artist Sophie Abbott!" exclaims Hudson. "Sophie is from our very own local Lexington High School.

She wants to be a singer-songwriter and has been taking summer classes to prepare for when she graduates. We have invited her here today to grace us with her beautiful voice."

Everyone stands with all eyes on Sophie as she stands next to the flag so beautifully in her long flowing floral-print dress. She is of average height, but by the way she carries herself, you would never know. I am also sure her four-inch heels help, too, just a little. She has beautiful shoulder-length auburn hair that she tries to curl the front and sides of, to break up the straightness. She is always very ladylike. She is a great singer, which shows when she flawlessly sings the national anthem. When she finishes, she takes a bow, the crowd clapping and whistling as she does.

Now, Sophie is my bestie, which in adult language is *best friend*. We have been friends for as long as I can remember. We do almost everything together. She is my rock. We are like the yin and yang, Bonnie and Clyde. She's the PB to my jelly. I would most definitely be lost without her.

We hear Hudson, the announcer, as he asks the riders to take their places at the gates. "Today we have in our lineup the following, from gate 1 through to gate 8: Dawn of the Ages, a three-year-old standardbred; Vanilla Sky, a three-year-old quarter horse; Dusty Daze, a three-year-old Thoroughbred; Red Petunia, a four-year-old Morgan; Speed of Lightning, a four-year-old Thoroughbred; Moon and Stars Collide, a three-year-old Arabian; Everybody's Dream, a four-year-old American paint; and last but not the least, Sands of Tyme, a two-year-old Araloosa who, we would like to mention, has been taking our wonderful track by storm! Not only is she and her rider, Chase Payne, stealing hearts and capturing the eyes of all who watch, but they are racking up quite a collection of trophies as well! They are the fresh, new team to watch at the track this season and the youngest duo here yet, with Chase at fourteen. They are the power team to beat!"

He continues, "They are ready to start today's race. Get ready, riders…get set…" You hear the gun go off with a *bang* as he finishes, "Go! They are off and givin' it all they got!

"Sands of Tyme starts off in the back as they all huddle to push for the front. Everybody's Dream has the lead, with Red Petunia right behind. Vanilla Sky is in third, with Dawn of the Ages holdin' in fourth. Look out, folks, today is proving no different for Chase! Here he comes on Sands of Tyme, making their way through the ranks, and is keeping the lead with Dusty Daze, Moon and Stars Collide. And Everybody's Dream has slipped back but is hot on their tails! Dawn of the Ages moves to third, with Red Petunia slippin' farther back the pack. Vanilla Sky is neck and neck and making moves for the front. Sands of Tyme is slowly pulling away and leaving her counterparts in the dust. Here they come around the last corner, Sands of Tyme, Dusty Daze, Everybody's Dream, followed by Moon and Stars Collide, Red Petunia, Vanilla Sky, Speed of Lightning, and Dawn of the Ages! It's gonna be a close one, folks, as they start to close in on the finish line!" Hudson quickly states, trying to keep up with the pace of the horses. "There ya have it, folks. Sands of Tyme and Chase Payne have pulled it off again!" Hudson proclaims as the crowd cheers loudly.

"Yes, they did it!" Hudson shouts out with glee. "They have taken yet another race this season, with this as his fourth win within his first six races! They are definitely the team to beat, just to watch and follow to see how far they can go."

"Yes! We did it, Sands of Tyme! Great job, girl!" Chase says to her as he rubs her neck. He sits up high and straight and waves to the crowd proudly.

As they make their way to the winner's circle for pictures and the winner's ceremony, Chase sees Mr. Parker Ashcraft coming to congratulate him on another spectacular win. Normally, Chase has to look up to get a glimpse of his smiling face, but from sitting up high on SOT, he can see it plain as day. It doesn't surprise Chase to see Mr. A in his Sunday best at the races, and he has never seen him without his fancy white cowboy hat with black rim strap, matching white cowboy boots, and beautiful pastel suits, which today is light blue, with a sharp black leather belt.

"Congratulations, Chase! You are an amazing young rider. You keep this up, boy, and I may just have to adopt you!" Mr. A proudly states. "Not sure how my little filly, Sydney, would take it, but she loves to ride as well. I wish I could get her here to see SOT race. After all, she has trained and raised her from a filly. They have nothing but pure love and respect for each other. It surprises me that SOT takes to you so well, Chase," explains Parker. "*SOT* is what we call Sands of Thyme for short."

"Thanks, Mr. A! I'm sure your daughter Sydney and I would get along well," Chase replies. After photos, they move to the stables to prepare for the ride back to the Ashcraft ranch.

It's a short trip to the ranch, and once they arrive, Chase gets out, unloads SOT, and walks her to the stables. Mr. Ashcraft meets him in the stables, where he brushes SOT and says his farewell to her till their next race.

"Here's your part of the winnings for today. You did good out there, Chase. Keep up the great work." As he starts to walk away, he continues to speak, stopping for a moment to turn to Chase. "Chase, you have a way with horses. Just where do you get your experience from? Do you live on a farm?"

"Mr. A, you can kinda say I live on a farm. I've grown up with horses all my life. We have a farm in our family too, but you see, my family wouldn't allow me to ride because they say it's too dangerous. But it's in my heart. It's in my blood. I just feel I can't breathe without horses as part of me," he stated with a slight tear in his eye.

"Okay, son, sounds good. You are welcome here anytime to ride for practice if you would like to. Now, I must go see if I can find my little filly. If she would ever be home, maybe I could introduce the two of you!" he replies.

"Sure thing, Mr. A. See you! And thanks for the nonworking invite. I'm headed home."

As Mr. A rounds the corner, Chase takes his winnings, puts them in his pocket, and heads out on his bike. Chase stays at a cottage that isn't far from the Ashcraft ranch by car, but on his bike, it only takes a few more minutes.

Chase arrives at his cottage and parks his bike on the front porch. He stays in the cottage that he has made his home since his grandad passed away and left it for him. Chase will always cherish it. How he wishes his grandad were still here. This tiny cottage sits tucked away in the pines by an amazing lake. This lake is well stocked with all kinds of cool fish, from small to large, and has some of the best fishing in the area for that very reason. Not far from the cottage's back door is a bench by the lake that his grandad had designed and carved himself and put there for them to fish from. It was always their go-to spot to sit and fish this secluded slice of heaven, drink a pop, and talk about life.

This lake isn't known by anyone but the family, so it has an untouched beauty that any wilderness lover can appreciate. It is as close as Chase can get the ocean for now. Till then, this cottage has all the amenities that one could need. When you walk in the front of the cottage, it is all open. There's a beautiful stone fireplace to the left, with a small couch in front and a big furry rug. His grandad used to always pick on him, saying it was a bearskin rug. The kitchen is to the right, with a few cupboards, a sink, and a minifridge. There's a hot plate on the counter. As you go toward the back of the cottage, there's a small bedroom to the left, with a small bathroom just across the hall. When he is here, he feels so in touch with his grandad. It's been a good, long day, and as he prepares for bed and thinks back on the race today, he takes his winnings from his pocket. Today has landed him about $5,000.

To most teens his age, this is a dream, but for Chase, it's a new beginning. As he puts his winnings in the lockbox and places it back under the bed, he thinks about a future dream of a cottage with a beach front property. It's been a dream for as long as he can remember, just to stroll on the beach, feel the sand beneath his toes and feel the waves on his feet, and collect shells. Chase thinks about the calming sound of the waves and knows that it's the waves and God's beauty that have his heart dreaming of the day. Either way, he has great memories here of his grandad and him by the lake till then. As he settles down to sleep, he almost instantly drifts off.

CHAPTER 2

At the Lake

As I walk in the door, I hear my dad yell from the kitchen, "Is that my little filly?"

I state back, sternly, "Dad! Please stop calling me that! I'm not a little girl anymore!" I say this with a huff and a sigh.

"How was your stay with Sophie?" he asks. "Did you get all your studies done up for your big final?"

I snap quickly, "Umm, yeah, sure. I guess I'm ready."

He stares at me for a minute and then states, "Grab some breakfast, would you? And have a seat with me. I have something I wanna discuss with you."

I roll my eyes and reply, "Dad, I'm not hungry. I just wanna go out with SOT!"

He quickly and happily responds with, "That's what I wanted to talk to you about," as he rubs his chin and looks down at his food for a second. He looks back up at me and prepares to explain what is so important. "So I'm not sure if you remember that we were looking for a jockey for SOT or not."

He looks at me with a smile, and I shrug my shoulders. "I guess so. But what's that have to do with me?" I ask with an attitude, like I do not even care.

"Well," he says, "you have raised SOT from birth, and you have a way with her like no other. And I really wanted you to meet her new rider, Chase Payne." Then he asks, "Do you know Chase? Is he from your school?"

"Dad, I do not recognize the name. And I'm sure we will meet up eventually," I say with a slight attitude. "Can I go now, please?" I ask. "I would really like to go see SOT!"

He looks at me and states unwillingly, "Okay, but I still want to talk to you about meeting Chase!" He practically shouts the last part at me as I walk away.

I mumble under my breath, hoping he can't hear me, "Not if I can help it."

He hollers back at me, asking, "What was that, honey?"

I reply, "I love you, Dad!" roll my eyes, and keep walking briskly so he can't try to stop me yet again.

I hear him, though faintly now, yelling back, "I love you too, my little filly!"

I shout out loud, "Dad!"

As I make my way to the barn, I spot Oliver Beavin, a.k.a. Obee. He's always wearing his blue jean bib overalls with his worn Dallas ball cap. He is our ranch hand. I walk over to him and say, "Hey, Obee, what's up?" As I jump and reach up for a high five. I feel like such a runt 'cause everyone is all so much taller than me, from my dad to Obee, to Emma, except my bestie, Sophie. She's on the short side like me.

"Not much," he states. "How's everything with you? Did you enjoy your time with Sophie?" he asks.

I wink at him and smile. "It was okay. I missed SOT, though. Have you been taking good care of her in my absence?" I ask.

"Well, if you were ever home lately, maybe *you* could take care of her," he remarks jokingly.

"All I hear is blah, blah, blah," I say back to him while laughing. "So did you meet Chase?" I then ask Obee.

"I did. He seems like a nice kid. He stole another race yesterday. Man, you better be careful. He's bonding with SOT, and you don't wanna lose your bond with her," he says while shaking his finger at me as if to scold me.

"Nah! No worries. It *will* never happen," I say with confidence.

"Care to place a bet?" Obee asks.

I am all over *his* confidence. "Aww, come on now, Obee, you know better than to ask me to bet with you!" I say, laughing. "I would hate for you to lose to me yet again, because I can guarantee you this time you are wrong!" I add with attitude and arrogance.

Obee chuckles as he makes his way to the barn to clean the stalls. I follow right behind him on my way to see SOT. "Good mornin', SOT! How are you, beautiful?" I ask her. I grab a brush and start brushing her. "Obee?"

"Yes, Syd."

"Do you think there is a heaven?" I suddenly ask.

"Most definitely, Syd! Now, what it looks like, I can only imagine."

"Where do you think Grandad is?" I ask softly.

"You know he's in heaven. Why? Is he on your mind again?" he asks as he stops mucking the stalls and comes closer to me to be within a good earshot from me.

"Yeah, you know he's always on my mind. I miss him so much. Some days it just hurts so bad, though, Obee. I always wonder if he's proud of me. If he is watching down on me every day," I say as tears form in my eyes, and I hang my head. I reach around SOT's neck, giving her a pat and a hug. "I love you, girl!" I kiss her neck and turn to look at Obee. "Hey, Obee?"

"Yeah, Syd."

"Do you think I'll ever see Grandad again?" I ask, hoping for some positive feedback.

"Why, sure, Syd! I can guarantee you will get to see him again someday. And I can definitely promise you that he watches over you every day. He was always so very proud of you!" he replies, grinning from ear to ear. "Ya know, Syd, I was out here in the barn the other day, and I found something I know your grandad would want you to have." Obee walks down to the last stall on the left. That was Grandad's stall. He had a small oak desk in there that he always came out to sit at when a trip to the lake was too far or the weather was too bad to go too far from the house. He had a special drawer in the bottom just for me, full of candy. Usually, there would be Neapolitans, Root Beer Barrels, Peanut Chews, plus many more.

Oh, how I remember the days of sitting out here in the barn with Grandad, listening to his stories of all the exciting things happening on the farm and from when he was a kid. He even told me one day I would own this estate.

Obee snaps his fingers and says, "Syd, come here. See what I found?"

"Coming, Obee. Whatcha got?" I ask excitedly.

He picks up something a little bit bigger than a jewelry box. "Go ahead and open it, Syd," he says as he hands the little box to me.

"Oh, Obee, I can't wait to see what it is!" I exclaim as I take the ribbon and bow off the box to open it. "Oh, Obee! Really?" I ask, my eyes filling up with tears. "This was Grandad's pocket watch. He had a pic of his favorite horse, Black Boots the Appaloosa, carved on the front when he was just a colt!" I say lovingly.

"Syd, look inside," Obee quietly adds.

So I open it, only to see that Grandad had it engraved on the back side of the lid:

Syd the Kid
Dream big
Ride hard
Love, Grandad

"Obee, thank you for finding this and seeing that I got it!" I say as I reach out to Obee for a hug.

"Ah, come here, kid. Give ole Obee a hug!" He grabs me securely, and we hug and sob together.

"Hey, Obee, you know what would make this even better?" I say, full of enthusiasm.

"What's that, Syd?" he asks back, laughing.

"If I help you when we get back, do you think we could ride out to the lake and do a little fishing, just you and me? Like Grandad would do with me?" I ask as I dance around. "Please, please, please, Obee? It would make my day so complete!"

"Oh, okay, but how about we clean these three stalls first so when we get back, then we only have those four to do today?" he asks in a let's-get-it-done kinda way.

"Oh…okay, Obee, I guess so," I say, feeling bummed, hanging my head.

Obee directs me to get the push cart while he starts piling up the straw and bedding from the stalls. Once we get the stalls cleaned, I grab SOT and her saddle, while Obee grabs PB Cup and her saddle. We saddle them up and grab some poles and the tackle bag.

"Obee, do we have anything in the barn fridge for snacks that we can take with us?"

"I think there may be some water and some sammiches." Obee has a way with words when he's in a goofy mood.

"Okay, I'll grab them, Obee. I am so excited! This is the perfect way to end this perfect day!" I shout as we mount the girls and head for the lake.

My family owns this estate and has for many generations. It was my grandad Jack Jones's grandad's. So that would be my great-great-grandad Sawyer Payne. It's a twenty-acre horse farm estate. We have a barn with seven occupied stalls, three of which house top-trophy, prize equines, Black Boots, PB Cup, and Tall Leaps.

When I was just about ten, Grandad asked me to pick which stallion I wanted to be my dad horse and which mare I wanted to be my mom horse, and I wanted Black Boots and PB Cup to make my beautiful ride, SOT. They tried for a few years, till *finally* SOT was born. SOT is mostly white, with caramel brown spots on mostly the body, but black spots on the legs only. She has an old, antique-gray-colored mane and tail.

Of course, I chose Black Boots the Appaloosa 'cause he was my grandad's. Black Boots is mostly white, with black spots all over, knee-high black boots on every leg, and the most gorgeous black tail and mane. I chose PB Cup the Arabian 'cause she was my mom's. PB Cup is a beautiful caramel brown, with creamy white tail and mane.

We have a lake that sits on about three-and-a-half acres, and it is tucked away in the pines, with a little cottage with clapboard siding. There's a special bench that grandad hand-made outta two strong old pines that were knocked over in a storm. He sawed the tops of the stumps that were left so they had just a slight trough in them. Then he took the tree and cut out a nice long piece to cut it in half for the seat. He laid it on top of the stumps, and he drilled holes down through the seat and stumps to secure them together with big wooden spikes that he hammered in. He then cut more of the tree to make two nice posts for the base of the hitching post. He dug holes to stick them in and packed the remaining hole with stones and dirt. He then finished off the tops just as he did the bench—only he left the top piece whole. Grandad didn't like to waste things. He cut up the rest of the trees for firewood.

This was where Grandad and I would hide away so we could sit and fish to our hearts' content. We would even hook up Black Boots with one of the carriage carts and ride together to the lake, or sometimes we would even just saddle up a pair of horses and ride up, just like Obee and I are doing, but of course, Grandad would wanna race to see who could get there first. And of course, I would *always* win. Sometimes I thought he was just letting me win.

I break from my thoughts to ask, "Obee?"

He responds, "Yeah, what's on your mind?"

"Oh, nutin'," I reply.

"Come on, Syd. I know better. What's got your mind lost and not here riding with us?" he asks, as if he already knows what I wanna say but just can't find the heart to say.

"Oh, I was just thinking again. You know how I am. My mind never shuts off. That little monkey up there is doing some overtime lately," I reply.

With sincerity, he says, "Well, I am here for you if you ever need anything. I made a promise to your grandad that I would be there for you with no judgment. Just a calm and peaceful place for you to vent about anything. And it'll stay right here between us. Don't you forget that! I will be here whenever you are ready to chat," he remarks.

"Thanks, Obee!" I say, smiling.

Suddenly, just ahead, in a small clearing, I shout with excitement, "Look, Obee! Look up ahead!"

"Yes, I see we are almost there," he states. We see the bench by the hitching post. We hitch the girls and prepare to fish from Grandad's bench. "Syd, do you mind if I take a look around the cottage? It's been a while since I've had the opportunity to come out here. I just wanted to check how it's holding up out here all alone in Mother Nature," says Obee as he heads for the cottage.

"Sure, Obee, but don't be too long. I wanna do a little fishing before we have to head back to finish up the stalls," I say, hoping that he doesn't hear me.

This has always been my happy place; such great memories exist here in this little corner of paradise on this estate. It's the closest I can get to the beachfront property I am dreaming of.

Obee isn't gone long before he comes back and grabs a pole and casts it way out into the lake. He mentions that the cottage looks as though someone's been there recently. I just shrug it off and keep fishing. All of a sudden, I get a hit that feels like a fifty-pound fish has taken my bait on a journey across the lake.

"Obee, Obee, I got something! Something big!" I scream as we both jump up off the bench and reel and wait. Reel and wait. Just waiting for the fish to tire out and give up so we can land it.

"Syd, I hope you have your phone. This is gonna be one we are gonna need pics for proof we caught it!" Obee shouts while trying to help me reel in this gigantic lake fish. *Finally* we land it! It's an eighteen-pound, forty-inch muskie.

"Here, Obee!" I scream happily as I toss him my phone. "Quick, get a pic!" I say as the fish squirms around.

"Sure thing, Syd," he replies as he opens my phone and clicks a picture just in time, literally right before it jumps off the hook. "Oh boy! Just in time!" says Obee as he hands me back my phone.

"Okay, Obee," I reluctantly reply, "a promise is a promise. Let's gather up our goodies and head back. Don't want Dad upset with you 'cause I had to run off for my own adventures again." I say this sadly, faking a smile.

Obee smiles back at me and winks while we clean up and prepare for our ride back to the barn. Our ride is a quiet one, but it's okay. Obee has been on the farm for as long as I can remember. He's basically family. He was Grandad's right-hand man, and now my dad's.

He looks over at me and whistles to get my attention. I look his way and smile. He puts up his fist, looking for a bump. So I bump him back.

By now we are back at the barn, stalls are cleaned, horses are fed, and we are headed in for dinner. Obee has a room on the estate with not much in the way of a kitchen, so most nights he eats with us.

Emma Howard is the lady of our house. She is an older lady who absolutely loves taking care of us and caring for our home. She takes pride in everything she does. She has beautiful brown hair with highlights of gray. She always has it up in a big bun. Mom always said she has to have some really long hair for that big of a bun. She *always* has an apron over her dresses. She must have one for every day of the week, 'cause she always has a different one on.

She does all the caretaking for our Victorian mansion. She has again filled our home with amazing smells of dinner. Tonight smells like adobo chicken, roasted garlic potatoes, and peas. Yum, my favorite! After dinner, I go wash up. Obee goes to his room. Before I go to sleep, I get down on my knees, just like Grandad taught me, and say a prayer to God:

> Dear God, Obee says Grandad Jones is up there with you. Can you please keep him company till I can see him again? And please thank him for his pocket watch. I will always carry it with me. Thank you, God, for my wonderful time at the lake today. Love, Sydney.

Grandad always told me to say my prayers 'cause God is listening and God is good!

I hop into bed, switch off my light, and drift off to sleep.

CHAPTER 3

Buzz around School

Buzz buzz.

The radio announcer says, "Good morning, Lexington! And what a beautiful morning it is! If you can, it would be a great morning to just get outside and take in some rays! It's a beautiful seventy-six degrees out there, and traffic is calm."

I slam my hand down on the radio to hit Snooze.

Five minutes later, the radio announcer continues, "And in other news, Chase Payne took another trophy this weekend at the Keeneland Raceway! I don't know about you, folks, but I think we have an equine superstar in the making! This young man just came outta nowhere with a mission to prove. And well, so far I think he's spot-on!" The news anchor seems intrigued by Chase.

I lie there smiling and wanting to stay in my soft bed for a little while longer, but I hear Em down at the bottom of my stairs, hollering, "Sydney? You awake? I have breakfast in the kitchen for you. Let's hurry, little lady. I have to stop at the post office on the way to school this morning. Come on, up, up, up, and away, I say!"

"I'm up, Em! Give me a few and I'll be right down!" I say it like something is killing me. I hear her laugh as she walks away.

I pick out my clothes for the day and make my way to the shower for a quick one. I come barreling down the stairs to the kitchen, and Em shouts, "Dear Lord, child, slow down 'fore you break a leg or sumthin' worse!"

"Sorry, Em. I don't wanna be late today! And you have errands to run before I can even get to school," I say to her as if I were mocking her.

"Okay, come on, let's go," she says as she hurries me out the door. So I grab the egg wrap she made for me and out the door I go as she smacks me from behind.

Em is so fun. She can't replace my mom, but she can almost tie for her place. She and my mom were good friends right up to the end. But that's another story for later.

As we pull up to the post office, I see my friend Sophie. I open the window and yell out, "Sophie!" She sees me and runs over to the car.

"Hey, Syd, what's shakin', bestie?"

"Just waiting for Em to come outta the post office."

"So, Syd, do you wanna walk the rest of the way to school?"

I think about it and say, "Sure, but can we wait till Em comes back out? I wanna let her know. And then we can go."

"Ten-four, bestie," she says as she laughs. That means "okay, sure, no problem," but that's just Sophie. She's so crazy and cool. She doesn't let anything or anyone get to her.

"Ah, here she comes!" I say when I see Em headed for the door. I get out of the car and head up to her with Sophie.

"Good morning, Sophie. It's good to see you!" she says as we get closer. She looks at me and starts to speak before we rudely interrupt her.

"Em, we would like to walk the rest of the way to school. Is that okay?"

She gives us a look as she stands there and thinks for a minute before she says, "I don't know, girls. Why don't you let me drive you?"

"Come on, Em, it's beautiful out here today. Can't we just walk? It's not that far," I plead. "Please, please, please?" Sophie and I both say in unison.

"Girls, I just don't know. If your dad finds out that I let you girls walk, Sydney, I would be toast! And I just don't know if I could—"

I cut her off and say quickly, "It's okay, Em. We will be fine. Please, I won't tell Dad. We will head straight there and look both ways, *twice*, before we cross any road!"

She hesitates before she responds with, "Okay, *but* just for today." She points at us, saying the words loud and quickly. "But if your dad finds out, I will deny it and say you ran from me. Girls, you are both so beautiful. Please be careful," she says with sincerity.

"We will, Em. You can even sit here and watch if you want. It's okay with us," I say, reassuring her. And with that, we turn and head up the street to school. We stop at each street crossing, and we even turn back to wave at Em before we look both ways and cross the street.

As we get closer, we find more students on their way and chatting up all about Chase Payne. Sophie looks at me, winks, and nods at me in agreement as I put my finger to my lips to silently motion "Shhh." We keep walking as we head to our first class, world history.

Yuck! History class sucks, but we have been talking in the most recent classes about things that happen, how they affect the future, and the things that we can learn from the past to change the future. It has had my attention, but only because I am all about trying to make a change, get noticed for something amazing, and make some life-changing history. My mom did something for our community that was life-changing, and I want to be like her. Grandad always said, if you want something, you gotta get up and go get it. You can't just sit here on your li'l bum and wait for it to come to you. Lord knows you would be waiting a long time! That's what he would say. Grandad always had a way with words that would really make ya think, and they would make a lot of sense.

So one of our projects is to make a difference in the world, either for ourselves or for our families or for the greater good of humankind, both men and women alike. It hasn't taken me long to pick my choice, and so far, it's catching on. When class is over, we head to our next class, and in the halls all you hear is, "Chase Payne is so awesome!" "Chase Payne, wonder where he's from?" "Does anyone know if Chase goes to school here?"

"Well, if Chase went here, I would want him on my football team! Chase Payne is riding for the Ashcrafts, and speak of the devil, look who we have here, boys." He puts his arm around me, talking like he's from *Lifestyles of the Rich and Famous*. "It's li'l Sydney Ashcraft! Do tell, Syd, what's it like having a new, up-and-coming rider plowing through the ranks with one of your very own horses? Please do tell. Inquiring minds want to know," says Lucas Devinshire, the lead football quarterback.

For most girls, he is a dreamy, tall-dark-and-handsome type, but built fine for a football player. He has the right amount of muscle curves in all the right places. But to me he's an arrogant, selfish know-it-all who *just* has to know everyone's business.

"Well, Lucas, if you must know, why don't you just ask him yourself?" I say as I kick him in the shin and walk away smiling sarcastically at him, with my tongue sticking out.

Sophie comes running up beside me and says surprisingly, "Syd! Wow, where did that come from? And why?"

"Sorry, he had it comin', Sophie. He's lucky that's all he got," I bravely respond. "Sophie, wanna come back to the farm after school? We can take the horses out for a ride and hang out for a while. I can even ask Em if you can stay for dinner?" I ask playfully as I wink and smile at her.

She gets out her phone and starts texting someone on our way to our next class. "Done!" she says, chuckling.

"Okay, let's get this day over with and let the fun begin," I say, skipping to the split in the hall. "Okay, luv. See ya after class for lunch! Miss you, miss me," I say as we part ways.

She calls back at me, "Love and miss you too, babes!"

We get through the rest of the day without any more mishaps. At the end of the day, we meet up in the hall to walk out to the front of the school together. As we are waiting out at the front of the school for Em, I pray she hurries so that we do not have another run-in with Lucas.

As we see her pulling up, we make our way to the curb. "Hello, girls! How was your day?" she asks.

Sophie and I both just look at each other, simultaneously and quickly say, "Good!" and I continue to ask, or rather state, "Em, I hope it's okay I invited Sophie to come hang out and have dinner with us." Before she can say anything, I quickly add, "Also, she has already asked her mom if she could come over to hang out and eat dinner with us."

Sophie chimes in with, "Yes, I did, and she said it was okay and to have fun. She also said she could come pick me up later, or if it's okay with you, she's okay if I spend the night."

"Well, it seems like we are having a special guest for dinner, Sydney," Emma says kindly. "Any special requests for dinner, ladies?" she asks as she looks in the rearview mirror at us.

Sophie and I look at each other, and I say, reassuring her, "Not really, Em. Your food is always the bomb!"

"I was thinking fish or meatloaf…"

She doesn't have to wait long for us to both say, "Fish, please!"

"Fish it is," she repeats.

As we head back to the farm, Sophie and I are filled with joy. Once we arrive, we both jump out of the car and head straight for the barn, with Em yelling behind us, "I'll call for you when dinner is ready!"

Our voices trail off as we say, laughing, "Okay, Em!"

We decide to saddle up SOT and PB Cup to head out to the cottage.

On the way out, we race each other, and I let Sophie win. She cracks off with, "What was that?"

I just look at her with some sass and reply, "What was what?" Then I look at her puzzled, like I don't know what she means, waiting for a response.

"You know what I mean!" she sternly replies. "You clearly let me win!"

I act as though I am letting a little air outta my head with a "Psst" and respond with, "I do not have a clue what you mean," as I start to laugh.

"So do you think they know?"

I look all around us as if someone is listening in and quietly say to her, "They are blinded by the beauty," as we hitch the girls and go inside.

It's not long before Em sends me a text.

Emma
Dinner is ready.

Sydney
We are on our way.

So we go out to mount up as I say, "Okay, you asked for it! You better get ready to eat your words, Sophie." And we race again. This time I give Sophie a run for her money! She holds up almost right beside me. When we get back to the stable, Sophie shows off PB Cup with a little sidestepping before we unsaddle the girls, then she starts boasting, saying, "That's what I mean, girl! Give it all you got! Nice run, Syd!"

"Well, looks like *you* are ready for racin', my luv!" I happily inform her. "I have just the thing for you!" I whisper.

As we head into the house, she quickly and quietly says so only we can hear, "If only girls could race, that would be amazing!"

I giggle and respond with, "Yeah, as if!"

Em hears us enter as we head to the kitchen and politely asks us to wash up. We quickly go to the hall half bath to wash up. Then we get seated to eat.

"Would one of you girls like to say grace?" Emma asks.

"I will, Em." We bow our heads and fold our hands, and I pray:

> Dear Lord, thank you for this amazing food that Ms. Emma has prepared for us this evening. Thank you for her love and affection for our family. May we be blessed with her presence for a long time. Thank you for your miracles and blessings. Amen.

"Well, thank you, Sydney, for the beautiful prayer. Now, let's eat!"

We dig in, and Sophie praises Em for her amazing five-cheese mac-and-cheese dish. "Ms. Emma, you make the *best* mac and cheese this side of the Mississippi!"

Emma blushes and nods. "Thanks, Sophie. I will have to be sure and send some home with you."

Sophie smiles. "Thanks! That would be awesome!"

We finish up and make our way to my room on the third floor. "Syd, you are so lucky to have the top room all to yourself," says Sophie with a little envy.

I roll my eyes and reply, "Eh, it's okay. Dad doesn't bother me as much up here. At least you have a sister to share yours with. You are the lucky one." I look out the window toward the direction of the cottage and think how I miss my mom coming up here to sit and just chat.

"Syd...earth to Syd?" She snaps her fingers to get my attention.

I snap outta it and respond, seemingly lost, "What's with all the snapping?"

"Girl, I don't know where you just were, but damn, girl, can you take me with you next time?" She laughs. "Hey, I have an idea! Let's wait till everyone is asleep and go to the cottage to sleep. You game?"

"Nah, not tonight. It's been a fun, crazy, long day, and I just wanna sleep," I tell her as I lie down and close my eyes.

"Oh, okay, I understand. Sweet dreams, Syd," she says as she cuddles up next to me.

"Night, Sophie."

"Night, Syd."

CHAPTER 4

Dreams What May Come

"Syd? Syd the Kid!"

"Grandad, is that you?" I try to look and feel around for my grandad. "Where are you? I can't see you! It's so foggy!"

"Over here, Syd. Follow my voice."

I start to walk toward Grandad's voice. When the fog clears, I realize we are in the barn, at Grandad's desk. I think to myself, *How did I get out here?*

"Grandad, you look so good! But how...I mean you're...oh, please explain to me what I am seeing!" I scream. "This can't be! You're in heaven and I am on earth, but you are here on earth," I say, so confused. "What's it like in heaven? Is it as beautiful as they say?" I then ask excitedly while patiently waiting for confirmation.

"It is *everything* you can dream of and more. So vibrant and colorful! Everyone is young, happy, and healthy! No pain, no stress, just total happiness." In his calm voice, I hear him say, "But it's okay, Syd. I am here with you now. I was here yesterday, and I will be here tomorrow as well. God spoke to me and said I should pay you a little visit. So here I am!" He has a delightfully huge smile on his face.

"Wait!" I pause for a moment. "God talked to you about me?" I am puzzled and confused. I think, *Wow, God does really listen to our prayers.*

"Yes, Syd. By the way, you are welcome. I had my watch engraved for you when I was sick and knew my time here on earth was shorter. I also knew that one day Obee would find it and see to it that you would get it. You are the very spitting image of your mother," he says so softly, like I remember. He has always had a calming and gentle voice that would make me feel so safe.

"Wait! Grandad, Mom…how is she? Is she with you? I miss her so much, as I do you as well!" I sadly say with tears in my eyes.

"She is here, my child, and she says to tell you she is so proud of you and the amazing courage you possess. She knows you will get what you are looking to achieve. You always do! Way to go getting out there off your bum and making a difference I see! What a creative way to accomplish it!"

"Really, Grandad? You think? You always told me to go get what I want 'cause it won't come to me. I have been given the chance to prove myself. I just pray it will work out and not be a waste of my time!" I say as I hang my head.

"Syd, why so sad, child?"

"It's just…Grandad, I know this is for a real change. I just hate how I have to go about it. I feel downright awful. I feel like I am lying to almost everyone around me."

"Sydney Ashcraft, now, you just need to have faith and be more positive. You *will* get the results you need. You are a trailblazer! Not just on a horse, but in all senses of the word. And sometimes trailblazers aren't always liked by all. But it's brave, amazin' people such as yourself that can make the necessary changes to make the world a better place. And I can bet that God has my back on this one."

"Grandad, you were always so wise. I hope I am as wise as you one day. I love you! Hey, did you see?" I say with excitement "Obee and I went to the cottage and I caught a whoppin' eighteen-pounder!"

"I did, Sydney. As a matter of fact, I was sitting there right next to you on the bench."

I start to tear up as he tells me that he was with me.

"I walk beside you every day. And I cannot say that I am very proud of what you did today."

"But, Grandad, he deserved it!"

"Remember, we do not judge, Syd. We leave that job to God."

"I'm sorry, Grandad. Can you forgive me?" I hang my head and close my eyes. When I look up again, we are in the training ring. "I don't understand, Grandad. Why are we here?"

"I just want to share some memories with you, Syd," he softly says to me. We are standing by the fence when here comes a much smaller version of me walking Black Boots, Grandad's favorite horse.

"Even back then, Syd, you had such a way with the horses. Almost as though you could speak with them. I knew when you picked Black Boots and PB Cup to make your new family that you were taking two amazin', prizewinnin' equines and makin' the one to beat!" He smiles and leans in to whisper in my ear, "You will blow them away with your talent, Syd. Just don't back down, and ride hard!"

"For you, Grandad, I will! I just want to make everyone proud! Then hopefully, I won't feel so guilty of my li'l white lies."

"Everyone will be beyond astonished and extremely proud! It may get rough and tougher, but all you have to remember is, I will be right beside you and God has both our hands in love, strength, courage, and wisdom! As long as you believe you will achieve it!"

"Grandad, I pray every day and my faith is strong. Even though I do not understand why God had to take Mom."

"Well, you see, Syd, God has a plan for each and every one of us. Whether we choose to see it or not. Some live to find our reason for being here on this earth. Some, well…some, it just comes naturally. Others just don't see it till it's almost too late. But at some point we all experience God and his love. It's then what we decide to do with it that makes all the difference in who we are."

"I love you, Grandad!"

"I love you too, Sydney. You are such a gift to the world. They just don't know it yet!"

All of a sudden, it's getting foggy again. "Grandad, what's happening? Are you leaving?"

"No, Syd. I want to go to one more place with you."

When the fog clears, we are at the lake.

"I should have guessed you would want to come here, Grandad."

"Sydney, when I built this bench, I built it for you to have forever to remind you of our times at the lake."

"Grandad, I didn't need a bench to remember our great times here at the cottage. But it sure helps to have a beautiful place to sit."

"I want to do something for you that I didn't get the chance to do before."

"Anything you want, Grandad."

"Syd, I want you to find me a pocketknife. Do you have your treasure chest key?"

"Yes, it's in the cottage, Grandad. I will go get it."

"Wait! What I need for you to do is open your chest and get me my pocketknife I hid there for you."

"Grandad, you hid your mini-Swiss knife in the chest? Where? I haven't seen it."

"It's there, Syd. Look in the bottom. There is a small pull cord. It opens to a small compartment in the bottom. My knife will be in there. Hurry now and go get it."

I turn and go into the cottage, to the chest. I unlock it, pull out the wigs and clothes stored inside. Then I see the pull cord. *How did I not see that before?* I think to myself. I pull open the secret compartment, and sure enough, in the bottom of this velvet-lined box is Grandad's mini-Swiss pocketknife. I have always loved this knife. We would always bring it fishing when we would come out here to the lake. Grandad would let me carry it as long as I promised to be very careful with it. *What's this?* I wonder. *He had his knife engraved too?* It says, "Love, Grandad."

"Aww, you are the best, Grandad!" I say out loud as I close the bottom, put everything back into the chest, and lock it up. I return to the bench to see Grandad sitting on the bench.

"Got it, Grandad! I see you had this engraved too! I will cherish it forever!"

"Now, may I see it for a moment, Syd?" he politely asks.

So I hand it to him, and for a minute I swear that I can honestly feel him touch my hand when he takes the knife from me. But this can't be; this is just a dream, I reason. Ghosts aren't real. I will wake up tomorrow and this will have been one of the best, worst dreams ever. But for now, I do not want to wake up. As long as I am asleep, I am with Grandad, and I would stay like this forever if I could!

He puts the tip to the bench and starts to carve something. I wait patiently for him to finish. When he's done, it reads, "God and Grandad love you forever!"

"Aww, Grandad, that is so beautiful! Now I will never forget it!" I lean in for just a moment to hug him, only to realize he has gone right into thin air. Like he was never there. But on the corner of the bench lies his pocketknife. I pick it up and put it in my pocket.

When I wake up, I realize he's gone and it's morning. The sun is just coming up over the horizon.

"Wow! What a dream! If only it were real. I just wanted to feel his touch, his loving hugs one more time," I say as I try to remember everything in the dream that seemed so realistic. If only there were a way to ensure it was *just* a dream. *Wait!* I think to myself. *His pocketknife—if it were a dream, I wouldn't have it on me!* I put my hand in my pocket, and sure enough, there it is! "No way!" I scream and scare Sophie straight up outta bed.

"Sorry, Sophie, but we have to go get dressed!" I exclaim without trying to wake up the entire house. "Come on, I will tell you all about it on the way!"

"On the way to where?" she asks with a confused look on her face.

So we make our way down the back stairs and out to the barn. We put the bridle on SOT, and we both ride bareback as fast as we can toward the cottage. Along the way, I tell Sophie all about my dream last night and how I was trying to see if what Grandad had carved in the bench is still there.

We arrive at the lake, and we both jump off SOT and I hitch her. Sophie runs ahead of me and shrieks, "Syd! No way!"

When I get to the bench, sure enough as it is daylight, there is Grandad's carving:

God and Grandad love you forever!

I just about pass out. I have to sit and really think about what happened. *How is this possible?* I think to myself. *It's like he was actually here. Did I sleepwalk all the way out here? Impossible! Can't be so.*

Sophie then says, "Syd, what about the chest?"

I think the exact same thing. So we both run to the cottage, right to the chest, and I unlock it. I empty it, and there it is, the cord. Sophie says what I am thinking: "Syd, I do not remember that cord being there before."

I look at her and say, "Me neither! But it's here now, and Grandad said it was always there."

"This chest *is* magical, Syd!" Sophie says with a shocked look on her face.

"Well, we better get back before Em sends a search party out after us. We can figure this out later." So we take SOT and head back to the house.

We sneak in the back stairs and up to my room unnoticed.

"Syd..." She pauses. "What *was* that?" Sophie asks as she holds up her hand in disbelief.

"Yeah, I do not have an idea other than a miracle from above," I say as I think about how awesome it is.

"Girls?"

"Yes, Em! We are up."

"Okay, breakfast is ready!" she shouts up the stairs.

"Okay, we will be down just as soon as we finish getting ready!" We hurry, get ready so as not to raise suspicion, and head downstairs.

As we come into the kitchen, we can smell eggs, bacon, and fresh, homemade blueberry muffins.

"Mmm, Ms. Emma! Breakfast smells amazin'!" Sophie says as she takes in a deep breath.

"Why, thank you, Sophie. It's the most important meal of the day, as Mr. Jones would say. So I am always up before the crack of dawn to prepare for breakfast. Mr. Jones said you can miss any meal of the day except for breakfast and it doesn't matter. But breakfast is a must in this house. So even though he is gone, I still try to keep up the tradition."

"I wish I had breakfast like this at my house. Some mornings I don't eat because I barely have time to even get a bowl of cereal," Sophie says with embarrassment.

"Well, Sophie, any time you stay here, you will have a healthy breakfast to start off your day."

As we finish up, Em asks, "Are you ladies ready for school?"

"Yes, ma'am," we say in unison. We grab our things and head to the car.

On the ride to school, Em asks, "How did you girls sleep?"

Sophie looks at me and gives me a look of "Oh no!" I wrinkle my face up sternly and slightly shake my head no. "We slept well, Em. It was nice havin' Sophie here to share my room with."

As we pull up to the school, Em says, "Have a great day at school, girls! I will be here after for you, Sydney, and if you need a ride, Sophie, I can take you home as well."

We smile as we get out and close the door. "Thanks, Em! Love you!"

CHAPTER 5

Encounter by Coincidence

I text Emma about what I plan on doing after school.

> Sydney
> *Em, could I go to Sophie's after school?*
>
> Emma
> *Is it okay with Sophie's mom?*
>
> Sydney
> *Yes, she said she would see that we get home.*
>
> Emma
> *Okay, just please let me know if and when you
> are headed home.*
>
> Sydney
> *Will do. Thanks, Em.*

"Okay, Sophie, I messaged Em. Can you message your mom?"
I ask.

And Sophie does text Allison, her mom.

> Sophie
> *Mom, could I please go to Syd's after school?
> Ms. Emma said it was okay.*
>
> Allison Abbott
> *Didn't you just spend the night last night,
> Sophie?*

Sophie
*Yes, Ma, I did. But she said it was okay to
stay again?*

Allison Abbott
*Okay, but remember, you have chores here to get
complete, and tomorrow after school, I need you
to babysit your sister.*

Sophie
*Ok, Mom. May Syd come over tomorrow to
help me babysit?*

Allison Abbott
Sure, she may come. Love you, Sophie.

Sophie
Thanks, Mom. I love you too!

"Okay, Syd, Mom is covered. But you gotta come help me babysit Eliza tomorrow," Sophie says as I take out my keys and give her one from my key ring.

"So we don't draw attention, we walk straight there after school. Go down the back alley a li'l bit up from there and I will meet up with you. When you get there, just go straight in the back door. This key will unlock the door. Got it?" I ask her to repeat what I've said to her to make sure she understands my instructions.

"Go straight from school to there, through the back alley, unlock the back door, go in and wait for you! Yes, I got it! See ya after school!" she says with excitement.

"Okay, let's get back to class and I will see you after school at the place!" I say to Sophie as I grab my bag and head out of the lunchroom toward my next class.

"Ten-four, bestie!" Sophie slightly whispers as she softly jabs me on my arm. We split ways and head back to class.

Why does it always seem that when you want something to happen, time drags its feet so bad? I think to myself. *But when you have absolutely nothing to do, it flies like an excited baby pig with new wings!* I watch the clock tick, tick, tick by.

Our days here at our school are different from days at most schools. I'm not sure as to why there is such a difference, but there is. Like with most schools, they have shorter days and go five days a week. We, on the other hand, go four days a week and are in school for a little bit longer each day. Which is one reason I feel our days drag on to begin with. But hey, at least we only have to go for four days, not five, so if it means I get an extra day to do what I want to, then I'm all for it.

I was so glad to see grandad last night. I just can't believe that God found him and told him about my prayer. How cool is that? I mean, of *all* the people in heaven, he found *my* grandad Jack Jones and relayed such an important message? *God, I know you are impressive, but I do not think that many people will ever truly know just how impressive you are. I want to thank you for opening my eyes to the fact that nothing is impossible with God truly in your life. Thank you, God!* I say in my mind to God. And with that, yet another miracle has happened: it's the end of the day! "Yes! Thank you, God, for you are amazing!"

I all but run to my locker to put away the things I don't need in exchange for the ones I do and slam it shut. When I turn to run for the door, I run right into my history teacher, Ms. Julia Dixon. She is beautiful, young, and a new teacher at our school. I'm in love with her gorgeous long blond curls. They look like she has invisible rods keeping them in place. Must take her hours to get ready in the morning. Not like me. I sometimes don't even want to brush my hair, but it looks good for being so short.

My mom had always had me in a short cut, so I just keep it short. I don't like it that way, but it was the way Mom liked it. Not sure why, but I keep it that way in her memory.

"Slow down there, Sydney. Where's the fire, li'l one?" she asks as she puts her arms up as if I were gonna fall and her petite little self would catch me.

"I am so sorry, Ms. Dixon. I'm just excited to have this day over with to go out and enjoy the amazing weather. I didn't mean to practically run you over," I say politely while smiling.

"Well, if you have a few minutes, I wanted to talk to you about your project. I haven't heard or seen anything about what you have goin' on," she says, concerned.

"Oh, Ms. Dixon, I am sorry I haven't turned in anything pertaining to my project, because I want it to have a bigger impact. I was afraid that somewhere someone would catch on to what I was up to and I would not get the chance to make the real difference I am tryin' to get accomplished with the same results. But I can guarantee you that when it's complete, you and everyone will be astonished and completely like, 'Where did that come from?' Oh, I should stop now before I accidentally give too much away! But please be reassured I am workin' on my project very hard and it will be so worth it for the community and the world. And if you don't think so, then you can grade me accordingly," I say with confidence.

"Sydney Ashcraft, I will take your word for it. And I am now so intrigued. I cannot wait to find out with everyone else what your project is. But can you please slow down in the halls so you can live to finish your project?" she asks.

As I turn to walk away, I say back to her, "Yes, Ms. Dixon!"

I head out the school and down the street. I walk about a block, and there I see my mom's beauty shop. We haven't had it open since the accident, but Dad can't let it go either. So I like to come here once every few weeks just to get a few supplies and sit and talk with Mom. I hope she hears me and knows how much I love her. As I get close, I turn to go back to the alley so I can come into the back door, hopefully unnoticed. As I come to the back, I hope that Sophie is already inside. I take out my keys and unlock the door. As I step in, I can smell different scents from shampoos and soaps being trapped inside.

"Sophie, are you here?" I ask quietly.

As I walk around the corner to Mom's old office, there sits Sophie at her desk.

"Hey, that's my seat, bestie," I say like *I'm* the one in charge as I pull up another chair on the other side of the desk for her to sit in.

She gets up to move seats and sits in the one I pulled out for her and, with sass, says, "It's okay, I like this one better, anyways." She and I laugh so hard.

"So did you go look around to find what you need?" I ask her.

"No, not yet. I wanted to wait for you. But I will now!" she says as she bursts off the chair with a smile.

I try to race her to the door of Mom's office and put my arm across the opening. "Wait!" I say. "Let me make sure the blinds are still closed up front. We can't risk gettin' caught in here, or everything will be ruined."

I put my arm down and walk out to where I can see the front of the store. The blinds are closed, so I wave Sophie to come out and look around.

"So take your pick. As you can see, there are plenty to choose from. While you look around, I will get you some other things to complete the look," I say as I let her look around. I quickly grab some other items from the shelves and stuff them in a shopping bag.

"Okay, Syd, I think I have it! What do ya think?" she asks, holding up a black wig.

"I think it's perfect! No one will know. Or at least let's hope," I say as we laugh together. "Okay, I think we are good. Let's get outta here."

Sophie asks, "Did you text Obee?"

"I did. He will meet us at the mini-mart. But we gotta hurry. He will soon be there!" I say in a hurry. We leave out the back and I lock up. We stay in the back alley till we get to the mini-mart. As we near, I see Obee pull up. We quickly get to the farm truck, get in, and he backs out and we leave.

"Hello, girls! How was your day?" Obee asks knowingly.

"Oh, just perfect with your help. I was hoping you would help us out!" I say with a smile from ear to ear.

"Syd, I told you what I told your grandad: I would be there for you. And I am keeping my word. As long as it's not illegal, I will help. Well, I'd probably help then too, *but* only if I knew ahead of time what y'all were up to. This isn't illegal, is it, girls?" he asks as if he is scared to know.

"Nah, it's for a history project *that* we can't tell you about just yet. We promise we will soon. Actually, you will be the first to know aside from us!" I say to reassure him.

"Okay, ladies, I will hold you to that! Here you go, cottage front door drop-off! Do you need me to cover for tonight?"

"Nah, we got it covered. But if you could maybe bring us some dinner, that would be awesome!" I say as we climb out of his truck. "Thanks again, Obee!" We wave and turn to go into the cottage. As he waves, he turns to drive away.

Once inside, we unpack the store bag and lay everything out on the floor. I grab my keys, open the chest, grab some things of mine, and lay them next to hers. I help her to get changed. She chooses a black wig with slight curls at the bottom. We pin up her hair and slip on the wig. With a li'l adjustment, it's a perfect fit. I make sure all her natural auburn hair is hidden. I take a brow brush and carefully darken her eyebrows with some black highlights.

"Okay, top looks great! Now we just need a name," I say, pondering what to call my bestie. Like a switch in my brain, it comes to me. "Aha, I got it! Wyatt Gentry! What do ya think, bestie?"

She thinks about it for a moment, shakes her head, and says, "By gee, ya gave me a cool name! I likes it." She smiles and motions to the rest of her. "So what about these puppies? Got a way to hide 'em?" she asks and laughs as she points to her chest.

"Yeah, I sure do. Take off your shirt and let's get this done!"

She takes off her shirt, and I hand her a chest wrap made of thin plain tee material to put on so she can take off her bra and we can get her wrapped. I get out this thick wide gauze, wrap her tight, and give her a boy's tee to put on. "Now, stand up and come over here to the mirror. I have one more thing for you, and I think you will be complete."

She gets up and comes to the mirror, and I hand her a small box that says *green*. She opens it and says to me, "Syd, green? Wow! I've *always* wanted green eyes. I can't wait to see how they look on me!" She takes them out and tries to put them in.

She looks in the mirror as I say to her, "Welcome., Wyatt Gentry, to the Ashcraft cottage. Now we just need one more thing." I look around the room and spot a cowboy hat in the corner on the coatrack. "Here, try this."

"Eh, I don't know, Syd. Do you have a baseball cap? Maybe that will look better," she states.

"Uh, yeah, sure. Let me look in the chest. Here's one!" I say, smacking it on my hand and handing it to her. "It was my mom's when she would train the horses. She said it made her look more like a man and the horses would respect her more. I would say, 'Nah, it's your personality they are attracted to.' She always denied it," I say, remembering back.

"Okay, I like it," she says. "Now, can we do you? I can't wait to see us done up together!" she squeals.

I grab my wavy red wig and slip it on over my brown hair. Thank God Mom always liked my hair short. I believe it was because she secretly wanted a boy. I mean, why else would she want her beautiful daughter to have such a short hairstyle? One day it will be long. Maybe just after my project I will start to let it grow.

Once I have my wig on, I take my brow brush and put a li'l red highlight in my brows. I take out my light hazel contacts and put them in. I put on my chest wrap and snake off my bra. I don't have quite as much to hide as Sophie 'cause our family doesn't seem to carry the "magic bubble" gene. I grab my thin blue plaid flannel and button it up. "Now that's how it's done! Grab your phone, Sophie," I say as I also grab mine. We stand beside each other in front of the mirror and snap a pic at the same time we hear someone at the door.

I just about drop my phone to run for cover when I hear Obee say, "Dinner for the li'l ladies. Ring-a-ling!"

"Obee!" I shout sternly. "Thanks for the warning!"

"Well, didn't y'all ask for dinner? I'm here to deliver. You are lucky—I thought I was gonna have to forfeit my dinner for you. But Ms. Emma left to use the ladies' room, and I scooped up some yums for y'all undetected!" he adds.

"Obee, you truly are the best!" I say as he looks at me puzzled and confused.

"Syd? Sophie? Umm, why is Chase here? Wait…nah, couldn't be! But seriously?" Obee is impressed yet so confused as to why we are standing there dressed like we are.

"Obee, may I introduce you to Wyatt Gentry? Of course you have already met myself, Chase Payne!" I say while we wait for it all to click with Obee. Sometimes he's smart, but he doesn't always see the apple fall from the tree!

"Oh my, Syd, or Chase. Umm, I kinda see what you are showing me, but what I don't understand is why. I mean, you li'l ladies are so purdy, and to dress up like boys? I don't quite understand." He thinks for a moment, and then it's like it *finally* hits that sweet spot that makes it click. "Syd! Chase! Oh, your dad..." He pauses for a minute, then continues, "Wait, that was *you* riding on the track? But whatever for? You are gonna get yourself hurt, or worse, out there!" He sternly scolds me as I quickly interrupt him.

"Obee! Shh!" I say with my finger to my lips. "I will be fine. This is part of my project, but you have to promise to keep quiet. I can't let anyone find out, not yet! Can you promise me, Obee? Please?" I say with determination.

"Syd, on your grandad's honor, I will promise to not tell anyone! But what I don't understand is, Why Sophie? I mean Wyatt Gentry? Am I missing something?" he asks, still confused.

"Well, Obee," I say like a teacher about to teach her class, "Sophie is a great rider, and...well, I thought maybe she could race with me. She's smart, strong, and good with PB Cup. So I thought I would bring her and ask Mr. A if he could use another rider."

"Syd, are you sure you know what you are getting yourself into? That's twice the trouble out there on the track! Your dad could get in a lot of trouble with the officials. I just don't know, Syd. Have you even thought about this Soph—"

Sophie quickly, and quite rudely, interrupts Obee. "It's okay, Obee. I am fully aware of the situation, and I am ready and willing to go out there and race to my fullest capability." Then she gets a little bit sassy. "And besides, it's for Syd's project, and if it goes anything like we expect, well, I don't wanna miss it for the world! I can't have her be the only one to take all the credit! So yeah, besties till the end, no matter what!" she says proudly as she pulls me in closer.

"Okay, girls, don't say I didn't warn you! Well, get outta those getups before someone else spots ya, and eat this food before it gets cold. I'm off to my room. Do y'all need a ride in the mornin'?"

"Obee, we would be honored if you would take us to school," we say as Sophie and I put our hands in together and wait for Obee to add his. "Come on, Obee, we're a team now, so in with the hand. It's our secret handshake, so you gotta do it!" I say as Sophie chimes in with the voice of a gangster from Brooklyn. "Or we gotta kill ya, ya see," she says, winking at Obee.

He nods and puts his hand on ours. We push down twice and say, "Go quietly, go proud, go team, for crying out loud!"

We make our fists bump and explode like fireworks!

Obee turns to leave but stops at the door and smiles. "Night, girls. See ya in the mornin' bright and early!"

"Night, Obee," we say together. And then I rush over to him and give him a huge hug, saying, "Thanks, Obee," as I wink and walk back to Sophie.

We clean up and put everything back in the trunk and lock it up. We eat and head to bed.

As we lie there, I can't help but feel something like a presence near me. I look around, expecting to see Grandad standing there, and nothing. Maybe it's my imagination.

We drift off to sleep.

CHAPTER 6

Dreams of Mom

It's been a while since I had someone stay overnight with me at the cottage. Sophie is a great choice, actually probably my only choice, since she is my main friend.

As I lie here thinking about all the progress I have made with Sophie's help on this project, I can't help but be curious what Mom would think of my decision. Would she be proud of me? Would she keep it a secret from my dad? She sometimes would keep things secret from my dad, depending on what it was and whether or not she thought he was worthy of knowing till the time was right.

All this time I am lying here thinking I'm awake and thinking about this craziness, only to come to the realization that I am in fact asleep. I figure this out when it starts getting misty, looking almost like last night. Could Grandad be coming to visit again? Oh, how cool would that be? I have so many questions to ask him.

By now I can barely see my hand in front of my face. I feel a presence, but this time it does not feel like when Grandad came to visit me. Could this be the big man himself? Oh, my heart races with the anticipation of who could be here with us! I wonder if Sophie will get lucky enough to catch any of this, this time.

I faintly see a figure a few feet in front of me. I see a dress light, almost-pale pink to white in color. Well, that's probably not God. But who could it be? The dress is flowing gently and almost seems to hover just above the floor.

"Hello?" I call out. "Who is there? Do I know you?" I hear a faint humming sound coming from the direction of the figure.

"Mom?" I softly, and with enthusiasm, say to the figure. "Mom, if that is you, I miss you…so much! I had a visit last night from Grandad Jack. He said you were up there with him. If that's you, Mom, can you give me a sign?" I wait patiently for some kind of a reply. The figure just hovers there, watching me, like it can't speak. Slowly now, the fog clears just enough that I can make out who it is.

"Mom! It is you! Oh, Mom, why don't you talk to me? I love you! Please, I just want to talk with you," I say as I start to cry because I do not understand why I was able to chat with Grandad but I cannot seem to have the same kind of connection with my mom.

"Please do not cry, Sydney," I softly hear her say to me. "I love you too, my dear, sweet child."

"Oh, Mom, how I wish I could just hug you and not let go. It's not the same without you here. It's not fair! Why did he have to take you so soon?" I say with a bit of anger in my tone.

"Sweetheart, I did my time here on earth, and God needed me here. So he brought me home. I know it does not seem fair, but one day you will understand. Till then, keep doin' the amazin' things you are doin'."

I look at her and she looks at me, and she can tell I am hurting, so her figure moves to the bed and sits beside me. She puts her arm around me, and I can almost feel her there with me, as if she were really here! I lay my head on her shoulder, and she wipes the tears away. She always did that when I would cry; she would come sit next to me, wipe away my tears, and tell me, "Everything happens for a reason, even if we do not see it at the current time, and everything will be okay. No worries needed. Just trust in God and you will see." Which she has just repeated to me as we sit here.

She then states that I need to make a trip to the shop again because she has something there in her desk for me.

I say to her, "Aww, thank you, Mom. Are we able to go now to get it? Like Grandad and I did?"

42

She simply states, "No I am sorry. I cannot go with you right now. But I promise you, even if you cannot see me, I am also always with you. And Grandad. We are both always by your side."

"Mom, I will do my best to go to the shop soon to get whatever it is that you have for me there." I hesitate. "Mom? Are you proud of me? Do you think what I am doin' is worth my time? Do you think it will even make a change in the world?" I ask eagerly, waiting for her response and approval.

"Sydney, I believe you are an amazin' young lady, and I am very proud of you. I cannot speak for how your dad is goin' to react at first, but I think he will eventually come around and understand why you did what you did. I think, once he sees the impact you will make, he will be the proudest father ever! You know how your dad is, always so formal and by the book. It's not that he does not want to go off the beaten path, it's just that he is old-school and sometimes it takes a little convincin' for old-schoolers to wake up and see the real world as it truly is right before their very eyes. They fear change, but once they see the change and how good it can be, most times they are okay with it, even if it takes a few days or weeks for it to settle in. But they eventually do come around for the good," she explains.

"Yeah." Then I smile and say, "Dad can be a li'l hardheaded, and I think he's literally got horse blinders on that stops him from seein' what's actually right in front of him. Do you know, Mom, that Dad didn't even recognize his own daughter when I was at the track the other day?" I say it like I am blown away by his actions.

My mom smiles and says to me, "Well, Sydney, I have to admit, you do a fine job makin' yourself into this Chase Payne fellow." She smiles. "So now I have a question for you, my child."

"Shoot, Mom," I say with anticipation of what she may ask.

"Well, Sydney, just where did you get such a name like Chase Payne?"

"Well, Mom, I thought you of all people would have known this one. Well, at least for the last name. I picked it from my great-great-grandad Sawyer Payne. And I am chasin' my dream of movin' to that beachfront home I always wanted, so I thought, What better name than Chase Payne?" I say to her proudly.

"Oh, I see. Well, I completely missed that one. You are right, I should have known that last name. Well, it makes plenty of sense. So why are you getting Sophie involved?" she calmly asks.

"Well, I figured it would have a bigger impact if we both did it," I state with heart. "And when she raced me the other day with PB Cup and won, well, I just knew I had to do something about that!" I smile. "So how do you feel about Sophie usin' PB Cup to race beside me at the track?" I ask her.

"Sydney, I would be honored to have Sophie ride PB Cup. But it's not me you need to convince, it's your dad! And I am afraid that's goin' to prove to be a bit of a challenge," she politely warns me, but then she adds, "But she did do very well with my sidestep, so maybe you should have her add that if she is able to. I am sure that will be what gets your dad's attention!"

"Nah, I think he will be just fine with it. I have a plan for that too!" I smartly add. "Dad is all about me meeting up with Chase, so I will tell him I already have and I am very impressed with his skills and I am so glad Dad found him to ride SOT for me. Sophie does have your sidestep down pretty good, doesn't she?" And I see her thinking about it, and she knows I am right.

"Yes, she does! Sydney, is there anything you do not have worked out? You have an answer for everything, like you have planned this for years and have every little detail figured out. So how long *have* you been workin' on this?" she asks.

"Well, Mom, we just started this subject in history about three or four weeks ago, and it's just been since then that I have worked this all out and put it all together. So not too much time. So far, I am thinkin' it is all just fittin' together like it is meant to be. So I say, so be it!"

"Really, Sydney Ashcraft? I am so proud of you and all you stand for! I wish I were still here with you, because I would put you in charge of my shop. Maybe after your project...maybe, you can reopen the shop? In my honor, I know you will be great, Sydney!"

"Mom, seriously? I would *love* to reopen your store. But that's one challenge I may have issues with, and I may need your help with that one. You know Dad won't go for that!" I say to her as she begins to fade.

"Mom, wait! Please don't go!" I reach out toward the direction of her figure, but the closer I get, the faster she fades.

"Oh, Mom, I love you!" I cry as she disappears along with the fog.

I wake up to Sophie shaking me. "Syd, wake up!" she says.

"I am awake. What's wrong, Sophie?"

"Syd, you were talkin' in your sleep and crying so bad I thought you were havin' a nightmare! I was worried. I am sorry, I didn't mean to wake you," she says as she sits next to me on the bed.

"It's okay," I tell her. "I just had another strange dream, with another visitor."

She looks freaked out. "Another visitor?" she quietly shouts.

"Yes, my mom. She would be honored if you would ride PB Cup in the races with me. She also said that Dad may be a challenge, which we already knew, so you are to do her sidestep! We both feel that this is what will hook him! *And* she said that there is something for me in *her* desk that she wants me to get," I say to her as I catch my breath to continue what Mom said. "And she also said she wants me to open up her shop after we complete this project, in her honor as well!"

Sophie just sits there staring at me like I am on crack or doing some kind of drug and have lost my mind. "Get yourself together, woman! Breathe before I have to call 911!"

"Well, I will need an assistant. Are you game, or do I have to ask another bestie to help me?" I sternly say to her.

"Yes, yes, yes! Wait, what other bestie do you have? Before you answer, I will do it! Mom said I need a job soon, and that would be absolutely perfect!" She pauses for a moment and then sadly says to me, "But, Syd, what about when I have to babysit? On the nights Mom works late, I wouldn't be able to come help."

"No problem! You can just bring Liz with you! She's not too small, and I think we can find something to keep her busy for a few hours. So is that still a yes?" I exclaim with ultimate joy.

"Ten-four, bestie! Times two!" she replies as she laughs and puts up her hand with two fingers up.

"Okay, then, we are a team, and this is goin' to be a blast, I can tell already. Okay, we need to get a li'l more sleep," I tell her. "We can talk about this more tomorrow."

She shakes her head and says to me, "No, nope, no way!"

"What do you mean no way?"

She looks at her phone and shows it to me. "Syd, have you not looked at the time?"

"Ugh, really? I'm not ready to get up!" I say as I grumble under my breath all the way to the bathroom.

"Well, won't Obee be here soon?"

"Ugh, yeah, in, like, thirty minutes! Okay, I will get a quick shower, and then you can get ready. I really need some more sleep. We have three more races this week!" I say as I drag myself to get ready.

We both finish up and are ready just as Obee pulls up outside. He takes us to school a little early. We wait for him to drive away, then we quickly run to the mini-mart for some coffee and doughnuts.

"Syd? Do you think we have time to go to your mom's shop to see what she has left for you there?"

"Well, I did think about that, but we can do it later. I do not want to take a chance of bein' late and having our parents find out. So later for sure!"

CHAPTER 7

The Day Before the Next Race

Today was an interesting day, to say the least. The final that Sophie and I supposedly studied for was today. I think I did well enough to pass, which isn't too bad, considering we didn't study too much. It was a math final, and there really was not much need to study. Basically, a refresher is good enough.

Of course, Lucas tried to start with me again, but I just told him to back off before I did more damage this time and really show him up in front of the rest of the football team. And his response did not surprise me. He was like, "This is not over, Sydney Ass-crack!" I just shook my head and walked away. I think Grandad would be proud of how well I handled the situation.

It's lunch by now, and I am waiting for Sophie to come into the cafeteria so we can sit together. I see her on the other side of the room. I wave my arms back and forth so she can hopefully see me. She spots me and rushes over to me.

"There you are!" she kinda screams as she gets closer. "How's your day goin'?" she asks.

"Well, not too bad. I almost had another run-in with Lucas. He just thinks he's all that. I put him in his place for now. Call it a feelin', but I don't think he's done messin' with me just yet."

"Sorry to hear that, Syd. Hey, I was wonderin', so that thing your mom left you at her shop?"

"Yeah, whatcha thinkin', Sophie?"

"Well, I was wonderin' if you wanna stop by on our way to my house and get whatever it is? I am so curious, *and* it's not even for me!" she says as she laughs and tries to be discreet at the same time.

"Shhh!" I say to her. "Keep it down. I don't want anyone knowin' that we may or may not be goin' there!" I sternly say to her.

"Sorry, Syd," she whispers. "I'm just so excited! Aren't you?"

"I am. But we don't want the wrong people to overhear and make problems for us. So shhh, calm down. And sure, I think we can quickly stop by," I say. She looks like she is quietly doing a cheer with no words. "*But* we gotta be quick!" I tell her. Sometimes I think she gets more excited about things that happen to me in my life than I do.

Lunch is over, and we go to our next class. Before we know it, the day is over. We quickly and quietly head to my mom's shop. We sneak back down the alley to the back door, and I unlock it. We quickly dart in, shut the door, and wait just a moment to make sure no one followed us. Seems to be clear.

I ask Sophie to guard the door while I try to find whatever it is my mom has left for me.

I search all over her desk, pulling out drawers and lifting things up, but I do not see anything. *Mom, what did you leave here?* I ask in my head. Then suddenly I realize that one of the drawers seems shorter than the others. So I pull it all the way out and examine it. Sure enough, this has a secret compartment. *What is it with my family and secret compartments?* I think to myself.

I open it, and inside is a locket on a chain with a picture of my mom holding me as a baby, and my dad holding me as a baby on the other side. Engraved on the back side are some letters:

$$IA + PA = SA \; \heartsuit \; 4EVER$$

"Aww, that is so sweet!"
There's a note here with it:

For you, Sydney, on your 16th birthday.

I'm puzzled. I still have about two years for that! I wonder what or why she wanted me to have it now.

I quickly close up the drawers and get to the back door. We exit through the back and are walking through the alley when Sophie asks, "So what was it? The suspense is killin' me!" She acts as though she is dying.

So I show her the locket. She says to me, "So what's with all these special gifts all of a sudden? Like, what is goin' on here, Syd?"

"Well, for some reason, these things are important for something. I just can't see it yet. But like Grandad always said, 'everything happens for a reason, even if we don't see it. We will soon enough,'" I say to Sophie, and she agrees.

"Yeah, my grandparents say that *all* the time. Must be an old-people thing." Sophie laughs.

"Yeah, they do think a li'l differently from our generation, that's for sure, but a lot of it makes sense, besides the fact that they are pretty cool words to live by."

Sophie agrees as we walk to her house. Sophie lives in the north end of town, but on the outermost part, almost where the sidewalk ends. We get there about ten minutes before her little sister's bus arrives.

Sophie's sister is about eight years old. She's about a head shorter than me, with brown hair and green eyes. Maybe that's why Sophie has always wanted green eyes. Makes sense. She's a spunky little spitfire, but she always means well. I wish I had a little sister just like her.

Her bus pulls up, and she gets off, then we go inside Sophie's house. They live in a small one-floor tan brick rancher with a two-car garage. When you enter, you are in the living room on the left side, and the kitchen and dining room on the right. There is a small hallway about halfway back that cuts either direction. We go to the left, and there is a full bath shared between two bedrooms. Sophie and Eliza share the very back bathroom. It's a pretty big bedroom. They each have their own bed and side to the room. We drop off our things, go to the basement to hang out, and watch her little sister till her mom or dad gets home.

We decide to put on cartoons and play some pool. Now, Sophie and Eliza can kick my but shooting pool 'cause they can practice *any time* of the day. But I enjoy shooting just to shoot, so I do not really care if I win or lose. We all already know what my game is.

"So, Eliza, got any *boyfriends*?" I say, acting like they are ewwy, yucky, gross.

"Eww! Yuck! Boys are for losers!" she replies. "I don't want a boyfriend. All they do is take your money."

I laugh and say, "Funny, they say the exact opposite about girls."

We rack up the balls, and Eliza takes the first shot. The balls crack so loud when the cue ball hits them. "You can definitely tell she gets some practice with the power she puts behind that ball," I say to the girls in astonishment as the balls scatter *all over* the table. And of course, the little pool shark gets three in on her first shot!

"Nice shot there, Eliza. So you got in two stripes and a solid, so I'm guessing you're goin' with the stripes?" I ask her like I already know her answer.

"Nah, I'll give you the advantage, and I will go with solids," she says as she laughs with a touch of evil.

"Yeah, there it is," I say. "I see it now."

"Oh yeah, what do you see, Syd?" She smirks with her chest out to me.

"Well, when we got here, you had a halo, and that currently seems to be shrinkin' a li'l bit, because I can see some horns growin' in its place, and it's just hangin' out on top of the tips," I say like I *actually* see some horns growing outta her head.

She freaks out and runs to look. She comes back, saying, "Syd, you must be blind, 'cause ain't nutin' growin' from anywhere outta my head," she states with sass.

"Oh, my bad, 'cause I can plainly see them. How about you, Sophie? Do you see them, or is it that I am blind?"

"Nope, I see 'em too! And man, are they ug-ly!"

"Well, I can't feel 'em or see 'em, so they aren't there!" she screams and stomps her foot.

"Okay, whatever you gotta tell yourself, kiddo," we say as we laugh about it.

Even with the help she gave me, she took out almost half of her solids within her second shot. I was lucky to get one in, and it'll probably be my only one, I think to myself as I chuckle.

Eliza asks, "What's so funny, Syd? You know I'mma wipe you up, right?"

"Yes, yes, I do. That's why I'm chucklin', because I am being slaughtered by the town butcher! It's okay, though, 'cause I bet you wouldn't last against me in a horse race!" I say, laughing back at her. "We are all good at something, and when we figure out what it is, we should strive to do our best so we can be the best at what we do," I say reflecting back on another great quote of Grandad Jones. I tell Eliza, "That was compliments of Jack Jones, best grandad ever!"

Sophie smiles and says, "Syd, your grandad was a book of amazin' wisdom full of quotes to get one's attention in such a way that they don't even realize they are learnin' something."

"Yes, he definitely had a way with words. Maybe one day I could write a short book on all his amazin' words of wisdom!"

"Well, I don't know how short it would be, but it would definitely be worth a read! I would buy one just so you could sign it, then I would have Grandad Jones's wisdom *and* your *famous* signature!"

"Ah, yeah, *whatever*," I say with attitude. "I do not have a famous signature, so good luck with that one, bestie! I am just a nobody!" I laugh.

"At the *rate you are going*, in a few more days, you will be known for something, my dear friend! You can mark my words on that! Then you will be famous!" she assures me.

We hear a noise upstairs, and then Mrs. Abbott hollers down to us, "Girls, are you here?"

"Yes!" we all say together.

"Okay, I'm makin' dinner, homemade pizza. How's ham, pineapple, and bacon on one and mushrooms and pepperoni for the other sound?" she asks.

"Good!" Sophie and Eliza both say.

"Sounds great, Mrs. Abbott!" I add in.

"Please, Sydney, call me Allison. We don't need any of that formal mess in this house. Okay, girls, I will let y'all know when it's ready!" she shouts down to us.

"Okay!" we shout back up to her.

We have been having such a great time shooting pool and laughing for a little while when Allison comes down to see what all the ruckus is about. She sneaks down the stairs and stands there and watches us for a few minutes without our knowledge. And we are having so much fun we don't even notice her.

Suddenly, she says, "Girls," quickly and loudly to scare us.

And it works.

I swear Eliza must have jumped, like, three feet in the air—okay, I may have exaggerated just a tad. And as far as me, I grab my chest and scream, "Allison, you scared the life right outta me!"

Sophie says, "*Mom!* Are you *tryin'* to give us a heart attack?" She's laughing so hard she's almost gasping for air.

"Well, I heard all the commotion down here and had to come see what was up! Also, to let you know dinner is ready!" she says as she waves us all to head upstairs. "So come on, let's get cleaned up!"

We clean up and get seated around their massive wooden table.

"Mmm, smells amazin', Allison!" I say as my tummy growls.

"Momma, may I say grace?" Eliza asks.

"Would you please, Eliza?"

We fold our hands and bow our heads as Eliza says grace for us.

> Dear God, thank you for my momma's yummy pizza and my sister and her friend Sydney. Amen.

"Short and sweet. Thank you, sweetie. Well, it sounded like Sydney needs to eat!" She laughs as she adds, "Dig in, girls!"

I go straight for the Hawaiian because it's my *favorite*! She has so many toppings piled on some fall off as I pick up my piece to eat it. "Mmm, Allison, it tastes even better than it smells! It's ah-maz-zing!" I say with food in my mouth as I try to swallow it and stress just how amazing it is for me.

"Syd," she says, smiling, "you are gonna choke. Oh, if your mom could see you now." She pauses a bit. "So what have you girls been up to? I haven't seen you, Sophie, in a few days. Are you girls stayin' outta trouble?" she asks, wondering.

"I'm sorry, Allison. She has been helpin' me with my history project. It's a pretty big deal. I couldn't think of a better person to share it with!" I say to her as I look at Sophie and smile and wink so that Allison can't really see me wink.

"Hey! What was that, Syd?" Eliza sees me wink and says this for everyone to hear.

Sophie quickly jumps to my defense. "She wasn't winkin' at anything or anyone in particular, sis. Sometimes her eye just randomly blinks or jumps outta her control."

Wow that was close! Sophie is always quick to respond, and she makes it sound good to cover my bum. I smile at Sophie and pretend to kinda look away and wink again. She catches it and smiles back. Not much gets past Eliza, but I do not think Allison is as quick to catch on. Not that she isn't smart; it's just that she's always so busy with work and preoccupied to pay close attention to little things right in front of her.

Allison is a realtor. And she is a good one. Right now she is the one in charge of my mom's shop if Dad ever decides to sell. But after last night, I have to try to find a way to change his mind to keep it. Maybe after my project he will see that I am mature enough even for my age to take on her responsibility at her shop. With his help, of course.

"Allison, I was wonderin' if I may spend the night since I am already here? I will help to clean up after dinner," I say so as to persuade her toward a favorable decision.

"Sydney, I would be so happy for you to stay! Will you please let your dad and Emma know just to make sure it's okay first?"

"Of course. I will text them now," I say as I quickly grab my phone and begin texting them. Emma responds almost immediately and says, "Have fun!" adding that she will see me soon.

"Em said it was okay!" I relay to Allison.

"Great! How about some dessert, then, ladies?" she asks.

We all say, "Not now. Maybe later. We're stuffed!"

Sophie asks, "May we please be excused, Mom?"

"Yes, go have fun, girls."

"I will be down in a minute. I promised that I would help clean up!"

"Okay, Syd, we will see you down there."

As I help Allison clean up, I say to her, "Thanks again, Allison, for everything! It really means a lot to me that you allow me to be a part of your family, especially since my mom has passed. I just want you to know just how much I appreciate it," I say as I hug her.

As Allison returns the hug, she says, "You're welcome, Sydney. I love you as much as I loved your mom, and I wouldn't have it any other way! We have always considered your family as our family!"

When I am done, I head for the basement again to have more fun and pool lessons from Eliza.

After a little while, we decide we want dessert, so we go upstairs. Sophie asks, "Mom, can we take you up on that offer for dessert now?"

Her mom nods, opens the oven, and we can smell she made brownies. She get out bowls and spoons. She goes to the cupboard, gets peanut butter and fudge, and sets them at the island bar. She goes to the fridge and gets the ice cream from the freezer. Eliza gets superexcited, shouting while jumping up and down, "Brownie sundaes! Thanks, Mom! I love you!"

"I love you too, sweetie. Now, can you settle down, or no sundae for you?"

She instantly stops and climbs up on a stool and patiently waits. She says, "Momma, you can give Sydney hers first, since she is our guest today?"

I say, "Thanks, Eliza. You are so sweet! But how about I let you get the first one this time?" I go over to hug her and kiss her forehead.

"Sydney, you are just as sweet!" Allison says to me. She cuts the brownies and places a square in each bowl with a scoop of ice cream. She gives us each a bowl to top as we want. I go for the peanut butter. *Yum!*

We finish our sundaes and head to wash up and settle down for the night. Eliza says her prayers, and we do ours. Then we get into bed and go to sleep.

CHAPTER 8

Mom Returns with a Message

Parker, Sydney's dad, sends her a text message.

> Parker
> *Hope you had a great day, Syd. Good night,*
> *Syd. Sweet dreams. I love you!*
>
> Sydney
> *I did, Dad. Thanks! Good night, Dad. I love*
> *you too!*

Parker goes to the kitchen for a cup of coffee before he settles down for the night. He fills up the water and puts in the grounds and starts it. He decides to read the paper while he waits. When the coffee is done, he pours himself a cup and sits down to read it a little more. When he gets to the classifieds, he sees his ad for a rider is still posted. "I thought I told Emma to call and cancel this!" he says with a bitter tone.

Just then, he hears footsteps and looks to see who could be headed toward the kitchen.

"I thought I smelled coffee out here. You know what I told you about eatin' and drinkin' before bed!" she scolds him like a child. "Why can't you sleep, Parker? I figured you would be in bed by now," Emma says to him.

"I don't know why I could not sleep, but I wanted to say good night to Syd. Anyway, Emma, I have something I want to ask you. A few days ago, I thought I asked you to take down our want ad for a rider?" he asks sternly.

"Yes, sir, you did, and I called the paper and asked them to remove the ad. Is it still in the paper?"

"Yes, it is. Can you please call to check out why it hasn't been pulled yet?"

"Yes, Parker, first thing tomorrow mornin', I will be on it as soon as the paper opens," she states to him.

"Thanks! Good night, Emma. I am headed to bed now. I have a big day tomorrow. I am hoping Chase can pull off another win, and I hope Syd will be here," he says before he walks off into the darkness toward his room.

"Good night, Parker," she says as he walks away. Emma cleans up and heads back to bed as well.

When Parker reaches his room, he strips down for a quick, relaxing, warm shower. He stands in there soaking up all the warmth and steaming up the bathroom. He gets out later, dries off, and dresses for bed. He brushes his teeth and walks into his room, slips off his slippers, sits on the edge of the bed, and picks up a picture of his wife, Ivy. He talks to her, tells her good night, that he loves her, kisses her picture, and sets it back down on the nightstand. As he lies back and covers himself, he thinks about all the nights he laid next to his wife in this bed, how soft her skin was, and how good she smelled. He says before he closes his eyes, "I love you, Ivy Blue Eyes."

He's been asleep for a little while when he hears footsteps walking nearby. He squints to try to see, but it's foggy. *Did I leave a window open?* he thinks to himself. *I haven't seen fog like this in a long time.* He continues to hear footsteps. "Who's there?" he hollers out. There's no reply. The footsteps stop. He smells a faint smell of something he's smelled before, but he can't quite put his finger on it. *Where have I smelled that before?* he thinks to himself. He feels a presence, with the air thickening.

He tries to make his way to the window to open it for fresh air or at least see if it's foggy outside. He finds a window, but it's foggy outside too. "There must be a window open," he says out loud. He tries to follow the wall around to the other windows, but they are all closed. *That's strange. Where is this fog coming in from?* he thinks to himself.

The footsteps continue to move around the room. Suddenly, they stop almost right in front of him. He softly hears a faint voice say, "Parker, it's me!"

"I'm sorry, but who is *me?*" he asks the voice. "Can you show yourself?"

With that, the fog slowly lessens just a bit. Enough so he can make out the figure of a woman standing there in a long white satin gown flowing as though she is hovering just above the floor. "Who are you? Do I know you? Why are you here?"

A hand comes through the fog and reaches for him. He reaches toward the hand and almost touches it before he quickly pulls his back away. "What am I doin'? This cannot be real! I have to be dreaming. Emma said not to have coffee and food before bed, but I *never* listen!"

"If only you were here, Ivy!" he shouts out. "I miss you so much, my love!" He puts his head down and starts to cry.

He hears a faint voice again. This time he can make it out a little better. "I am here, sweetheart," the voice says, so softly and sweetly.

Parker tries to stop crying so he can listen more closely to the voice. *Did I just hear what I thought I heard?* he thinks to himself. "Okay, I *seriously* have to lay off anything food related before bed," he says out loud to himself.

"Parker, my love…my dearest, can you hear me?"

"I hear you, but I am tryin' to decipher if what I am hearin' is real or not. You can't be my wife, because she died a few months ago!" he shouts at the figure. "So *go away* and *stop tormentin'* me! Just let me be in peace!" he screams as he picks up one of his slippers and throws it at the figure.

"My sweet Parker, please, it's me, Ivy. Do not be frightened. I came to visit with you and talk to you about Sydney. Do you not wish to speak with me?" she asks.

"No, I am sorry, it's just…I do not understand why or how you are here. I don't believe in ghosts!" he shrieks.

"I am just a heavenly figure. I am not here to hurt you. I only have a little time before I must return, and I wanted to tell you to trust in Sydney. She is doing great things. I watch her every day."

Parker interrupts her and says, "Well, at least one of us is. She has been at Sophie's more than here lately." He says this with noticeable envy.

"I can reassure you, my love, she is not in any trouble. She has a miracle in the works, and I want you to trust and believe in her as you did in God and me. Because she will make you very proud. Also, when the young man comes tomorrow to ride PB Cup, please accept and allow him in my honor! It would mean just so much to me! Can you do that for me, sweetheart?" Ivy asks him.

"Ivy, I will do whatever you would like me to. You always knew best for our li'l filly. That's just one of the things I miss, you being here for Sydney, for me, for us. Also, when we would go ridin' with Syd, our game nights, just everything. We just miss you so, so much! Some days it hurts so bad. I think about those last moments we spent together every day. Those dances were absolutely amazing! You were so beautiful! That SOB should have to pay for what he did. He took you from us! Damn it, why did we have to go out that night? Maybe you would still be here for me to love and hold if we had just stayed home. What I would give just to have you here with us as a family again! There is so much we didn't get to do together! It's just not fair!" he shouts out in anger. "Ivy, can I ask you something, my love?" he then asks politely.

"Anything, Parker. What is it that you want to know?"

"Well, since you have passed, we haven't had the shop open, and I was tryin' to decide what to do with it. I do not want to get rid of it, 'cause it was your dream! But I can't, in good conscience, let it just sit there and just let everything go to waste either! So since you are here, can you please tell me what *you* would like me to do with it? I was thinkin' about talkin' with Allison to see what we could do as far as renting out the space, whether it's someone with something new or just to take over your supply shop. Please tell me your wishes, my love," he says to her in desperation.

"My love, I also wanted to chat with you about this very situation. What I would like for you to do is to open it up in the afternoons and let Sydney run the store in my honor. Let a small percentage go toward research for cancer. It would also generate some money for you."

Parker interrupts to quickly say, "Like I need the money, sweetheart! I do not need that money!"

"Okay, Parker. After all expenses are paid, I want you to please donate 20 percent to cancer research and see that Sydney gets paid well for her time! This way, the store will be open for the public. If they have any needs that they need to have filled, they will be able to. These are my wishes!" she exclaims.

"Ivy, I do not think that Sydney is such a good choice for runnin' your shop."

"Parker, have you not listened to a word I have spoken to you here tonight? Did you get too much fog in your head? I want Sydney to do this. She is ready! And please give that beautiful friend of hers, Sophie, a job as well! And if Allison needs Eliza to come and hang out there, allow it! These are my wishes. So please follow them for me?"

"Okay, I am sorry I forgot you can see things that I can't, and if you say Sydney is doin' well, then I just have to trust what you are tellin' me. It's just she's barely..." He pauses as Ivy puts her finger to his lips.

"Parker!"

"Yes, I know, Ivy, honor your requests. Okay, I just hope that I do not live to regret my decision!" he says with an attitude under his breath and in disbelief that he's even listening to a ghost.

"Parker?" Ivy softly asks.

"I already told you, Ivy, I will do it!" he says as he hangs his head.

"No, Parker—"

"What do ya mean no!" he shouts rudely, interrupting her.

"Parker, please just listen. I wanted to tell you that I love you, and I want to let you know you are *never* alone while you sleep in our bed." She pauses, waiting for a reply, but he doesn't give her one. "Parker? Did you hear what I said to you?" she asks politely.

"Yes, I heard what you said, Ivy. I am sorry. I do not mean to be so difficult. It's just...I miss you so bad, and it's just been difficult without you here. It seems that Syd doesn't want to be here with me anymore. Then you show up in my dreams and say everything is goin' to be all right?" He pauses for a minute to gather his thoughts. "I just do not know how to handle *all* this. And by *this* I mean this right here right now! You know my beliefs. So you must know just how hard this has to be for me! To see you, to hear and listen to you speak to me right here, right now! It's more than my mind can handle! It's complete craziness!" he says in a state of complete confusion.

"Parker, what this is is nothing short of an absolute miracle. A miracle from God! He has granted me this wish to come down here to speak with you. For you to be able to see me, hear me," she says passionately as she reaches for his hand. "To touch you," she says as she touches his hand.

His eyes widen. "I can feel your touch, but I…I cannot believe it! There's a subtle warmth. But how? Your hands are just as soft as I remember, if not softer!" Tears start to form in his eyes.

"Parker, believe it, for it is a miracle. I am a gift from God right here, *right* now! Do you believe in God, Parker?" she asks.

"I did, till…" He pauses again to carefully choose his next words. "I mean I do, and again, I am so sorry I have been so difficult to you for your being here. I am so grateful that God has given you the ability to come here and to speak to me in such a way as to try to open my eyes and see what I needed to see to restore my faith in the Man oh Mighty. My new MOM!" he exclaims. "You are still so amazing, my love. Just now you are absolutely heavenly! Thank you for wanting to come and speak to me. Would you please be sure to relay the same message to God on my behalf, that I am so very grateful for all he has given me, what he has allowed me to have in life, and for this most precious of moments right here? I am most grateful for this, and my faith is restored! With God's love, anything is possible, Ivy!" he proudly says as he stands up and turns to her. He then reaches for her hands. "Please stand with me as I vow my heart and soul back to the Lord and make my new motto 'With God's love, anything is possible!'" he shouts as he pulls Ivy in and starts to sway and dance back and forth. For a slight minute, he even seems to be floating in the air just above the floor.

"I love you, Ivy." As fast as he says that, the door flies open, the fog and Ivy are completely gone without a trace, and he falls straight to the floor with a loud thud. "Ouch! What the...," he says as he wakes up and sees Emma standing there in her robe and nightgown.

"Mr. Parker, is everything all right?" she exclaims. "I heard shoutin' and screamin', so I just had to come make sure that you were okay, sir!"

"Well, thank you, Emma, but I am just fine," he says as he starts to get up and brushes himself off as if he got dirty. "And since you are here, I want to tell you that there will be some changes made from here on out. To our farm, our home, the love we share in this home!" he proudly tells her.

"Why this new, sudden change of heart, sir?" she asks.

"Emma, let's start with, from now on, I am just Parker, no more *mister* or *sir*! We are family. *You* are family. Lord knows you have been with us for a few decades now, so let's act like it and be the family God intended us to be! For with God's love, anything is possible!" he shouts out loud, as if he were standing on the rooftops, proclaiming his love of God to the world.

"Mister—I mean, Parker, shush, you are gonna wake Oliver!" she says while trying to shush him down a few notches.

"No, Emma, no! I do not care who I wake up! This is the start of a brand-new day!" he exclaims. "Where are you goin', Emma?" he asks as she gets up to walk away.

"I'm headed for my medicine bag, 'cause you are obviously runnin' a fever or you hit your head when you fell outta the bed," she says sternly.

"No, Emma, I am fine. No, I am *great*! I have not felt this good since before my love, Ivy, passed," he says while hanging his head. "No, I said I would be grateful!" he suddenly exclaims.

"Grateful for what, Parker?" she asks with confusion. "I really think you hit your head just a li'l too hard just a moment ago! Let me go get my bag and some ice."

"No!" he shouts. "I am sorry! No, I do not need ice. Please just listen. I am fine. I am more than fine! I am grateful because my beloved Ivy came to me in a dream!" Parker says with such excitement that he is acting like he is high. "She was talkin' with me and tellin' me things I need to do! *We* need to do! You and I have to go to the shop today! We need to get it ready for the new, spring reopenin'!" he says, breathing fast as he tries to quickly get his thoughts out.

"Parker, you have a race to do. I can take the car to go in and work on gettin' things ready! But are you sure about this?" she asks. "Who will run this?"

"Yes, Emma, I am 100 percent sure. Sydney, Syd will run it. In the afternoons after school! It will be a *great* experience for her!" he explains. "Okay, now, just what time is it?" he asks, still feeling just a li'l tired.

"It's 3:00 a.m.!" she says, laughing. "As wired as you are, I bet you won't be able to sleep now!" she says as he gets back in bed and pulls the cover back over himself. "Good night, Parker. See you in a few hours," she softly says as she turns to look and sees, sure enough, that he is passed out and softly snoring already. "Dang, he must have been tired," she softly says as she shuts the door and heads back to bed herself.

CHAPTER 9

The New Beginning

As Parker hears his alarm, he smells the most amazing breakfast ever. *Mmm, wow, I am so hungry!* he thinks as he quickly gets up so as not to waste another minute of the day. As he's making his way into the kitchen, he says out loud, "What is that *amazin'* smell that is fillin' this beautiful house, my beautiful Emma?"

"Yep, I knew it! You *definitely* hit your head too hard! Shoulda let me ice it last night!"

"Emma, I am just fine! I have a new outlook on life, though. That's why I am this way, not because I want or have to be, but because I just am! Ivy came to me in a dream last night!" Parker tells Emma with full sincerity.

"Now, Parker!" Emma pauses to gather her thoughts so she doesn't offend Parker with what she wants to say. "You know my faith is strong with the Lord. You also know I am a believer in miracles. But this, Parker, this already seems so far-fetched, even for you! So out with what you are *really* up to," she commands, shaking a rolling pin at him. "Or maybe I will just whack ya over da head and fix ya up right, huh?"

"Nah, there will be no need for whackin' me, or my head, for that matter. Seriously, we will find out just how okay I am, Emma, and here's how. So apparently, there is a boy to be comin' here today. Do you know *anything* about this?" he asks.

"No, I do not believe I know anything of any young man comin' here. Do we know him? Has he been here before?" she asks.

"That's the thing, Emma: I have no clue. But Ivy stated that when this boy comes here today, I am to let him ride PB Cup in today's race in her honor. Now, you know that she is a prizewinning mare. I just do not know, first, how I am supposed to just let some boy that I do not know come here, and second, how I'm just supposed to let him take one of our prize horses to the track, and third, how I'm just supposed to let him race her! So what do you think, Emma? What would you make of this?" he asks, looking for a direction to go.

"Well, if Ivy were here, I would do what she says. Only because she usually was a very good judge of character. She had a good reason for the things she did and how she did them. But you are still hangin' with how she came to you last night and told you this is what's supposed to happen?" she asks, as she believes this is all from hitting his head last night and he is now making all this up from being so delirious.

"Well, she said some other things, but once this one *huge* thing happens, then I will tell you more about the others. Only because you and, well, I, too, are havin' such a hard time believin' what we have come to know." He pauses. "So when will you be callin' the newspaper?" Parker requests.

"I was plannin' to call when they open." As she looks at her watch, she adds, "So in about thirty minutes, they should be open. I will call them then. I will head out to the shop a li'l later today. I have some things I would like to get done here first, if that is okay with you?"

"That's perfect, Emma! I will see if Sydney can come out with you to give you a hand. I do not think there should be much to do, but just give it a good straightenin' and a good look-over just to make sure nothing needs refillin'. Chase should be here soon. Then he, Obee, and I will be headed to the track in a few hours. I am praying Chase can pull off another win today. But he can't win *every* race—that would look rigged!" he states. He eats his breakfast and gets up to head to the barn.

On his way out, he says over his shoulder, "I'm headed out, Emma. I will catch up with you later!"

"Okay, Parker!" she says as she cleans up breakfast.

By now, the newspaper office is open. Emma looks up the number and calls to check on why the ad was not taken down. As she's on the phone, she sees two people walking down the lane. "Okay, thank you very much. Bye." She hangs up and walks out to the barn to look for Parker.

As she nears the stables, she sees him on the other end putting bags of feed away. "Ah, Parker, there you are! I wanted to update you on the paper. The newspaper said we paid for a specific length of time, apparently? And when the time is done, they will pull it. But I also wanted to let you know there are two people walkin' in the lane. I couldn't make out who they were just yet," she tells Parker.

"Thanks, Emma! I will see who it could be." He puts down the last bag of feed and walks out around the barn, only to see Chase and another young man. "Well, hello, Chase! Who's your friend?" Parker asks as Emma stands off to the side, shocked at what she is seeing.

Parker said that Ivy came to him in a dream and she said that a young boy would come here today. I thought he was crazy. Oh my, what a miracle! she thinks as she walks over to introduce herself. "I'm sorry, I do not mean to interrupt, but I am Emma, the lady of the house."

"Hello, Mr. Parker and Emma. So I have met Sydney, and she tells me that you are still lookin' for another rider. This is Wyatt Gentry, my longtime friend, and he's a rider too! I was wonderin' if it would be possible for him to show you how well he rides? And maybe possibly let him enter the race today?" Chase asks.

Parker looks Wyatt up and down and is beginning to think about what Ivy had said to him the night before when Emma begins to speak.

Emma says, "Oh, how nice! Well, good luck today, Chase, and if Parker says it's okay, good luck to you as well, Wyatt, did you say?"

"Yes, ma'am! It was a pleasure to meet you! And thank you!" Then he turns. "So, Mr. Ashcraft, what do you think?" Wyatt asks, unsure of what kind of response he may get.

Emma walks away to go work on house things, just as Parker says to the boys, "Well, Chase and Wyatt, let's take a walk out here to the trainin' ring and see just what Wyatt has to offer." As they walk out, he already wants to say yes because of what Ivy told him last night. But he wants to see just how good Wyatt is before he just says yes to them. "Okay, boys, you wait here and I will bring out a horse for you to try, Wyatt."

As Parker walks away, Chase looks at Wyatt and winks. Wyatt nods back at Chase. They fist-bump and wait for Parker to come back out. Just then, here comes Parker with PB Cup all saddled up and ready to go. He opens the gate to the ring and asks Wyatt to follow him in. "Chase, can you please shut the gate, son? Thanks!"

"Sure thing, Mr. A!" Chase jumps off the fence and closes the gate behind them.

"Okay, Wyatt, this is your time to shine. Now, I must tell you that this is, or was, my wife's favorite horse. Not to mention PB Cup is a prizewinnin' Arabian who has many trophies under her saddle. So I will go sit on the fence while you show me what you got!" Parker gets up to sit on the fence.

Wyatt starts off just walking, then he does some galloping, trotting, even some slow-running. But what gets Parker is when Wyatt does a sidestep with PB Cup. Parker's jaw drops. Chase catches this and knows it's a done deal, all while saying, "Mr. A, whatcha thinkin'? Do you like Wyatt's moves? Can he race today?" Chase asks this knowing the answer already.

"Well, I do have to say that I am very impressed with your moves, Wyatt. I do have to ask, though, that sidestep? Where'd you learn that? My wife used to do that with PB Cup *all* the time! You did very well makin' her move *just* like my wife used to do! I am more than impressed!" Parker says, still not believing what he is seeing.

"Well, sir, I have experience with horses. I honestly do not know what else I can tell you. I ride at Chase's farm all the time. We have been together for many years. I would be honored to ride your wife's horse in the race, if it's okay with you, sir," he states.

"Well, I would be absolutely honored to have such a fine, talented young man riding my wife's horse! I guess that means we need to get ready and get goin' soon, so we can get you signed up. How old are you, by the way, Wyatt? Just so I can tell them when I sign you up. Also, are your parents okay with this? Maybe I should talk to them first?"

"Ah, it's okay, Mr. A. My family is great with it! There's no need to bother them with anything. They said they would try to make it to the race to see if I was able to ride, so we can talk with them later," Wyatt says, hoping he doesn't ask too many more questions about his family.

"Chase, would you mind gettin' SOT ready to load? Wyatt, can you stay with PB Cup while I get the truck and hook up the trailer? I will be right back, boys." Parker goes for the truck, and Obee comes around the corner just in time to help Parker get the trailer hooked up. Once they have the trailer hooked up, Obee starts opening the tailgate so they can load the horses. Parker then goes to the boys. "Okay, Chase and Wyatt, I need you to bring your horses over to the trailer so we can load up and get outta here."

"Yes, sir," the boys say.

Once the horses, saddles, and supplies are loaded, Parker tells the boys to get in the truck a while.

As the boys are walking to the truck, Chase says to Wyatt, in a whisper, so that Parker doesn't hear, "So far, so good!" They both nod to each other at the same time that Obee comes around the truck and winks at both of the boys. Everyone gets in the truck, and they head to the track.

On the short ride, Parker begins to speak. "I am sorry, Wyatt, I don't remember how old you said you were."

"Oh, sorry, sir, we got busy and I forgot to tell you I am fourteen, sir," Wyatt states.

"Okay, boys, from now on, no more *sir*. We are family! Just call me Parker. That will be great, thanks!" he says, smiling from ear to ear. He whispers under his breath, "I love you, Ivy!" He thinks about *everything* that he and Ivy had spoken about the night before. He is so excited to see how things work out since this was so important to her and is going so well so far. He can only imagine how everything else will work out.

"What was that, boss?"

"Oh, nothing, Obee! I was just thinking out loud. I'm sorry."

"No need to apologize. I just wanted to make sure that you weren't talkin' to me. My hearin' isn't so good lately as I age."

"Okay, we are here! Let's get unloaded and I will go sign you up, Wyatt!"

"Awesome, Parker! Thank you for everything!" Wyatt says.

"No thanks needed, son," Parker says, full of joy. "Just do well out there today, and if you do well, I will be thankin' you!"

Parker stands at the registration booth, waiting to get the boys signed in. "Next!" Hudson calls out. "Ah, Mr. Parker Ashcraft! It's great to see you today, sir. Will you be signing up that superstar that you have racin' for you?"

"As a matter of fact, yes, Hudson, I will be! The same as last time, he will be ridin' Sands of Tyme. But I also have another rider today. Is it too late for new rider sign-ups?" Parker asks.

"Well, I would say normally yes, but it so happens that we had a cancellation just a few minutes ago and we are in need of a rider to fill the spot," Hudson states. "So another rider? Let's hope you have *another superstar* on your hands!" he says, chuckling.

"Well, from what I have seen so far, he could very well be! Well, it must be our lucky day, then. This is truly amazing! Say, could our new rider ride on, say, my wife's horse today?"

"PB Cup? Are you bringing her out of retirement?" Hudson asks.

"Wow! You remembered, Hudson. That's awesome! No, she never retired. We just stopped racin' her when Ivy passed. But if he does well enough, PB Cup may be a regular again. So I thought, what the heck, let's give this new rider of ours a shot and see how he works out!" Parker says. "So his name is Wyatt Gentry. He's fourteen. Hudson, this is a special, in-memory-of-Ivy run I am doin' today. Can we please let the crowd know? And we will be reopening her shop soon too!"

"Thanks, Parker. Wow, another young one! How do you always pick 'em so young?" Hudson states. "Okay, you, or they, rather, are all signed up and good to go. Good luck, Parker! Also, I will make an announcement for you, Parker, in hopes to generate you some business. I got you taken care of, Parker," Hudson says.

"Thanks, Hudson! You are the best announcer I know on this side of the Mississippi!" Parker walks back to the boys. "All right, you two are signed up and ready to go! This is a special race for you, Wyatt. This is the first race PB Cup has been in since my wife, Ivy, passed away. So ride her like you own her, and go for the gold!"

"Thanks! I will, Parker. I will do my best to make you very proud, sir!" Wyatt says.

"What am I, Parker? Chopped liver?" Chase says, laughing.

"No, you are not, Chase. I want you both at the top of the board! So both of you give it all you got! I will see you after the race. I'm headed up to the stands for a seat," Parker says as he walks away. Since Parker is always in his Sunday best, he doesn't spend too much time in the stable area with them, perhaps from fear of getting too dirty. So he always comes to say his good wishes to Chase—well, now the boys—and makes like the wind and just disappears up to the stands.

Obee walks up and gives them a good luck and winks. They wink back and get ready to walk to the gate.

"Good afternoon, ladies and gentlemen! Welcome back to the Keeneland Racetrack! Today, folks, is a special day here at the track. We have a special request that I have decided not only as the announcer but also as the president of Keeneland Racetrack to up the request with a special gift. So for a few years we had a mare here that had received many trophies but hadn't been at the track lately due to a tragic family accident. But many of you may remember her as a five-year-old Arabian. Well, folks, I am proud to announce that PB Cup is back for a special run! The Ashcrafts have another young racer, named Wyatt Gentry, fourteen, who will be ridin' PB Cup today!"

"As the riders prepare for their walk to the gates, let's all stand for our national anthem." After the anthem plays, Hudson continues, "Riders, take your places at your gate. Our lineup today, starting with gate 1 through 8 is as follows: Speed of Lightning, a four-year-old Thoroughbred; Ain't No Chicken, a three-year-old quarter horse; and returning today, Dusty Daze, a three-year-old Thoroughbred. Our fourth spot goes to our special guest. Welcome back, PB Cup!

She is a five-year-old Arabian. Then we have Blue Bell, a three-year-old Appaloosa. Next up is our up-and-comer, Sands of Tyme. She's a two-year-old Araloosa. Then Sassy Steps, a four-year-old Tennessee walker. Lastly, we have Coal Miner, a five-year-old Tennessee walker. Those are our racers today! Are all riders in their gate and ready to go?" Hudson waits for the flag to drop, letting him know that they are ready. The flag drops, and Hudson continues, "Racers, are you ready? Get set..." *Bang!* "Go! There they go, folks! Ain't No Chicken takes the lead as Sassy Steps and Coal Miner close in! There's another race behind the front group with Sands of Tyme, PB Cup, and Dusty Daze! Oh, they are all over the place! We now have Blue Bell, PB Cup, and Dusty Daze pushing to the front! Ah, here she comes, folks! Sands of Tyme is pushing through the pack, with Dusty Daze and Speed of Lightning hot on her tail! *Agh!* Here comes PB Cup! Looks like she's gonna give Sands of Tyme a run for her money! Little quick trivia, folks. Sands of Tyme is PB Cup's filly! Here they come around the last corner, folks! Man, this is gonna be the closest race ever with a three-wide front pack with Sands of Tyme, PB Cup, and Sassy Steps! Tryin' to push up through them are Speed of Lightning, Ain't No Chicken, and Coal Miner! With Dusty Daze and Blue Bell in a tight third!"

The crowd goes wild as they watch the horses cross over the finish line, with Hudson reporting the winner.

"It's gotta be some kinda miracle, folks. Sands of Tyme has done it again, with PB Cup takin' second place, then Sassy Steps, Coal Miner, Ain't No Chicken, Speed of Lightning, Blue Bell, and Dusty Daze. That's the finishing order, folks! If you have time, please stop by and congratulate our superstar, Chase Payne, and get pictures with Sands of Tyme! Also, a major thank you to PB Cup for her return. Hopefully, she will have many more as it's clear she still has what it takes to race! Also, we hope to have back as well our newest young rider, Wyatt Gentry! Congratulations, young man. For your first time here, you have blown our minds! Welcome to the Keeneland track family! Before I forget, the special gift is, 50 percent of the proceeds from today will go to the cancer society in honor of Ivy Ashcraft!"

The crowd cheers and chants, "Ivy! Ivy! Ivy!" as Hudson gives the news of the special gift.

"Please remember to check out Ivy's beauty shop in town for its grand reopening, also in her honor! Have a great rest of your day, folks! See you at the next race! This is your announcer, Hudson Hammond. I'm out!" he says with pride.

Parker quickly makes his way to the winner's circle, where Chase and Wyatt wait for him with SOT and PB Cup. Flashes are popping in every direction as people snap pictures left and right. Little kids are coming up to hug them and ask to sit on SOT and PB Cup.

Wow! Chase thinks to himself. *This is crazy! Everyone wants to be next to Wyatt and me. We are a huge hit right now!* He then sees Parker trying to politely push his way through the crowd.

"Chase! Wyatt!" Parker shouts as he makes his way closer to them. "*Congratulations*, boys! I am beyond excited for you both! I have to ask you, Wyatt, would you please join our team and race for the Ashcrafts from here on out? I will even let you ride PB Cup! My wife would be so *proud* and *honored* if you would accept it. I just know it!" Parker asks as he feels just pure joy. When Ivy spoke to Parker, he never dreamed how much of a miracle he was about to be a part of. He feels so glad she came to him and he *finally* listened to her.

Wyatt responds to Parker with, "Yes, *yes*! I will do it! Thank you, Parker, for this opportunity. I promise you that you won't regret it!"

After all the pictures and autographs are done, they pack up and head back to the ranch.

CHAPTER 10

Shop Party

Emma is at the ranch, finishing up chores for the day. She is just about to make her way into town to Ivy's shop to clean up per Parker.

She grabs her phone, keys, and purse and heads out to her car. As she prepares to leave, she sees *the guys* headed in the lane. She waits to hear the results of the race. As Parker drives up to the barn, he sees Emma in her car, so he pulls up beside her. Obee puts his window down as they pull up. Emma sees and puts hers down too.

"Emma!" Parker shouts out Obee's window. "We took first and second place today! And I have asked Wyatt to join our team!"

Wyatt puts his window down and says, "I happily accepted," grinning from ear to ear.

"Welcome aboard, Wyatt! It's great to have you with us," Emma says. "So who took first and who stole second?"

Chase says, "First!" as he raises his hand.

Wyatt copies and says, "Second!"

"Great job, boys!" she says. "Okay, great job. Goodbye! I'll be back in time to make dinner a little later." Then she drives off.

"Okay, boys, let's get these girls out of the trailer and into the pasture. I'll get you paid and get you on your way," Parker says as he backs the trailer into place for unloading. "Chase, can you please do me a favor? If you happen to see Sydney, would you please let her know that Emma is at the shop and could use her help to clean up to prepare for the grand reopening?"

"Sure thing, Parker! I can definitely tell her if I see her," Chase replies.

After the horses are unloaded and in the pasture, the saddles and other equipment are unloaded and put in their proper places. Parker comes to the boys and hands them their portion of today's winnings. "Chase, for you," he says, handing his winnings. "Thank you again for another amazing race!" He turns. "Wyatt, for you." He hands him his winnings too. "Thank you for an amazing first race with us. May we have many more together! Okay, boys, I have some things I want and need to get accomplished. Thank you both so very much! I will see you soon!" He then disappears outta sight.

Chase sees Obee and waves him over to them. "Obee! We need a favor. Can you please help?"

Obee says, "Sure! Whatcha y'all need?"

"We are goin' back to the cottage. Can you please pick us up and take us into town to Mom's shop after we change?" Chase asks politely.

"Definitely. Just text me when you are ready to head into town, okay?" he replies.

"Oh, that's awesome! Thank you so much, Obee!" Chase says as he and Wyatt prepare to head out the lane. As they walk out the lane, they open their envelopes with their winnings and look inside.

"Wow! There's a lot of money in here! Oh, how am I gonna hide it from my mom?" Wyatt asks.

"Easy! You can keep it in my lockbox! Your name is on it. I think there is some tape at the cottage that you can use to secure the envelope. So whatcha think? How much did you get? Looks like I have about…" Chase counts the money in his envelope. "Looks like $6,000. *What!* Wait! I have never gotten that much! Wow, Parker must have given me a raise, kinda?" he says.

"Looks like he gave me around $3,000! Wow! Holy cow!" he says, dancing and singing like Chase has never seen or heard from him before! "Thank you, Syd, for askin' me to be a part of your experience! I just do not know what I will do with all this money!" she exclaims.

*****

I lean over and whisper to Sophie, "I do! Buy a car! When you are old enough, of course!" She nods in agreement, then we both begin to laugh so hard.

We make it to the cottage, and I quickly text Obee.

> Sydney
> *Just got to the cottage. Give us 15 to change and wash up and we should be ready. Thx! Syd*

"Okay, we gotta make a move on it! I told Obee that we should be ready in about fifteen. I will wash off my face while you change, and that way the sink will be free for you as soon as you are ready," I say in a hurry. I quickly run into the bathroom, soap up my face, scrub it real good, and rinse it off. "Okay, done! Bathroom is free!" I shout as I run out to change quickly.

"Ten-four, bestie! I will make my way in there in just a minute. Here, Syd, take my money to put in your box," Sophie says as she hands me her money on her way to the bathroom.

"Okay, no problem!" I say as I take it and pull out the lockbox. I get my keys, unlock the box, then place Sophie's winnings in for the day. I open mine and take out a few bills. Then I put mine in, lock it back up, and slide it under the corner of the bed. I tear off my clothes as quickly as I can. "Sophie, time check!" I shout back to her.

"Eight more minutes!" she hollers back.

"Okay, we got this! I am so excited! Sophie!" I say.

"Yeah, I know! Me too!" she says as she walks out from the bathroom. "Today was such a rush out there on the track, just feelin' the adrenaline pace through your body. It was like I was flying with PB Cup beneath me! It was nothing like when we raced here. She just had the spirit to wanna just mow over the other horses! Oh, it's such a rush that I have never felt before! Thank you so much, Syd!" Sophie says with excitement.

"Well, I have an idea! I will talk with Dad and make like Chase and Wyatt spoke with me and wanted to know if he, too, can come have nonwork ride time. So we can ride together at the farm in our disguises and get the girls ridin' together to push each other more!

We will also ride them with you and me together. This way, they will be used to pushin' each other, and I think we can rule that track! What do you think, Sophie? You game?" I ask.

"Heck yeah! I'm all for it! Syd, I think Obee just pulled up," Sophie says.

So I get up to look, and sure enough he is. "Obee is here. Let's hurry!" I say as I wave her out the door.

"Hey, Obee! Thanks again for helping out with everything! Here's a li'l something for your troubles," I say as I smile and wink at him.

"Yes, Obee, thank you for being such a gem! Syd is *so* lucky to have you in her life. You are by far a godsend!" Sophie chimes in.

"Oh, girls, thanks, and, Syd, this is *way* too much! I am sorry, but I can't accept this!" he says as he tries handing it back to me.

"No!" I sternly say. "That is for you. First off, you did not ask to be dragged into this mess, and you have *more* than gone above and beyond my expectations once you did join us! So no, it's yours!" I say happily.

"Okay, I understand all that, Syd. But really, it's just *too much*! It's more than I get paid for a month!" he states sincerely.

"Well, without you, Obee, I would not be as good with horses as I am and I wouldn't be gettin' the money I am, so yes, please just take it. I want you to have it. It's a onetime you-are-a-*kick-A*-awesome-friend payment!" I say.

And Sophie chimes in with, "Yeah, we want you to have it. Syd, I want to give you half of what you gave him!" she proudly says.

"Nope! Consider that your friend payment for stayin' with me through this crazy ordeal!" I respond.

"Ten-four, bestie! That's what friends are for!" Sophie says, hugging me as we pull up to the front of Mom's shop.

"What you two can do for me is pay it forward to someone who needs something. It's a selfless gift with no expectations. The gift of God!" I say to my friends Sophie and Obee.

"Thanks again, Obee. See you later back at the ranch!" I say as we get out of the truck and head inside.

"We are here!" we shout as we enter the shop. "Emma!"

"Back here, girls! I'm goin' through the inventory. So glad you could make it!" Emma says, out of breath.

"Looks like we are just in time too! Emma, why don't you play the foreman and direct us what to do *while we* do all the busy work? You sound like you need a break!" I say with concern.

"Yep, sounds good to me," Sophie says with a smile as she puts her arms up, trying to make big muscles. "See, I brought the big guns," she says. "Well…" She looks at her arm muscles and adds, "Okay, the li'l guns, but I brought 'em to help! Let's get to boogie'in'! Do we have any music we can turn on?"

"Yeah, I think there is a sound system for the shop we can turn on. Let me look," I say to her. "Are you good with some country?" I shout out to her.

"Ten-four, bestie!" She smiles and starts to dance her way to putting merchandise in their correct spots.

We work with Emma for most of the afternoon, working to put out new supplies that never made it to the shelf just months ago, before Mom passed. Finally, I ask Emma, "If you don't mind me askin', Emma, why are we doin' this? We don't even have the shop open anymore." I say it sadly, too, with misty eyes.

"Well, girls, I want to be honest with you, but I also don't want to step on your dad's toes, Sydney, and misdirect my authority. So I bet if you are patient enough for just a few more hours, you may find out at the dinner table tonight. With that said, Sophie, do you think that Allison will allow you to have dinner with us tonight?" she asks. "Because I think you will want to be there, too, when Parker discusses what his plan is."

"I am pretty sure Mom will say yes, but let me just ask," Sophie says as she starts to text on her phone.

> Sophie
> *Mom, Ms. Emma would like to know if*
> *I could possibly eat dinner with them this*
> *evening?*

> Allison
> *Sophie, that would be great, but I just had a*
> *client ask to see one of my listed homes. So I*
> *am sorry, I just cannot say yes. You have to take*
> *care of Eliza! As a matter of fact, where are you?*
> *I need you to get home to her now so she's not*
> *alone when I leave.*

Sophie
Mom, I am at Ivy's shop with Emma and Syd.

"Mom says I have to go. She has a showing, and I have to watch Eliza," Sophie says, hanging her head.

"Sophie, that is great!" Emma says as Sophie looks at her, then me, all confused. "Would Allison like me to come get Eliza?" Emma asks.

"Umm, I do not know. Let me ask," Sophie says, trying to figure out what Emma is up to.

"It would be great if Eliza could come, too, for dinner!" Emma says quickly before Sophie texts her mom back.

Sophie
Mom, Ms. Emma said she will come get Eliza.
She would love for her to come to dinner too!

> Allison
> *Okay, well, I will save her the trip. I can just*
> *drop her off at the shop since I will be goin' right*
> *past there. Is she sure?*

Sophie
Yes, she wants Eliza to come too!

> Allison
> *Okay, I will be there shortly.*

Sophie
Okay, love you, Mom!

> Allison
> *Okay, love you too, kiddo!* 😊

77

"Emma, Mom said she will save you a trip and drop her off when she passes by here," Sophie tells us.

"Okay, sounds like a real girl party now!" Emma says, smiling.

When Allison drops off Eliza, she thanks Emma for the help. Allison leaves, and Eliza finds the kids' corner and plays around in there as we finish up just a few more things before we head back to the ranch.

On the way back, Emma thinks about what's for dinner. When she thinks about what she has enough of for everyone, she says to us, "Great job today, girls. Since we have a few extra guests for dinner, I was thinkin' about makin' spaghetti and some fresh, homemade garlic bread with cheese. How does that sound to you, ladies?" Emma asks us.

We all nod in agreement, and Emma says, "Spaghetti it is! Parker will be so glad we have you girls over tonight! So I am sure he will break the news to y'all!" She smiles.

When we get back to the ranch, we hurry inside and up to my room. Eliza says, "Wow, Syd, your room is *so* big!" as she twirls around in all the open space I have. "I wish my room were this big! Don't you, Sophie?" she asks her sister.

"Yeah, she is lucky, isn't she, Liz?" Sophie says.

"So, ladies, wanna paint our nails? Or brush one another's hair? Play a board game? Watch a movie?" I ask the girls.

"Nah, I'm just hungry," Sophie says.

Eliza says, "Me too!"

Like magic, Emma shouts up the stairs, "Dinner!"

Sophie and Eliza run so fast to the door they beat me to it and head down the stairs, skipping steps on the way down.

"Whoa, slow down, girls! We have a speed limit here at the ranch! You can't run faster than our horses, or out in the pasture you go!" She laughs out loud. "Please wash up before comin' to the dinner table."

"Okay, Emma," we all say as they follow me to the bathroom just off the kitchen. While we wash up, we discuss who will say grace tonight. Sophie volunteers.

As we make our way to the table, Dad comes in to wash up and meets us at the table. "Tonight, ladies, I will say grace," he states with excitement. We girls all look at one another and shrug in unison as Dad continues to speak. "Let's pray, ladies," he says.

Dear God, thank you for all your messages,
no matter how they are sent. Everyone is such a
gift, and we are very grateful for the messengers
and their messages. You are truly the greatest!
And with you, all things are possible! Amen.

Dad looks around the table and is so happy. I can't remember when the last time he seemed so happy was. I think it was before Mom passed. "Let's get our food and talk, ladies," he says. As we dig in and fill up our plates, he starts to talk a while. "So, ladies, I wanted to let you know that we will be reopening Ivy's shop sometime within the next few weeks. But there is one slight issue that I will need to fix, and that is, I need beautiful ladies to run the store in the afternoon. I was wonderin' if you might know of any good-lookin' ladies lookin' to earn some money and experience?" he asks us.

We all three look at one another in complete shock and all jump up and flock to Dad, giving him one *big* group hug. We all excitedly say, "Us! We will do it for you!"

"Okay, ladies, let me breathe. You are squeezing me so hard I almost can't breathe!" Dad says, gasping for air. "It's a deal. You are *all* hired! I will let you know when I need you to start. It will probably be just after race season, just because it has all my extra time consumed at the moment. Thank you, girls! Our grand reopening will be in Ivy's honor, and from here on out, we will donate 20 percent of our proceeds to the cancer society," Dad says proudly.

"That's awesome, Dad!" I say, tearing up. "I would be honored to run Mom's shop!"

"Same, Parker! I have always loved your wife's shop, and it would be my pleasure to help run it!" Sophie says.

"Parker, I am too young to help run it, but I would love to hang out with my sister when she is there. Thank you!" Eliza states.

"Eliza, li'l one, you are too cute. But I know we have just the right job for you so it feels like you are helping us, but in reality, you will be helping the customers. There is a small nook in the back of the store with kids' toys. Did you see it when you were there today?" Dad asks Eliza.

"Yes, sir, I did. I put all the toys together and cleaned up the area for Emma," Eliza replies.

"Oh, good, you know where I mean. Well, how about we give you the job of helpin' out with any small children while their parents shop? Would you like that job, Eliza?" Parker kindly asks her.

"I will ask my mom if it is okay. But I think I can help you," she says so sweetly.

"How about I talk with your mom and you just have fun? How's that sound?" he says, lookin' at Eliza as she gets so excited, but in a calm way, so as not to show it.

"Yes, I would like that, Parker," she says.

"Okay, ladies, it's set, then. Thank you for an amazin' day, and you all have a great rest of your evenin'! I have a few things I need to do out in the barn. Good night, ladies," Dad says as he excuses himself from the table.

"This has been a day from heaven, ladies, and again, thank you for all your help at the shop! If you are done, you may get up from the table. Sophie and Eliza, would you like me to take you home?" Emma asks.

"May we stay a li'l longer?" requests Sophie.

"Sure, no problem. I will take you home in a li'l while. Go have fun, girls," Emma tells us.

Emma cleans up the dinner mess and goes into the living room to sit and relax on the recliner for a bit. She almost starts to drift off when she decides she better get up and get the girls home before she falls asleep. Emma shouts upstairs to us, "Girls, can you please come down here?"

When Emma asks, we go down to see what she needs. "What's up, Em?" I ask.

"Sydney, I am so sorry, but would you please ride with me to take the girls home? I hate to cut your time short, but I have had a very long, busy day, and I just need to go to bed," Emma states, starting to yawn.

"Yes, I will!" I gladly tell her.

"We are okay with leavin' now, Emma. Thank you for lettin' us stay this long," Sophie politely says.

We get in the car, take the girls home, come back, and head to our rooms for bed.

CHAPTER 11

One Fateful Night

A few months ago, an event happened that changed our lives here on the Ashcraft ranch forever. These are the events of that dreadful night.

*****

"Emma, would you be a doll and go pick up Sophie and Eliza? Allison called this afternoon and asked if the girls could come hang out while we all went out tonight. I told her absolutely!"

"Sure thing, Ivy. I will go now. Sydney?" she hollers up the stairs to her.

"Yes, Em? I'm coming!" Sydney says as she starts down the stairs. "What's up, Em?" she questions her.

"I'm headed to get Sophie and Eliza. Would you like to ride along?"

"Yes, please!" Sydney shouts. "When will you be leavin', Mom?"

Ivy slightly raises her voice so Sydney can hear her from her room. "We should still be here when you get back, dear."

"Okay, great, 'cause I want to say goodbye before you guys leave!" Sydney says as she heads to the front door.

Em and Sydney walk out to the car. Well, Em walks; Sydney skips her way to the car. They get in and take off out of the lane. "So what would you like to do with the girls when we get back to the house?" Emma asks.

"Well, I would like to maybe watch a movie. But they are our guests. Can we ask them what they would like to do? If they want to ride, can we?" Sydney asks.

"Well, I do not have a problem with it, but let's check with your dad before they leave to make sure he's okay with it. Is that fair?" she reasonably asks.

"Yes, sure, that seems fair, Em. I pray Dad says yes!"

As they pull up in Sophie's driveway, Sydney has her hand on the door handle, ready to jump outta the car. "Please wait till I stop, Sydney!" Emma cautiously asks.

"I will, Em. I'm just excited to see Sophie!"

She comes out as Emma stops the car. Sydney jumps out; they hug and dance around together. "Where's Eliza?" Sydney asks, expecting her to be right on her heels.

"I'm right here, Syd!" she says as she comes running toward Sydney, who tries to catch her to slow her down, but Eliza is so spunky and full of energy while being so loving and sweet she almost knocks Sydney completely over. If it weren't for the car, she would have been on the driveway.

Allison comes out the door and says, "Thank you, Emma. We are so grateful for you and all you do for us and our girls, as if they are Ivy's too!" She then turns to the girls. "Girls, please be good for Emma. Don't make too much trouble for her."

"Allison, they are no bother. They are a great pair of girls you have there! I would love to have them over anytime. But as for you, please have a good time tonight with the Ashcrafts. I pray you all have so much fun!" replies Emma. "I can bring the girls back tomorrow mornin' or even in the afternoon, if that suits you better."

"Yes, Emma, I think the afternoon would be best. We will try our best to have a nice night out. Lord knows we haven't had one in quite a while! So that makes us all due for one. We will try to make the best of it!" Allison says with anticipation of a fun night ahead. "You need a fun night out too! Maybe we can talk the guys into watchin' all the girls so we can all have a women's night out. What do you think?"

"Okay, that sounds like a good game plan, Allison! We best get going, girls," Emma says, trying to get us all loaded up for the drive back. "Hurry, girls. Let's get in so we can get going. I still need to talk with Ivy and Parker before they leave for the night." They all wave at Allison as they get in the car to leave.

Eliza watches out the back window at her mom till she can no longer see her. Then she turns around, sits down, grabs Sydney's hand and Sophie's hand, and puts them together in her lap. She's looking forward and smiling like she has some devious plan in the works. Sydney looks over at Sophie as Sophie looks over at her, and they just look at each other like, "What does the little one have up her sleeve?" Sophie shrugs and smiles; Sydney can't help but laugh.

Then Eliza turns to Sydney and asks, "Syd, what's so funny?"

She smiles and tells her, "Nothing, Liz. I was just thinkin'." So she turns and continues looking forward.

Then suddenly she shrieks, "We're here, we're here!"

Sophie says, "Eliza, shh. Not so loud! Yes, I see we are here!"

When they pull up, as Em stops the car, they get out and Eliza runs up to the fence where PB Cup and SOT stand watching them pull up. Sydney walks over to give SOT some love. "How's SOT? She's such a beautiful girl, yes, she is," Sydney tells her as she rubs her neck and hugs her.

"Can I ride her?" Eliza asks.

"Let's go ask my dad," Sydney tells her.

They head to the house to ask Sydney's dad if they can ride the horses. He's in the kitchen with her mom. "Dad, can we ride the horses for a bit before it gets dark?"

He thinks about it and asks, "Ivy, have you seen Oliver lately?"

"He was out in the barn," she tells him.

"Come on, girls, follow me. We're walkin' out to the barn," Parker says to them.

"Honey, please be careful to not get dirty. We do not have time to change you before we leave," her mom says as she watches her dad take them to the barn.

"Emma, I love that man with all my heart! Do you think he even knows it? I know he knows I love him, but do you think he knows to the extent of how much *I love him*?" she asks with misty eyes.

"Ivy, he is so lucky to have such a beautiful lady such as you by his side. I think he knows," Emma reassures her.

"Emma, I am not sure how late we will be tonight. I am okay, though, with the girls stayin' up a li'l later than normal, but not *too* late!" she tells Emma. "Good night, Emma. I love you! We will see you in the morning," she says as she walks out the door to find Parker. She walks through the stables to get to the training ring, where Parker stands with Obee and the girls. "Honey, are you just about ready to go?" she asks so softly.

"Yeah, dear, just about. So remember, girls, as long as Obee is right here with you, you may ride the horses. Obee, have fun with the girls tonight, and we will see you in the mornin'. Come give Mom and me some quick lovin' so we can go, Sydney," he asks as he waves her to hurry over to them.

Sydney goes to her mom and dad both and gives them big hugs and kisses, and then she turns to her mom and gives her one more great big hug and kisses. She tells her, "Mom, I love you very much! You are the best Mom in the world! Have fun tonight. I will see you tomorrow!"

Then Sydney turns to her dad, "I love you too, Dad. Please give Mom the night of her life! I will see you tomorrow too!" Sydney says as she hugs him one more time and they turn and walk away. She stands there watching them walk to the truck to leave. Obee, Sophie, Eliza, and Sydney wave to Sydney's mom and dad as they back out, pull away, and drive out the lane. No one ever knows when the last they see their loved ones will be, but if Sydney would have had any clue that this would be the last she would ever see her mom, she would have begged them to stay.

"Obee, let's ride out in the pasture. Please?" Sydney asks him.

"As long as you guys stay with me, sure, we can do that. Let's get some horses saddled up and go for a ride."

As they go for a ride, Emma is inside, making brownies for the girls as a treat. She also has dinner in the oven.

Meanwhile, in town, her mom and dad have reached the club across the street and just down from her mom's shop. They park the truck and wait for the Abbotts to show up. "I will text them and let them know we just got here and we are waitin' for them," she tells Sydney's dad.

Ivy
Hello, Allison. Just wanted to let you know
we are at the club. Just got here and are
waitin' for you to arrive.

Allison
Okay, sounds great. Can't wait to see you guys.
We will be leavin' in about five minutes.

Mom tells Dad, "Allison and Greyson will be here shortly. While we wait, could we drive over to the shop real quick?"

"Sure, sweetheart, not a problem," he says as he turns the truck around and drives down the street. "Is everything okay, Ivy?"

"I just need to check on a shipment that was to be delivered this afternoon. I haven't had confirmation that it was delivered yet, and I would like to just make sure," she says as she quickly gets down out of her husband's truck and walks around back. She comes right back out.

"No, it has not been delivered yet. We can check on our way home later this evening. Right now, though, we need to get back. The Abbotts should be there by now, and if not, they will be very soon," she tells Dad.

"Yes, dear, we are off for the night of a lifetime! I wanna have so much fun with you. Just relaxin' and tearin' up the dance floor," he tells her as they turn back into the club.

The Abbotts are not quite there yet, so Parker decides to profess his love to Sydney's mom. "I just want you to know, you look absolutely gorgeous this evening. There's a twinkle in your eyes that I have not noticed before. You smell so delightful! And I do not know *how* you got your skin so soft, but it's like satin. I just want to hold your hand *all* night! I also want you to have this. I have had this for a li'l while, just waitin' for the right time to give it to you, and well, tonight seems as good as any. It sparkles almost as much as your eyes do tonight." He hands her a long skinny box with a beautiful blue bow and ribbon that just happens to match her dress for the evening.

Ivy takes the box, smiling so beautifully, and opens it. "Oh, Parker, these are absolutely beautiful!" She puts on the earrings and necklace. She hands the bracelet to Parker for him to put on her wrist. He puts the bracelet on her wrist, then he softly kisses her hand. Ivy blushes as Parker pulls her in for a soft, sensual kiss, only to be interrupted by the Abbotts tapping on the windows.

"Get a room, you two lovebirds!" Greyson says jokingly.

"Hey, man, I gotta show my woman a good time. I don't care who sees me makin' out with my beautiful woman! We can get a room later," Parker says, jabbing Greyson on the shoulder.

Allison and Ivy walk in together. Then Parker and Greyson follow in behind them, together. They stop at the hostess booth and wait to be seated. This is a restaurant-style club. There are tables with seating like in restaurants with waiters and waitresses to take orders and bring food. They have a wooden dance floor with a disco ball and live music every Friday night. Club Cowboys and Cowgirls is a multigenerational club. The crowds are more formal, with a mature, sophisticated group on Friday nights than Saturdays. The Saturday crowd is younger, more redneck, wild, with more chaos and ruckus type. Ivy has wanted to go to this club for some time.

They get seated and place their orders. While they wait, Parker goes up to the DJ, hands him a $20, and asks for a song. You can see Parker talking to him and the DJ nodding in agreement. Parker returns and asks, "My beautiful lady, Ivy, would you give me the pleasure of a dance while we wait?" He puts out his hand to hers. She gladly accepts, and they walk out to the dance floor while they wait for the music to start. Parker stands there holding Ivy, just waiting for the right moment to make his move.

Ivy hears the beginning and begins to tear up. "Honey, you remembered," she says as they start to move with the music. In the background, "I Cross My Heart" plays as they slow dance in the middle of the dance floor. Parker gently wipes away her tears and looks deep in her eyes. He sings to her the chorus. As he sings, she smiles at him. He wipes her tears again, and she lays her head on his chest. They slow dance for the length of the song. When it's over, she starts to turn to walk back to the table, but Parker stops her, shakes his finger at her, and shakes his head no. She returns to his grasp as a more upbeat song begins to play, "Forever and Ever Amen." She just smiles and whispers in his ear, "You have my heart forever and ever, I cross my heart." She puts up her pinky and waits for his. "I pinky promise!" she says as she wraps hers around his.

When the song is over, they take their seats.

She then gets a text stating her package has been delivered. "I'm sorry, everyone, but I have to make a quick run to my shop, where my package was just delivered. Since I am not sure how long we will be, I don't want it sitting out. I promise to be very quick," she tells everyone as she excuses herself from the table.

"Sweetheart, do you want me to come along?" Parker asks.

"No, honey, please, I will be just fine. Stay with the Abbotts so they aren't here all alone," she states to Parker as she kisses him before she leaves.

She walks out the door and down the street. She makes it to her shop, places her package inside, and makes her way back to the club.

As she walks down the street, she comes to the alley, and out of nowhere comes a car flying down the street, swerving back and forth. She tries to move out of the way.

Meanwhile, inside the club, the food has been delivered to the table. "Will there be anything else?" the waitress asks.

Parker and the Abbotts state, "No, we are good. Thank you!"

They begin to eat and are making small talk when someone comes running through the door screaming to call 911. Parker hears and jumps up and screams, "No, Ivy!" as he runs toward the door.

The bouncer stops him dead in his tracks. "Sir, please, you don't understand. My wife, Ivy, is out there! I need to make sure she is okay!"

The bouncer says, "Sir, please. You must wait here!" He puts his hand out to stop Parker.

Greyson sees what's happening and comes up to Parker. The bouncer says to Greyson, "Sir, stop!"

"I'm with Parker here. His wife, Ivy, went outside just down the street to put a package in her shop that was just delivered. Can you please just check to make sure that whatever is happening out there, it's nothing to do with her? She is wearing a long light-blue dress with spaghetti straps, and a blue tulle wrap. Please, sir. I will make sure he stays put if you could just do us this one li'l favor," Greyson asks the bouncer.

"Okay, I will see what I can find out, but you two must stay here till I return!" the bouncer demands.

Allison comes up to Parker and Greyson. "What's goin' on, Greyson?" she asks.

"We don't know. I asked the bouncer if he could go make sure it wasn't Ivy."

Allison states, "Whatever it is, it must be bad. There are sirens comin' from all directions and lights flashing everywhere off every surface like it's the Fourth of July! Oh, I do hope that Ivy is okay and that bouncer returns soon with some info!" Allison has a worried look on her face. "Dear," she says to Greyson, touching his shoulder, "I am takin' Parker back to the table. When the bouncer returns, let us know what he tells you. Come on, Parker, let's go sit for now and say a prayer that it's not Ivy but for whoever it is to be okay," she says as she guides Parker back to the table.

Just as they get seated, the bouncer returns. "Sir, did she have curly brown hair?" he sadly asks.

"Oh, dear God, yes! Is she okay? Please say she's okay!" Greyson pleads with the bouncer.

"Sir, I am sorry, but the police are gonna wanna talk with your friend. I will send them in. He will want to stay in here. It's not pretty," the bouncer warns.

Greyson gets sick to his stomach and asks, "Sir, just how bad is it? Is she responsive? Can my friend Parker ride with her to the hospital?" he asks, trying to fight back the tears as he feels frustrated that he can't do anything to help Ivy.

"I'm sorry, but they had to call the coroner. There was a hit-and-run. A witness said the car was swerving all over the road and she tried to get out of the way when it hit her. I am so sorry. I will send the police in to speak to your friend. What was his name again?" he asks.

"His name is Parker Ashcraft. Her name was Ivy Ashcraft. Oh my, this is gonna crush him. Okay, thank you, sir. I will try to go inform him somehow. Thank you," Greyson sadly says. He stands there for a moment and tries to collect himself.

He turns to look at Allison, and she sees the fear in his face. "Parker, I will be right back," Allison says to him as she walks up to Greyson. "Please, Greyson, please tell me Ivy is okay," she says without much hope.

"Allison, it was Ivy, and I don't know how to say this, but…"

"But what, Greyson?" Allison quietly demands an answer. "Greyson, please tell me right now. Just out with it!"

"Allison, there was a hit-and-run, from what they believe was a drunk driver. From what the witness said, she tried to get out of the way but the driver hit her. Allison, they had to call the coroner," Greyson says as he hangs his head in disbelief.

"Oh no! Okay, I will go try to break the news to Parker."

"Allison, wait! The police want to talk with Parker. The bouncer went out to let them know who she was and that her husband was in here. I just can't believe this, Allison. They were havin' such a great time tonight. It was such a much-needed night out." Greyson closes his eyes and grits his teeth. "I just wish there were something I could do to help," he says, feeling hopeless.

"Well, right now we have a friend over there who needs us, so let's go comfort him," Allison says respectfully.

As they turn to walk away, an officer comes in, loudly announcing he is looking for Parker Ashcraft. Parker hears this and runs up to the officer. Allison and Greyson join them.

"Sir, I am Officer Baskett. I am sorry, but there was a hit-and-run this evening. The witness stated that the car was swerving back and forth over the road and Ivy, your wife, tried to get out of the way. I'm sorry to tell you she was hit and is unresponsive."

Parker just about hits the floor! His knees get weak, and Greyson catches him in time to help him to a chair. "Officer, may I see her?" Parker asks.

"I'm sorry, but at this time, that may not be such a great idea. This is unlike anything I have ever seen before. Can you just wait here for a moment? And I will be right back," the officer warns Parker.

"Greyson," Parker says weakly.

"Yes, Parker, what can I get for you?"

"My Ivy is gone. What am I gonna do? What about Sydney? Oh, how my heart aches already!" Parker says, crying uncontrollably.

Greyson reassures Parker, "Buddy, we are here for you, and we together will and can get through this with God's love."

Parker stands and screams out loud, "With what? God's love? What god? What kind of God would take a perfectly healthy woman from a perfect marriage with a child and a husband and leave our hearts empty?" Parker says with anger. "I am done with God. He is ridiculous!"

Allison takes Parker's hand. "Parker, please, you are hurting right now! But you will see, and you already know that everything happens for a reason, even if we don't know why. We will eventually figure it out. I'm sure God has a *very good reason* for this. Trust me and God, for I pray you will know soon enough." She tries to reassure him of his love for God and God's love for him.

"Please, Allison, I just want to be alone right now," Parker rudely states.

"Do you want us to take you home, Parker?" Allison calmly asks.

"No! I want to be alone! I will be fine!" He pushes his way to the side entrance of the club and gets in his truck and takes off outta town.

"Greyson, I am worried. Should we follow him?" Allison wonders.

"No," Greyson sadly states. "I am sure I know where he is headed, so I will let him go and I will go tomorrow morning and check on him. Let's pay the bill and get home for now."

When they go to pay the bill, the manager comes over to them and states, "There will be no charge today. And we took it upon ourselves to make you fresh food to take with you. We are so sorry for your loss. Please do come back sometime with meals on the house."

"Oh, thank you, sir. Have a good night!" Alison says as they make their way out to the side entrance to their vehicle. They head home and try to get some sleep. Tomorrow is gonna be a hard day for *everyone*.

CHAPTER 12

Search for the Hit-and-Run Driver

"**H**IT-AND-RUN SEARCH IS ON. It's a sad day here in Lexington. Last night we had a fatal tragedy. The family of the victim is seeking help to find the driver of the car that hit one of their own. They ask that their name remain anonymous at this time. If you were in the area of Club Cowboys and Cowgirls last evening around seven and saw anything that can help the police, please call the station," states the front page of the newspaper.

Emma puts the paper down and goes to the front door. She looks out the window and doesn't see Parker's truck. "Oh, I hope everyone is okay. I better put this paper away for now, just till I hear from Ivy and Parker to make sure all is well."

She starts to prepare breakfast. As she does so, she can faintly hear the girls get up and stir about. She sets the table while waiting for the French toast to brown. Emma is living up to her normal standard when preparing food. The house smells amazing. The smell has managed to make it all the way up to the top floor.

"Mmm, what is that smell?" Eliza asks, rubbing her belly as she silently zipper-locks her lips and throws away the key. "Shh, sissy, don't tell Mom, but her cookin's don't *never* smell like that!" she exclaims.

"Eliza, *don't* or *never*, but not *don't never*," Sophie says, laughing as she corrects her. "I can promise you that if it smells that good, it tastes *even* better!"

"Well, what are we waitin' for? Have we all pottied and washed up?" I ask them. "I know I am good!" I say, smiling.

Eliza and Sophie both say in unison, "We are good!"

"Well, then, let's go eat, 'cause I am *starving*! And smellin' this ah-maz-iness is makin' me even hangrier!"

"Me too!" Eliza says, dragging her feet like she's outta energy and the breakfast will be the *only thing* to restore her to movable status.

"I am famished! Can't wait to dig in. I can't promise you that I can eat with manners this morning," Sophie says, laughing.

We all make our way downstairs calmly. As we get closer to the kitchen, Eliza takes off running for the kitchen. "Mmm, Emma, breakfast smells *so* good!"

"Thank you, li'l one. I think you will absolutely love it. Have a seat. I will get you some. Today we have homemade blueberry muffins, French toast, scrambled eggs, bacon, and whatever you would like to drink. So what will you have, ladies?" Emma asks us.

"Eliza, why don't you tell her first?" I gently command.

Eliza makes a fist, and as she states what she wants, she opens a finger like she's counting her food. "French toast, eggs, muffins..." She pauses for a moment. "Umm, do you have strawberry chocolate milk?" she asks so sweetly.

"Strawberry chocolate milk? Hmm, that's a new one."

Emma is about to say no when Sophie quickly states, "It's just strawberry milk," chuckling. "At our house we have chocolate and strawberry syrup that we put in milk, and she thinks she has to say chocolate. We don't know why she says that, but yeah, she just wants strawberry milk, please," Sophie reassures Emma.

"Okay, so for Eliza, how about one slice of French toast, half of a muffin, a scoop of eggs?" she says, handing the plate to Eliza. She turns for a glass and spoon, sets them on the table, and goes for the syrup and milk. "One glass of strawberry chocolate milk," she says, smiling and winking at Eliza.

"Thank you, Emma!" replies Eliza as she now sits and waits patiently for everyone to have their food and prayer.

I motion for Sophie to choose next. "Oh, okay. I would like French toast. May I just have the other half of the muffin? And eggs and apple juice, please," she kindly requests.

"Sure thing, dear." Emma selects her order, pours her juice, and hands her what she asked for. "The usual, Sydney?" she then asks me.

"Yes, please. So who wants to do grace?" I ask.

Eliza raises her hand like she's in school. I nod in agreement, and we all fold our hands, bow our heads as she begins:

> Dear Lord, thank you for Ms. Emma and her
> amazing food! Shh, please don't tell Mom. Amen.

Sophie chuckles. "Sorry, sometimes she can have some of the cutest prayers. I don't mean to laugh. I love you, Eliza!" Sophie professes to everyone.

"It's okay, sissy. I love you too," she says, blushing.

"Okay, ladies, let's eat! So what do we want to do today?" Emma asks.

"I was thinkin', if it's okay, that we could hook up the medium carriage and take it out to the lake to do some fishing. Would that be okay, Em?" I ask, hoping for a yes.

"I think that would be just fine, Syd. Can you please ask Oliver to help you hook everything up so it's done correctly?" she asks kindly.

"Yes, I will," I tell her. We all finish up, and I ask, "May we be excused, Em?"

"Yes, girls, go have fun. I will text you when lunch is ready."

As we girls get up and head outside, Emma quickly gets up and texts Oliver.

Emma
Oliver, the girls are headed out to you, but I need to talk with you. Do you think you can come inside for just a moment?

Oliver
Sure thing, Emma. Can you give me just a minute?

95

Emma
Yes, see you in a few. Thank you!

Emma fixes a plate for Oliver and cleans up the rest of breakfast. When he comes in, she has the paper lying with a plate of food. He looks at it and says, smiling, "Mmm, you have outdone yourself again, Em. Food smells amazin'! And I even get the paper this mornin'." He quickly eats his breakfast.

"No, Obee, I have a bad feelin' way down deep in my gut. Read the front page," she instructs.

He reads it and says, "Why? Do you think something happened to Parker and Ivy or the Abbotts?"

"I don't know. I just feel like something's off. And Parker and Ivy didn't return last evening. Can you ride out to the lake with the girls and keep them busy fishing for a while, so I can go into town and try to figure *something* out?" she asks worriedly.

"Sure thing, Emma. Here's the paper back, and thanks again for the most amazin', tastiest breakfast ever!" Obee says as he gets up and heads back outside.

Emma gets ready to head to town while Obee hooks up the bigger carriage and loads us all up. Em comes out to leave and shouts over to us, "Girls, I will be back. I have to run some errands and pick up some things for lunch. I will be back shortly. Love you!" She blows us multiple kisses.

We wave and all say, "Bye," and return air-kisses.

We all take off on the path to our destinations. We make it to the lake, and Obee helps Eliza set up her hook while I help Sophie. We cast out and wait. Eliza is the first one with a bite. "I got one! I got one!" she screams, jumping up and down, waving her arms everywhere. She almost smacks Obee in the face.

"Eliza," Obee says, trying to get her focus back on the rod and fish. "Here, let's reel it in and see whatcha got!" he says. They both are reeling together. She lands it, and it's a pretty big pumpkinseed sunny. We continue to fish.

Meanwhile, back in town, Emma goes straight to the Abbotts' to see if they are home. As she pulls up, there is only one vehicle in the driveway. *Maybe one of them is home,* she thinks as she parks her car and gets out. She walks up to the door and knocks. Allison comes to the door and invites Emma in.

"Emma, please come into the kitchen and sit with me for a li'l while. How are you this morning?" she asks.

"Well, I am okay, I guess. Well, I was till I read the paper this morning. Now I can't shake this feeling something is wrong, very wrong. So Obee has the girls at the lake, fishing, and I figured I would come see if maybe the Ashcrafts had come here to stay. Please tell me they got a room?" she cautiously asks.

"Oh, Emma, where do I start?" Allison states, and she looks away, trying to hold back the tears a bit longer. "Let me say that last night was amazin' as it began. We had seats right up front by the dance floor. Parker had the DJ play 'I Cross My Heart,' and they slowly danced so beautifully together, caressing each other. Then they danced for one more song, 'Forever and Ever Amen,' and stepped up their dance moves to match the beat. When they came back to the table, Ivy had received a text stating that the package she had been waiting for was delivered. She left to go secure it inside the shop…" She pauses and can't hold back the tears any longer. She gets the box of tissues and takes one for herself and one for Emma and hands it to her. "Emma, that was when the night turned very bad. We still do not know *all* the details, but from what I gather, a witness saw a car swerving in the street, Ivy trying to move to safety, and apparently, she did not make it out of the way in time. She was struck, and by the time help could arrive, it was too late," she sadly relays to Emma.

Emma's heart drops, and she clenches her chest. "Oh my, dear Lord, where is Parker? Is he okay? He never came home last night. He probably didn't want to worry us, but where is he? He didn't stay here?" she asks in a frantic panic.

Allison reaches for Emma's hands. Emma gets even more emotional, so Allison gets up and pulls her in for a secure, loving hug. Allison tries to calm her and continues with the story. "Emma, all I know is Parker was a wreck, as would be expected in this sort of situation. He wasn't able to see her last night because Officer Baskett advised him otherwise. When Greyson tried to comfort him, he took off out the side door of the club and tore off in his truck. Now, Greyson mentioned that he may know where he was headed, so he left outta here early this morning to go check on him. That is what I know for now, Emma. I am so sorry to have to deliver such horrific news so early in the day, or even at all." She sadly regrets things. "We asked the officer to keep it anonymous for now to give it time for the shock to kinda buzz down a li'l, not that it will anytime soon, if ever. And to give the police time to catch who may have done it. Is there anything we can do for you?" Allison asks.

Emma sits there hanging her head, at a total loss with what to say. "I…I don't know how I will tell Sydney and the girls. Have you checked with Greyson to see if he made contact with Parker?" Emma asks, feeling empty.

"I will ask him now." She picks up her phone.

> Allison
> *Greyson, have you found Parker?*
>
> Greyson
> *Yes, I have. We are just sittin' here, talkin'. I'm tryin' to help him decide what to do for right now. We are headed back to our house. See you in a bit. Love you, love me.*
>
> Allison
> *Okay, love you. BTW, Emma is here.*
>
> Greyson
> *Okay, I will tell Parker.*

"Greyson is bringing Parker here. They will be here in a bit. Can I get you something to drink?" Allison asks.

"Just water, please," Emma requests.

Allison goes to the fridge and gets a bottle of water for Emma. And a cup of tea for herself. Just then, Greyson pulls up, and sure enough, Parker pulls up right behind him. The door opens, and Emma goes to Parker, wraps her arms around him, and says softly, "I am so sorry. We will get through this with the love of God—"

Greyson abruptly interrupts. "Emma, that's a sore subject for him right now," he promises.

"Well, sore or not, I completely understand why he feels this way. He has the right, but I will pray every day from this point on for Parker to remember his faith and that *everything will be okay!* Because with God's love, all is possible! And one day, I pray, soon he will be okay with this decision that God has bestowed upon him," Emma states to them in the Lord's name.

"Thank you, Emma. I pray one day I can get past this too. But right now, I just don't see it. I have lost my one true love, my better half, my Eve, my one true Ivy Blue Eyes," he says, wiping his eyes. "There will never be another to replace her!"

Allison hands him a tissue and gives him a gentle hug. "We love you, Parker, and will do anything you need. Please don't hesitate to just ask," she passionately relays to him. "Truly, anything, anytime."

"Well, actually, I was wonderin' if I may steal Greyson for a bit. I need to go to the morgue and verify that it's definitely Ivy. I know it is, but they say it's protocol," he says, teary-eyed. "I just do not know how I can even bring myself to do this, Allison."

Allison responds, "I know deep down you still believe in God, as much as you say you hate him right now. He will still be with you today as you have to go do the hardest thing anyone must have to endure. Also, Parker, Greyson is yours all day. I can catch up with him later. Just promise to give him back at some point." She smiles and rubs his arm and kisses his forehead.

Parker actually gives the tiniest of smiles and says to Allison, "Thanks, Allison, but I don't think Greyson will want to be with me long, anyways, 'cause I was the worst half!"

Emma quickly reacts. "I'll have you know, Parker, that before you and Ivy left yesterday, she professed her love for you to me. She loved you so deeply, and I honestly feel that she would kick your bum sayin' you are the worst half. Sir, I should take ya outside and whoop you *all* over the yard!" She laughs as she exclaims.

"Thank you, Emma. It means a lot to know she told you that. I am sorry. I won't say I'm the worst half anymore. God knows I wouldn't want her or you to kick my bum." Parker tries to joke but just can't find the effort.

Greyson says respectfully, "Come, Parker, let's get this over with so we can move on to the next phase beyond this. Allison, Emma, we will return shortly."

Greyson and Parker leave to head to the morgue. The morgue is in the back of the police department. When they get there, they meet the sheriff, Colton Hutchins, at the counter. "My condolences to you, Parker. I was totally shocked to hear about last evening, and even more shocked when I saw for myself. I'm sorry to do this, but even though you were both well-known around town, *we* can't legally verify the body. It has to be one of a family member. Is there any particular way you can verify her? Any scars, tattoos?"

"It's okay. I want to see her. Don't try to sugarcoat an already-bad situation, Colton," Parker says grudgingly. "I'm sorry, it's not your fault, but I just want to get this over with, please."

"Okay, boss, whatever you want. Follow me this way," Colton states.

They all head back the hall toward the morgue. When they get there, Colton pauses for a moment before he opens the cold metal door, slides out the drawer. He pauses for another moment. "Are you ready, Parker?" Parker nods, and Colton begins to unzip the bag.

Parker stands there, making fists to control his anger as he grits and grinds his teeth, trying to hold back the tears. Once the bag is open, Parker just stands there for a moment, just staring at Ivy. He begins to tremble as he slowly moves closer and reaches for Ivy. He gently caresses her face, trying to wipe away the dried blood. He leans down and ever so gently kisses her one last time. He whispers to her, "I love you, Ivy Blue Eyes. Please watch over us." He stands back up and motions for Colton to close the bag back up. Then he motions to stop. "Wait! Please wait. Colton, may I have her jewelry? I had just given her those pieces last night before we went to dinner." Greyson puts his hand on Parker's back to show his support.

"Um, sure, Parker. Would you like me to take the pieces off, or would you like to?"

Parker looks at Greyson for what he should do. "Buddy, you do what you feel in your gut!" Greyson assures him.

"I will do that, Colton. Thank you for the choice." Colton unzips the bag so Parker can remove her jewelry. He starts with her earrings, then her necklace, and he stands there and pauses, trying to get up the energy to ask Colton to unzip the bag further so he can get her bracelet and watch. Parker looks at Greyson again, and Greyson figures out what he is unable to say.

"Colton, can you please unzip the bag further for Parker to get her watch and bracelet?" Greyson kindly asks.

"Sure thing. I am so sorry, sir." He unzips the bag more.

Parker reaches in and takes her arm, so cold and stiff, to retrieve her watch and bracelet. He gently lays her arm back down. Then he remembers her wedding rings, so he takes her other arm out and pulls off her rings as he starts to break down, so teary eyed he can barely see. He puts her other arm down but doesn't want to let go even though it's not the warm, soft hands he held just the night before on one of the greatest nights they have had in quite a while.

Greyson Starts to get misty-eyed watching Parker hurt so bad. He wants to just take him away, but he knows he needs this for closure.

Parker finally lets go and just stands there, taking in his last moments with Ivy, the sweetest love of his life. He leans in and gives her one more last kiss. He then backs away and motions for Colton to close her up.

Parker and Greyson watch as Colton zips up the bag, pushes in the drawer, closes the door, and latches it.

"Again, Parker, I am so sorry. If there is anything we can do, please just ask," Colton states with a heavy heart.

"Yeah, there is something you can do for me," Parker angrily requests. "Find the SOB who did this and make him pay!" Parker then walks away.

Colton follows him and says, "Parker, I want to assure you we are doin' our best to find the perp. We have a statement in the paper. We are takin' calls and checkin' out *all* leads. As soon as we know anything, we will let you know. Till then, please know that you and your family will be in our thoughts and prayers. Also, feel free to call and ask for updates as often as you wish," Colton informs Parker.

As Parker and Greyson make their way to the location of the counter. Officer Marlow motions for Colton to come over his way. "Just one minute, Marlow. I have to make a receipt of Ivy's belongings that were returned to Parker."

After Colton gives Parker his receipt, he walks over to see what Marlow wanted. They can be heard whispering between them, but Parker can kinda make out a small amount of what's being said, along with his reading Officer Marlow's lips. "Dylan...wrecked...front end...garage...last night...something big...and drunk!"

"Okay, thanks, Marlow." Colton walks back over to Parker and Greyson.

"Was that a lead, Colton?" Parker demands.

"It was. I sent Marlow out to investigate. When he reports back, I will call you if it leads to any important info," Colton says, trying to get them to leave. "Okay, you will have to excuse me, gentlemen. I have something I have to get to. I'll be in touch," he says as he turns to walk away and leave.

Parker and Greyson head out to Greyson's truck. "What was that in there, Parker?" Greyson asks, puzzled.

"Greyson, right now I am hurtin' and you are my one true friend. You said I can ask you for anything. Well, did you hear anything from that conversation between them?" he asks Greyson.

"I have to say no, not really. Were you able to hear anything?" Greyson asks.

"Yeah, that's what I was whispering and reading from Marlow's lips. Wanna take a trip?" Parker asks.

"If it'll help you get through this, sure, anything, friend," Greyson proudly states. "Where are we off to?"

"Do you know where Dylan's garage is?"

"I sure do! He has done some work for me. But what's with his garage?" Greyson questions.

"Well, let's take a drive by and see. If what I think I heard was correct and I piece it all together, then someone who was drunk, hit something big, the vehicle is at Dylan's with front-end damage.

So I just want to drive by and see if I recognize the car," Parker says painfully.

"Okay, let's go! Can you text Emma to let her and Allison know what we are up to?"

"I'm on it!" Parker states willfully as he quickly grabs his phone.

Parker
Emma, we are on a lead. We will be back soon.

Emma
Okay, be safe, you two. I will tell Allison.

"Greyson and Parker are following up on a lead. They will return in a bit," Emma tells Allison.

"Okay, I pray it's a good lead." Allison is hopeful.

CHAPTER 13

Guilty by Association

Parker and Greyson pull up at Dylan's garage. "Look, Parker!" Greyson points to a small car sitting out in the open in front of the garage with front-end damage.

"Stop, Greyson. I want to go in and take a look. No one seems to be around. I need to look over the car," Parker says with hope.

Greyson stops, and they get out. Parker walks up to the car and gets real close and looks it over real good. "Greyson, look!" Parker says quickly, pointing to some light-blue fibers and a few strands of hair. "This is the car! It's the car that hit Ivy!" Parker starts to weep again as he takes out his phone and snaps pictures of the evidence.

"Parker, do you know what this means? We have to call the sheriff and report this! Have them test the hair with Ivy's. Hopefully, they can find out who was drivin' this car," Greyson states.

"But we need a plan. How did we just show up here? You know they are gonna ask," Parker reminds Greyson.

Greyson thinks and says almost immediately, "We will just tell him we were out drivin' around, lookin' to waste some time, talking, and we happened upon this car. It's sittin' next to the road, so who-ever parked it here either doesn't have brains or was so drunk they didn't think ahead."

Just then, Dylan comes around the corner and sees them at the car. "Hey! Get away from there! Who said you could come here? You better get off my property!" Dylan shouts as he slightly stumbles. "Did you not hear me? I said scram!" he sternly advises them.

They hold in their places as Dylan moves closer. With each step he takes, it becomes apparent that he's not sober. "So you feelin' okay, Dylan? You are lookin' a li'l green behind the gills there, my friend," states Greyson.

"That's it, I'm calling my brother! He will arrest you fer bein' there on my property," he says belligerently.

Parker eggs him on, saying, "Go ahead, call. We were just about to call them ourselves. So you are just doin' us a favor, friend."

Dylan takes out his phone and drops it trying to unlock the screen. "Let me get that for you, Dylan," Parker states. As he gets close to pick it up and hand it back to Dylan, he notices that he smells worse than a bar on St. Patty's Day. When Parker moves back, he comments on this to Greyson as Dylan dials 911.

"Wow, I think someone has had more than his share of liquor. He smells just like he's still plenty wasted," Parker whispers to Greyson. So Greyson gets the wise idea to secretly video Dylan's actions for further evidence.

"Yeah, these two quacks are on my property, snooping around my lot," Dylan tells the 911 dispatcher. "I don't know why they are here. I didn't invite them, if that's what you are askin'. Looks, I just want them gone," he states, slurring his words. "Whatya mean am I drinkin'? I am talkin' to you on the phone! I haven't drank tonight since yesterday!" He stumbles and drops the phone. "Hold on, I dropped my phone. Givesame a minute."

As he tries to get up, Sheriff Hutchins pulls in.

"Boys, didn't we just have a chat? Whatever are you doin' here? I received a call that you are here harassin' my brother. Why don't you just leave?" Colton stresses.

"Sheriff, we were just out talkin' and drivin', tryin' to make sense of all this, when we happened upon this car sittin' here next to the road. So we simply just stopped to look at it. And *your brother* just came around the corner, stumbling, slurring words, smellin' worse than a bar at St. Patty's Day, and just trying to keep us from simply lookin' at this car to see if there was a chance it could have been the one from last night. Your brother is the one acting like he can't stand on his own and has something to hide. So are you gonna arrest him,

Sheriff? He's obviously above the legal limit of intoxication," Parker states directly to Colton. "You said you were willing to help, but there you stand. Do something!" Parker shouts.

"Look, Parker, I know that you are going through a lot right now, but I will take care of my brother. You just need to get in your truck and leave at once," he commands them.

"I tell you what, Sheriff? my friend Parker and I will go sit in my truck and not interfere with what you need to do, but you need to take samples from that car! There is hair on it that looks like Ivy's, and a piece of blue fiber like her dress. Your brother, I think, knows something, so he should be taken in for questioning. At the very least, put in a cell to sleep off his drunkenness. So no one else in this town has to get hurt today!" Greyson demands

"Just cool yourself, Greyson, and stop insinuating that my brother has anything to do with Ivy's hit-and-run. Now, if ya want to sit in *your* truck and wait, I will be takin' Dylan in for questioning, but another word from ya and I will get *ya* and your *friend* for tampering with evidence and obstruction of justice! Now go! Let me do my work!" Colton sternly advises them as he points to the truck.

"Yes, sir," Greyson respectfully says as he and Parker return to the truck. When they are in the truck, Parker states he has a strong feeling that Dylan is somehow involved. They watch Colton go to Dylan and cuff him.

"Dylan, now, ya know that this is only protocol, so I have to take ya in. Ya really need some help, kid. Ya have to stop all this drinking. It's gonna be the death of ya one day. I don't wanna lose my brother. Like Parker lost Ivy. Okay, let's go to the car and I'll give ya a ride downtown. I think I'mma take Greyson's advice and lock ya up, but just till ya are sober," Colton says as he puts him in the back seat and shuts the door. He goes over to the car, looks at it, and makes a call to the station. As Colton turns to get in the driver's-side door, he stops and nods at Greyson and Parker, gets in, and drives away toward town.

"Greyson, can we go park somewhere close?" Parker asks. "I want to watch and see if an officer comes out to collect the evidence."

"Yeah, there's a spot across the road just up a piece. We can sit there. At the very least, we can see when or if they come." Greyson moves up the street. They haven't been sitting there too long when, sure enough, a car pulls up. Greyson opens his glove box and pulls out a pair of binoculars. "I just knew these would come in handy for something," he wisely says to Parker.

"Whatdya see, Greyson? Who came out?" Parker asks in wonder.

"Looks to be Officer Marlow. He's got an evidence bag, and he is pickin' off the fibers and strands of hair," Greyson sadly says.

"Okay, can we just head back to your place?" Parker asks.

"I'm on it, friend." They pull out into the road and drive back past the car. About a mile down the road, they pass a tow truck headed toward Dylan's. Greyson says, "Did you see that, Parker?"

"Yeah, I did. Do you think that it is headed to Dylan's for the car?"

"That was my thoughts. All we can do is hope so and that there is more evidence within the car to nail whoever was drivin' it."

The rest of the ride back to the Abbotts' home is a quiet one. They get out and walk inside. When they walk in, they head to the kitchen, where Allison and Emma have prepared food for lunch. "I know it's not a good time, Parker, but I called Obee and asked him to gather the girls and bring 'em here so we can all eat as a family. And hopefully break the news to Sydney easier. Or at least I hope to," Emma says thoughtfully.

"It's okay, Emma. I want to see Sydney, anyways. I have to let her know how much I love her. How soon will she be here?" Parker asks.

"I'm guessin' they should be—"

She's interrupted by the front door opening.

"They're here now!" she continues.

"Parker, do you want some privacy, or do you want us with you when you break the news to Syd?" Allison softly asks so, hopefully, Syd doesn't hear.

"So I don't hear what?" Syd asks as she sees everyone sitting around like they are an intervention. "What's goin' on? Where's Mom?" she softly asks.

"Allison, yes, do you…?" Parker starts to ask, and Allison picks up on what he's asking and motions for him to follow her. She leads them back the hall to Sophie and Eliza's room. "Syd, come with me," he tells her. "Thanks, Allison," Parker says as he shuts the door behind Sydney. "Sydney, I want to tell you just how much I love you and just how special you are to me, but I have something to tell you."

As the Abbotts, Obee, and Emma wait for them to come back out, Greyson starts to tell them what he and Parker had found out at the station and the car they found.

Suddenly, there's a muffled scream from the back room.

"No! You're lying!"

They hear more talking, but they can't make it out. They all look at each worried about how Sydney is taking it. A few minutes later, they both come out from the room. They are both crying and wiping their faces. Sydney does not want to look at anyone. Allison suggests for the girls to take Sydney back to their room and just try to get her mind on something else. Sydney reluctantly goes with the girls. Almost as soon as they leave, Eliza returns and asks politely, "May we please have something to eat?"

"I'm sorry, I almost forgot! Yes, this time you may take lunch back to your room. Here are sandwiches, a little bag of chips for each of you, and some bottles of water. Can you handle it all, Eliza? Or do you need me to help?" Allison asks.

"Can you carry the water, Mommy?" Eliza asks so sweetly.

"Sure, I'll be right back, guys," Allison tells everyone.

When Allison returns, everyone is peacefully sitting around the table, so quiet you can almost hear a pin drop. After about twenty minutes, Emma pipes up. "Do you know what I loved about Ivy? I loved that no matter how classy she ever seemed, she wasn't the least bit afraid of gettin' dirty." She smiled, thinking back. "She especially loved plantin' her flowers all around the house. I will have to see if I can get Syd out there with me to keep up her tradition."

"Emma, the girls and I would love to help when you are ready to plant this year. Just let us know."

"Thanks, Allison. I will do just that."

"I remember her beautiful voice in church, in the car, in the shower. She could belt a tune to soothe the ears of the meanest beast," Parker says like he's still listening to her sing.

"She always had a beautiful smile to light up a room! No matter how down you would be. Just one look from her with that smile would melt away all the sadness…well, most of it. I'm gonna miss that smile," Obee says, teary-eyed.

"I loved how she and Allison could go shoppin' and no matter how much stuff Allison brought home, she barely paid much for it. She had such a way of bargain-shopping. I really hope Allison *learned something* from those trips," Greyson says with appreciation, winking at Allison.

"Yes, I do remember the days we would go on those trips. We would be gone for hours and travel halfway across the county lookin' in *every store* we came across. It didn't matter if it was a li'l mom-and-pop shop or a bigger chain store like Someone Else's Laundry. She loved those stores. She was good friends with the owner of the three local stores in the area! Guess I will continue our tradition with Sydney, Sophie, and Eliza," Allison promised. "We would love it if you would accompany us too, Emma!"

"I would love that, Allison. I'm sure it won't be the same without Ivy, but I will do my best to try to live up to her expectations!"

As they sit there, reminiscing about all the good times spent and had with Ivy, Parker's phone rings. Everyone gets quiet as he answers and puts the phone on speaker. "Hello?"

"Parker, it's Sheriff Hutchins. I had Officer Marlow go and collect samples from that car at Dylan's. I had a rush put on the samples to compare them with samples from her body. I have news. The samples are a match. It is definitely the car that hit Ivy. It is with a heavy heart I deliver this information to you. We already took the next step and had the car brought to the impound yard for further investigation. Again, our sympathies are with you and your family," he states sadly, relaying his findings and sympathy.

"Thank you, Sheriff Hutchins. Please find the SOB who did this. I want to make them pay!"

"We will do our best. Goodbye, Parker," Colton says as he hangs up.

"Well, you all heard it for yourselves. Greyson, that was the car. I just hope they can find out who was drivin' it. Yeah, it's not like they can check the plates for an owner. There were no plates even on the car!" Parker says disgustedly.

"I'm sorry, Allison. Can you please see if Syd would like to stay here for tonight? Emma, I just have to head home and get some rest. I didn't sleep last night," Parker tells them.

Allison gets up and goes to the girls and asks about Sydney staying. When she returns, she says, "They all agreed that she was going to stay here. Listen, Parker, if you need anything, even though you have Emma and Oliver, if there is *anything* they can't do, please don't hesitate to ask. Even if you just wanna come hang out, we are here for you," Allison reassures Parker.

"Thank you, Emma, Oliver, Allison, and Greyson, for everything. I'm sorry for this, and I will try not to be a burden on y'all. It really does mean a lot, even if I don't show it. Just please understand, I am very grateful, and I will apologize now for any rudeness I may show unintentionally in case I forget to later when or if I do get nasty." With that, he turns to head for the door.

"Wait, Parker." Greyson attempts to get his attention. "Wait up, man. None of this is your fault, and you are never a burden. Come here," Greyson says, reaching out to give him a big, manly bear hug. As they embrace, everyone lines up to share the love. They each send him on his way with a big hug and words of love.

He turns, walks out the door, and leaves. Emma and Oliver follow suit, saying their goodbyes, and they head home too.

CHAPTER 14

Still No Answers

It's been such a struggle since Mom's passing for everyone. For me, my grades dropped almost soon after she passed, because I didn't want to go to school. If I did go, I wasn't doing my homework. Now my grades are slowly improving, and I am hoping this project really helps to bring at least my history grade up.

Dad, until yesterday, was kinda distant and nonexistent. I'm not sure where he goes, but his job is here with the ranch and he's just never around. He doesn't even come to every meal to eat. So either he isn't eating or he is eating somewhere else. So I am not sure what recently changed him, but I truly hope it's not just a one-day fluke.

Obee just keeps himself busier than normal, polishing saddles—if he polishes them too much more, I'm afraid he will polish away all the leather! The horses have *never been* cleaner. I'm really surprised that the horses don't have dry skin as much as they get bathed now. But he does take time to go fishing with Sophie and me from time to time. He also has been helping us with my project now that we've secretly made him a member of Team Make a Difference. He's who we call when we have a transportation issue or something else that we cannot ask any of the other adults to help us with. He's always happy to help.

Emma just prefers everyone around all the time. Especially when I ask for Sophie and Eliza to come over. I think she really enjoys our company. Mom always did spend a lot of time with Emma, talking, baking, gardening, and even a little crafting from time to time. Next to Allison, Emma and my mom were really close. Mom was almost always with either Emma or Allison if she wasn't with Dad or me.

Now, Allison takes my mom's place and hangs with Emma whenever she can. Allison always has a bunch of houses listed and moving ownership frequently. Today she wanted to come check out some of the Someone Else's Laundry stores. Sophie and I wanna go with Emma and Allison, but we have to make sure that they will be back in time for today's race.

Sydney
Do you know when your mom wants to leave?

Sophie
She said early, b4 any of her clients have a chance to need her.

Sydney
Are we comin' to you, or are y'all comin' here?

Sophie
I think we are comin' to get y'all, so be ready. We gotta go so we can get back later.

Sydney
Yeah, I know. That's what I was thinkin'. See ya soon, bestie!

Sophie
Ten-four, bestie!

I run to check on Emma. "Em? Are you almost ready? Allison and Sophie will be here soon!"

"In the kitchen, Sydney. Come grab a quick bite to eat!" Emma shouts. I head right to the kitchen, sit down, and eat a little bit so I won't be hungry till later.

A few minutes later, Allison, Eliza, and Sophie pull up outside. "They're here!" I scream, jump off the stool, and run outside. "I'm so excited to go shopping today! How about you, Sophie?"

"Yep! I was *so happy* when Mom asked me to go with today!" Sophie says as she gets close to me, then begins to whisper, "I talked her into just one store today. I told her we would go another day soon, and I would see if you and Emma would like to join us?" She says this as if she were asking a question as Eliza tries to listen in.

I return my reply with a whisper, "Yeah, I think that's a great idea!"

"Mom! Sophie and Syd are up to something!" she shouts, trying to get us to let her in on whatever we were talking about.

Sophie returns a shout to her mom. "No, we're not, Mom!"

As I see Emma on her way out, I shout out to Dad, "I love you, Dad! See you soon!" I wave, and he waves back. Emma, too, waves as she comes out. Then we load up and head off to the store.

"I was askin' Sophie about y'all goin' with us on another shopping excursion soon because she said we should limit our trip today to one store in case I have clients who may need me. Would you like to join us?" she asks Emma and me.

Emma says as she turns to look at me for agreement, "It's okay with me, Allison. I normally don't have too much extra goin' on, so it's pretty easy for me to make time for just about anything." Then she asks me as Sophie pokes me in the ribs and smirks, "Sydney, how do you feel about it, sweetheart?"

I turn to Sophie and whisper under my breath, "Ouch, love!" I turn to Allison and Emma, smiling. "Sure thing. I love to go shopping with y'all! Especially if it means I can carry on Allison and my mom's tradition, then I am all for it!" I exclaim. "I wouldn't want to miss it for the world!" Then I ask Allison, "Maybe one day we could do a circuit like y'all used to do?"

"Sure thing, Sydney. Sounds like a date!" replies Allison.

As we make our way to the store, Sophie and I overhear Allison ask Emma, "I'm sorry to ask today of all days, but have you and Parker even heard anything more about who was drivin' the car that night? I don't mean to pry. It's just…Greyson and I were talkin', and we kinda came up with our own conclusions as to who was drivin' that night. He mentioned it to me to ask and put a li'l voice in your head with our thoughts of it," Allison says, worried she may ruin today's trip with painful memories.

Emma folds her hands in her lap and sighs. "I'm sorry, Allison, it took them a few weeks to search the car, research what they found, and they say that they still aren't any closer to a suspect. Parker had mentioned that he would talk to Greyson, but it sounds like he didn't get a chance to for whatever reason. If you have time after our shopping trip, we can sit down and discuss your theories. I don't think you makin' mention of it has ruined today yet, so let's just save that for later," Emma says while quickly changing the subject. "Well, that's good timin', because we are here, girls!" Emma tries to say with a little excitement to calm the thickness in the air.

As we exit the car, Allison says to Sophie, Eliza, and me, "Girls, go have fun lookin' through the clothes, tryin' them on, and load up the cart. Today's trip is on me," she says to us, pointing for us to head into the store, then she says to Emma, "That includes you, Emma! I want to pay for yours too!"

Emma, feeling like a burden, says, "No, Allison, it is okay. I will pay for mine."

"Emma! I am not hearin' that! I will pay for yours as well. You need a treat every now and then too!" she states, refusing to take no for an answer.

"Okay, if you put it that way, this time I will allow it!" Emma agrees.

We all head in the store and split off in different directions. Eliza heads for the toys and books, Allison and Emma head to the women's area, while Sophie and I head for the boys' department first. "Let's see if we can find just a few more pieces, and then we can go to the junior misses area," I say to Sophie. She nods and starts looking. We each find two pairs of outfits and move to the juniors department.

Off in the corner we hear Eliza having a great time with the toys. We continue to look, showing each other things that we think the other would like. I usually wear jeans and T-shirts, but once in a while, I change it up and dress up a little. But I feel so much more comfortable and myself when I dress down.

Sophie is the exact opposite—she would rather dress up than down, and usually when she wants to dress down, we do it together, and it's the same way when I wanna dress up. We coordinate and try to match either in color or the type of outfit we choose.

Everyone seems to have found something. Allison comes to us and asks us to finish up so we can get back. So we gather our outfits and head to the register. Sophie and I hope that Emma and Allison don't question our boy selections. We've devised a plan in case they do. We would tell them that we have a jeans-and-T-shirt day or "dress opposites" day at school. Thankfully, though, they don't ask, so diversion is averted. Allison grabs everyone's bags and hands them off to us. We go out to the car and head back to the ranch.

When we get back, Sophie and I head up to my room, with Eliza hot on our heels. We get to the top of the stairs and slam the door shut quickly. Eliza starts screaming bloody murder. "Mom! Sydney and Sophie won't let me in!"

We try to shout through the door, "We want to try on some of our outfits!"

Allison asks, "Eliza, honey, can you please come down and let the girls get dressed? Come on!"

Emma hollers up, "Want a cookie?" Then she quickly whispers to Allison, "Is that okay?" Allison nods.

We quickly grab our clothes and check to make sure the coast is clear, and then we make a beeline for the stables. We see Obee, and I ask him, "Where's Dad?"

Obee says, "He had to run to town quickly. So what's up, li'l ladies?" He thinks for a moment and quickly says, frantically, "Girls? Wait! The race? What about the race?"

"That's what we wanted to ask you about. Can you possibly get us to the cottage like yesterday?" I ask politely but with urgent demand.

"Sure! Syd, help get the carriage hooked up. I will take ya out to the cottage, and then after the race, I will come back to bring ya back here," Obee commands.

So I quickly help Obee hook up Black Boots to the covered carriage. And off we scoot. As we near the cottage Obee states, "Syd, Sophie, when I slow down, just jump out. I'll get back quick before anyone misses me. See ya in a bit, girls!" Obee slows down, then we jump out of the carriage, wave goodbye to Obee, and run into the cottage.

Sophie and I change very quickly into Wyatt and Chase. We look each other over just to make sure we look like our alternates. We give each other a thumbs-up, go out, get the bikes, and head back to the ranch. As we are pedaling in the lane, suddenly we hear a vehicle behind us. We get over to be out of the way, only to see it's Dad! He slows down to talk with us.

"Hey, there, Chase and Wyatt! Need a lift back to the ranch?"

"Thanks, Mr. A—I mean Parker. Sorry. We are good. We will see you back at the ranch," I say, trying to get him to keep moving so I can talk with Sophie.

"Okay, boys, see ya in a few!" he says as he drives off.

"Wow, that was close, Wyatt!" I wink at her. We hurry and pedal faster to get to the ranch faster. As we gain on the ranch, we see Dad, Parker, walking out to meet us.

"So are you boys ready to race? Hudson called me and mentioned a meet and greet of sorts today with some boys your age from our local school. He wants you two to talk about your backgrounds and why you chose to race. To help encourage other young riders to join. Just lettin' ya both know so you can think about what you would like to say. Obee's loadin' up the horses, and I think everything else is good to go. You may get in the truck a while and wait while we load up the girls."

Just then, I see Eliza peeking her head out the window by the front door, and I try to get Sophie to look. "Oh no," she whispers to me. "What if she comes out here?"

"Let's just pray that Parker and Obee hurry!" I whisper back. Just as I say that, Obee jumps in the truck, followed by Parker.

Parker waves at Eliza, she waves back, and we are off to the races!

When we get to the track, we see a tent set up where there usually isn't one. Parker says, "Boys, I think that is where you are to go. Over to that tent. We will stop and letchas out while we go unload and I register the two of you."

"Okay, thanks, Parker," we say as we get out of the truck. As he pulls away, I say to Wyatt, "So are we ready for this?" I am nervously shaking.

"Are you shakin', Chase?" Wyatt asks me.

"Yeah, I'm just nervous. What if Lucas is here? I'm just worried about which boys will be here for this *event*," I say, clearing my throat.

"It'll be okay, Chase. I will be there, and I got your back!" Wyatt says as we make our way to the tent.

We hear Hudson talking with the crowd the closer we get. When he spots us, he gets excited. "Yes, here they are, folks and youngins, Chase and Wyatt! Welcome, boys! Are you ready for your meet and greet? There are some young boys here who are interested in your thoughts on racin' and why maybe they should give it a try!" He moves the mic from his mouth and covers it as he whispers to us, "Are yas ready?"

I look at him and stutter out, "A-as ready as one c-c-can be for such s-short notice." I stop and gather my thoughts. "Sorry, Hudson. Yes, I am just nervous, but I do believe that I am ready."

Wyatt says, "Ten-four, bestie!" I quickly give him a look of "Oh no, you didn't!" He quickly states, "Sorry, cuz. Didn't mean to steal your line, if you are here listenin'." He winks at me, and I nod and whisper, "Nice cover! Now, shall we?"

"We shall." She smiles as she whispers this back.

"Welcome to all you, young enthusiasts. We are Chase, that's me, and this is my best friend—"

Wyatt cuts me off and says, "I'm Wyatt. Welcome! So let's start with a li'l about us, and then we can open up for questions. I'll let my good friend Chase start."

"Thanks, Wyatt, and yes, again, welcome. I am Chase Payne. So quickly, I grew up around horses all my life. It's basically like second nature to me. It's in my heart. It's in my blood. I just feel I can't breathe without horses as part of me. My family didn't want me to ride for fear of fallin' and gettin' hurt, or worse, but I race with my friend Wyatt all the time and we are still here. I've been ridin' since I could walk. There's no better feelin' than you and your horse cuttin' across the fields, with the wind blowin' through your hair. It's amazin'! I highly recommend gettin' riding lessons if you don't have any horses at your home that you are familiar with. Thank you. Now, here's my friend Wyatt."

"Thanks, Chase, and welcome, everyone! It's a pleasure to be here and chat with y'all! I am Wyatt Gentry! I have been around horses almost as long as Chase has been. We do ride frequently together. I unfortunately do not live on a farm, but Chase and I are almost inseparable. And if I am ever missin', my family knows right where to look at Chase's house. I agree with Chase that when you form a bond with your horse, there's nothing that beats the feelin' you get when you ride full steam ahead. So now, any questions?" Wyatt asks the crowd.

A hand comes up in the back.

Wyatt says, "Yes, the person in the back with the cowboy hat. What's your question?"

"Yeah, so this question is for Chase. I was told by Sydney Ashcraft to ask you how you like to race her horse. I mean, she's gotta be your girlfriend, right? Why else would you be ridin' her horse?"

"Ah, Lucas Devinshire! Nice to finally meet you. I've heard all about you and your arrogance. I just don't think that horse ridin' is up your alley. So do we have any other questions about horse racing?" I ask the crowd as another hand comes up right next to Lucas's. "Yes, what's your question?"

"So does Sydney ride you, or do you ride her? Talk around school is that she wears the ridin' pants so she would ride you!" Jaxson interrogates Chase.

"Ah, yes, I've heard about you too, Jaxon Milburn, friend of Lucas Devinshire. Look, this has nothing to do with Sydney. So you can leave her out of this. This is a question-and-answer session for those who are seriously interested in ridin'. So if there aren't any more questions about racin', I believe we will end this session till after the race. Goin' once...goin' twice..." After looking around and seeing no hands come up, I say to the crowd, "Thank you!" Then we wave and walk back to the horses.

*****

Meanwhile, back at the ranch, Allison and Emma talk about Greyson's theory. "So, Emma, here's what Greyson's theory is: it was Dylan who hit Ivy that dreadful night."

Emma thinks about it and responds with, "So I'm sure that you guys have more to back your theory? Not just that you think that he is guilty."

"Yes, Emma, we do. So first, that date kept stickin' with me. It was the anniversary of when Dylan and Misty got into an accident on a stormy night when he had been drinkin' but supposedly not a lot. But they swerved for something in the road, hit a tree, and she died. So we think that he was drinkin to the point of no return and went out in that car and hit Ivy. But if there was any evidence in that car, we will never know, because of Sheriff Hutchins. That's his brother. He was over the legal limit of intoxication the very next day, and all he got was time in prison to sleep it off. He's been out since to possibly destroy another family if he would do it again. He definitely has a drinkin' problem! I just wish we knew for certain. I mean, there's enough possible evidence just with the fibers from her dress, her hair. He was wasted that night, and still was the very next day, and that car was in his lot on his property. Someone just had to have seen him drivin'!" Allison says in disgust.

"Come to think of it, I think I remember the night you are talking about. It was so sad when Misty passed. She was such a sweet young lady. So do you think anything would be done if you turned over your theory to the police?" Emma says in wonder.

"I doubt it. They would probably find a way to just cover it up." Allison hates to say it. "You hate to think that way, but the Hutchinses are a tight-knit family and would lie their way outta anything that would cover anything up that could and would incriminate them."

"Well, I pray that the suspect is finally brought to justice soon!"

"You and I both! That's all we have been praying for! I know it won't bring Ivy back, but justice would definitely be nice. And whoever it was won't be out there to harm another family!"

CHAPTER 15

The Calm before the Storm

"There ya have it, folks! Chase Payne with Sands of Tyme and Wyatt Gentry with PB Cup! They did it again, first and second place!" Hudson proudly shouts through the loudspeaker. The crowd goes wild; one-half of the stands is chanting, "Chase!" while the other half is chanting, "Wyatt!" "Chase!" "Wyatt!" "Chase!" "Wyatt!" They scream as they blow whistles, clap, cheer, and sing!

Things couldn't be better. We are at the top of the racing charts, and *everybody loves* us! It's been a good day, almost like the calm before the storm. So as Wyatt and I make our way to the winner's circle, we have all kinds of people congratulating us and wanting to shake our hands or just touch us! We are like young legends. When I started this project, I never dreamed this would get this big! I just wanted to make a small impression on the horse racing world, but this is gonna make an even bigger impact than I had anticipated.

At the winner's circle, people are snapping pictures from every direction and just about blinding us. This must be what it's like on the red carpet. Even though Wyatt is in second place, I've asked that he be present with me at the circle because we are a team and I want to share this moment with him. We are going down in history! After pictures and all the commotion settles down for a bit, we make our way to the stables.

"What a race, Chase! You did great out there!" Wyatt says, encouraging me.

"Nah, I couldn't do it without you. All that practice is paying off, dontcha think?" I ask Wyatt.

"I thought it could help, but I never dreamed it would be to this extent. So we gotta keep it up!" Wyatt expresses to me.

"Well, let's see what we can do about more practice time at the ranch. We'll have to ask Parker. Even though he said yes, we just need to double-check," I say to Wyatt as I hear a chuckle from behind us. I turn, and of course, it's the football freaks. "Oh, sorry, I thought I smelled something. Don't y'all have a game to get to?" I say antagonistically.

Lucas steps forward, with Jaxson Milburn and Camden Owens close behind. "Hey! Chase! Give Sydney Ass-crack a message from me."

I quickly interrupt. "She doesn't want to hear anything you have to say. So don't waste your breath, dude."

"We'll just see about that! And tell her to watch herself in school! Come on, boys, let's go. I'm done with this loser trash!" Lucas says ignorantly as they walk away.

"Chase?" Wyatt asks. "Umm, what was that?"

"That was the start to his butt-whoopin'!" I say to Wyatt. "Come on, let's get goin'. Don't let that blade of grass bother us. Look, there's Parker. Let's go over and see how soon we are leavin'." We head over to Parker and Obee.

"Great job guys," Obee says, slightly winking so Parker doesn't see. We carefully nod back. "I think we are just about done here, if y'all wanna get in the truck a while. I'mma let Parker know we are ready," Obee says as he walks over to chat with Parker. We see them talking and nodding with another rancher. It isn't too long and they are both headed back to the truck.

As Parker gets in, he says to us, "Wow! Great job out there today! What a race! I couldn't have asked for better! This spring season is almost over. Then we have a few months of practice and we will start the fall season. I'm not sure where you two came from, but you must be a gift from God! Here, I want you to both have your winnings now! And again, congrats, boys!" He hands us our envelopes, which feel thicker than normal. As we open them for a slight sneak peek, Parker continues to speak to us. "So how was the meet and greet?" he asks.

I look at Wyatt and kinda cringe. I can't tell Parker, a.k.a. Dad, that a football player was there harassing me about Sophie. I just kinda brush it off as it was nothing much. "It was okay, Parker. Nothing too excitin'," I add. "But I can honestly say it felt good to race again today!" I happily inform him as I smile.

By now we have reached the ranch. We help unload the horses, brush them down, help feed them, and empty supplies from the trailer. "Parker, Obee, we will see you soon. We are headed home."

"Thanks for everything, boys! See ya next week for our last two races!" Parker says proudly.

We turn and head out the lane with our bikes. We book it to the cottage. Once we are there, I send a text to Obee.

> Sydney
> *Obee, we made it to the cottage. Come out as soon as you are ready. Thanks! Syd*
>
> Obee
> *Okay, Syd. I will be out soon!*

I head to the bedroom to get my lockbox. I bring it to the kitchen table. I hand a pen to Sophie so she can label her envelope. "I counted mine, and I got $7,000 this time!"

Sophies counts hers, and she shrieks. "Arrgh, $5,000! Wow, thanks, Syd!"

"No problem! We only got two more races, so we have to win those too! Okay, we have to get changed before Obee comes back!" I say as I put our envelopes in the lockbox and put it back under the bed.

Sophie already has used the bathroom to wash up, so I quickly go wash up so I don't get too excited or busy and forget. We change outta our Chase and Wyatt attires, then wait for Obee. We walk out to the lake and sit on Grandad's bench. "I wish we had some rods out here. I may have to give Obee a li'l money to go buy us some, because days like today are too beautiful to just sit here and not fish."

A few minutes later, Obee comes out on the carriage to pick us up.

"Great run today, girls! Way to show 'em how it's done! So back to the house we go."

We get in the carriage, and we head off.

"Obee, we were thinkin', maybe if we give ya some money, you could go to the store and get us a pair of rods for the lake to keep at the cottage. I'm not sure why we don't just keep 'em out there. It's not like we go fishing anywhere else. I mean, we have the best lake in the area, for cryin' out loud!" I say with confidence and bragging rights.

"Sure thing. I will see what I can do for you, Syd. And don't worry about the money. I'm all good!" he brags as he smiles. "You girls have given me more than enough money!"

"You are the best, Obee!" I say as I lean over and hug him.

"Okay, guys, act normal. We are back," Sophie says, laughing.

"There you girls are! We've been lookin' all over for ya!" Dad says.

"Sorry, sir," Obee says. "You should have said something. I didn't know anyone was lookin' for them. I took them out to the lake for a li'l."

"Yeah, sorry, Dad. We just wanted a li'l girl time. I should have told you. But we thought you would make us take Eliza," I say, hanging my head.

"Syd, I know that li'l girls can be *annoyin'* sometimes, but it's usually just because they like you and look up to you. They wanna be doin' what you're doin', and that's why they seem like they are constantly up your backside. So please, next time, just let someone know. Can you please go tell Emma? She's worried sick too!" Dad says with sincerity.

"Okay, Dad. Sorry. We will go talk with Em." I hang my head and walk into the house. Sophie follows me.

"Oh, thank God, there you girls are! We were so worried. Now, wherever did y'all run off to?" Emma says, relieved to see us.

"Sorry, Em. We just wanted to go to Grandad's cottage. We didn't mean no harm. We just wanted to do girl chat and stuff without Eliza. I promise we will let you know where we are goin' next time," I say with empathy.

"Grandad's cottage?" she quickly shrieks. "I didn't even know it was still standin'. I thought when those two pines came down, that was the end of it. Well, how does the old place look? I bet it needs a good cleanin' before you girls go out there again," she says, all concerned, like we are gonna catch something if it wasn't cleaned spotless.

"Em, it's fine, and no, the two pines didn't even hit it. They just came close. Those are the trees Grandad made the bench and hitchin' post out of, those that are out there. And no need to worry. With the nicer weather upon us, Sophie and I were out there cleanin' up so we can spend more time out there, especially fishin'. We will have to take ya out and show ya sometime soon!" I proudly tell her.

"Sydney, you are growin' up to be a fine girl! You too, Sophie. I think Eliza would have loved to come help you girls."

Sophie quickly jumps in and says, "Ah, no, she has allergies to dust, and we made a bunch of dust. So it may not have been such a great idea to have her tag along out there while we were stirrin' up so much of it."

Emma nods and says, "Oh, okay, I didn't know that about your sister." She then asks us. "So what are your plans for the rest of the day? Wanna go get Eliza and make cookies?"

We look at each other and simultaneously shrug. "Sure, we really don't have anything else to do. Sophie, can you text your mom? And, Em, can we go get Eliza?"

"Ten-four, bestie. I'm on it!" Sophie says, smiling.

"Yes, we can get Eliza. Let's go get in the car," instructs Emma.

Sophie
Mom, we are on our way to get Eliza. Love you!

Allison
Little lady! Where have you been? We looked all over for you!

Sophie
It's okay, Mom. We went to the cottage to
clean it up so it wasn't so dusty for Eliza.
Now that the nicer weather is here, we
wanted to be able to let her come out with us.
I'm sorry I worried you, Mom.

Allison
Okay, I'll have Eliza ready. I love you!

"Okay, I told Mom. She will have her ready," Sophie states.

We get to Sophie's house and pick up Eliza, then we head to the store for a few supplies. When we have everything we need, we head back to the ranch.

It is a great rest of the day, and we make bunches and bunches of cookies! After we make cookies, we all settle down for bed, brush our teeth, say our prayers, and go to sleep.

When we wake up, Emma has the house smelling of a huge breakfast waiting for us to devour! We quickly get dressed, wash our faces and hands, then head downstairs. Eliza goes flying down the stairs, and Emma starts to yell till she sees it's Eliza. "Eliza, honey, we have to watch how fast we come down the stairs. You could slip and fall and hurt your bum!"

"Sorry, Em. I'm just hungry, and your food is makin' me hungrier," Eliza says shyly, laughing and smiling.

"Let's eat, ladies. I thought today we could just go open Ivy's shop and see what business we generate, without makin' it known that we will be open. What do y'all think?" Emma asks.

"Sure, Em. Sounds like a plan," I say, ready to have some girl fun.

"Can I be in charge of the toys like Parker said?" Eliza asks.

Emma smiles. "Sure thing, Eliza. That will be your job to keep other li'l ones busy."

Eliza claps and smiles from ear to ear.

We finish up and help Em clean up. Then we all pile into the car and head to Mom's shop. We spend most of the day there, and we have about five customers all day. But it is a good first day. As we go to leave, we have a visitor waiting outside for us.

"Look who it is, boys. It's Sydney Ass-crack! So, Syd, did your *boyfriend* give you my message yesterday?" Lucas says, trying to pick a fight.

Emma comes out and tells Lucas, "Young man, you need to be on your way. We won't be havin' any of that kind of dealings around here." She points away from the shop.

"Look, boys, Sydney gots herself a bodyguard! Later, Ashcraft. I'm watchin' you," Lucas promises as they walk away.

"Has he been givin' you troubles, Syd?" Emma asks.

"Nah, it's nutin' I can't handle, Em," I reassure her. We all get in the car, then head to Allison's to drop off Eliza and Sophie. "Em, may I see if I can spend the night?"

"We can see what Allison says. I'm okay with it," Emma says as she pulls in their driveway.

The girls and I jump out of the car and run in to ask Allison if I may stay. We run back out, and I yell to Emma, "She said it was okay. I love you, Emma! Please tell Dad I love him too! Thanks! And Obee!" We run back in before Emma has a chance to speak.

"Thanks, Allison, for letting me stay," I say politely.

"No problem, Sydney. We love havin' you over! We can't let Emma have all the love, so I figured, girls, we will eat pizza tonight? I will call it in and have it delivered. You girls can go relax, have fun, or do whatever it is you girls do till it gets here," Allison states comically.

We all take off for the girls' room to sit, do one another's hair, and gossip. About forty minutes later, we hear the doorbell and we run out to the kitchen. Sure enough, pizza! Just as Allison turns and yells, "Pizza's here!" she sees us and says, "Ah, good. Are yas washed up?" We go wash up and come back to eat. Eliza does one of her silly, corky words of grace, and we eat.

Allison starts to question Sophie and me about school. "So, Sydney, Sophie says you girls have a big history project. How's it goin'? Are you close to gettin' yours finished?"

"Well, Allison, I love you so much, but all I can say is, my project is comin' along better than I had hoped. I pray, too, that it makes the big impression I am hoping for. But for right now, Sophie is the only one who *really* knows what my project is. It's only because she is my best friend and I have to tell someone, and she is who I chose! It's not that I think you will say anything, but you just never know who's listenin' that may take what I say and misunderstand what I mean or just turn it around. So I figured, to get the best impact, it was best I only told Sophie. Ms. Dixon doesn't even know!" I say, winking to Sophie.

"I am impressed, Sydney! I can't wait to see what your project is all about!" Allison says kindly.

As we finish up dinner, we chat more about school with Eliza, Sophie, and me, while we have some dessert. Homemade brownies that Allison made with huge PB chunks in it! "Mmm, I'm sorry, but these are the best, Allison!" I say while talking with my mouth full of brownie.

"They are made with love," she says, smiling at us. "And huge PB chunks!"

Eliza quietly asks, "May we have ice cream with them? With PB sauce, Mommy?"

Allison gets up from the table to go get the PB sauce and ice cream. "Here you go. Just a li'l bit. It's almost bedtime, and y'all have school in the morning," she says as she gives us each a scoop of ice cream and passes the PB sauce around. We finish up dessert, then head to get our showers. When we are done with showers, we say our prayers, lie in bed, and tell one another jokes and ghost stories till we fall asleep.

CHAPTER 16

A Minor of Storms

Allison knocks on the bedroom door as she opens it at the same time to wake us up. "Good mornin', girls! It's time to get up! Let's go grab some cereal and get out the door!" she says as she walks out of the room and down the hall.

"Ugh, I hate Mondays!" Sophie complains. "Why can't the school week start like Tuesday or Wednesday?" she asks with an attitude as she gets up and throws herself in her chair at her vanity.

"Sophie, you sound so ridiculous," I tell her. "You do realize that if we were to have any other day as our first day of the school week, it would just be the same ole thing with you? 'Ugh, I hate this day! Can't we have another day as the start to our school week?'" I say, trying to mock her as I hug her from behind.

"Yeah, yeah, I know, Syd," she tells me as she crosses her arms to hug mine. "I just hate school! I wish we didn't have to go!"

"Well, all I can say is, I'm glad we only have to go for four days and not five like the other ones around here," Sydney says, and we both laugh and agree.

Eliza looks left out, so I say to her, "Come here, squirt! Come on in here for a group hug!" We all hug, finish getting ready so we can go eat a little something for breakfast, and get off to school.

As we get to school, with the nicer weather, we see more people standing out and about than normal. We say goodbye to Allison and head up to the doors to enter.

Now, do you ever just have a feeling like someone somewhere is about to drop a hammer on you for something that you have no clue about? Well, today I just have a bad feeling in the pit of my stomach. Mom always said not to ignore this said feeling because it's my *woman's intuition* talking to me. So as we walk to our lockers, I keep an eye out for whatever beast lurks, just waiting to pounce on me. Once we reach our lockers, I put away what I don't need and get what I do. Then, out of nowhere, we hear yelling and screaming at the end of the hall. At first, it's hard to make out, but then I hear an angry voice that seems to get closer to us. "Where is she? I'm gonna show her. Who does she think she is? Gotta have her mommy call in and make a complaint about me. *Me!* Does she *not* know who I am? I am the freakin' lead quarterback! *Everyone* has my back!" I quickly motion for Sophie to follow me as he rants on, "I am Lucas Devinshire! I am what keeps this school on the map. Oooh, when I find her, I'm gonna show her!"

We have gone around the corner and are trying to make our way back outside when he spots us. "Hey, Ass-crack! Where do you think you are goin'? Come here! We need to talk!"

Sophie and I stop. She looks at me and, under her breath, says to me, "Syd, what are you gonna do?"

"Just watch, Sophie. Stay back here." I hand my things to Sophie as I turn toward Lucas. "What do you want, Lucas? I'm busy right now," I say like I don't care about him or what he has to say.

"Why you have your mommy callin' into school, sayin' I was threatenin' you?" Lucas says with his arms out.

I have learned from Obee that this is a scare tactic that bullies use to make themselves look bigger against who they think could be a weaker target.

But I don't back down, and I step closer as I say, "What did you say, Puke-us?" Lucas got drunk at a party once, and his nickname was Lucas Puke-us, but lately, it's not been so popular. I'm hoping when I kick his butt, it will make a savage return!

"You heard me, runt. Why! You! Have! Your! Mommy—"

He has started to act as if he is gonna cry when I interrupt him.

"First off, Puke-us, I don't have a 'mommy,'" I state as I make air quotations, "because someone's drunk uncle"—I take another step closer, poke him in the chest as he steps back a step—"hit her and took her away from me and got away with a hit-and-run! So I don't know what your problem with me is, but you best get off your high horse and leave me alone!" I then stomp my foot and stare him down.

"You take that back, Ass-crack! My uncle didn't have anything to do with your mom!" he screams in my face. He swings and punches me in the eye, and that gets my blood boiling! Obee taught me how to fight since I was an only child and didn't have siblings to fight with. But he made me swear to never start a fight or to back down if I was pushed into one. Well, I think this constitutes a fight that I didn't start, so no backing down.

When he hits my face, I kinda fall back, but I catch myself. When I get my balance back, I lunge for Lucas like a lion after its prey, and I rip Lucas up! I hit him so hard from fear, panic, and adrenaline rush that he falls backward and hits the floor. I jump on top of him while students are chanting and screaming, "Fight, fight, fight!" Some are cheering me on, while others are cheering Lucas on. *Wow!* I think to myself. *People are cheerin' for me? That's cool!* I start drilling him so hard he's starting to draw blood.

The next thing I remember is being pulled off him and being escorted to the principal's office. Sophie follows me as my main witness. She is good in school, and her word is considered gold! Sophie sits with me as I come down from my rage. Since my mom passed, I have had severe anger issues when I get my buttons pushed the wrong way. And Lucas *definitely* pushed my buttons today! As I sit there waiting for my dad and Emma to show up, I close my eyes and make a prayer to God.

> *Dear God,* I silently pray, *please forgive me for what I did just now. I didn't mean it, but you saw it for yourself, Lord. He had it comin' to him! I promise if I get off with li'l to no punishment, I will make this right. I'm not sure how, but I will do whatever it takes. Thank you, Lord. Amen.*

As I lift my head and open my eyes, I see my dad and Emma standing there. My dad has this look of disgust and is slightly proud at the same time. We get called into the principal's office.

Mrs. Cora Gossett is our principal, and she's almost too pretty for the principal position. I think principals are not to be so good-looking, and they should have a slightly meaner, monster look, in my opinion. That way, you can't sweet-talk 'em into not getting punished. 'Cause you'd be too scared to face 'em. So you would just take your punishment and do your best *not* to end up in their office too many times.

Mrs. Gossett asks Sophie if she was a witness to what happened. When Sophie nods, Mrs. Gossett waves her into the office too. As we talk with principal Gossett, Dad tries not to let the proud part show too much for fear of me getting in more trouble. But I know he's proud because his "li'l filly" just whooped a boy! Inside I am dying from pride and trying to show the exact opposite on the outside!

Mrs. Gossett speaks. "Where do I start? First, I want to let everyone know how I want to conduct this, and then once I have, I will have Sophie or Sydney go out to the main office to sit while we sit in here. Then I will have you two swap, okay? I want to ask you some questions of just what happened out there. You both know that this is not tolerated at our school!" she scolds us as we nod in agreement. "Okay, Sophie, how about you go out first? I'll have Sydney send you in when we are done."

Sophie gets up without one word and goes out to the main office.

"Sydney, I want you to tell me exactly what happened out there just now."

"Mrs. Gossett, I realize what I did was completely uncalled for, but he has been continuously bullyin' me and today he pushed my buttons too far. Apparently," I say as I turn to look at Emma. "Sorry, but someone called the school today and must have made a report of what happened yesterday. He decided to tell me that my 'mommy' called this mornin' and got him yelled at first thing," I say as Emma puts her hand down on my arm and slightly raises her other to intervene.

"Yes, I am sorry, I did call the school today, but only to have them keep an eye out that nothing like this happened. He did seem awfully mean to her yesterday. I am sorry, Sydney. I didn't realize it would turn out this way," she says so peacefully and softly.

"So, Sydney, this isn't the first time you have had a run-in with Mr. Devinshire?" asks Mrs. Gossett.

I hang my head and say, "No, ma'am. I always try to avoid this happenin', but when he mentioned my mom callin' in here today, it just sent me into a rage. But I did refrain myself from hittin' him at first. It wasn't till after he punched me that I tore him up. But it won't happen again," I sadly respond.

"Well, I think you need to have suspension and classes or counseling for your anger issues. I understand you lost your mom and it's hard, but we cannot take it out on other students. Mr. Devinshire is now in the nurse's office, in severe condition!" she sternly advises me.

"No, just wait one minute. I want to know what Lucas will be gettin' out of this. He started it! And she's been tryin' to avoid it for some time," Parker says angrily.

"Well, sir, your daughter doesn't look nearly as bad as Lucas, and she needs to be punished. That kind of behavior in this school is not tolerated!" she says as Parker rudely interrupts.

"No! The problem here is, he needs to be punished for the bullyin' that he did to her that led to her whoopin' his butt!" he says as he quickly stands and slams his fist to the desk.

"Mr. Ashcraft! I need you to sit back down! I won't have these outbursts in my office! Now, it is unfortunate that he has taunted Sydney, but he is the lead quarterback for our football team, and we can't have him with a dirty name," Mrs. Gossett says, which gets my dad superheated!

"No, *you* listen, and listen good to me!" Dad says. "If my daughter gets any discipline from this incident, you can mark my words I will have your job! Your school is supposed to be all about 'a bully-free zone,'" Dad says, making air quotations like a teenager with sass and attitude, "but it takes my daughter whoopin' her bully to get him to stop while you guys just sit here and try to protect him 'cause he is a freakin' 'lead quarterback'? Total BS! Come on, Sydney, I got better things to do with my time than to sit here and listen to this lie that they try to feed to everyone here! Emma, you too, let's go!" He storms off. We get up and follow Dad out of the office as he continues to complain about the "bully-free zone" and how it's total BS.

As I pass Sophie, I shrug my shoulders and keep walking. I motion like I'm talking on the phone, asking her to call me later. She gives me a thumbs-up and waves goodbye.

Mrs. Gossett gets up and tries to catch my dad as she passes Sophie; she points at her to wait a minute. Mrs. Gossett goes out in the hall and hollers at my dad. "Mr. Ashcraft, please come back!" He hears her say this, as he motions back to her something inappropriate but keeps walking.

Mrs. Gossett goes back into the office and has Sophie follow her. "Have a seat, Sophie. I'm sorry for that rude show of inappropriate adult behavior there just now, but can you elaborate on what happened to Sydney today, please?"

"Sure. So Lucas has been bullyin' Sydney for a while now, but she mostly brushes it off. Today, I think he went too far and Sydney tried to brush it off, but he just wouldn't let up. So when he punched her in the eye, she must have snapped, because I spent *a lot* of time with her and I have *never* seen her so angry. But he did say stuff about her mom, and I do know that is a tender subject for her. She misses her mom so bad some days. But that's what happened. May I go to class now?" Sophie asks.

Mrs. Gossett nods and fills out a pass and sends her on her way.

On the way home, Dad is furious. "That damn school, what is wrong with them? First off, to think that their own motto of bullying is okay? Second, to punish the bullied person? And third, to let a boy hit a girl and think, 'Oh, he's a lead quarterback, so it's okay'?" he says with sass like a girl. "It is completely effed up! I am sorry for the profanity, Syd and Emma, but this is unreal. What kind of society do we live in to think that this is okay? Now my beautiful young lady has to walk around with a black eye for the next two weeks!" Dad says as I start to panic.

"Two weeks!" I scream. I start to cry as I say, "Two weeks? Really, Dad? I can't have this shiner for two weeks!"

"Emma, can you stay here with Sydney? I have something I have to do! I'll be back later. I love you, Syd! Thanks, Emma!" he says as he scoots out the door in a hurry.

"Emma, now what? I can't have this black eye for two whole weeks! Can we do something about it?" I ask, worried it won't be gone in time for the next race.

As we get out of the car and head into the house, she says, "Well, let me see what we can do for that for ya." As I follow her into the kitchen, she puts her purse and keys on the counter and thinks for a moment.

"Hopefully, we have something that will work," I say, trying to be hopeful.

She goes to the bathroom and comes back out with a bag and goes to the freezer. "Here, Sydney, try this." She hands me a cloth bag full of ice. "Hold this on your eye for a few minutes and off for a few and back on again. See how that works."

I take the ice pack and head to my room. "Thanks, Emma! I'm goin' to my room."

"Syd, I am so sorry about today," she says sadly. "I never meant for things to get so far outta hand."

"It's okay, Emma. It's not your fault." And I disappear around the corner.

I get to my room and lie there, waiting for Sophie to call. I have ended up falling asleep for what seems like just minutes when I hear my phone ring.

Sophie says, "Sydney, how are you feelin'?"

"Hey, Sophie. Eh, my eye's a li'l sore. Emma gave me ice for it. How about you? Did you end up talkin' with Mrs. Gossett?"

"I'm good!" Sophie tells me. "Yeah, wow, you put a whoopin' on Lucas today! You were *all the talk* around school after you left. I think now people will think first before tryin' to fight you, Syd. So when are you comin' back?"

I huff, "Never, if I can help it. But you know Dad will make me! Ugh, why does school have to be so hard? I miss Mom!"

"Well, Lucas was at school all day. How come he was there and you weren't?"

"I don't know. I guess it's just because 'I'm a football player, I get to have no punishment, wah, wah, wah.' What a crybaby!"

"So do you think I can come over?" Sophie asks.

"I don't know. I have to ask Emma. Can you wait till I go ask?"

"For you, Syd, I will wait forever!" she responds. "But hurry, 'cause I wanna come over soon if I can."

"Okay, hold on."

I run down to the kitchen. It's almost always where I can find Emma. I think it's her favorite room of the whole house! "Em? Can Sophie come over? Please?" Nope, not here. Okay, where else could she be? Let me look outside. "Emma!" I shout. "Emma?"

I go back to the phone. "Sophie, I can't find Em. Let me look in one more place."

I go back in the house and look in each of the rooms downstairs. I finally go back down the hall to her room in the back of the house. Her door is closed, so she must be inside. I gently knock on her door. "Come in!" I hear from inside.

I start to talk as I am opening her door. "I'm sorry to disturb you, Emma, but could Sophie come over, please?" I ask, hoping for a yes.

"Well, Syd, I don't know. After what happened today, I should say no, not today, but I also know it was not 100 percent your fault. So if you promise to be good from here on out, she may come over," Emma says, understanding today's issues weren't *all* me.

"Yes, yes, I will do everything in my power to be very good. Thank you! Thank you, Emma. I love you!"

She nods and lies back down. I close the door as I leave her room.

I tell Sophie, "Sorry, she was nappin'. Yes, you may come over. Do you have a ride, or do I need to have Obee come get you?"

"Umm, if Obee can, it would be best! Mom has to take Eliza for swimmin' lessons."

"Okay, I will ask him, and I will text you back. Love you, bestie!"

"Okay, talk to ya soon!" Sophie says. "I'm so excited!"

I go out and look for Obee. He's usually easy to find; he's almost always in one of the barns. "Obee? Are you out here?" I ask.

135

"Hey, Syd, what's up? Oh, wow, what happened to you? Did you fall into a door?" Obee asks, shocked with my black eye.

"Oh, but you should see the other guy. Seriously, I whooped some bum today! But could you please pick up Sophie? Emma said she could come over," I say.

"Umm, sure. How soon do you need me to go get her?"

"Well, honestly, the sooner, the better, but I can wait if you are in the middle of something. Or I can help ya to finish whatever you are doin'? If it helps ya?" I ask patiently.

"No, I am good. I just wasn't sure when you needed to go. You wanna ride with me?" Obee asks.

"Do I ever! Thanks again, Obee!" I say as I run to his truck.

Obee gets in, and we head off for Sophie's. "So you wanna tell me about the shiner? Just *who* hit you, and *how bad* did you hurt the other guy?" he asks, like he's afraid to know.

"Well, you see, there's this boy at school who thinks he's all that and a bag of chips. But I crumbled him to dust today!" I subtly say.

"I'm afraid to ask, but would this boy just happen to be a football player?" he asks.

"Hmm, how'd you guess? Was it the fact he thinks he's all that?" I ask, laughing.

"Well, that was my first guess. So I know I taught you self-defense, but it sounds like you annihilated him to dust!" Obee laughs.

"Yep, that's a fact. It's Lucas Devinshire!" I say with confidence. "He tried to make himself look big and unstoppable, but I squished him! And they wanna suspend me and let him off! Pssh! Dad was not so happy when he heard that!"

"Well, I would really hate to see him. I can only imagine how bad he looks!" Obee says as we pull into Sophie's.

Sophie is already outside and waiting for us. She runs up to the truck, and I open the door for her. She climbs in, and we head back home. She's getting to see my eye for the first time since school.

"That looks like it hurts, Syd," Sophie says, like she thinks it's gross.

"Oh, it hurts, but it was so worth it! I just hope it's gone by next race day," I say with concern.

When we get home, Sophie and I scrounge around in the kitchen for some snacks. We find a bowl of homemade brownies. They have big white chocolate and big peanut butter chunks baked into them. "Mmm, are you thinkin' what I'm thinkin'?"

"Yes, yes, I am!" Sophie says, smiling. "You know me, Syd. I cannot get enough of a peanut butter brownie sundae! You do have peanut butter, right?"

"I think so. Em usually keeps that stuff stockpiled because I love it so much!" I look through the cupboards, and sure enough, it's there. "Yep! We got plenty! Do you want the softer, sauce kind or the kind that gets hard when it touches the ice cream?"

"Eh, I don't care. Just pick one, Syd. Just so long as it's peanut butter!"

We sit down and enjoy our sundaes and talk about the fight and things that happened today in school before we finish up and head to my room. We hang out, just chatting more about the day's events and the other upcoming days and events before we wind down for the night and drift off to sleep.

CHAPTER 17

Remembering Grandad

As I drift off, I think about when I was younger and when Grandad was still alive. The fun things we did together were endless. We never really went anywhere too far from the ranch, but he always made it so much fun when we were together that it didn't matter, 'cause I didn't have time to think about anything but us and what we were doing together!

I remember one summer, Grandad bought a little tent to take out to the far end of the lake. Yeah, the cottage was there, but this was a survival lesson. Grandad didn't want us to be able to cheat by using it and its supplies. So he felt that taking the tent to the far end of the lake would be best. We probably could have hiked back to the cottage, but it would have taken a good part of our day and time up.

Grandad's reason for this particular kind of trip, and the others to follow, was to teach me how to survive in the great American outdoors. He always thought that there would be some astronomical world devastation and we would need to know how to survive, and this was his way of teaching me the basics, so I wouldn't starve or go thirsty. He taught me how to hunt for food, whether it was with a .22 revolver that was his grandad Sawyer Payne's or to set snare traps for rabbits and squirrels. After we would hunt and catch our food, then he would show me how to clean them. He also taught me how to fish and clean what I caught. "Of course, now that we have our food to eat, we need to know how to cook it," he would say to me. He taught me that fish and meat from rabbits and squirrels would cook up differently, and how to make sure it was up to temp so I wouldn't get sick from undercooked meat.

He taught me what plants we could eat and which made for good medical purposes. So we would make a meal with meat, fish, and some greens that we would make into a little side salad with berries for a dressing. Most girls probably would turn their noses up at eating squirrel and rabbit, but actually, it was not all that bad. If it means living or dying, then I am eating it. Grandad even said that there were insects we could eat, but I told him, "I will save those for when I actually have to eat them." He would just laugh at me. He taught me different ways to collect water, from the rain to the lake, and to make sure it was drinkable.

He would say to me, "Syd, other than food and water, you also need good shelter and heat that you can cook with." We started off with the tent for the first few times, but as far as I know, still to this day, the little shelters we built are still up. I should take Sophie and go scouting one day to see which, if any, are still standing. We made about three good, sturdy ones that definitely should still be standing, but he also showed me how to make a few lean-tos as well. Those I doubt are still standing, or at least not all the structure. He told me that the kind of shelter you make depends on your surroundings, and a good shelter would protect you not only from wildlife but from the elements as well. Some we made the fire inside the shelters, and some we made outside. It was hard sometimes to get the fire started, but he said that it takes time to learn and be good at it. Once we got them started, though, he would show me how to keep them going. That was the easy part. He even showed me how to keep it going even in the rain.

That was the really nice thing about our farm; as big as it was, there was plenty of room for small game and wild berries and plants to make this all the more fun for us. That was half of the fun of these trips, to go out and explore and see just what was out there for the taking. I still do not think we covered a very big area even for the amount of times we would go and do one of these trips. It was all pretty simple and basic, but everything will definitely come in handy one day, if not for a crisis, then maybe just for fun with my kids someday.

Then there were days we would just ride out to sit by the lake and just chat about life. I would listen to Grandad's stories and his quotes full of wisdom. Some days we would fish together while we were sitting at the lake. It was always so peaceful and calming just sitting there with Grandad.

I also remember the times we would just saddle up Black Boots, and before SOT was born, we would saddle up one of the other horses and just ride around, enjoying the scenery. When I was younger, Grandad wanted me to be familiar with all the horses on the farm so they would be used to me and I would know their tendencies. He called me the baby horse whisper because I was always so good around them and they listened to me very well. "You have a way with the horses, Syd. They listen to you like no other," he would always say to me.

I think one of the saddest times I remember with Grandad Jack was when Grandmom Willow Jones had found out she had stage IV colon cancer. Grandad loved Willow so much. They had been married for all but seventy-five years. Back in the day, when my grandad was young, they dated at much earlier ages than the newer generations of my parents' time. So providing you were healthy, you could live to see a marriage make seventy-five years. From Grandad's stories, I believe they had been married for about seventy-two years when she started showing signs of a medical complication that landed her in the hospital. This was when they discovered the cancer. Grandad did his best to get her the best medical treatment available. But even with the best, they were unable to help her. By the time the symptoms had reared their ugly little head, it was so far throughout her body that they only gave her about two years to live. They said that was the best chance they could give her due to the severity of her cancer. They had mentioned that they could try to operate but they could not guarantee a much better chance. Grandad and Willow had decided it was best to just live life to the fullest and do everything they wanted to do but just never got a chance to.

We would pray with her every day in hopes the good Lord would allow her to see her seventy-fifth year with Grandad. That was one of the few wishes Grandmom had. They did make plans to go see all of God's wonders, or the things they called wonders, like out West to the Grand Canyon, to Yellowstone to see the geysers, to Great Wall of China, the Big Ben, the Eiffel Tower, the Stonehenge, the Pyramids of Egypt, the Leaning Tower of Pisa. They would make plans to go to an area and see all they could before they had to return. They truly tried to make the best of all the little time they had left.

The days turned to weeks, and weeks to months. She did not show any signs of getting better, but also no signs of getting worse either. She was able to celebrate her seventy-third and seventy-fourth anniversaries with Grandad. Then, about one month before their seventy-fifth wedding anniversary, she started to show signs of things not looking so well. She decided it was time to make out her will or at least update it. Grandad said she always had a verbal statement about her things and what she wanted done with them. So I guess she just wanted a more permanent will in testament. The pastor started to come to the ranch more regularly to bless her and read scripture to her, like she was getting her very own mini church service all to herself. We would sit with her as the preacher would read and talk with her.

The last week, there was a nurse who came to the ranch from hospice and saw to her pain and that she was comfortable. We continued to pray for Willow to get to see one more anniversary with Jack so we could have just one more big celebration of life and love before she passed. She would tell me in her final days how much she loved me and she would watch over me forever and ever. She prayed that I would grow up to make her and the family proud. I would tell her I would do my best and that I loved her as well.

The family planned a small gathering of friends and family to be prepared to come together for this last celebration. We wanted her to know she was loved and would be missed, even though we were pretty sure she already knew it. Mom had her favorite flowers delivered, huge bouquets of daisies and black-eyed Susans. Some were fresh cut, and some were potted so we could plant them around the house after she passed, in her memory.

Grandad and Grandmom sat and looked through photo albums and reminisced about their life together for the last few days. Grandad said how lucky he was to be with such a beautiful lady by his side. She made mention how it would be the gift of a lifetime to get to spend just one more anniversary with Grandad. Then, two nights and two days before their seventy-fifth, she woke up from screaming in her sleep. Grandad assumed that she was in pain and scrambled to get her something for the pain, but she stopped him and said to him, "No, Jack, I do not need any pain meds. I am not in any pain."

"Willow, what, then, is wrong? Why did you scream in your sleep?"

"Oh, Jack, I am sorry to worry you, but I was just startled, is all."

"Willow, my love, what had you so startled? Did you have a nightmare?" At that moment, my mom and dad came running into the room to see what was happening. Emma was close behind them.

"I am so sorry to wake everyone. I was just startled because I had a visitor."

"A visitor? Willow, I do not see anyone but the family here. Did they leave already?" Jack said, worried that she was going into delirium.

"Mom, are you feelin' okay? Why would you say you had a visitor when clearly there is no one here? Are you in pain? Can I get you something to drink, like a glass of water or some warm milk?" Ivy, my mom, asked her mom.

"I am fine, everyone. I am. Yes, Ivy, I would like a glass of water, please. I am so sorry to have woken you, but I had a visitor, and he is still here."

"Willow, my love, are you sure that you are not seein' things? There is obviously no one here but us."

"I am fine, Jack. I am not seein' things. Well, I am, but I know that what I am seein' is real. Even though you may not all be able to see him, he is definitely still here. My guest is Jesus. He is here to take me home. But I have asked to have a few more days, so I can get my one last request. Which he said he would honor. I am guessin' that was when I screamed out of excitement."

"Listen to me. You cannot have her just yet. Please, wherever you are, please, just let me have a few more days. We are not ready to let her go. Please, just a few more days, Lord, then you may take her home with you," Grandad said as he fell to the floor beside Grandmom's bed, sobbing as he reached for her hand, kissing it ever so gently.

"Jack, please come sit with me on the bed. Everyone, can you please excuse us for a li'l? I want to just lie here with Jack, holdin' each other, just for a while. We will come out in a bit. Thank you."

We all left the room, and Mom made a few calls to the Abbotts and a few of Willow and Jack's friends to get everything ready and set up for celebration, while Emma made breakfast for everyone. Emma decided it was the perfect time to make one of her huge breakfasts, which she loves to make for special occasions. Today seemed to qualify for a great day for a special occasion. With these particular breakfasts, if you walked away hungry, that was on you, because there was always a huge selection and plenty of everything. You name it and she probably had it made and waiting to be devoured. Today was no different. She even asked me to help do a few things to help her get everything done just a little quicker. "Syd, while I get the waffles and French toast started, can you please set the table? Please put a plate, bowl, cup, fork, knife, spoon, and napkin at every spot. Thank you, sweetie!"

"Yes, ma'am."

"Emma, what can I do for you?" Ivy asked.

"Would you mind gettin' out the eggs? I need some whipped for the French toast and another bowl of them whipped for scrambled eggs, please." Mom got busy with the eggs as Emma got the waffle iron out and made up the waffle batter.

"Ladies, is there anything I can do to help out with breakfast?" Dad graciously asked.

"Actually, Parker, could you please go to the deep freezer and get me some sausage links, bacon, and ham slices? Please and thank you!"

By the time Jack and Willow came out to be with the family, breakfast was just about served. "Emma, what a spread! You literally made a feast for the gods. Waffles, French toast, ham, bacon, sausage, eggs, toast, blueberry muffins, milk, juice, crepes, and fresh fruit! All my favorites! Thank you, Emma. You truly are the best cook who has ever blessed my palate with food! Shall we all eat, everyone?" Willow directed everyone to sit to eat.

The next two days were so somber with the realization that Willow's time here on earth was just about at its end. We had an amazing celebration for Jack and Willow. Everyone had got to say their goodbyes and flood her with love. That morning, just past midnight, Willow took the walk with Jesus to her new forever home to wait for Jack to join her.

Grandad took it hard the next few weeks. As would be expected with a long love life and relationship such as they had just going *poof*, gone forever. Grandad wanted to get away and not have to think about things too much, so we took a survival trip out by the lake and I showed him what I learned so far from all our other trips. It was enough for him to let loose a little and enjoy himself. He said I did very well and he was very proud of me.

They always say that when you really, truly love someone and they pass, the other spouse dies of a broken heart from being lonely. I believe Grandad passed away from a broken heart. It was only a few months after Grandmom passed that Grandad joined Grandmom. I think he knew when his time was up, because I heard him mention to Mom that he had seen Willow. She came to him in his dreams to tell him that she would be coming to bring him home in a few days. I made sure to let him know many, many times how much I loved him and how much I would miss him. I also asked him to let Grandmom Willow know how much I missed her and that I would always love her too! He promised he would and that he would be with me every day, to watch out for me.

The day Grandad passed, I was so sad yet again. To lose one family member after another, you begin to hate death and wonder why God takes your family one at a time if he truly loved us. But

Grandad always said everything happens for a reason, even if we don't see it at that time.

All this time I have been trying to remember Grandad. I hope I get some sleep, or I will be one tired little lady tomorrow.

I wake up to look at the time, and I still have time to grab a couple more hours of sleep. So I try to clear my mind and actually get a little more sleep.

CHAPTER 18

Round 2

Sophie and I get up, get ready, and head to the kitchen for some breakfast before we need to get off to school. Emma asks, "Am I to take you girls to school today?"

"Oh, I guess you can, Em."

"You guess? Well, it sounds like you already had someone in mind to take you, Syd."

"Nah, not really, but you do *always* take us, so I *was* thinkin' about askin' Obee. But you can take us if you would like. I can ask Obee another day."

"Are you worried about goin' back today after yesterday? Is that why you want to ask Obee to take you in today?"

"No, I am not worried. Can we just finish up so we can go? I just want to get this day over with."

"Are you okay, Sydney?" Emma asks, concerned. "You don't sound like yourself today."

"Don't worry, Emma, I am good. Just had thoughts of Grandad last night, and I am just missin' him today, is all. Sophie, you good to go?"

"Yep, I'm ready, Syd."

"Okay, girls, let me get my purse and we can scoot."

While Em gets her purse, Sophie and I head out to the car.

Emma comes out right behind us, so we all get in the car and head out the lane. I notice her keep looking in the rearview mirror; she acts as though she has something that she wants to say to either myself or us, but she continues to drive and not speak. It's very odd to ride to school with Em and not be talking about something, so I decide to break the silence.

"Em, how's everything goin' with the shop? Will we have it open soon?"

"Sydney, I think the plan was to have a grand reopenin' this weekend. Now, you should confirm that with your dad, because I am not 100 percent sure, though."

"Well, if Dad decides to open it this weekend after the races, I am game to open it with him," I tell Em. I honestly hope Mom's shop takes off again. I cannot wait to be the center of all of it!

"Sydney, you didn't try to cover up your shiner?"

"Nah! I earned this, kinda, in a way, and I am in no way embarrassed about havin' it." Well, that's what I tell Em. Truth is, I am so afraid it won't be gone in time for the races, and how will I explain this before I am ready to?

"Okay, well, I was gonna say we can stop by the shop and get some makeup to cover it up if you wanted to."

"Thanks, Em, but I should be okay for today. But maybe we can stop by after school?" I ask, hoping to not sound too eager and have her wonder why I, all of a sudden, changed my mind about it.

"Sure thing, Sydney," she says as we arrive out front of the school.

As we pull up, some kids have already seen us coming and have started to stop, point, and stare. I look at Sophie, and she looks at me, and we can already tell this may not end up being a very good day.

"Okay, girls, I will be here to pick you up later. Try to have a good day, okay, girls?"

"Thanks, Em!" we both say as we get out of the car and just stand there looking like a pair of new kids at a new school.

"Sophie, I pray this day turns out better than my gut feels like."

"You too? I just suddenly am not feelin' so well," Sophie nervously states.

We are both heading toward the doors when a group of "loser" students makes their way toward us. One of them steps forward as if they were the leader of the group. He has on thick black-rimmed glasses, greased-up hair, suspenders, pocket protector, a plaid shirt with khaki pants. Why is it that most nerds all have the same look?

"Hi, Sydney!" he says with a lisp. "I am Stanley Melman. I am basically our little group's spokesperson." He snorts and laughs at the same time.

Sophie and I just look at each other, and then I begin to speak. "Hello, Stanley. It's nice to meet you. What can I do you for?"

"Well, we just wanted to say that we would be proud to have you in our group, and your friend Sophie too! After watchin' you take out the trash the other day and stand up against one of the biggest bullies here at our school, we just knew we needed you in our corner!" he says with pure excitement like he was talking to a movie star.

I again look at Sophie, and I say to her, "I don't know, Sophie. What do you think?"

"Well, Syd, we have never been part of a group before. I kinda feel honored that you are askin' us to be a part of yours," she says, first looking at me, then at Stanley and his group of friends.

"I know, Sophie. That was my thoughts exactly. Stanley, we would be honored and proud to be a part of your group. If you ever need anything, just remember, we are now your friends and we will always have your back!"

"Wow! That's great!" he says as he turns to high-five everyone in the group and then turns to Sophie and me to high-five us too. "Sydney, Sophie, we have a club that meets after school, if you are interested. Just let me know. I am the president of it. Okay, I guess we will be gettin' to class. See you later! Oh, and if you have lunch with us, feel free to sit with us!"

"Thanks, Stanley, but I am about to be very busy after this weekend with my mom's shop, I think. I haven't had time to speak with my dad to make sure just yet. But I will let you know. As far as lunch, yeah, if we see ya, we can sit with y'all. Okay, see ya later." They no more than turn around to head for the doors to get to class than who happens to be standing there, blocking their way? You guessed it, the trouble-causing football jocks.

"Where do you nerds think you are goin'?" Lucas demands.

"Sorry, Lucas, we are headed to class. We didn't mean to get in your way. We will just go around you," Stanley politely says as he and his group turn to go around. "Come on, guys. See ya later, Sydney and Sophie!"

Sophie and I look at each other, and yep, there it is! My gut feeling kicking me in the throat! My head's saying, "Don't do it, Syd, don't do it. Think of Grandad!" But my heart says, "Step up to the plate and defend your friends." I can see Sophie with a look in her eyes like, "Just turn and walk away, Syd. He's not worth it!" And as we look away to see Stanley and his friends start to walk around Lucas and his jocks, it happens! Lucas jumps over in front of them again.

"I said, just where do you *nerds* think you are goin'? I did not say you could go past us this way!" Lucas rudely says and starts to act like he's gonna push Stanley.

I mumble under my breath, "Sophie, if he pushes him...!"

She whispers back, "Syd, we just need to walk away. This isn't your fight." She says this with a slight fear in her voice.

By then, Lucas does it! He hauls off and pushes Stanley. Stanley falls back onto the concrete, and I just snap inside, my blood boiling. I am doing all I can not to just run up and knock him out again! He would deserve it. *And I know Sophie is right, it's not my fight, but can I honestly just stand here and let Lucas push Stanley around like this?* I think to myself as I also say to Sophie in a whisper, "Grandad, please forgive me. Here, Sophie, hold my things again!"

"Syd! No!" Sophie sternly says under her breath.

Well, much to my surprise, Jaxson and Camden are standing back, keeping an eye on everything that is happening. When I hand my things to Sophie, Jaxson taps Lucas on the arm and his focus goes from Stanley right straight to me.

"Oh, hey, there, Ass-crack! Whatcha gonna do? Wanna start somethin'?"

"Nope! I'm just givin' my friend a hand to get up because some hothead decided to push him down."

"Your friend? Ha ha ha, Jaxson, Camden, do y'all hear this? Ass-crack is friends with the nerd!" They all start laughing as I help Stanley up. Lucas steps up and chest-checks me. Now, if you don't know what chest-checking is, I will tell you. It's when someone *thinks* they are bigger, better, and throws their weight around to make other people *think* they are tough! They push out their chest and push you with their chest. But we all know who's the tougher one here. And it's not Lucas.

"Yes, Lucas, my friend! Our friends! You should try it sometime. It's nice havin' friends who care about you and stand up for you!" I say, hoping one way that Lucas would step up to say he was sorry, or another way, he would step up to me so I could whoop him again! Some bullies just never learn—that's their problem.

"I know what friends are, Ass-crack. See, I have two right here always by my side."

"Well, then, you have a great day, 'cause we are late for class. Come on, guys, let's roll," I say as I try to coax everyone to leave.

But I can see that Lucas wants to roll and he didn't learn from our last encounter. "Yeah, Ass-crack, that sounds like a great idea. Let's roll. So come on. You think you can take me again? You just got lucky last time," Lucas says to try to intimidate me.

"Ha ha ha! Nah, I'll pass. I think I did enough damage to you last time. I wouldn't want to bruise your ego. After all, the football team needs you," I say loud and proud.

I guess he didn't like it and decides he's gonna try to take me again. He steps up in my face, and when I don't move, he hits me in the stomach so hard I will feel it for a while, I'm sure. But I instantly go from smiling proudly to instant rage! I get up and charge Lucas with everything I have, knocking him into Jaxson and Camden. Again, I just start nailing him so hard anywhere I can, just to get a hit in on him. His arms are flailing around like he's being attacked by bees or something. With every hit, I am saying, "You ever touch one of my *friends* or *me* again, or *anyone*, for that matter, and I will find you and I will see to it—"

Before I can get out the rest of my sentence, I'm once again being pulled off Lucas and being taken to the principal's office.

"You stay right here, young lady! I have had about enough of your actions for this week already!" says Mrs. Gossett angrily as she walks out of her office and slams the door. I turn to look, and she walks out of the office and toward the front doors. A few minutes later, she returns with Stanley, Sophie, Lucas, Jaxson, Camden, and Stanley's other friends that I haven't had the pleasure of meeting yet. I hear her through the glass telling them that they are all to stay seated and not to be talking with one another. She tries to separate everyone, away from one another. She then comes back into her office and starts making phone calls.

"Hello, good mornin'. This is Principal Gossett. We have a situation at school, and I need you to come in at your earliest convenience. Thank you." This is her side of the conversation with all the calls she makes, and I would have to say that she has called *all* our parents.

About twenty minutes later, parents and guardians start showing up out in the main office. I turn to see which parents have all showed up, and of course, there stand Emma and my dad! Mrs. Gossett waits a few more minutes, and then she gets up and goes out to speak with all the parents. I can't make out what she is saying this time, but everyone is getting up and headed out into the hallway when she comes to get me.

"Ms. Ashcraft, would you please follow me?"

I get up and follow her and everyone else to an empty classroom. We all take a seat and prepare to listen to what Mrs. Gossett has to say.

"You are all probably wonderin' why I called you here today. Well, it seems we have some issues that we thought we had worked out from yesterday, but turns out I was misled. So now we are *all* involved, and we need to find a solution to this problem today! It seems that one young lady has taken it upon herself to start fights. This makes two in as many days."

Dad knows she is talking about me and jumps up and cuts Mrs. Gossett off. "Now, you just wait one minute. Are you seriously gonna stand here and try to put this all on my daughter *again*? I thought I made myself clear yesterday this was not her fault. She doesn't just go around pickin' fights and startin' problems!"

Emma grabs his arm to settle him down, saying softly, "Parker, would you please sit down? Let Mrs. Gossett talk."

"Thank you, Emma! Now, like I was sayin' before I was so *rudely* interrupted, we need to come together, the parents and the students, to work out a solution to the situation at hand here. Now, I want *everyone* to have a chance to speak their opinions. So one at a time, we will start and go around the room. Let's start up here with Lucas. Go ahead and say what's on your mind, Lucas," Mrs. Gossett gently says.

"Thank you, Mrs, Gossett, for the opportunity to start this off. So I just want to say that I was outside, just mindin' my business and talkin' with my friend Stanley, and Sydney just comes up and gets in my face. And well, here we are," Lucas says with a smirk on his face.

Next, Jaxson and Camden make their comments, which pretty much mock what Lucas said.

Then it is Stanley's turn to talk. "Mrs. Gossett, Lucas came up and got in my face and refused to let me come into the school. Lucas pushed me, and Sydney offered me her hand to get up. Then Lucas chest-checked and hit her. She was just defendin' me. I did not ask her to, but he was bullyin' me and she did what any good friend would and should do," Stanley states while Lucas gives him the evil eye.

Stanley's other friends tell the story just as Stanley did. Mrs. Gossett looks at Lucas and his friends. Then she looks at Stanley and his friends.

"Well, it's obvious that we have two very different stories here. And we only have two more stories to hear, and I can only *imagine* how they will go. So go ahead, ladies. It's your turn," she says to Sophie and me.

"Well, Mrs. Gossett, I will go first. When Sydney and I got here, Stanley and his friends came up to talk with us. When they were finished, they turned to leave, and that was when Lucas and his friends were standin' in their way. Stanley and his friends went to go around them, but Lucas jumped in front of them. Lucas pushed Stanley, and Syd went to help him up. Then Lucas chest-checked her and punched her in the stomach. Sydney was only defendin' herself and Stanley."

"I second that, Mrs. Gossett. I was only plannin' to help up Stanley and walk away, till Lucas got in my face. Even then, I was plannin' to walk away. But when he punched me, that was where I drew the line! Someone has to teach him that just because he's a football player doesn't give him the right to pick on anyone he pleases. Now, I promised Emma I would be good from here on out. And even though he pushed my friend, I held my cool. I am so sorry, Emma, I failed you," I say as I hang my head.

"Well, this seems to be a control issue for you, Sydney, I think," Mrs. Gossett starts to say when my dad lets her have it again.

"Look, Mrs. Gossett, what seems to be the problem is *you* have a failed the 'no bullyin'' policy here at your school! If you are someone in sports, especially football, then you and your actions are overlooked! So I think you need to fix your policy before you think about punishin' those who are bein' bullied. It's not fair to keep letting Lucas and his buddies off with no recourse for their actions. So now the question is, What are *you* gonna do about this?" Parker, says sternly.

"Parker, as I have stated before—"

"I am sorry, but I don't care who he is, if he's on the football, basketball, or chess team! I don't care. Right now, it's about one student against another student. Student for student! Let's treat it that way!" Parker says as he gets more pissed off.

"Mr. Ashcraft, one more outburst and you will be escorted off the school premises. Now, it seems as though, Lucas, you are goin' to have to receive some kind of punishment. This is twice in as many days that you have instigated a fight with Sydney. If this happens again, you may risk bein' let go from the football team. Now, Sydney, you really need to control your anger, as we spoke of yesterday. Stanley, I am sorry you were dragged into this. Are you okay? Do you need to go to the nurse?" she asks.

Lucas is sitting there, getting cocky, because obviously, if anyone needs a nurse, it's him. I put a big whoopin' on him again. But he definitely deserved it again this time!

"Is there a problem, Lucas?"

"No, ma'am."

"Now, what I think we will do is just for you all involved here today. We are goin' to set up a special teamwork class for you to learn to work together and get along. If you all complete it, then this will be the end of it. Case closed. But for those of you who do not complete this class, then you will receive one week's suspension, with no after-school activities. Do you all agree?" she asks us, looking around the room. We all nod in agreement, and she releases us to go to class, except for Lucas, Stanley, and me. "Do any of you need to visit with the nurse?"

"Nah, I'm good," I say.

"I should be okay but would like the opportunity, if I start to not feel well, to go to the nurse then," Stanley asks.

"That's fine, Stanley. Lucas? What about you?"

"I'm fine," Lucas says like it doesn't matter, anyways.

"Okay, here are passes for you all. Can we please get through the rest of the day without any more problems?" She hands us our passes, one group at a time. As we each get our passes, we head to class.

"Now, are there any questions from the parents?" she asks.

"I think what you need is a class like that for the entire school. Then maybe there wouldn't be any of this kind of behavior at school," Parker says to Mrs. Gossett.

"Well, Parker," she says as she writes something down on the tablet, "I think that would be a great idea! We could use someone to come in to help organize it. Would you be interested?"

"No, I am not a teacher. Sorry, not my forte."

"I would be interested in helpin' with that, if I may say," Emma says, accepting Mrs. Gossett's offer to Parker.

"Okay, I will get with you, Emma, and we can get this set up. I will let you work with the students from today as your startin' class."

"Okay, great. I will work on some team-building skills that I feel will do the most help. And I will present them to you when we get back together. Now, if you don't mind, I have some errands to run. Thank you, Mrs. Gossett. Till I hear from you again," Emma says as she gets up and leaves.

"Mrs. Gossett, I want to thank you for takin' the time to listen and understand that this wasn't all Sydney's fault. I also would like to say I am sorry for the outbursts from me today. But do you see where I was comin' from yesterday and today?"

"Yes, Parker, I do, and I am sorry for not seein' things sooner. I just hope now, with Emma's help, maybe we can turn things around for some of the students. Thank you again for the short notice and for comin' in. Hopefully, we can stop meeting up like this," she says as she walks Dad to the door.

CHAPTER 19

Ashcrafts versus Hutchinses

When Parker leaves the school, he goes to see if Greyson is available to assist him in a special errand. When he gets to the Abbotts', he sees Greyson's truck in the drive. He pulls in and parks his truck behind Greyson's. As Parker gets out and shuts his door, he hears the garage door start to open.

"Hey, I thought I heard someone out here. Is everything okay, Parker?"

"Well, Greyson, to be honest, I just stopped by to see if you would mind goin' on a special errand of sorts with me."

"Ah, sure thing, Parker. What are ya thinkin'?"

"Well, there was another situation at school, and I wanna stop it at the source. I was wonderin' if you would mind goin' along just in case things start to get a li'l outta hand. So I have a witness. Ya know what I mean?"

"Well, I will probably say yes, but can I have a li'l more info, Parker?"

"Sure thing. We are makin' a trip out to see Dylan, Colton, or maybe even Claire, because they need to get some kind of authority over Lucas. This boy is pushin' the limit lately. Yesterday he hit Sydney, and today he hit her once more. He's gettin' off with a slap on the wrist yet again! I just can't believe that the school is *allowin'* this to continue. So maybe if one of his home influences were aware of his school behavior, then maybe he will change. Or at the very least, I hope it will make some kind of a difference."

"Yeah, sure, so where do you wanna go first?"

Parker thinks about it and then says, "What do you think about goin' to see Claire first?"

"I was kinda thinkin' the same thing. So do we wanna take my truck?"

"Sure. Let me move mine."

"Okay, I will close everything up and meet ya back outside here," Greyson says as he goes back in the garage.

By the time Parker has moved his truck, Greyson comes back outside. They get in Greyson's truck and head toward Dylan's.

Claire is Lucas's mother. She is also Dylan and Colton's sister. She doesn't work because she lost her husband when he was in the military and she now gets his pension for life. So unless she's out shopping, she should be home.

"So hopefully, Claire is home, and Dylan too. That way, maybe we can talk with them together. I know how Lucas feels about losing a family member, but I just don't know why this kid has to take it out on the other kids around him. Especially a young lady like my daughter, Sydney."

"Well, Parker, you kinda do the same thing, whether or not you want to believe it. But not to the extent that you would hit someone over it. Though you definitely get a li'l moody, we will say." Greyson laughs.

Parker thinks for a minute, then he says, "Greyson, I am sorry. I didn't realize. Well, maybe I can get Claire to let me talk with him and let him know that I know how he feels. Maybe that's what may work. Maybe she will even let me bring him back to the ranch to do some fishin'?"

"Yeah, maybe. So when are you gonna invite me over to fish your secret lake?" Greyson jokes.

They pull up at the Hutchinses' residence. There are three homes all close to one another behind Dylan's garage that make up the Hutchins property.

"Which one do you think is Claire's?" Greyson asks Parker.

"Well, if I had to guess, I would have to say the one with all the flowers. It looks as though it has a lady's touch," Parker notes.

They walk up to the more neatly manicured home and knock on the door. They can see someone coming through the curtains on the door. The door comes open.

"Hello, gentlemen. Just how may I help you?" Claire says.

"Hello, Claire! I am Parker Ashcraft. I was hopin' to speak with you today about Lucas. May we please come in?"

"Ah, sure. Would you guys like anything to drink? I have water, beer, milk, juice?" she offers.

"No, I am good. Greyson?"

"Thanks, but I am good, Claire."

"Okay, have a seat. So what's this about?" Claire is wondering.

"Well, Claire, I want to say I am sorry I never had the chance to say I was sorry for your loss," Parker sincerely states.

"Well, I believe I can also return the condolences to you and your family."

"Well, I am by no means pointin' any fingers, 'cause both families have been through enough, but there has been some issues at school with Lucas and Sydney. I just thought I would come by and see if there was anything I could do to talk to him to let him know that I, too, feel his pain and that in time it does get a li'l better." Parker pours his heart out to Claire.

Then Claire says something that makes even more sense but that Parker never even thought of. "Well, Parker, I completely understand where you are comin' from, but I think there could be a li'l more to it than either of us had anticipated. So I was cleanin' Lucas's room the other day, and I found something quite interestin' that I have kept to myself. I didn't even want Lucas to know that I knew." Claire gets up and starts to leave the room when she says, "I'll be right back. Let me get what I found."

She disappears for a few minutes and then returns with a piece of paper. She hands it to Parker. As she does, Parker gets his first look at the paper and his jaw drops.

"Umm…wow! Okay, this is not what I was expectin', but it makes a li'l more sense," Parker says as he thinks about today's events.

"Oh, okay. Can you please tell me what it is you are talkin' about? Seems like there's more than what I know?" Claire asks, afraid of what Parker is gonna say.

"Well, where do I start? Because it sounds like you do not know what has been happenin' the last two days," Parker says. "So yesterday, Lucas punched Sydney in the eye. He gave her a real good shiner."

"Well, Parker, that answers my question of what happened to Lucas. Was it Sydney who put a whoopin' on my boy?" she asks angrily but like she's not surprised.

"As much as I hate to say it, yes, it was Sydney. But that's not all. Today, she was talkin' to another boy and I guess Lucas must have gotten jealous, 'cause he pushed the boy and Sydney stepped in to help the boy and those two got into it again," Parkers says with embarrassment.

"Are you embarrassed, Parker?"

"Well, yeah, kinda. I mean, my girl is whoopin' your boy!"

Claire laughs and says, "Parker, I am so proud of Sydney for havin' the…well, you know, to stand up to Lucas. She was just givin' him what he deserved. Since his dad passed, he just walks all over me. He doesn't listen, there's no respect, and he is just all-out rude and hateful most days."

"Well, you should go talk to Mrs. Gossett. She thinks he's an angel and he can do no wrong. She keeps puttin' the blame on Sydney," Parker says as he hears the door opening behind him, and he quickly pushes Lucas's drawing to Claire to hide in case it's Lucas.

"Ah, I thought I smelt something rotten," Dylan says.

"Dylan, these are my guests, and you will treat them as such. Now, what do you want?" Claire demands from Dylan.

"I wanted to see why these companies you have were here. Are they snoopin' again?"

"What do you mean, Dylan? Snoopin' again? Ain't no one snoopin' anywhere. They are here to visit with me as friends. Now, if you don't have a good reason to be here, then I suggest that you leave. Just take your drunk ass home!" Claire demands.

"Yeah, they were here the night I hit that woman and tryin' to raise suspicion to get me mad at Colton," Dylan says, making no sense except for one thing.

Apparently, Greyson picks up on it too. "Dylan, will you excuse Claire and me for a minute?" Parker asks as he motions for Claire to come to the other side of the room.

"I'm sorry, Claire, but did I hear what I thought I just heard? That Dylan hit a woman?" Parker asks with tears filling up his eyes.

"Well, Parker, as much as I hate to say it, yeah, I heard it too. I want to call Colton to come out here. He needs to deal with this. I'm sorry, I didn't know sooner. I know you have been wantin' to put closure to all this."

Greyson keeps Dylan busy while Claire and Parker chat in the corner. While Claire calls Colton from the other room, Greyson and Parker keep an eye on Dylan.

Claire says, "Colton, it's sis. I hate to make this call, but you know I wouldn't do it if it weren't true. I need you to come arrest Dylan. He is drunk again and just basically blurted out that he hit a woman."

There's dead silence on the other end of the phone, then Colton says, "Who all heard it, sis?"

"Parker, Greyson, and I. Like I said, this isn't the call I wanted to be makin' to ya."

Colton asks, "Parker and Greyson? What are they doin' there?"

"Well, they came to me to talk about Lucas. Then Dylan came in here all drunk and was spattin' off. Please just hurry."

"Okay, Marlow and I are on the way."

"So we are all set," Claire says as she winks at Parker and Greyson.

"All set for what?" Dylan asks.

"Don't you go worryin' yourself with that, Dylan. Why don't you just have a seat and take a load off for a few minutes?"

They finally get Dylan seated and settled when there's a knock on the door. Claire gets up to go to the door. Faint talking can be heard coming from the front door area.

"Where is he?"

"He's in the kitchen."

Then three pairs of footsteps echo as they walk closer and closer. Then, through the entryway, Colton and Marlow just stop. Dylan doesn't even know that they are standing there. Colton motions for Claire to get him talking, to see if he will say anything with them there.

"Dylan? Hey, can I ask you something?"

"Claire? What dontcha want to know?"

"I was curious about something that you said earlier? And what you meant by it."

"I meant what I said. But what did I say?" Dylan says, slurring his words.

"Did you say that you hit a woman? When did you hit a woman? Where did you hit a woman?"

"Shhh, that woman doesn't want me to give it away. It was, like, a few months ago in my li'l car that someone came and took."

"Dylan, you have the right to remain silent." Dylan doesn't even have a clue what's going on. "Anything you say can and will be used against you in the court of law. You have the right to an attorney. If you cannot afford one, one will be appointed for you. Do you understand these rights as I have told them to you?" Colton waits for a response. "Dylan?"

"No, Misty, come love my back!"

"Okay, come on, Dylan. I bet that you don't even know what day it is. I'll be right back. Let me take him to the car. Marlow, can you get the doors, please?"

"Sure thing."

They take Dylan out to the patrol car, and a few minutes later, they return.

"Parker..." Colton pauses for a moment as tears start to form in his eyes. "I...I am truly sorry. I should have listened to you that day."

Parker stops him. "It's okay. You weren't 100 percent sure, and I wasn't either. I didn't want him to go to jail without knowin' for sure that he had done it. I knew by the love of God that we would figure out who hit her one day. *I am* just sorry to find out that it was Dylan," Parker says as he slowly relives the night in question over again in his mind, his eyes beginning to well up.

"I think, because he was my family, I just wanted it *not* to be true. For that, I am very sorry. Can you please forgive me for my ignorance?"

"Yes, yes, I can, Colton. You were only doin' your job, and I completely understand that. Like I said, no hard feelins. Thank you again for everything. Marlow, the same to you, man. Thank you! For your awesome work, you are a great officer of the law."

"Thank you, Parker. I give you my condolences as well. If you do need anything, please just call the department and I will do whatever I can. Bye, Claire! Parker, Greyson."

As we walk them to the door, we realize it's getting late. So we say our goodbyes to Claire. "Thanks for the info you showed us earlier. It does help to understand a li'l more of why Lucas is acting the way he is."

"No problem, Parker. Just remember," she says as Parker continues to head for the front door.

"Yes, I will not say anything. This was just an informational visit that answered a *whole* lotta questions. But hey, would you mind if I came and took Lucas back to the ranch one afternoon? We have a private lake that is so beautiful tucked away in the pines that has to be at least three acres big, if not more, just filled up with *all* kinds of fish for the catchin'!" Parker asks, hoping to get to speak with Lucas alone and one-on-one.

"Sure. I think that could be arranged. Thank you!"

"Okay, we will be in touch. And again, I am sorry about today with Dylan and all," Parker says.

"It's okay. I should be the one apologizin'. Okay, bye now," Claire says as we walk out the door.

When Greyson and I get up into his truck, we both just sit there for a moment. Greyson looks as though he just lost someone with that look on his face.

"You okay, Greyson?"

"Me? What about you, Parker? I mean, we came here to talk about Lucas and straighten out that whole mess, and then this happens. I don't know whether to be happy, relieved, or sad right now. I mean, shit, man, you *finally have the answers* that you have wanted and needed for these last few months. So like, we should be happy. But it hurts all over again, like it just happened again."

"It's okay, Greyson. We *can* have all those feelins. It's just for me, I…" Parker tries to gather his thoughts, but he just keeps reliving that night and the following days over and over in his mind like it's on a fast repeat. "I just miss Ivy. Now I can try to let go of this part of everything. I no longer need to wonder who took her life. Now I have to live with *knowin'* who took her life. To be honest, Greyson, I don't know which is worse." Parker pauses as he has a sudden urge to just cry like he never has before and tries to push it deep down. "The knowin' or not knowin'."

"Well, let's just get back to the house so we can try to plan where we go from here," Greyson sadly says as he starts his truck and gets turned around to leave the Hutchinses' place.

As they drive to Greyson's house, Greyson puts his hand on Parker's shoulder to show him some support.

"Do you need to go anywhere or do anything else before we get back to my place? I can take you if you would like?"

"No, Greyson. But thank you. I think I have done enough today." Parker turns to look out the window before continuing, "I just need to go home and gather all my thoughts up and decide how I want to provide this newfound information to my family."

"Well, if you need Allison and me to come be with you and your family when you do decide, just let us know. We would be happy to come over," Greyson says as he pulls in his driveway.

"Actually, Greyson, can you and Allison come over for dinner tonight? I think it would be appropriate that you are both with us when I tell the family, since you *are* family," Parker says as he gets out of Greyson's truck and heads for his.

"Yeah, I will let Allison know not to make any plans for this evenin'. Will we see you later? Like, six?"

"Yeah, I think six is fine. Thanks again, Greyson. I couldn't have asked for a better friend!" Parker says as he gets in his truck and backs out the driveway and pulls away.

CHAPTER 20

The Closing No One Expected

Parker is calling. "Emma, can you please put together a meal for this evenin', say, for six? I have something I need to discuss with everyone. Also, I have invited the Abbotts as well. Is there anything you need? I can pick it up on the way home." He listens. "Okay, sounds good... Drinks and dessert, got it!" He hangs up and heads to the store.

As he comes out of the store, his phone rings, and it's Emma. "Hello, Emma, I'm at the store. Did you need me to get you something else?" He listens as she speaks. "Yes, Emma, I can get the girls. Not a problem. Okay, see you soon. Yep! Bye now."

Parker heads to the school to get the girls for Emma. He's not been sitting there long before students start to make their way out of the school. He wipes his face, takes a few deep breaths, and tries to calm himself before Sydney sees him in such a wreck. A few minutes later, he spots Sophie and Sydney. He toots his horn with one quick bump to get their attention.

Sydney and Sophie hear a horn honk and look around to see Parker sitting next to the curb. They wave and make their way to his truck.

*****

"Dad, is everything okay? Where's Emma?" I ask, worried that something happened to Emma.

"Hey, girls, everything is okay! Emma is fine. We are havin' your family over with us tonight, Sophie. So Emma asked me to get a few things, and you girls were part of it," Parker says, trying to laugh but finding it hard to do.

"Dad, are you sure everything is okay? Also, can we stop by Mom's shop? Emma was gonna stop so I could get some cover-up for this gnarly eye of mine."

"Yes, everything is good, and sure, we can stop by the shop. Do you need me to let you in?"

"Nope. I got it. Thanks, Dad."

When Dad pulls up outside, Sophie and I run in and grab what I need and come right back out. "Okay, we are good to roll, Dad!"

We head to the ranch. Dad puts his hand on my knee and says, "Syd the Kid, I love ya so much. So how was the rest of your day, girls? You didn't let her whoop anybody else up, did ya, Sophie?"

Sophie laughs. "No, Parker, no more fights. And in my defense, I told her not to."

"Thanks, squealer. I did what Grandad said, only fight when necessary. I thought Lucas pushin' Stanley more than qualified as a necessity."

"Well, hopefully, we won't have any more of these happenins at school. Do you understand, Sydney?"

"Yes, sir," I say as I hang my head.

"Syd, I know why you did what you did, and I'm not scoldin' you for that. I'm just sayin' that you need to try harder to not have this happen again."

"But, Dad!"

"No, Syd, no *but*s!"

"Sir, if I may say?"

"Yes, Sophie?"

"Well, she does try very hard every time, but it's when Lucas hits her that she returns the fire."

"Yes, I understand that, Sophie, but she just needs to not let it get to *that point* next time."

"Dad! That's what she is tryin' to say. Every time, I do my best to redirect either myself or Lucas, and he just isn't havin' it. It's like he *wants* to have some kind of contact with me."

Parker thinks back to the visit with Claire earlier and thinks, *Maybe Syd is right.* So he just returns a reply with, "Okay, Syd, all I am askin' is for you to continue to try the best that you can."

"No problem, Dad. It's all I have been doin'."

We are finally home at the ranch. Dad pulls up, parks, and shuts down the truck as he says to us, "Go have some fun, girls, till it's dinnertime. Oh, but first, girls, can you please take these items into Emma? I have something I need to do before I come in."

"Okay, Dad, I love you!" I say as we take the drinks and dessert and run into the house.

Parker gets out of the truck and makes his way to the barn to Grandad's desk. He pulls out the chair and sits down like he has had the hardest day ever. Obee comes around the corner just in time to see him sit.

"Hey, boss. You okay? You took a heavy seat there just now. Anything you want to get off your mind?"

"Hey, Obee, um, yes. Well, yes, but not right now. But could you please come to dinner with us tonight? I have some news I wanted to share, and I would love it for you to be present when I do. After all, you are family, and this is a family matter. Say, six?"

"Well, yeah I think I can do that. May I ask without steppin' outta line what it's in regard to?"

"Well, Obee…" Parker pauses for just a moment and goes to open his mouth, but the words just can't or won't come out.

Obee sees the tears forming in Parker's eyes. Obee says, "It's okay, Parker, I can wait. I'll let you be so you can have some time to yourself. I have a few things to get done before dinner, anyways. See ya at dinner!" Obee then walks away.

Parker opens up the top desk drawer, where Grandad always kept pictures of his loved ones. Grandad would come out to the desk when no one was around, or so he thought no one was around. He would open the drawer, and he would take out pictures of whomever he wanted to talk to, and he would sit there and hold a conversation with them, telling them whatever it was that was on his mind. I guess it was his way of rehearsing what he wanted to say to them to make sure it sounded all right.

Parker takes out a picture of Ivy. As he sits there, looking at her beautiful face, he starts to talk to her. "Ivy, my love, my blue eyes, I miss you so much! I am so sorry you died so tragically. Today, I am sure you know that we found the driver from that night. I had my suspicions all along, but how would it look on me to blame someone without hard-core evidence? Well, today, whether I wanted to know or not, I found out. Now, I have to tell the rest of the family. I don't want you to think that this means that I won't ever think of you again, 'cause to be honest, sweetheart, my heart breaks for you every day. And it will for the rest of my breathin' days. Can you please stand with me later as I tell the rest of the family the news Greyson and I found out today? It would mean so much to me. I love you, Ivy!" he says as he kisses her picture and places it back in the drawer.

As Parker walks out of the barn, he sees Greyson comin' in the lane. He walks over to his truck and waits for them to get parked.

"Hey, Parker, we thought we would come over a li'l early. Are the girls inside?"

"Yeah, I'm guessin' they went up to Syd's room. You may go on up, Eliza," Parker says, smiling.

"Be good, Liz," Greyson tells her. "Honey, I'm gonna talk with Parker for a few minutes. Do you mind?"

"Nope, not at all. I was actually wanting to go see if Emma could use my help," Allison says as she walks toward the house.

When Allison gets in the house, she calls out, "Emma? I'm here to lend a hand if you need it."

"I'm in the kitchen, Allison. Come on in," she says kindly.

"Hey, there, how are you?" Allison says as she reaches for a hug.

"I'm doin' well, I think," she says as she hugs Allison. "So do you know why Parker suddenly wants us to have dinner today together?"

"Well, all I know is that Greyson and Parker found out some information today and he wants to share it with us all at once."

"Oh well, I hope it's some good news."

"Me too! Lord knows we need some," Allison says. "So what's for dinner, Emma?"

"Well, I thought we would have comfort food for a meal. How about meatloaf, mashed potatoes, and mixed vegetables, with an apple pie?"

"Well, that sounds very yummy! I hear you make some amazing meatloaf! So I will be so excited to try it."

Meanwhile, outside, Parker and Greyson are talking about the events that happened earlier today at Claire's. "I just don't know how everyone else is gonna take this. And I have to be careful not to let the wrong things slip."

Just then, Obee walks around the corner and hears what Parker says. "Let the wrong things slip? Do I even want to know what that's all about?"

"Ah, Obee. Umm, well, how do I say this? I mean, I know *you* won't say anything, but we have to be careful that no one else is within earshot, 'cause I promised that I would *not* say anything."

Obee waves them to follow him. They walk way out past the barns, where they have a clear sight of anyone who would be around. "Okay, boss, I provided you with the privacy, so come on, spill the beans."

"Obee, what I am about to tell you cannot leave this circle of three. Or I will have to fire you!"

"Right, my lips are sealed."

"Okay, so I do not know how much you know about what's been up with Syd lately."

"Oh, Parker, I am sorry, but I do not know what you mean. Can you please just stop with the riddles and just tell me, please? I promise I won't say a word!" Obee vows

"Okay, okay, so we went to Claire's today, and she showed us something that Lucas drew, and now we think we know why Lucas has been actin' the way he has been actin' toward Sydney. We think he's crushin' on her!"

"Wow, I did not see that comin'! Wait, that would be Syd's first boyfriend! Agh!"

"Calm down, Obee. They are not dating. If anything, I think we are quite a ways away from that. Okay, now we are done with this conversation. Let's go see how dinner is comin' along."

The guys head back to the house to wash up and gather everyone together in the kitchen. "Girls, can you please wash up and come down to the kitchen?"

Faintly they can hear, "Yes, Dad, be right down!"

A few minutes later, they hear the girls come stomping down the steps.

"Okay, now that everyone is here with us, I would like to first make mention of many thanks for all the love and support you all have given me since Ivy's passin'. It has meant so much to me, and I appreciate everything from everyone! Now, let's get our food and have a seat to pray!"

Everyone takes their plate, gets their food, then takes a seat around the table. Once everyone is seated, Parker asks for everyone to hold hands and bow their heads as he prays:

> Dear Lord, thank you for all you have provided for me and my family and friends. From food, jobs, money, a roof over our head, and much, much more! Thank you recently for the news I have to share with my family. Thank you for my family. Please keep us safe as we go about our lives every day. Amen.

He pauses.

"Now, I am sure that you are all wonderin' just why we are here tonight together! Well, it just so happens that today, after the situation at the school," Parker says while looking at Sophie and me, "we made a trip to see Claire to try to see if she could help with gettin' Lucas under control. But that aside for now, I just want to tell you the information I found out by complete accident, and finally, bein' in the wrong place at the right time has kinda paid off for once. So I am glad that everyone is sittin' down, 'cause this may floor some of you." Parker has to stop and get himself under control for a moment before continuing. "I'm sorry," he says as his eyes start getting teary. "So this is bittersweet, in a way. But today, when we, Greyson and I, were at Claire's, she had a visitor. Dylan came in, and he was completely wasted again. He wasn't makin' any sense, with the exception of one thing." Parker gets choked up as he waves to Greyson to finish up for him.

"So what he was tryin to say was, Dylan confessed today that he hit Ivy," Greyson says with a heavy heart.

The room goes completely quiet as everyone takes a minute to consider the information they have just been told.

Emma is the first to speak. She clears her throat. "So when he confessed, what happened next, Parker?"

"Well, I pulled Claire aside and confirmed she heard it too. She did. She called Colton. Colton came to arrest him just after he heard the evidence from Dylan's lips. The Hutchinses apologized and gave their condolences again. And here we are."

"Wow, Greyson, you said it was big, but I am at a loss for words! I had no idea. So what happens next?" Allison asks.

"Well, that's the thing. We do not know as of yet anything other than what we have just stated here tonight," Parker states.

"Dad, what were you doin' at Lucas's mom's house?"

"Syd, like I stated just moments ago, we went there to talk with his mom, to ask her to get Lucas to back off. But once again, everything happens for a reason. Whether or not we see it just yet," Parker says as he looks at Greyson with a "Whew, we made it!" look.

"Okay, who's ready for apple pie?"

The kids are first to say they want a slice. So Emma gets out the pie, cuts it into eight slices, plates one up for everyone, and sends them around the table. "Would anyone like a dab of vanilla ice cream?" Everyone seems to nod in agreement. So she gets a scoop, the ice cream, and she walks around, giving everyone a scoop to eat with their pie.

After dinner and dessert, the Abbotts go home, Obee, Emma, and Dad go to their rooms, and I go to mine with Sophie. Her parents say she can stay the night so I am not alone after the news we all received this evening.

CHAPTER 21

School Is Not the Place for This

As we wake up for the day, I just want to lie here and not move. It saddens me so much to know that my mom died so brutally. I just feel so empty inside after I just started to feel a little bit normal again. I don't feel like having to deal with anyone today.

"Syd, are you awake?" I hear coming from under the blankets.

"Ugh, no! I do not want to get up! Can we just stay home today? I am really feelin' it from yesterday between Lucas tryin' to relocate my internals and findin' out about my mom. I just don't want to move!"

"I wasn't even punched, and I feel like poop. I agree, we should just stay home."

There's a knock on the door. "Girls, are you awake?"

We just grumble back.

"Em, can we please just stay home today?"

"Syd, now, unless you are sick, you know you have to go."

"Okay, we are gettin' up, Em. Come on, Sophie, let's get ready so we can get some breakfast before we have to go to school today."

"Oh, all right, Syd."

We both drag our feet, trying to get outta bed. "Sophie, I hope and pray that today goes better for us than the last two days."

"Amen, Syd."

As we get our things and ourselves together, we *finally* make our way downstairs to the kitchen for some breakfast.

"So, ladies, what do you want for breakfast this mornin'?"

"Do we have any breakfast leftovers in the fridge, Em?"

"Well, let me see, Sydney. Looks like we have some French toast and a few pancakes. Does any of that sound appealin' to ya, Sydney? Sophie, how about you?"

"Em, I will take a few slices of French toast. Don't even bother heating it up. Just give me the plain French toast, please."

"I would like some pancakes, please, Emma."

"Okay, French toast, cold, no warm-up for Syd, and pancakes for you, Sophie."

Emma gets our breakfast together and then hands it to us. We eat and grab our things and head out the door. As we are walking to Emma's car, Dad sees us and comes over to us.

He reaches in to give me a hug as he says to me, "Syd, how are you this mornin'? Did you get plenty of sleep?" He kisses my forehead and takes a step back.

"Eh, I slept, Dad, but I wouldn't say it was a good sleep. I wish I didn't have to go to school today. I just want to lie in my bed and rest."

"Well, I am sorry, Syd, but you do need your *edumacation*, unless you want to be talkin' like me." He laughs, trying to get me to laugh.

"I know, Dad. I was just sayin' I *wish* I could stay home. Okay, we gotta go now, Dad. I love you! I will see you soon," I say as I get in the car.

"Bye, Mr. A!" Sophie says as she waves.

"I have a few errands to run on my way back, so I will return as soon as possible. If you need anything, just text or call me."

"Okay, Emma. See ya soon, Sophie. Love you, Syd!" He waves as we drive out the lane.

"So, Sydney, are we goin' to have any issues today at school?"

"No, Em. I will be on my best behavior," I say like I am so tired of all this already, and it's only been two days—well, three, if you count today, but today hasn't officially started, so I don't count it.

"I didn't think so, but I was just curious. So I am not sure if you ladies know, but I am goin' to be teaching at your school for a few days a week. I may even have you in my class. What do you think about that?"

"Seriously, Em?" I try to say like I even care or am excited. "Why would the school have you startin; to teach so close to the end of the year?"

"Is there a teacher who's sick that you will be replacin' till they come back?" Sophie asks.

"Well, no, Sophie, and I'm startin' now 'cause they have a new class startin' up and I have been asked to teach it."

"Really, Em? A new class? They *never* start a new class so late in the year. Really, what are you really teachin'?"

"Mrs. Gossett asked me yesterday to oversee this new class, and I graciously accepted. Are you not proud of me, Sydney?"

"No, it's not that at all, Em. I am very proud of you. I honestly do not know where you will find time to do even *more* stuff. Your plate is *so* full already! What am I goin' to have to give up or sacrifice or lose because of it?" I ask like a spoiled brat.

Em pulls over and stops the car. "Sydney, first off, I want you to know that your tone with me right now is just not goin' to be tolerated. So I suggest you calm yourself right now. You are not a spoiled brat, and I do not know where this attitude is comin' from." Emma stops herself for a minute as she realizes that she is now the one stepping out of line. "Sydney, I am sorry, you are not a spoiled brat. You are a very lucky girl who hasn't had to want for anything *ever*! But that doesn't entitle you to everything *all* the time. To be grateful for what we have when we have it means understanding what it means to have to do without sometimes. We came here with nothing, we leave here with nothing. It's how we react in the times when we usually have something, and now we don't, that defines who we really are. Now, with that bein' said, I do not, at this time, see you havin' to do *without* your normal day-to-day as you know it, *but* I'm not sayin' that it may not happen either. Do you understand, Sydney?"

"Yes, Em, I am sorry. I am sure I will be just fine, and I am sorry for bein' a brat."

"You're not a brat. So please do not think you are."

"Okay, I may not be a brat, but I was *actin'* like one. And I am sorry for that. I hope you like your new position, and I hope to see you sometime around school. But, Em, if we don't get to school, Dad is not goin' to be happy with you, and the school may revoke your new job before you even have the chance to actually start it! So we gotta roll!" I say with just a little more spunk than I had been show-ing earlier in our ride.

"Oh my, yes, Sydney, you are right. It's okay, girls. I will get you there on time!"

"Without gettin' a ticket, Emma?" Sophie adds while laughing.

"Yes, dear. See, here we are, and you still have a minute or two to spare. Guess that doesn't leave a lot of time for any mischief. I will see you girls later. Love you!"

We wave and run toward the school. "Ugh, I thought she would *never* quit talkin'," I say to Sophie.

"Let's just get to class."

As we go through our day, everything is kinda quiet and peace-ful. Well, that ends real quick. Here we are at lunch, and I have a really bad feeling down deep in the pit of my stomach again. And I do not think it's because I am hungry. We get our food and sit down. *So far, so good,* I think to myself.

"Syd?"

"Yeah!"

"Do you feel like somethin's off?"

"Yeah, I was feelin' it too," I say under my breath. I scan the room to see who's all near and see if everything looks as though it should. I don't see Lucas or his group. No sign of Stanley. "Eh, maybe we are just overthinkin' things, Sophie," I quietly say to her so that I don't disturb the force.

"Yeah, maybe you're right, Syd."

We eat our lunch as more students still make their way into the cafeteria. Something catches my eye, and I try not to look or let it be known that I looked. Sure enough, it's Lucas and his jock friends. "Sophie, do *not* look up. Just keep eating as you are. Lucas has just entered the cafeteria, and I would like to eat in peace and leave in peace," I say very softly so hopefully only she can hear.

"Ten-four, bestie," she whispers and winks with her eye that's closest to me.

Now, today isn't a bad lunch, but in one line we have soup and sammiches; the other line has sloppy junk. Sloppy junk is *never* the same. One time it could be pork, and next it could be beef or chicken. We both opted for soup. They usually have three choices, and today's choices are chili, corn chowder, and tomato bisque. I got the corn chowder. Sophie got the chili.

They say that just before you get struck by lightning, you can feel the hairs on your neck rise up. Well, it's not storming outside, but I have an overwhelming feeling that I am about to be struck by lightning of a different sort.

"Well, well, well, look who we have here!"

"I think they look hungry, Lucas, don't you?" Jaxson says, poking Lucas.

"Yeah, that's what I was thinkin' as well. Why don't we give 'em something to eat, boys?" Camden suggests.

"We are good. Maybe another time, thank you," Sophie says without looking at them.

Just then, I guess they don't like Sophie's offer, because they decide to dump their soup all over us and our things. They must have ordered extras, because they dump more than a bowl's worth on us—not just a bowl each, but two bowls each. And let's just say that it's a bit of a hot mess that I have decided isn't hot enough. I quickly look at Sophie, wink, and stand up, throwing my chair backward right into Jaxson's shins. I turn and just go after all three of them. Hitting, punching, kicking, and swinging as fast and as hard as I could, trying to get my soup-covered self all over them. Next thing I know, Sophie and Stanley, who I had no idea where he came from, join me in whooping some jock butt!

Apparently, they've picked a good time to fight, 'cause it seems like an eternity till some kind of authority shows up to split us apart. Next thing I see are teachers shutting and locking the cafeteria doors to keep everyone and all the mess inside.

"*Great* way to go, Lucas! Guess you don't like the football team too much!" I say as I start to laugh.

175

"Shut up, Syd! This is all your fault."

"*My* fault? What the ugh! Are you completely delusional? *You* and your dumb jocks dumped your soup on our heads and things. I do not see that as our fault. We were mindin' our own business, like usual."

"Well, this is about *all* that I am takin' from you two! You are both suspended for a week! Sophie, seriously, you decided to fight them too?" Mrs. Gossett says, looking at Sophie and me. Then she turns to look at Stanley. "Stanley, what were you thinkin'? This is *enough* from *all* of you! Do you understand? This is not what our school is all about! Those of you with soupy clothes can call home to get dry, clean clothes, and, Sydney, Sophie, Lucas, Jaxson, Camden, and Stanley, just stay put! Do not touch or speak to one another. Do not even *look* at one another!" she says, pointing her finger at us.

Mrs. Gossett leaves and does not return for what seems like forever! We all just sit there, smelling like soup and getting stickier by the minute as it starts to dry on us.

Well, I guess Mrs. Gossett called our parents, because Claire, Greyson, and Allison have just walked in. And now Emma and my dad. They just stand outside the cafeteria, looking in, and they do not look happy. Stanley's, Jaxson's, and Camden's parents are now here too.

"Okay, let the show begin," I very quietly whisper to Sophie as I notice Mrs. Gossett unlocking the door and ushering the parents into the cafeteria, where we, soup-drenched students, all sit.

"So you all know this is the third day of this, and I have decided that Sydney, Sophie, Lucas, Jaxson, Camden, and Stanley will all be suspended for one week."

Dad steps forward, pointing a finger and steaming mad as he says, "It looks to me like the ones who need to be suspended are the jocks! Lucas, Jaxson, and Camden! To take this out on the others is a fault of yours, Mrs. Gossett!"

"Parker, student for student? I believe you said so, did you not?"

"I did, but this is definitely different. You can clearly see that the soup was dumped on the girls. For starters, I am quite sure that Stanley here did *not* do any dumpin'. So that just leaves these three half-wits. Sorry to your parents. This isn't their fault. You three clearly knew what you were doin'!"

"Parker! The reason they are all gettin' suspended is that Stanley, Sophie, and Sydney returned fire."

"No shit, Sherlock! Tell me, if someone dumped hot soup on you, you would just stand, rather sit, there and *just* take it?"

"No, I would just walk away."

"Doubtful. Apparently, you have never been bullied! Otherwise, you would answer differently," Parker says, shaking his head in disbelief.

"There will be punishment for all. I will re-evaluate the situation and pass along the results of my findins later. For now, get these kids home and cleaned up. Allison, Greyson, Parker, please let me know if the girls obtained any burn marks from the soup. You may all be excused. Emma, may I talk with you for a few minutes, please? In my office. Thank you."

"Sure thing. I will wait for you there."

We all get up to leave when Dad stops Claire and pulls her aside.

"Do you mind if I take Lucas back to our place for a li'l fishin'?"

"Well, let me take him home and get him cleaned up, then I will bring him over."

"Okay, I will see you all later."

"Sydney, let's go"

"Can Sophie come over, please?"

"Ah, I think we need to go home and have a talk. Dependin' on how it goes, maybe she can come over later or you can come to our house either way. We will have her call you later," Allison says as they turn to walk away.

Sophie says bye and waves as she leaves with her parents. I wave in return.

Dad and I walk out and leave to head home. It's an interesting ride home. Dad doesn't yell at me or scold me; he just drives us home. When he pulls in the driveway, he gets to the barn, parks, and sits there for a minute and just stares straight ahead.

"Dad?" I ask softly, hoping he doesn't blow up on me. "You okay?"

"Yeah, I'm good, Syd." He probably thinks about what to say to me without giving away the tiny piece of info he has. He turns to me and just stares at me. "You are so beautiful, just like your mother. Even covered in soup puke." He laughs.

"Well, Dad, that's a matter of opinion. I just pray I can get it all outta my clothes. I may need Em for that."

"Well, for now, just get them soakin' in some cold water. You can talk with Emma later on how to treat them."

"Okay, Dad, I'm on it. I'll be out a li'l later," I say as I get out of his truck and go to my room.

*****

Parker goes to the barn to look for the fishing rods. "Obee, are you here anywhere? Oh, Obee?" *Where did he put those rods?* Parker thinks they're always sitting here in this one corner of the one barn stall.

Parker hears whistling, and here comes Obee flying around the corner. "Whoa, slow down, Obee. Where's the fire? Hey, have you seen the fishin' rods? They used to sit right here in this corner."

"Oh, sorry, boss," Obee says, laughing. "Oh yeah, I took them out to the cottage. Syd and Sophie asked me to take the fishin' supplies out there since that's the only place we ever use it. So I thought, yeah, that it was a good idea, so I did. I'm sorry."

"No, Obee, you are fine! That's great that you did it! I may be takin' a li'l ride out there later this afternoon and was thinkin' about doin' a li'l fishin'."

"Wait, you, do some fishin'? What's the occasion? You barely ever went or go out there. Why the sudden change of heart?"

"Well, I may be takin' a…" He pauses to choose his words wisely. "A friend out fishin' with me. For a li'l one-on-one time."

"Oh, so, Syd! She is gonna love that."

"No, not Syd. Just please do not say anything. I was hopin' to get out there and back without this bein' a big deal."

"Oh, wait!"

"Obee, please stop! If you are around when they get here, you will know! What I am askin' is for you to just please keep quiet about it, whatever you end up knowin' or seein'! Please?"

"Oh, umm, sure," Obee says, scratching his head in confusion. "I think I can do that."

"You think? Obee, come on. I'm not jokin'!"

"Yeah, sure, boss. Yes, my lips are zipped."

"Okay, now I wonder if Emma has any sammiches in the fridge?"

"I think I saw some earlier when I was in it."

"Thanks, Obee. I will go look."

Parker goes to look for a small lunch bucket, ice packs, sandwiches, and bottled water. He is looking forward to having the chance to talk with Lucas. He hopes that Claire brings him over later. He walks up to see what Sydney is up to. Her door is closed. He softly knocks. He doesn't hear anything. He calls out to her, "Syd, are you awake?" Silence comes from the room. He figures she has laid down for a nap, so he goes back downstairs.

He hears Emma coming in when he gets to the bottom of the stairs. "Emma?"

"Yes, Parker."

"I have something possibly planned for later. If anyone needs me, just text. But I would prefer not to be bothered. Also, if you see anything, please keep it to yourself. I will explain later. I just came in for some sammiches and drinks."

"Oh, okay, so secretive. I will try not to bother you once you walk out that door."

"I told Syd that you would help her clean her clothes. She should have 'em soakin' in cold water as we speak. Also, if she wants to go hang with Sophie, I'm okay with it."

"Okay, Parker. Have fun with whatever it is that you are up to."

Parker nods and walks back outside. He goes to saddle up a few horses and get everything ready for a quick escape. A few minutes later, he hears a car coming in the lane. He walks out to check it out. It looks like Claire's car. He stands by his truck. Claire pulls up and parks. She and Lucas get out of the car.

"Mom! Why am I here?"

"Lucas, please just behave."

"Hi, Lucas. I am Parker!"

"Yeah, I know who you are. But *why* am I here?" Lucas screams.

"Hey, Lucas, it's okay. I asked your mom if she would bring you here," Parker says as Lucas looks around like he's afraid someone may see him.

"Mom, can I just go home?"

"Lucas, please just listen to Parker for just a moment."

"Lucas, have you ever gone fishin'? Or even horseback ridin'?"

"No, I haven't. Why? Do you think you are gonna take me?"

"Well, I was hopin' to show you. Would you like to at least try? Who knows, you may just like it?" Parker asks Lucas, hoping he would say yes so they could get going.

Lucas turns to his mom. "Mom, do I have to?"

"Lucas, I think it would be fun. You should just do it for me just this once. Please. If you don't like it, I will never ask you to do it again. Promise!"

"Fine. Sure, Parker, I will go. But just because my mom wants me to."

"Thank you, Lucas. Claire, I will bring him home when we are done. Thank you."

"Anytime, Parker. I love you, Lucas. I will see you later. Please try to have fun."

"Whatever, Mom! Can we just go get this over with so I can go home?"

"Well, sure, let's getcha on a horse and we will ride out to the lake to fish." Parker leads Lucas to the horses he has saddled up and waiting to go. "So I am givin' you Sydney's horse to ride. Her name is SOT for short. Her racin' name is Sands of Tyme. I am on Black Boots. He was Syd's grandad's horse. Okay, let's get goin'."

They take off out through the trails to the lake. As they are making their way, Parker notices how well Lucas is doing.

"Lucas, are you sure you have never ridden before?"

"That's what I said."

"Well, by the way you ride, I would have never known. You carry yourself so well. Ya know, I have two young riders that ride for me, and they make money doin' it. Do you think you would be interested? I am curious just how well you would do."

"Nah, I'm good."

"Hey, just humor me for a moment. Let's just take off and see how it goes for ya. Come on, just join me. Try and keep up!" And with that, Parker and Black Boots just take off, and to keep up with them, SOT takes off too, almost knocking Lucas off the rear.

"Whoa, slow down, Mr. Parker!" Lucas screams.

"Nah, just grab the reins and show me what you got!" Parker yells back.

Well, it must have worked, 'cause Lucas gives it all he has, and when he catches up with Parker, he just keeps going, and then he is way ahead of Parker. *Well, he's got that down,* Parker thinks to himself. The lake is growing ever closer for Lucas, and Parker is about to see if he can stop her. As he gets closer and closer, Parker sees him trying to figure it out. *Well, SOT never was a fan of the water, so this should be interestin',* Parker thinks to himself.

"How do I stop her?" Lucas screams.

But before Parker could tell him to pull back on the reins, SOT gets to the water's edge and abruptly stops. Well, you can only imagine where Lucas went! Right straight over her head and right in the lake. *Well, that's one way of stopping!* Parker thinks to himself as he starts laughing.

When Parker gets up to Lucas, he has finally made it to his feet and does not look very happy at first. But when Lucas sees Parker smiling and laughing, then he begins to laugh too.

"Lucas, I'm sorry, I don't mean to laugh, but if you could have seen when she stopped and you flew up over her head! Oh, man, I am so sorry. Come on, let's go in here and see if we can find ya something to dry off with."

"Sure thing. Thank God it's not cold out."

They walk to the cottage and go inside. Parker finds a towel in the bathroom. "Here's a towel. Hopefully, it's good enough for now. Get yourself dried off some, then come meet me at the bench by the lake. And we'll see how you do with fishin'." Parker chuckles and walks outside.

Parker grabs two fishing rods and the tackle box from the back porch, then heads down to the bench. He decides to sit there and wait for Lucas before doing anything. He turns around on the bench and sees Lucas coming out of the cottage.

"Parker, I'm sorry I was an ass to you earlier. I want to thank you for offerin' me to come hang out with ya. But I have to know why you even thought about askin' me. I mean, I thought you didn't like me because of my situation with Sydney?"

"Son—can I call you *son*, Lucas?"

"Umm, sure, I guess so."

"Well, where do I begin? How about, for starters, I have always wanted a son? And I know you recently lost your dad. So I'm not tryin' to be your dad, but I know how important it is to have an adult man in a young boy's life. So I am available any time you need someone to talk to. How does that work for you so far?"

"Well, I mean, I do miss my dad, and I guess it wouldn't be so bad to have another male adult in my life since I recently lost another one. Well, I think you know what I mean. And honestly, you are pretty fun so far."

"Yes, I do. So next is, we have both recently lost someone for whom we have much love. Agreed?"

"Yeah, I guess so. So you kinda know how I feel, then, right now. The rage and anger. Parker, do you have issues keepin' it under control?"

"Well, if you ask my friends, they would say yeah, most likely. But I feel like I try to keep my anger and hostility under control. So yeah, I know what you mean, though. Let me ask ya, Do you ever take it out on anyone you like or love but don't mean to?"

Lucas hangs his head. Parker puts his hand on Lucas's shoulder. "It's okay. You can tell me. I will not tell anyone. Promise, my lips are sealed, son. What happens here at the lake stays here at the lake."

"Sir, I am sorry. I haven't meant anything lately that I have done to your daughter, Sydney. Sir, the truth is that I..." Lucas stops and won't say another word.

"Lucas? What were you goin' to say just now? You can trust me. I won't tell anyone. Or if you are not ready, my son, then that's okay. Whenever you are, I will be here, ready to listen."

"It's okay, sir. I just had to man up first," Lucas says as he stands and faces Parker. "Sir, the truth is, I have hurt someone that I like and that I love. I haven't meant to, but I just do not know how to handle these pent-up feelings. Some days I have such rage and hurt."

"Lucas, my son, I do know exactly what you are feelin'. Some days it hurts so bad I just want to end my life. I get in my truck, and I just drive around, lookin' for anything to take my anger out on. Or something to do to use up all my energy so I am too tired to do any harm to anyone or anything because I am so drained. It is so hard some days, though, to even function, but I try to dig down deep so I can be strong for Syd."

"Sir?"

"Lucas, please, you do not need to call me *sir*. You can call me anything but *sir*."

Lucas puts his hand up, pointing at Parker when he says, "Sir, I have to call you that, for I want to show you respect that you deserve for what I am about to say. Sir, I like Sydney. I like her a lot. And I feel she may not return the feelins because I *am* just a stupid jock and I just want to be liked by everyone. But I think if Sydney liked me, I wouldn't care if anyone else did. So you see, sir, what my issue is? I have royally effed up! Can you please help me fix it?"

The look on Parker's face is blank. "Lucas, I am speechless right now. I never expected to hear that from you. You literally just dropped a bomb on me, son! So how about you and I do a li'l fishin' so I can have a few minutes to think about how I can help you out with this?"

"I'm sorry, Parker. I didn't mean to spring this on you like that. But hey, now is as good a time as any, right?"

"Well, when you put it that way, I guess so. Hey, you hungry? I brought out some sammiches and water."

"Sure thing. Yeah, let's eat, please!"

Parker gets out the lunch bucket and lays out all the food on the bench. "Go ahead and take what you want."

They continue to bond and have a great time. Turns out that Lucas is pretty good at fishing too! When they get done, they ride back to the barns. Since there's no water, Parker decides to teach him how to stop so he doesn't run into a barn, or worse. When they get back, they jump in the truck and Parker takes Lucas home. On the way, Parker wants to say a few things to Lucas before he drops him off.

"So, Lucas, do you think that you would like to try out the race tomorrow? I mean, even if you don't win, at least you can get a shot at a new thrill of ridin'."

Lucas thinks about it and says, "No, thank you."

"Okay, well, I just thought you would enjoy it. So I had a great time today, and I would love to hang out again sometime. If that suits ya?"

"Sure thing, Parker." Lucas sits there just gazing out the window. As they pull into Lucas's driveway, Lucas says to Parker, "Second thought, if you can spare me a horse, I would give the race thing a try. Tomorrow, you said?"

"Wow! Yes, that sounds great! I will do my best to get you signed up for tomorrow. If they would be full, then I will make it for the race the very next day. Okay, tell your mom I said thank you! I am gonna go now so I can talk with Hudson. See ya, Lucas!"

CHAPTER 22

The Cat's Out of the Bag

"**S**ophie, come on, get up. I do not want to be late."

"I'm up! Ugh, I cannot wait for summer to be here so I can sleep in!"

"I know! I was thinkin' the same thing. But at least this is our last couple of races. Then we won't have to get up this early anymore till school starts again. We can just be us!"

"Well, for now, we just need to get ready." I go to the chest and get out our clothes and disguises. We quickly get dressed and close up everything and leave the cottage. We get on the bikes and ride them to the ranch. As we are riding in the lane, a car I don't recognize comes up behind us. We get off the side to the lane and let them go by. As the car passes, I look in the passenger side and I see Lucas!

"Sophie, did you just see what I saw?"

"I think I did. But the real question is, Why?"

"Yeah, for sure. Well, let's get back here and see what's up."

We pedal as fast as we can to get back to the ranch. As we are pedaling back, the car comes right back out. Sophie and I look in the passenger side.

"Syd!"

"Yeah, I saw that too! Oh, this isn't very good!"

As we get close to the ranch, Parker sees us and makes his way over to us.

"Hello, Chase and Wyatt. I am so glad to see you! We have a new rider this mornin'. Meet Lucas Devinshire. He's just given it a try to see if he likes it or not."

"Ah, yeah, I think we have met already. Right, Wyatt?"

"Yeah, weren't you at the meet and greet the other day? I believe you were heckling us about Parker's daughter, Sydney."

"Umm, yeah, about that. I am sorry. I didn't mean anything by it."

"Well, I hope not, because we are friends with Sydney."

"Do you need us to help load up today, Parker?"

"Yes, please! I do not know where Obee is, but he needs to get himself ready and get outta here."

"Okay, we will load up the horses, saddles, and other such supplies a while."

Parker goes to look for Obee. Chase and Wyatt load up the trailer. Lucas gets on his phone and makes a call.

"How did you like that one, Wyatt?"

"Oh, you mean that we were Sydney's friends?"

"Yep. I did that hopin' that she kicked his butt enough not to bother us too much."

"Well, fingers crossed, let's hope it works!"

"Fingers crossed!"

"Ten-four, bestie! Whoops!" Wyatt says, laughing.

Once we have everything loaded, we get in the truck to wait for everyone else. After waiting a few minutes, we see Obee and Parker coming toward the truck. Parker waves for Lucas to come over to leave. Lucas quickly ends his call and runs over to the truck. Once everyone is in, we head to the track.

As we near the track, Parker says to us, "Good luck out there today. I will meet up with you all later after the race. After I park, I am goin' to get everyone registered."

Wyatt and Chase get out of the truck and go get their horses out of the trailer. Lucas hangs in the truck as he makes another call.

"Wyatt? Does something seem fishy with Lucas? I mean, who does he keep callin'?"

"Yeah, I was thinkin' the same thing. We will just have to keep an eye out on him. God only knows what he has up his sleeve! Yeah, let's go get our stable."

"Obee? Are you gonna get Black Boots, or is Lucas?"

"Yeah, we will get him. Go on and get yourselves a stable."

Wyatt and Chase head to the stables. They notice that there are a bunch of different riders today that haven't raced in a while.

Meanwhile, at the registration booth, Parker is getting the boys all registered. "Hello, Hudson. How are you today?"

"I'm good, Parker. So who do you have racin' today? Did I hear that you have another, new rider?"

"Yes, you heard right. I have Lucas Devinshire. Agh, I forgot to get his age. Let me text his mother quickly. While I do, I also have Chase and Wyatt with me again today!"

"Okay, I will work on those for now."

> Parker
> *Claire, I forgot to get Lucas's age, and I do*
> *not have a contact number for him.*
>
> Claire
> *I'm sorry, Parker. He is 15.*
>
> Parker
> *Okay, thanks, Claire.*

"Okay, Hudson, Lucas is fifteen. I thought as much, but I wanted to make sure. Also, he will be ridin' Black Boots."

"So you are bringin' another one out of retirement? Okay, Parker, you and the boys are all set to go. Good luck out there today!"

"Thanks, Hudson!"

"Good afternoon, everyone! Welcome back to the Keeneland Racetrack. We have an exciting lineup for you today! I am your announcer, Hudson Hammond, and here is the list of racers, listed from gate 1 through gate 8. Today we have Rugged Trails, a four-year-old Thoroughbred; comin' out of retirement for today, Black Boots, a five-year-old Appaloosa; returnin' today as well, PB Cup, a five-year-old Arabian; and it's a family affair with Sands of Tyme, her two-year-old Araloosa, who has been stealin' all the hearts here in the last few weeks. Next, we have Ain't No Chicken, a three-year-old quarter horse; Lion's Pride, a four-year-old quarter horse; Dreamin' Big, a five-year-old standardbred; and last but not the least, Babes Mare, a five-year-old quarter horse. Riders, take your places. While we wait, here are a few words from some of our sponsors."

As the riders take their places, Hudson plays the sponsors' commercials. Once the commercials are done, Hudson gets the sign that the riders are ready, and he continues, "Ladies and gentlemen, would you please stand for our national anthem?" Hudson states proudly.

After the anthem, everyone sits and Hudson continues again, "Okay, riders, on your mark...get set..." *Bang!* The gun cracks as Hudson says, "Go! There they go! They're off to a fine start! We have Rugged Trails, Sands of Tyme, and Black Boots pushin' the lead for first. Followed by PB Cup, and Lion's Pride hot on their tails, with Ain't No Chicken and Dreamin' Big up next, followed by Babes Mare pullin' up the tail end. Oh, the move is on with Black Boots, PB Cup, and Sands of Tyme makin' their way to the lead position. Hot on their heels are Rugged Trails, Ain't No Chicken, and Lion's Pride. Followed by Dreamin' Big and Babes Mare. Rugged Trails makes his way back into first for a four-way, with Sands of Tyme, Black Boots, and Ain't No Chicken, all tryin' to take the win, with PB Cup, Lion's Pride, and Dreamin' Big in a tight second. Here comes the last turn, with Sands of Tyme sandwiched between Rugged Trails and Black Boots. It's gonna be a close one again today, folks! With PB Cup and Ain't No Chicken in sharing second. And it's a picture-perfect finish! Sands of Tyme has done it again by a nose!

"Whoa! Folks, there seems to have been an accident on the track! Medics are on the track as we speak. Seems just as they crossed the finish line, one of the horses wasn't very happy. Not sure what happened just yet. Let me give you the rest of the lineup, and maybe we will know by the time I am finished. From second place down, this is how they finished, folks. We have Rugged Trails, then PB Cup, followed by Black Boots, then Ain't No Chicken, and Babes Mare. Next is Lion's Pride, and ending with Dreamin' Big. What a spectacular race here today! Give me one second, folks!" Hudson shuts off the mic while he gets details on what has happened down on the track.

"Okay, folks, it seems we have a tiny bit of an issue. Chase Payne was thrown from his horse and is bein' taken to the hospital. At this time, we have no further word on his condition. So that wraps it up here for today. One final note, there will be an auction later this evenin'. If you are in need of any great horses, we have some mighty fine mares and stallions on the list for later. Stop by and check them out back at the stalls. Thank you all for your participation, and we shall see you later for the auction or tomorrow for our next race, which just so happens to be the last spring race, so please come join us! Have a great day, folks!"

When Parker hears it's Chase, he immediately finds Obee and asks him if he can gather up the horses and get his truck home and be ready for when he calls for him to come to the hospital.

Wyatt is already with Chase on the track, and when Parker comes up, Wyatt asks to ride along. Parker agrees, and Obee takes PB Cup and Sands of Tyme back to the stalls. Lucas follows Obee but stops for a moment.

They load up Chase and put him in the ambulance. Parker and Wyatt get in to ride with Chase to the hospital. As they get in, Lucas stands there with a look of *mission complete*, before Obee yells back to him to hurry and catch up. They close the ambulance doors, and they drive away.

Inside the ambulance, all the attention is on Chase. "Chase, I am so sorry, son. I hope you are okay. I wouldn't want your parents to kill me!"

The nurse in the ambulance says to Parker, "Sir, is this your son?"

"No, sorry, he just rides for me. To be honest, I am not really sure who his parents are. We were supposed to meet—"

Sydney interrupts Parker. "Dad! It's okay, it's me!"

"I'm sorry, Chase. He must have hit his head, nurse. Can you check?"

"No! Parker, what she is tryin' to say…" Sophie stops talking for a minute, and they both take off their wigs at the same time. "This is what she was tryin' to say. You know our parents 'cause, well, you *are* hers and mine are your friends!" Sophie says as she kinda partially hangs her head and looks up to see Parker's reaction.

Parker sits there with a completely blank look on his face, like he was just super duped!

"Sydney?" He pauses. "Sophie?" He buries his face in the palms of his hands. "I do not understand what's goin on here," he says, so confused.

"It's a long story, Dad, but it was part of a history project that was not supposed to be exposed this way. But now the cat's outta the bag. So I am sorry, but surprise, Dad! Are you mad at me?"

"Syd, I am so emotional right now I do not even *know* where to begin! I am sad that you couldn't tell me that you were doin' this. Happy because, oh my, you are an amazin' rider! And relieved 'cause your mom said you were gonna be doin' something amazin' and I would be proud. And *wow*, she was right again!"

"I'm sorry, Dad, if I had told you, it wouldn't have been as good of an experiment as it has turned out to be. And Mom told you? When did you speak to Mom?"

Parker whispers so the nurse doesn't think he's crazy, "She came to me in a dream, Syd. And she told me about this. Well, not *this* exactly, but that you were up to something that would make me proud! I'm not quite sure how we will break this to Hudson, though."

"Well, if you want, Dad, I can say something to him for you. After all, you didn't know, and I do not want you to look like the bad one, or worse."

"Well, let's just get you to the hospital to get you checked out for now."

"Dad?"

"Yes, Syd."

"I cannot help but feel like this was a setup to get me outta the race. But I do not know why. Am I disliked that much?" Syd says with tears starting in her eyes.

Parker thinks about the recent days and events as he says, "Well, I can't say for sure, but I have a feelin' that I may possibly know why this happened. But I do not want to say before I know. So what actually happened out there, Syd?" Parker asks.

"Well, it was a tight race at the end, but I feel as though Lucas and Noah both moved in toward me at the same time. It happened so fast I honestly cannot say for sure. But that's what it felt like. Dad, again, I am sorry. I hope I don't get you in too much trouble."

"You were amazin' out there, and don't worry about me. I will be fine! Remember, everything happens for a reason, and with God's love, anything is possible! How are you feelin'?"

"I just feel like I had the wind knocked outta me, but otherwise, I think I am okay."

"Okay, well, I think I need to call Allison and Greyson so that they know where you are, Sophie. Are you ready to deal with your parents? 'Cause I am assumin' that they don't know either?"

"No, Parker, they don't," Sophie says, hanging her head. "Do you want me to call them? That way, I don't get you in trouble."

"I can, but if you want to, then maybe you should."

"Should I call now or wait till we get to the hospital?"

"Maybe you should call now so that they can meet us there a li'l sooner than if you waited."

"Okay, here goes." Sophie takes out her phone and calls her mom. There is no answer, so she leaves a message. "Mom, it's me, Sophie. I am okay, but I am headed to the hospital with Syd. I will call Dad now. I love you!"

Then she proceeds to call her dad. It rings and rings, then he picks up. "Dad? It's me, Sophie. I am okay, but I am in an ambulance with Syd and Parker, headed to the hospital. Can you please meet us there? Okay, I love you!"

"He didn't say much, but he is headed to the hospital," Sophie tells Parker.

A few minutes later, they arrive at the hospital, and they wheel Sydney into the emergency room. A nurse comes in to evaluate Sydney. She does the normal routine stuff of BP, temp, oxygen level, then she jots down a few things and says, "Give the doc a few minutes and he will be in." She smiles and walks away.

Out in the hallway, we hear what sounds like Allison and Greyson. "She's in here. Right this way." The curtain opens, and they come in.

"Wow, do I even want to know how y'all ended up in here?"

"Well, Dad, you see..."

"No! Sophie, please let me. Allison, Greyson, I am sorry. I never wanted it to happen this way, but the cards that I have been dealt planned it out a li'l differently than I had planned. Allison, do you remember when I mentioned about my history project?"

"Yes, Sydney, I do." Allison pauses for a minute and gets curious for a moment. "But, Sydney, what does this have to do with you bein' here in the hospital? Y'all didn't try some stupid stunts, did ya?"

"No, it's nothing like that, per se. So my project is simple: I just wanted to ride in the races. But everyone thinks that a woman can't do it or it's too dangerous."

"Well, you are in the hospital, aren't you?"

"Yes, but I never meant to be. I think someone had me set up."

"About that...umm, Syd does have a point, but we do not want to accuse anyone just yet, because we don't know exactly what happened," Sophie adds.

At about that time, the doc comes in. "Hello, I'm Dr. Gossett. Who's our patient today? And what seems to be the issue?" he kinda jokes.

"Dr. Gossett? You wouldn't happen to be any relation to Principal Gossett, would you?"

"Actually, yes, she is my lovely wife. Do you know her?"

"Do I ever! I'm Sydney Ashcraft. It's nice to meet ya! She is my principal."

"Well, then, let's see what's wrong with you. Just what did you get yourself into today?"

"Well, sir, I was racin'!"

"Racin'? Like a dirt bike or scooter?"

"No, horses!" Sydney proudly states with a huge beautiful smile across her face.

"Horses? You don't say? Well, not on the big track, I'm sure."

"Actually, she has been racin' almost all month, unbeknownst to myself. And she won most of her races. Even the one today!" Parker says proudly.

"Well, I thought females were frowned upon at the track?"

"Well, yes and no. Females do race, but very rarely, because the males taunt and harass them. So most don't race," Parker informs the doc.

"And that's what my project was about, showin' them that females are just as good as the males. So why can't we race too? Today I got sandwiched between two other riders, and I got thrown off my horse."

"So when you got thrown from your horse, did you get stomped on by any of the horses? That's my main concern right now."

"No, sir, I did not. I was lucky in that aspect 'cause, growin' up around horses all my life, I know what damage they can do to someone. I can praise the Lord I did not get stomped," Sydney says, laughing.

"Well, it seems like you are in good spirits, so you must be okay. Let me just check your lungs. Sit up straight for me and take in a few deep breaths," he instructs Sydney.

She breathes in and out four deep breaths, and he responds with, "You got yourself a good set of lungs there! Everything sounds good. So I will release you with these words: Please be safe, child. And get some rest!"

"Sir? I have a quick question."

"Yes, li'l lady, shoot!"

"I have one more race. Can I please participate in that one last race? Do you think it would be okay?"

"Well, I tell you what? If you promise to keep yourself outta my emergency room, I think you can enjoy your last race. How's that sound?"

"Wow, that sounds awesome! Thank you, sir! Can you also please tell Mrs. Gossett thank you? And I will do my best *not* to be back in your ER!"

"Sure, but if she asks, What are you thankin' her for?"

"Well, just tell her for puttin' up with me. I promise, things will get better soon!" Sydney says, smiling as she high-fives the doc.

"Okay! Go on, get outta here. Please do not come back anytime soon," Dr. Gossett says with sincerity.

"I will try not to. Thank you!" She waves as she leaves the ER.

"Okay, everyone, how about we have everyone over for a cookout to celebrate?"

Allison and Greyson both nod in agreement.

Sophie says, "May I spend the night?"

"Only if Eliza comes too!" Parker says.

When they get outside the hospital, Emma and Obee are already there, waiting. Emma gets out of the car and comes running up to Sydney so fast she almost knocks her over.

"Syd, I am so glad you are okay! Allison called me and told me that Sophie and you were headed to the hospital. I was worried. But you look just fine!"

"I am just fine. Just had a li'l wind knocked outta me, is all. Dad wants to have a cookout. Is that okay, Emma?"

"Sure thing!"

CHAPTER 23

Celebrating an Accomplishment

"**D**ad, since we are havin' a cookout, could I invite some people over?"

"Sure thing, Syd! The more, the merrier! Who were you thinkin' about invitin'?"

"Well, if you give me a second, I will be right back!" Sydney takes off for the ER entrance. She's only been gone for a few minutes when she returns.

"What was that all about, Syd?"

"You will see!"

"Is there anyone else?"

"Actually…" Syd waves for her dad to come closer, and she makes a whisper in his ear.

"Sydney, are you sure? I mean, after everything?"

"Yes! Can you just please ask?"

"Okay, if that's what you want." Parker takes out his phone and makes a text message and sends it. "Okay, Emma, do you have a list of things we need from the store? Sydney and I will stop and get them while you go and get other things ready."

"Well, I was wonderin' if Sydney and I could go."

"You know what? Yeah, sure. I'm sorry, Emma! That definitely makes more sense. I will go get the grill ready, and I will see y'all at home. I love you, my li'l filly!"

"I love you too, Dad!"

Parker thinks to himself, *Wow! I called her "my li'l filly" and she didn't crack back at me? That's odd for her. Just what does she have goin' on up there in that pretty li'l head of hers?*

Parker gets ready to head home with Obee when he says, "Greyson, do you have anything goin' on till later?"

"Not that I am aware of. Allison, do we have anything goin' on, sweetheart?"

"No, I think our calendar is clear. I was actually thinkin', maybe you could go give Parker and Obee a hand and the girls and I will go help Emma and Sydney with the grocery end, if that's okay?"

Parks says, "Allison, I like your thinkin'! That was what I was gonna ask. So what do you think, Greyson?"

"Sounds great to me!"

"Emma?"

"Yes, Parker, sounds like a great game plan! Allison, would you and the girls wanna ride with us? We have plenty of room."

"What do you think, girls?" Allison asks.

"Yes, yes, we would like to go with them, please!" Eliza says, and Sophie nods in acceptance.

Parker, Obee, and Greyson head to the ranch to get the picnic tables and the grill out and ready, while Allison, Emma, Sydney, Sophie, and Eliza head to the market to get eats for the cookout later.

"Okay," Emma says, "this is a big deal, so let's have an all-out cookout with the works! I'm thinkin' hamburgers, hot dogs, chicken, maybe some sausage for our meats? How about baked mac and cheese, broccoli salad, potato salad, baked potatoes—for those who aren't a fan of the potato salad—chips, baked beans for the sides? And for dessert, how about either Hawaiian delight or Watergate salad, brownies, some cookies, pies, like an apple and a blueberry? Fruit is usually good too. How about a watermelon, honeydew, some grapes, and pineapples?"

"Dang, Emma, that's a lot of food!" Eliza says, shocked, with her eyes real big.

"Emma, do we really need that much food?" Allison asks.

"Umm, yes, Allison, we do! This is a special occasion that requires a celebration. And I have extra guests comin', at least four, and with the four in my family and your family having four, that's, like, twelve people. A lot of people calls for a lot of food!"

"Okay, Sydney! Then let's help Emma get what she needs!"

Emma tears up the list and gives out things for everyone to get. "Here's a small part of the list for you girls, and Allison and I will get these things. Let's meet out by the registers when we all have what we need."

"Emma, what about drinks?" Sydney asks.

"Syd, good idea! Grab some lemonade, sweet tea, and some root beer. I will grab some more water bottles. Okay, ladies, see you up front in a few." Everyone takes off like they were roaches and someone just turned on the light in the night. They scatter so quickly!

A few minutes later, they regroup up by front registers.

"Okay, ladies, do we have everything?"

"Emma, I grabbed cheese and rolls because I am sure we are low on both at the house."

"Great thinkin', Syd! Can we think of anything else, ladies?"

"Emma, do you have plenty of condiments? And paper plates and cups?"

"Actually, Allison, could you please be a sweetheart and go just over to that aisle and grab a stack of plates and a stack of cups? There's no sense in me cooking *and* doin' dishes. So we can use paper!"

"Sure thing, Emma. Any particular kind?"

"Nope, just the cheapest works for me!"

"Okay, I will be right back!" After just a few minutes, she returns. "Here ya go, Emma. This looked like the best deal."

They put all their findings in the cart and make their way to the register to check out, and $135-plus later, they make their way out of the store. They load up Emma's car and head back to the ranch.

On the way back, Emma asks, "So, Syd, when do we get to know who your guests are?"

"When they show up!" Sydney says, laughing and smiling from ear to ear as she looks out the window, trying to be secretive.

"Well, then, I guess you told me," Emma says, laughing back. Then everyone starts laughing and having a good time.

They get back to the ranch, and everyone grabs a couple of bags and they carry everything into the kitchen. Parker comes in to check on how things are going.

"Wow, Emma, did you get enough food?"

"Yes, sir! Syd said we will have about twelve people attendin' for the cookout, so I wanted to make sure we had enough food and choices for everyone."

"Looks like we will have a great spread. I have the grill cleaned up and ready to go. Whenever you are ready to start cooking, let me know and I will come get the meat and get it goin'."

"Sydney, did we set a time for our guests?"

"I told them about four o'clock. Did you tell my other guests that too, Dad?"

"Yes, ma'am. So I guess I better get this meat out there now." Parker chuckles. Emma hands him all the meat, some cooking utensils, and some spices.

"Just in time, Greyson! Can you help me carry these things out to the grill?"

"That's why I came in. I figured the ladies were stackin' ya up with grill goodies!" Parker shares some of the items with Greyson to carry out to the grill. They head out a while. Emma realizes that she forgot to give them the foil.

"Syd, could you please take this foil out to the guys?"

"Can I help and take it out, Emma?" asks Eliza.

"Oh well, of course you can, sweetie."

"Okay, Syd, we need bowls for everything else. Can you help me by gettin' out the big party bowls we normally use?"

"Yep! Sophie, you wanna help me?"

"Ten-four, bestie!" she says with two thumbs up.

"Allison, would you like something to drink?"

"Actually, Emma, could I have a bottle of water? That would be great!"

Emma hands Allison a water as Syd starts to hand bowls to Sophie, who then puts them on the table. Emma picks them up and decides what will work best in each bowl by its size.

Just then, a car comes into the lane. Allison notices it and says, "Emma, I think one of Syd's guests is here."

Sydney quickly goes out to welcome the first guests. It's Dr. and Mrs. Gossett. "Hello, Dr. and Mrs. Gossett! Thank you very much for comin' to our li'l celebration cookout. We are just so glad you can make it!" Sydney says with much excitement.

"Well, I have to say, Sydney, when my hubby came home and said we had plans with someone I knew very well, I was a little confused at first. But thank you for invitin' us! By the way, this isn't a bribe, is it?"

"No, ma'am! I hope you enjoy yourself, and could I offer either of you a drink?"

"Water is good for me. How about the doc? Honey? What would you like?"

"A water for me too, Syd."

"Okay, two waters for the Gossetts. Dad, Obee, Greyson? Would any of you like a drink?"

"Syd, just bring out a bunch of waters, please."

"Okay, Dad, be right back!" Sydney runs in to get a bunch of waters and brings them out and hands them out to everyone. Sydney goes back into the house. Just as she goes in, another car is making its way down the driveway.

"Sydney, there's another car, dear."

"Thanks, Allison! Sophie, can you please come out with me?"

"Ten-four, bestie!"

As the girls go outside, Sophie spots who's in the car, and under her breath she says, "Syd?"

"Yes, Sophie?"

"Umm, why is he here?"

"Just trust me, okay?"

"Ten-four, bestie. If you say so."

"I do! Now, be nice, please?"

"Hello, Claire and Lucas. Welcome to our celebration cookout. Can I get you a drink?"

"Water for us, please?"

"Okay, two bottles of water. Food will be ready in a li'l bit. I will be right back with your water." Sydney goes to get two more bottles of water and to let Emma know that everyone is present for the cookout.

Sydney returns with water for Claire and Lucas. "Here you go, guys. If I could please have your attention. Everyone, all the guests are here. Most of us know one another. But I can introduce everyone when I return. I will be right back."

"Sydney?"

"Yes, Lucas?"

"May I have a moment of your time?"

"Umm, sure. How about after we eat? Is that okay?"

"Yeah, that should be good. Thanks."

Sydney goes back into the house to help carry out the rest of the food.

While the ladies inside get everything ready to bring outside, Claire goes up to have a word with Parker. "Parker? May I have a moment of your time? I just want to ask a quick question."

"Sure, anything. Ask away, Claire."

"Well, I wanted to thank you for allowin' Lucas to join you the other day and for allowin' him the chance to ride in a race. He seems very interested in riding more and asked me if I could get him a horse, but we do not have the room for a horse. Could you please help me find one and I will give you the money to buy it? Also, could we board it here?"

"I will do ya one better. There is an auction tonight, and I can take Lucas up and tell him what I think is a good horse and let him pick. And I will try to buy it. He can come here and work with the horse and work it off! How's that work for ya? And he can work off the boarding fee too! I will give him a good discount."

"Wow, Parker, would you really do that for us?"

"Sure thing. If he's honest about really wantin' to ride!"

"Well, you see, the truth be told, I think it's because of Sydney that he wants to ride. But I do not see the harm in it."

"Well, he is a natural. So why not? I say! Sure, we can give it a shot!"

A few minutes later, Emma, Sydney, Sophie, Allison, and Eliza are headed out with the rest of the food. Lucas runs over to Sydney and offers to help carry some of her items.

"May I help you carry something, Sydney?"

"Umm, sure, Lucas." Sydney hands him a bowl of food.

Sophie walks by and says, "Yuck, get a room, you two!"

"What are you talkin' about, Sophie? He was just offerin' to carry some of the food for me."

"Ten-four, bestie." Sophie starts to laugh as she says under her breath, "I'm sure that's all he wants."

"Do I hear a tad hint of jealousy in your voice, Sophie?"

"Nope, not a lick of it!"

"Well, I have known you long enough to know that you do sound just *a bit* jealous," she says. Then she thinks to herself, *And are looking a li'l green with envy.*

"Nah, I'm good, Syd!" Sophie says, laughing like, "Ha! Yeah right, I'm so jealous!"

When all the food is cooked and placed on the table, Syd makes a quick comment. "Hello, everyone! I would love to thank my dad and my family for allowin' me to have this get-together. I would also love to thank everyone who is here with me today! These last few months have been hard on myself and all of you as well. So I thought, what better way to have a great time with family and friends than a huge buffet-style cookout! I would also like to say that this week I have a report to give on my project, and I would like as many of you as possible to be present to hear what I have accomplished. Now, could we please have a prayer so we may each enjoy this amazin'-smellin' food? Is there anyone who would like to say grace?"

Eliza raises her hand. "May I please say grace?"

"I am okay with it, Eliza. Everyone, let us hold hands and bow our heads so Eliza may say grace."

"Thank you, Syd," she says.

Dear God, thank you for all this food!
Thank you for the farmers who grew it. Thank
you for the people who cooked it. Thank you

for the people who are gettin' to eat it with me!
Amen.

"That was very nice, Eliza," Syd tells her. "Okay, everyone, let's eat!"

When everyone is done filling their plates, Syd asks a favor. "Okay, can we start with that end of the table, work our way around, and please say who you are and how you know my family and myself? Thank you."

"Hello, I am Allison. I am our local realtor. I have known Sydney since she was very li'l. Her mom, Ivy, and I were very good friends."

"Hello all! I am Greyson, and Sydney is my amazin' daughter Sophie's friend. I'm also Allison's husband. Parker is my friend."

"Hi, y'all. I am Emma! I have known Sydney for most of her life. I am the lady of the house. I help with the house care. Also, most recently, helpin' to care for Sydney."

"Hiya! I'm Oliver, also known as Obee. I am a farmhand here. But I feel like family. I've been here for many, many years."

"That's because you are family, Obee!" Sydney proudly chimes in.

"Hi! I'm Claire. I am Lucas's mother. We are friends of the family."

"Umm, hi, I am Lucas. I go to school with Sydney."

"Hey, there, everyone, I am Parker. I am Syd's dad."

"Hello, I am Cora Gossett. I am Sydney's principal."

"Hi, again, everyone! I am of course Dr. Henry Gossett, Sydney's ER doc. Thank you for invitin' my wife and me, Sydney. It was very nice of you!"

"I am Sophie. Hey to y'all! I happen to be this girl's bestest friend!" she says as she pulls Syd in for a hug.

"Thanks, Sophie! I love you, bestie! Obviously, everyone knows me."

"Syd, don't forget about me."

"I didn't forget, Eliza. I just saved the best for last. Eliza, it is now your turn. So go ahead."

"Hi!" Eliza says, waving to everyone. "Thanks, Syd," she whispers. "I am Eliza. Sophie is my sister, and Syd is her friend, so that makes us friends."

"Okay, now that everyone is acquainted, let's finish eatin' and just have a great time."

When everyone is done eating, the women start chatting and the men get together and start having a conversation. The girls and Lucas make their way out through the barns to the pasture to see which if any of the horses will come up to them.

SOT comes up to them, and Eliza and Sophie are giving her all kinds of love; that's when Lucas tugs on Sydney's sleeve. Sydney turns to him and motions for him to wait a sec. Then she goes to Sophie and tries to whisper so Eliza doesn't hear. "Lucas wants to talk with me, so I will be right back. We're just gonna go to Grandad's desk in the barn."

"Ten-four, bestie. Don't do anything I wouldn't do!" Sophie laughs.

Sydney waves Lucas to follow her. They walk over to the barn to Grandad's stall and go to sit by his desk. "So what did you want to talk about, Lucas?"

Lucas starts getting nervous and shaking a bit. He says, "I...I just wanted to say that I am sorry." He looks down and away from Sydney, trying to think about what he wants to say next. "I didn't mean to be so nasty to you. It's just...well, you see, I lost my dad kinda like you lost your mom."

"I know. I'm sorry for your loss. It hurts so much when we lose a loved one. Especially when they are close to us."

"Yeah, sometimes it hurts so bad I just get so angry, and I didn't mean to hurt you, Sydney." He looks away and hangs his head.

"Lucas, are you okay?"

"Yeah. Umm, Sydney, I have to tell you something."

Just then, Eliza comes running at Lucas and Sydney, with Sophie running after her.

"Eliza, stop! Sorry, guys, she figured out you disappeared and came lookin' for ya."

"Sophie, it's okay. We were just talkin'."

"Lucas, if you ever need to talk, I am here. If I may have your phone, I will put my number in it so I will be just a text away." She puts her hand out for him to lay his phone in it.

He picks his phone out of his pocket and hands it to Sydney. Sydney puts her number in and returns it to him. "Thanks, Sydney."

"No problem! We should see if we can take one of the carriages out to the lake. What do ya think, guys?"

Lucas nods as Eliza jumps up and down while Sophie tries to hold her still. "I think Eliza wants to go, but if some li'l lady doesn't settle, she won't be able to go," Sophie tells her. She settles just as Obee, Parker, and Greyson come into the barn on the other end.

"May we take a carriage out to the lake to fish for a li'l bit?"

"Well, Syd, I came in to see if Lucas would like to go to the auction house and see what horses are goin' through tonight."

"Really, Parker? You are gonna buy me a horse?"

"Well, I will see if there are any there that are worth buying. And you can board it here, *but* you have to come help out and work off the price. Speaking of price, I believe I owe you kids some money from today's race." He hands each of them an envelope with cash in it. "Now, don't spend it all in one place."

"Parker, would it be rude of me to just let you pick the horse for me? That way, you are pickin' one you think is right for me. I will be happy with whatever you are able to get me."

"Well, Lucas…" Parker thinks for a moment, and then he responds with, "Yeah, sure, that is fine, and yes, Syd, you all may take out a carriage *as long as* you are very careful and you are the one in control the entire time."

"Yes, sir, I can do that! Let's go ask your parents if you all can come too!"

"Sophie, ask your mom, but I am okay with you girls goin' out."

"Okay, Dad, thanks!" Sophie says as the kids all walk out to ask Allison and Claire if they may go out to the lake. The women are all cleaning up, so the kids grab some things to help carry into the house. When everything is cleaned up, they ask.

"Mom, may I ride in a carriage out to the lake with the girls?"

Claire thinks about it and remembers his drawing, so she looks at them and says, "Sure, Lucas, but please be careful and have a great time. Do you want me to take you home? I can wait for ya if you want."

"Yes, please wait for me. We shouldn't be too long," he says as he hugs his mom. "I love you, Mom!"

"Aww, please don't ever grow up! I love you too, Lucas."

"Dad already said he was okay with us goin', Mom, but he wanted us to still ask you too!"

"Yes, sure thing. Have fun! Be safe. I love you, girls."

"We love you too!" they say as all the kids turn to go outside to hook up a carriage and head out.

When they get out to the barn, Obee helps them to hook up and gets ready to help everyone inside the carriage. As they are hooking up the carriage, Cora and Henry walk over to the kids. "Thank you again for invitin' us. We had a good time. We must be goin' for now. I hope we see more of you at school behavin' like this," Cora says, smiling.

Lucas gets up and walks over to her. "Mrs. Gossett, I just wanna say I am sorry for my behavior lately. I promise to be better."

"Why, thank you, Lucas. I appreciate your apology. And I will hold you to that!" she says as they turn to walk away.

"Goodbye, kids," Henry says back to them.

"Okay, kids, your carriage awaits." Obee chuckles as he helps them all into it. "Text me if you have any issues."

"Okay, Obee," Syd tells him as she takes the reins and they head off to the lake.

As the kids head off, Greyson and Parker prepare to go to the auction house. When the kids get to the lake, Lucas jumps out of the carriage first to help each of the girls out. Sydney hitches SOT, and she says, "Lucas, Eliza, the rods are on the back porch. Sophie and I have to do something quick. We will be right back." Sophie and Sydney go into the cottage to put their winnings in the lockbox under the bed, then they return outside with Lucas and Eliza. "Grab a rod, Sophie, and let's go show these kids how to fish!"

They have fished for about an hour when they decide to head back for the day. They all put their rods and gear back, then Lucas helps each of them back up into the carriage. When he gets to Sydney, he stops and looks her in the eyes like he wants to pour his heart out to her but won't because Sophie and Eliza are with them.

By the time they get back, Parker and Greyson are back.

"Lucas, look!"

"I see, Sydney. What a beautiful horse!"

"Yes, for sure! Do you have a name you would like to use yet?"

"No. I wanted to see what your dad found first."

"Let's go see what Dad says!"

They get parked and secure SOT till they can get her unhooked. Lucas helps each of the girls from the carriage, and they hurry over to Parker and Greyson. Standing by them is a beautiful Thoroughbred stallion.

"Wow! Parker, is this my horse?"

"Yes, sir, Lucas! What do you think so far?"

"Well, sir, he is stunning. Such a handsome Thoroughbred!"

"Well, I must say, I am impressed! You sure do know your horse breeds, Lucas!"

"Yes, sir, I have been recently studying up on the different breeds," Lucas says as he looks at Sydney.

Sydney notices and blushes, and she says, "That's a great racin' breed. Guess I'mma have some competition."

"Hey!" Sophie smacks Sydney and says, "What am I, chopped liver?"

"No, but I've *been* racin' you! And besides, Lucas gave us *both* a run for our money today out there on the track! So we *both* have competition!"

"True, very true, bestie!"

"So, Lucas, what do you think for a name?"

"Oh well, Parker, it's a simple name, but I think it fits just perfectly. How about Loads of Luck?"

"Okay, Loads of Luck it is! So how about we getcha saddled up tomorrow and you can take him around the pasture for a while so you can get to know each other better? If you two get along and work well as a team, maybe, just maybe, I can get you two in the last spring race just to see how it goes?"

"Oh, that's definitely a great game plan, Parker! I can't wait! Well, I guess I better get goin' so I can come back tomorrow. I will be sure to be here bright and early! Bye, everyone! Bye, Sydney!" he says as he waves and turns to go look for his mom.

"Bye, Lucas!" Sydney smiles, trying not to blush.

"Well, don't make it too early. This old man's gotta have my breakfast before I make my way out here!" Parker says, laughing.

"Okay, Parker! Maybe I can have breakfast with ya?"

"I tell you what? Why don't you and your mom both come for breakfast tomorrow mornin'?"

"Oh, really? Aww, man, that would be, like, so cool! I will ask Mom and have her text you later. Okay, see y'all later!" he says, trying to hurry and get to his mom so they can go home.

"Syd, please don't let me forget to let Emma know that there's a possibility that they both may be here for breakfast tomorrow mornin'."

"Okay, Dad, I will just go tell her now. Come on, Sophie." Sydney grabs Sophie by the arm and pulls her to follow her. Eliza struggles to keep up as she runs along after them.

As they make their way inside, they hear Lucas talking with Emma and Claire. "So can we, Mom? Parker said it was okay!"

"Lucas, sure, I guess so. We can join them for breakfast." Just then, Claire spots Sydney and Sophie, who have just walked into the kitchen. Claire nods to Lucas that the girls are behind him.

He turns and acts startled. "Oh, hey, girls!"

"Hey, Lucas. So your mom said yes to breakfast tomorrow? That's so awesome! You will absolutely love Emma's breakfast food! It'll leave you wantin' more, and of course, you should not be hungry once you leave our table!" Sydney makes big eyes at Lucas while rubbing her belly.

"Okay, cool. I can't wait till breakfast then, okay mom can we please go?"

"Yes, Lucas! Okay, Emma, Allison, Sydney, Sophie, and Eliza, was it?"

"Yes, ma'am!"

"Okay, well, we will see you all tomorrow mornin'. Should I bring anything?"

"Oh no, Claire, please, I got this. Just bring yourself and Lucas. I will take care of the rest! Our treat! Just come with a hungry belly is all I ask!"

"Will do! Okay, let's go, Lucas. Bye, everyone!"

Everyone waves and says goodbye.

"Sophie, we have to go take care of SOT! In all the excitement, I completely forgot about her! Be right back, Em!"

As Sophie and Sydney go head out, they hear Eliza start to talk with Emma. "Emma, Mom, would you mind if I stayed in here with you guys? My sister and Sydney are way too fast for me," she says like she's out of breath.

"Sure, Eliza! Have a seat on the stool while I finish cleanin' up here."

"Honey, you are always—well, almost always—welcome wherever I am. You know that."

As Eliza tells Emma and Allison all about her fishing experience, Sydney and Sophie are out talking with Parker and Greyson while they work on disconnecting SOT from the carriage. Once they have SOT unhooked, Greyson and Parker manually park the carriage. Sydney takes SOT to the pasture, while Sophie stands by the fence and waits.

"So is it just me, or do you think Lucas is actin' strange?" Sophie asks as Sydney closes the gate.

"You noticed that too? I thought it was just me."

"Nope, huge yellow flags are wavin' all around that boy. Syd, if I didn't know better, I would have to guess he wants to ask you something serious!"

"Nah! You're crazy!"

"Am I? Care to wager?"

"What are we wagering? Money? Or something else?"

"We can do money. So how sure are you? I say we wager $100! You in?"

"Sure! I'm in, and I up the ante to an additional $50!"

"So $150 it is!" Sophie reaches for Syd's hand for a shake, and they start laughing. "May the best take the prize, and that shall be me!"

"You seem so sure of yourself, Sophie. I think I will win!"

"Nope, I will, because you are so blind to the truth, Syd!"

Just then, Parker and Greyson come around the corner and startle the girls. "There you girls are! Sophie, are you ready to go home?"

"Dad, I was wonderin' if I could stay the night here with Syd?"

"Let's go ask your mom before I say yes."

"Okay, we will go ask!" And the girls take off toward the house. Greyson and Parker follow them.

"Mom, may I please stay over with Sydney tonight? Please!"

"Well, Emma, is it okay with you? And what did your dad say?"

"He said that we needed to ask you before he could say yes."

"That's what I told her, Allison. I just wanted to make sure that you didn't need her for anything before I committed to sayin' yes."

"Well, I'm okay with it, and if you want Eliza to stay as well, we would be delighted to have them both! You are racin' in the last race tomorrow, aren't you, Sophie?"

"Oh yes! Mom, Dad, can I please?"

"Well, who are we to stop you? Sure, but only on one condition! You gotta come share some love and be good to your sister!"

"Oh, thank you, Dad!" Sophie says as she hugs Greyson. "Thank you too, Mom!" And she hugs Allison as well. "I think I can be extra good to Eliza!"

"Okay, with that note, then Allison, what do you say we hit the road and get home so we can get rested so we can watch our daughter race tomorrow!"

"I thought you would never ask! Emma, Parker, girls, we shall see you tomorrow. Eliza, come give us some lovin', and we will be on our way!"

"I love you, Momma," Eliza whispers in Allison's ear as she hugs her. Then she reaches for her dad and he bends down as she hugs him and whispers to him, "I love you, Daddy!"

"We love you too, Eliza and Sophie!" Allison and Greyson say simultaneously and then turn to leave.

"I love you too, Mom and Dad!" Sophie shouts out to them as they leave.

"Sophie, Eliza, wanna go up to my room?"

"Sure!" They all run upstairs.

"Night, Emma! Tomorrow is a big day. See ya when the rooster crows!" Parker chuckles.

"Night, Parker!" Emma says as she and Parker both head to their rooms.

Meanwhile, upstairs, the girls get ready for bed and say their prayers before lying down to sleep.

CHAPTER 24

The Last Spring Race

Sydney, Sophie, and Eliza wake up to the sound of the doorbell chiming away.

"Who do you think it is, Syd?"

"It has to be Claire and Lucas."

"No, but it could be my mom and dad."

"True! Well, what are ya waitin' for? Let's go see!" They hurry and get ready for the day.

"Come on, Eliza, let's go see who's here. Hurry, get dressed and come down stairs!" Sophie tells Eliza as she and Sydney take off downstairs.

"Wait! Wait for me!" Eliza screams as she comes running down the stars, almost falling near the bottom.

"Slow down, Eliza. No one's leavin' without ya!"

When the girls get downstairs, Claire is in the kitchen.

"Where's Lucas?" Sydney asks.

"He's outside with Parker. Apparently, if Loads of Luck does well with Lucas, Parker is goin' to let them be in the last race together. So Lucas was excited to get out there and try to bond a li'l before the race. He was so excited last night, that all he kept talkin' about was comin' here to ride Loads of Luck and comin' to ride over the summer."

"That's awesome. I hope he does well, Claire. It will be nice to have more new competition that can actually give some good experience!"

"Hey! I'm a li'l offended!"

"Sophie, chill. I meant it for us, not just me! We both can use a new challenge. It'll be great. I can promise you that!"

"Well, Syd, you wanna go peek to see how well he's doin'?"

"Sure! We need to know what we are up against!" They both laugh as they head outside.

"Don't be too long, girls. Breakfast is almost ready! Can you tell everyone else too, please?" Emma yells out to us.

We return with a yell over our shoulders, "Okay! Will do!" The door slams behind us, and we make our way to the barn. We sneak through the barn to see if we are able to catch a glimpse of Lucas riding Loads of Luck in the training ring.

"Would you look at his form! Dang, Syd, I gotta hand it to him. We are in some serious trouble! He must have ridin' in his blood! Or he has had ridin' classes and just never mentioned it?"

"You mean like me? It's just beginner's luck. I bet that's why he named his horse what he did! So when he wins, he can say it's the horse."

"To be honest, Syd, I can totally hear him sayin' that in his cocky li'l voice! So are we gonna let him win today or what?"

"Oh, no way! It's not happenin'! Not today! Let's go tell 'em it's time to eat. Then we can eat quickly, come back out, race to the lake and back for some practice. What do ya think?"

"Okay, that's a great game plan!" They high-five each other as they make their way to the fence.

"Hey, guys, Emma said to tell ya it's time to eat! So hurry in soon before it gets cold!"

"Okay, Syd, we will be in soon!"

"Come on, Sophie, let's go," Syd whispers, and then they take off running for the house.

As the girls go running into the house, Emma shouts out to them, "Girls, did you tell everyone out there it's time to eat soon?"

"Yes, ma'am! Dad said that they will be in then."

Just then, there's a knock on the door.

"That must be my mom and dad. I'll go look." Sophie heads for the door while shouting out to Emma, "I think it's my mom and dad, Em, so I will check to see who's at the door!"

"Okay, Sophie!" Emma shouts from the kitchen.

Sophie heads to open the door. It's Allison and Greyson. "Hey, Mom! Hey, Dad! You're just in time to eat! Hurry before it gets cold."

"Oh, that was good timin'," Greyson softly says to Allison. "Emma, breakfast smells amazin'!" Allison and Greyson walk into the kitchen and take a seat at the table.

"Thanks, Greyson! I usually get that my breakfast is amazin'! I just hope I am up to your standards," Emma says, laughing.

Just before Greyson was able to comment back on Emma's comment, Sophie comes running into the kitchen. "Dad, you will love Emma's food! It's to die for!"

"Well, Emma, how do I get a plate of this amazin' breakfast?"

"I will plate you up some food. All you have to do is sit there and eat it."

"I think I can handle that."

"Em? May Sophie and I get ours next? We really wanna go ride a li'l before we leave for the race."

"Okay, here ya go, Greyson. Sophie and Sydney, I will work on yours next. And li'l Eliza? Where is she?"

"Right here, Em!"

"I will get you yours as well. How about you, Allison? Would you like me to fix you a plate as well?"

"Just a li'l bit, please. I'm not all that hungry right now."

"Okay, no problem. Sydney, Sophie, here you girls go. And now for Eliza! There you go, sweetheart," Emma says, smiling as she hands plates to everyone. "Sydney, did you tell Lucas and your dad about the food?"

"Yes, ma'am! Sure did!"

"Okay, sorry, Sydney, I guess I already asked you that, didn't I? Well, okay, I will fix them a plate and hope that they come in soon." Just then, the front door opens. "Parker, Lucas, please wash up and come get your food. I already plated yours up, and I don't want it gettin' cold!" Emma shouts out from the kitchen.

"Comin, Em! We are starvin!"

"Em, we are done. May we please be excused?"

"In a minute, dear."

"Did I hear someone wanted to be excused from the table already?" Parker asks as he walks around the corner to go into the kitchen.

"Yes, Dad. Sophie and I wanted to go ride for a li'l before the race."

"Well, just be careful not to overrun them or tire them out too much before the race. Or someone else may just take your place," Parker says as he winks and nods at Lucas.

"Okay, Dad, we won't. May we please go out?"

"Sure!" As Sydney and Sophie get up and go outside, Lucas and Parker take a seat to eat their breakfast.

As Sophie and Sydney close the door and head toward the barn, Sophie says, "So, Syd, do you think that we have anything to worry about with today's race?"

"Nah. Lucas just got lucky with his first race! But we are way better and have way more experience. I don't think he will have a chance. I mean, he could place in, like, the top five maybe, but I don't think he will do much better than that. I mean, he's only been with Loads of Luck for, like, today. So seriously, what are his chances? Right!"

"Well, I tend to think a li'l differently. Think about it, Syd. He has never really ridden, and he just shows up here and wants to ride? Parker let's him take out Black Boots and Lucas takes fourth place? Which, in your defense, is within the top five."

"You do have a point! Ugh, I hate it how you may just be right! You have a way of makin' me look at things from a different perspective. But that's one of the reasons that I love you so much! My one and only bestie! Well, let's get a few steps in before we have to go to the track and I have to do my best to try to prove you wrong!" Syd smiles, and they get on the mares and ride off through the pasture.

"So how do you think everyone is goin' to react to the news that we aren't boys but girls and we have been whoopin' butts and takin' names and trophies?"

"Well, hopefully, it will be a good reaction since we have made such a strong impression on the racin' community so far already! I'm just hopin' this has made the impression I was goin' for."

"Syd, I think we made such a huge impression that they just have to love us! I can almost guarantee they will be shocked, and they will never forget you and me!"

"I can second that just as you will be second to me," Syd says, laughing as she kicks SOT and takes off, running across the pasture. "Catch up if you can!" she shouts back over her shoulder.

"Oh, it's on, bestie!" Sophie kicks PB Cup, and she takes off, catching up to SOT and Syd quickly. "Boo! I see you!"

"Well, it took ya long enough!" Syd laughs as she adds, "Come on, let's get back before Dad thinks we've run off." They head back to the stables just in time to see Lucas and Parker walk up to the pasture gate.

"Did you have a good run? Are you ready to go racin', ladies?"

"Yes, sir, Dad, we are ready! Let's go see how the community will like us bein' who we really are."

"Load up the girls and we will get Loads of Luck and meet ya over at the trailer."

While Sophie and Syd load up the girls, Parker helps Lucas get Loads of Luck rounded up. "Lucas, for now I think we will just let you use Black Boots's saddle and gear. I will work on findin' you your own set of gear soon. How's that work for ya?"

"Great! Parker, thank you so much! I really hope we do well today. By *we* I don't just mean Loads of Luck and I. I mean Sydney and Sophie too! I am so glad that even though I treated them so badly, they are at least tryin' to be good to me. They are probably bein' better to me than I deserve."

"Lucas, my thoughts on that matter are that you have seen the error in your ways and you have made the correct first steps to fix your wrongs. Now, it's how you continue from here that truly counts. Have you talked with the girls and let them know how you feel?"

"Well, I kinda started to tell them, but I haven't completely finished relayin' just how I feel. Something just keeps comin' up. Plus,

I am so afraid of what they will think of me. I don't want to weird them out, but I do want to tell them just how sorry I am."

"Lucas, I have an assignment for you. Today, I don't care when, but by the end of today, I really want you to get with the girls and tell them how you feel. I can assure you that after you do, you will feel better, and I think that your relationship with the girls will improve. Can you make me this promise?"

"Sure thing, Parker. I will do my best. Thanks for bein' willin' to let me live my dreams. You and your family have opened your hearts and home to me. I have always wanted to ride, but we just never had the money or the room for a horse. And then Dad passed, and I definitely never foresaw this to ever be in my future. Thank you for all you have done for me! I can never repay you enough. I just hope I can continue to do well at the track."

"Lucas, you are an amazin' young man, and I am so impressed with your level of skill already that even if you don't do well today, it's okay. We have all summer to work on next season! You just go out there and ride with no expectations. That will make me very happy. Okay, let's get goin', or we will be late."

"Yes, sir! I wouldn't want to steal away Sydney's thunder. I hope she does really well today! Can we celebrate later if she does?"

"Let's see how everything goes and we can decide afterward."

They get everything loaded, and the horses are all hooked in as they close the trailer gate and climb in the truck. "Okay, kids, let's get y'all to the track! No pressure today. Just go out there and ride! It would be amazin' to have all three of you at the top, but it's okay if not."

"Good luck, everyone! Let's give 'em all we got!" Sydney says as though she is blessing them all.

"Sounds like a plan, bestie!"

"Good luck, girls. Don't run me over out there. I would like to make it to next season," Lucas says, chuckling.

"Well, don't get in our way. Syd has to keep up her image more now than ever 'cause she will be racin' as a girl!"

"Sophie! Down, girl. Chill. What I think she meant to say, Lucas, was, good luck out there."

"No! I said what I me—"

Syd elbows Sophie to make her shut up.

"Ouch! Syd!"

"I'm sorry, bestie, but it's time to zip it!" Syd says as with each word her voice gets sterner and progressively quieter.

"Fine!" Sophie says as she crosses her arms and huffs.

Parker just smiles as he nears the track and announces their arrival. "Okay, so let's get parked, and we can walk over to talk to Hudson together to get this all sorted out and get y'all signed up."

"Dad?"

"Yes, Sydney?"

"I would like to do the talkin' with Hudson, please? I mean, I don't want to get you in trouble, and you honestly didn't know. So I feel I should be the one to speak with him. Is that okay with you?"

"Well, okay, I guess so. But I will be there so if you need me to do anything, I can and will."

"It's okay. I should be good. Just stand and listen, Dad, and thank you for understandin'."

"I love the lady you are growin' into, Sydney."

"I love you too, Dad!"

Parker parks the truck, and they all get out and follow Sydney to the registration booth to see Hudson.

"Dad, I don't feel so good." Sydney states as she rubs her stomach.

"It's okay. It's just your nerves. Hudson is a great guy who will listen and do his best to understand. Don't worry, sweetheart, just be brave and you got this."

"Thanks, Dad! You are right, it's time to suck it up, buttercup!"

"That's the spirit!" Parker says, laughing.

As they wait in line to talk to Hudson next, Syd is running what she wants to say to him over and over in her head so she doesn't screw it up.

"Next!" Sydney steps up to Hudson. "Well, hello, li'l lady. What can we do ya for?"

"Well, sir, my name is Sydney Ashcraft. I would like to start by sayin' that I am sorry." She hangs her head a little.

"Sorry? Sorry for what, li'l one?"

"Well, I'm sure the name Chase Payne rings a big bell for you?"

"Yes, of course, it does. He is a great rider. Do you know him? Wait, of course you do. He rides for your family."

"Correct. Well, kinda. See, I am Chase Payne. I had a history project at school. I was to make a difference in either my life, my community, or for someone else's life to be better. I thought about the fact that there are not many female racers in the race community, and I decided I wanted to prove that females are just as good a rider as males. But to make my point without argument, I dressed as a boy and fooled everyone right down to my dad, who also had no idea."

"Hudson, she is correct. I cannot believe she fooled me."

"Well, you definitely fooled me, and everyone! You definitely did show that determination can get you anything. Even in this crazy world of horse racin'. This is odd, and the horse race community shouldn't be too cruel, if at all. So I will announce the change today, and we will see how it goes. Hopefully, no riots."

"Well, sir, can you also fix my friend Sophie Abbott? She was Wyatt Gentry."

"Is that so? Hmm, well, you gals are a piece of history for sure! I am proud that you were brave enough to do what you did. I think for the most part, you will have more support than you anticipated. Simply because you proved yourself then came clean. It's not exactly how I would have gone about it, but I'm an old-timer." Hudson chuckles as he writes down their info. "Good luck, girls! I assume that you will be ridin' your usual horses?"

"Yes, sir, SOT for me and PB Cup for Sophie!"

"Okay, got it. And you, young sir, are also returning from last week? You are a male, correct?" Hudson looks hopeful as he awaits Lucas's response.

"Yes, sir, I am 100 percent a male. But this week I would like to add a new horse that I will be ridin'. His name is Loads of Luck. He's a four-year-old Thoroughbred." Lucas leans into Hudson and says quietly, "Thanks to Mr. Parker, he is my horse."

"Okay, that is awesome! I have all your info, and you may all go get saddled up for today's race."

"Thank you, Hudson," they say as they hurry off for the stables.

"Yes, thank you, Hudson. I just pray that the fans and the horse community see it like we do and take it easy on them," Parker says, worried.

"That's for sure. You have one brave li'l gal there, Parker."

"I know. That's what scares me. Well, I better go get my place in the stands. Thanks again," Parker says to Hudson as he waves and jogs away toward the stands.

Meanwhile, back at the stables. Sydney, Sophie, and Lucas work on getting their horses saddled up. When Sydney and Sophie notice a small group of boys headed toward Lucas, taunting him.

"Look who it is, boys. It's Lucas Puke-us. What are you doin'? I thought you only raced the last race to take out your li'l girlfriend."

"I told you she's not my girlfriend. Can you guys just go? I have to get ready for the race. We can talk later."

"Nah, I wanna talk now, or I go to the curls and spill my guts," the boy taunts him, then pushes him and knocks him down.

"Syd, do you think we should step in? We can't just stand here and let them do that to him, can we?"

"Just wait. Let me think. Finish gearin' up. Don't let them see you lookin'." They go about their business, acting like they don't have a clue what's goin' on. When they hear what sounds like someone kicking something, Sophie turns around and grabs Syd's arm.

"Syd, we have to step in."

"Wow, okay, yeah, let's go!" The girls head over to all the commotion by Lucas. "Is there a problem here?" Syd asks.

"Everything is good, Sydney. Please take Sophie and head back over to your horses."

"Yeah, you heard the mutt. Get lost!" the unidentified boy says to Sydney and Sophie.

"Well, I am sorry to tell you, Lucas, but friends don't let friends get bullied. Friends stand up for friends!" Sydney says to the boy straight in his face, not backing down from him or his size. He towers her by at least a foot. He has her on the size too; he would be classified as a plus-size dude, but she isn't afraid of him. "So step back and take a hike. We do not need your kind here."

Sydney does a quick step forward as if she were trying to pounce on him, and he flinches. "Chicken wow, not what I expected from a boy of your size! So get steppin'!"

"Lucas has his girlfriend doin' his dirty work for him!" says another boy from the group.

Almost simultaneously Lucas and Sydney respond to the second boy, "She's not my girlfriend," "He's not my boyfriend." They both look at each other as if they *were* boyfriend and girlfriend and had just broken up.

"Awkward," Sophie mumbles under her breath. She steps up to the friend plate and puts her two cents in as well. "You heard the woman. Now scram! You don't want her whoopin' up on ya. Just ask her boyfriend, Lucas. He's felt her wrath." She feels eye daggers deep in her back. "Sorry, Syd. I'm just pickin'."

"Now's not the time for pickin', bestie!"

"Yeah, she will put a hurtin' on ya. I know, 'cause I've been there and done that! It wasn't a pleasant feelin' either."

"Fine, we're goin' but we ain't done with you, Puke-us! Watch your back, 'cause you never know when we will be there," the first boy says as he motions for the others to round up and split.

"Thanks, guys. It means a lot, especially from you, Sophie. I know you don't like me very much, but I am truly sorry for my actions toward you two. I would like the opportunity to chat with you guys later, if that's okay? 'Cause right now we have a race to get conquered!"

"You are right, Lucas. Come on, Sophie, let's get ready. Are you good to get ready, or do you need help, Lucas?"

"Don't worry about me. I will be just fine. See ya on the track."

"Okay, see ya in a few." The girls go to check on the last of their final checks for the race.

Just then, you can hear the mic key up. "Testing, testing, testing, one-two, one-two, three-four." Then Hudson says, "Good afternoon, ladies and gentlemen! Welcome, one and all, to our last of the spring races here for the Keeneland Racetrack. So we have some amazin' news that may just shock most of you as it did me! It's a long story, but I'll give it to ya straight and short to the point. They will be no more Chase Payne or Wyatt Gentry!"

As he states this info, the crowd goes a bit silent, then the boos and chants start. "Chase!" "Wyatt!" "Chase!" "Wyatt!"

"Ladies and gentlemen, if I could have your attention for just a moment, I can explain the situation to you." The crowd slowly settles for just a bit. "The riders will still be here today, but they will not be known as Chase and Wyatt. They will be Sydney Ashcraft and Sophie Abbott! So can we give them a big round of applause, please?" Just as he finishes his comment, there's a hush of sighs over the stands. Just as quickly as the silence hits the crowd, though, it is broken by what sounds like a few people who start clapping. Sydney and Sophie are sure it's their families. Then slowly the momentum picks and there's cheering, clapping, stomping on the bleachers so hard the girls can feel the stomps on the ground at the stables. The girls look at each other and start hugging and dancing around.

"There was something about a project for school, and it is what it is and that's an amazin' miracle. These two young ladies decided to take a chance and disguise themselves just to prove a point that very well could have backfired. To be honest, I was even a bit wary as to how the community would take it. Seems as though you all are in agreement that this is nothing short of amazin'. So with all that said, let's get this race started and see how they finish today!"

The crowd roars with excitement and joy. Hudson clears his throat and takes a drink of water as he prepares to key up the mic and read the list of riders for today. He decides to speak what's on his mind. "Folks, this is the craziest day ever. I can't even remember a time with so much excitement here at this track! So let's keep it goin'! Here is the lineup for today. Startin' at gate 1 through 8, it's as follows: Blue Bell, a three-year-old Appaloosa; Stars in My Eyes, a four-year-old American paint; Loads of Luck, a four-year-old Thoroughbred; Sands of Tyme, a two-year-old Araloosa; PB Cup, a five-year-old Arabian; Cups of Courage, a five-year-old standardbred; Pocketful of Posies, a four-year-old Appaloosa; and last but not the least, Gentle Eyes, a three-year-old Arabian. There you are, folks, that's your lineup! Let's show 'em some love for our last spring race!"

The crowd goes wild; whistles and screams are all that can be heard.

"Riders, take your places," Hudson says. "If I could have everyone's attention, please stand for the national anthem!"

Everyone stands, facing the flag, as the anthem plays over the intercom. When it's finished, Hudson says, "Thank you all. You may be seated."

Meanwhile, down at the gates, Sydney looks to her left at Lucas, then her right at Sophie, and says, "Good luck! See ya at the finish line!" They both nod and get ready.

"Get set..."

Bang!

"And they're off this beautiful Sunday! We have Blue Bell and Stars in My Eyes neck and neck in first. Next are the Cups," Hudson states, chuckling. "PB Cup and Cups of Courage pushin' for first from second. Sands of Tyme and Pocketful of Posies are fightin' for third, with Loads of Luck and Gentle Eyes bringing up the rear. Stars in My Eyes has pushed to first with Cups of Courage, knockin' Blue Bell to second place, with Sands of Tyme makin' a move up one to second as well. Oh, would you look at that! Blue Bell took her spot back in first with Stars in My Eyes. That shifts Cups of Courage back to second place with Sands of Tyme and PB Cup for a three-way race. They are pushin' so hard, and here they come for the finish line. And just who will make it today?

"Oh, folks, it looks like Chase, or rather Sydney, got knocked back this week, but it's still not a bad finish, with PB Cup takin' the race today! Let's give them a big round of applause, ladies and gentlemen! And the rest is as follows: second is Sands of Tyme, Cups of Courage takes third, with Blue Bell in fourth, and Loads of Luck tops off the top five in fifth place. Stars in My Eyes takes sixth, seventh is Pocketful of Posies, and Gentle Eyes finishes off our last spring race in eighth place!

"Thank you, everyone, for makin' the trip here to enjoy this wonderful and eventful race today! You just never know what will happen here, so please mark your calendars for our first fall race, which will be the first Friday in October! If you are on our mailing list, we will send you info on all the happenings a li'l closer to time. Thanks again. Now, let's give one more round of applause to our winner, Sophie Abbott and her beautiful horse, PB Cup, and all the other beautiful horses and their lucky riders!"

The crowd cheers, and they make their way to the winner's circle for photo ops and the winner's circle ceremony. Parker tries to push his way through the crowd and rushes to meet his crew of riders. As he nears, he sees Sydney waving to him.

"Over here, Dad!"

"Comin', sweetheart!" he shouts across the crowd as he politely pushes his way through the remaining guests. "Excuse me, please. Thank you! Excuse me, excuse me, thanks!" When he finally makes it to his riding crew, he gives Sydney a big hug, and then Sophie. Lucas puts his hand out for a shake, but Parker pushes his hand away and reaches in for a big bear hug instead. "Come on, Lucas, you are not gettin' away that easily, boy. Give me a man hug!" Lucas gives in and smiles uncontrollably. When they are done, he looks Lucas in the eye and says, "You did very well out there!" He pulls him in close so Sydney can't hear and says, "You are gonna give Syd all kinds of competition this fall, I can tell! Good luck, kid!"

"Thanks, Parker! But I couldn't have done it without your help. So thank you so much! I will never forget it!"

"Okay, kids, how about we all go out to celebrate at dinner, wherever y'all wanna go?"

"Sounds awesome, Dad! Great job, everyone! I can't wait till this fall to see how much competition you are gonna lay on me then, Lucas!"

"Eh, I'm not that good!" Lucas says while hanging his head.

"Well, I happen to think you are!"

"Well, as much as I hate to admit it, Lucas, Syd is right. You did awesome out there today! I'm actually excited to see how you grow over the summer."

"Thanks, Sophie. I wouldn't have thought you would even care. Oh, and, girls, once we get outta here, I want and need to talk with you both, please."

"Okay, cool, no problem!"

While the photo ops are finishing up, Lucas and Parker start loading up anything that they aren't using at the moment. When the girls are all done and everyone is preparing to leave the track, Parker and Lucas help them get SOT and PB Cup loaded and hooked in the trailer. They close up the trailer gate, lock it, and hurry to the truck so they can head home.

As they pull away and leave the track grounds, Parker asks the kids, "So any ideas or suggestions where we can go for your celebration dinner?"

"Can we go for pizza?" Syd asks.

"I want tacos!" Sophie chimes in.

"Well, Lucas, you are the tiebreaker. Where would you like to go?"

"I hate bein' the tiebreaker. But can I think about it?"

"Sure, Lucas, you have till we get home and unload."

"Can Emma come, Dad?"

"Sure! Why don't you give her a heads-up so she can be ready?"

"Already on it!"

As they near the ranch, Parker looks at Lucas, hopeful that he has made up his mind about where he wants to go eat. Lucas looks back and just shrugs.

"I texted Emma, and she said she would love to come. I want Obee to come too! I'm sendin' him a message."

"Sophie, why don't you ask your parents and Eliza, if they don't have plans, to join us?"

"Are you sure? I mean, okay, I will!"

"Yes, I am sure! This is a big family affair. Let's all celebrate together. Same with you, Lucas. Please ask your mom to meet us. Just as soon as you figure out where it is you want to eat."

"Okay, Parker, I will ask her." Lucas picks up his phone and calls his mom. "Hey, Mom, whatcha doin'? Would you like to come out with all of us for some pizza?" He listens to her. "Oh, okay, see ya soon. Love you, Mom."

"So pizza it is! And that's perfect timin', as we are finally home. Let's get the horses unloaded and go wash up. We can get the rest out tomorrow sometime."

"I will let my mom and dad know to meet us at the pizza shop!"

As he parks, they all jump out. They go to the back of the trailer. Parker opens the gate, and each of the kids takes their horse and walks them to the pasture. Once the horses are out of the trailer, Parker closes the gate. While the kids go in to wash up, Parker disconnects the trailer from the truck before heading in to wash up too.

"Em, we are goin' for pizza!" Sydney shouts as they split up for two different bathrooms.

"Okay, Sydney, I am ready."

Just as Emma shouts back to Sydney, Parker comes through the door with the biggest smile on a father's face the world has ever seen!

"So you look like you won the lottery and are burstin' to tell someone!"

"Emma, if you could only have watched them race today! It was absolutely beautiful! I'm not meaning to put Syd down, but Lucas is goin' to give her a run for her money this fall! Loads of Luck and Lucas are like Syd and SOT! They are an amazin' team, and for them bein' together for the first time in an actual race, my mind is so blown! It's like it was meant to be!"

"So I do agree, this does call for a celebration dinner! So who chose pizza?" Emma asks, chuckling.

"Well, I was hopin' that they would pick something a li'l more formal, but kids will be kids, and I left it up to them. Syd wanted pizza—"

Before he can continue, Emma interrupts him. "I should have guessed Sydney would say pizza," she says, smiling from ear to ear in amazement.

"No, actually, she wanted pizza, Sophie wanted tacos, so that left Lucas to do a tiebreaker. He chose pizza. I think I know why too!" Parker winks and smiles at Emma with a nod and that look.

"Oh no, Parker, you aren't sayin' what I think you are sayin', are you?" Emma gasps. "From that look, I am guessin' so!"

"Emma, sweetheart, it is the very thing I am sayin'! I know a li'l something that no one knows I know about Lucas and his feelin's toward Syd."

"Oh my! Well, that's definitely something!"

Just as Emma finishes her comment, Sydney comes around the corner and says, "What's definitely something?"

"Oh, nothing, dear. Dad and I were just talkin', is all. Are you all washed up?"

"Yes, ma'am!"

"Well, I guess I better get washed up instead of standin' here gabbin'. I will be right back. Give me a few minutes!"

"Okay, but hurry, Dad!"

As fast as Parker heads out of the kitchen, Lucas and Sophie come in. "I'm all ready! Mom and Dad are meetin' us there."

"Same, my mom is meetin' us there too!" Lucas says. "So can I talk with you girls quickly before we go? It's important, and I don't wanna put it off."

"Sure thing. Em, can you let Dad know we will be outside, whenever he is ready?"

"Yes, Syd, I will let him know."

"Thanks, Em!" Sydney says as they all turn and head for the front door.

Parker comes into the kitchen just in time to see the kids go out the front door.

"So I think we need to give them a few minutes. Lucas wants to talk with the girls about something important."

"Yes, we can do that. He talked with me earlier about how sorry he was for how he treated them, and I said he needs to talk with them today and let them know. So I am sure that's what it is all about."

Meanwhile, outside, the kids have walked over to the pasture gate, and Lucas seems to have some trouble speaking. "Sydney..."

"Yes, Lucas? What's up?"

"I...I want to tell you something. No, I need to tell you something. Well, actually, Sophie, I should...I mean, I need to tell you too! I...umm...arggh! Why is this so hard for me?" Lucas puts his head in his hands and grabs his hair and screams as he starts to tear up.

"It's okay, Lucas. Just say whatever it is you need to say. We can sort it out after that, or whatever it is we need to do. It's okay."

"Why can't I just be a man and quit all this cryin'? I'm not a baby! But all I do is cry anymore, and it's drivin' me nuts!"

"Lucas, it's okay. When you cry, you show that you have compassion and actual feelins!"

"Yeah, Syd always says she's buildin' character when she cries. I think it's true, because every time she cries, she seems to grow more as a person. Sorry, Syd. Hope you don't mind me spillin' out all your secrets."

"Actually, Sophie, it's all good! But she is right. That's my motto since Mom passed. Every time I cry, I am buildin' character!"

"But I am a boy. I am not supposed to be soft!"

"Well, I believe differently! Lucas, you are a great person. I just know it. I can sense it! So keep cryin', my friend, and out with it! Come on, spill whatever is tuggin' at your heartstrings right now! We will get through this together as a team!"

"Okay, you are right! What I want to say is that I am so very sorry! I am sorry from the bottom of my heart! Sorry for pickin' on you, sorry for bein' a bully, sorry for thinkin' I was better than you! You two have no idea how grateful I am for you even bein' so nice to me when you obviously didn't have to even give me a chance. I truly don't deserve it. I will do whatever I can to make it up to you! Truth is, I am kinda jealous of your relationship with each other! I don't have a friend like that." Lucas hangs his head and continues to sob. "That's all I want, a friend who understands me. Since my dad passed away, I have felt so alone! We did everything together, and just like that, he's gone forever and never comin' back. So can you girls please forgive me? I know I don't deserve your forgiveness, and I understand if you don't want to."

Just like that, Sydney says, "Lucas, shut up!" She reaches to pull him into a hug, and Sophie joins in. "We are a team! We forgive you. Right, Sophie?"

"Yes, ma'am! We accept your apology, Lucas!"

As they separate, Lucas has a smile on his face, with Sydney wiping away his tears. "Careful, Syd. Don't wipe too hard. You might wipe away my new character!" Lucas says, laughing.

Just then, Parker comes around the corner of the barn. "Is everything okay out here?"

"Yep! Just great, Dad! Come on, you two. Let's go get some pizza." Sydney takes both Lucas and Sophie by the hand, and they walk toward Parker. "We are ready now, Dad!"

"Okay, let's get in the truck and get outta here. I don't know about you, kids, but I am famished!"

"Dad, do you think they will have the pizza bar open?"

"We can only hope so, Syd."

"Pizza bar? What is that?" Lucas wonders out loud.

"Well, Lucas, it is a buffet with all kinds of pizza flavors on it! If you can imagine it, most likely it's already on there, and if not, just ask and they will put it on it!"

"Awesome! We do not go out to eat pizza. Mom usually just has them deliver it. Sounds interesting."

"It is! You will love it!"

CHAPTER 25

The Perfect Project

When everyone has arrived at the pizza shop, they all go in for a table together. "How many?" asks the hostess.

"Ten, please," Parker replies.

"Okay, right this way." She shows them off to a table over in the corner. "What can I get for everyone's drinks?"

"Okay, what's everyone want?" Parker asks. "If a bunch of us want the same things, we can get some pitchers."

Greyson speaks for the Abbotts. "We are good with sweet tea, please."

"Water for us, please, Parker," states Claire.

"Emma, what do you prefer?"

"I think I will be good with water or sweet tea as well."

"Okay, can we have a pitcher of sweet tea and a pitcher of water, please?" Parker tells the hostess. "Also, we would like ten for the pizza bar."

"Okay, great, no problem. I will get you your drinks and pitchers. Please help yourself to the bar. Let us know if there's a flavor that isn't there that you would like. We will make it and place it on the bar for ya. Have a great night, and enjoy!"

"Thank you. We will! We are celebratin' tonight!"

"That's awesome. Do you mind me askin' what y'all are celebratin'?"

"Certainly, we are celebratin' a great year at the track and the fact that we have another amazin' rider with our team!"

"That's great. Well, congrats to your new team member! I wish them all the luck this fall! I will be right back with your drinks."

"Thank you. Okay, guys, let's eat!" They all get up and head to the bar.

"Thanks, Parker, for includin' Lucas and me this evenin'."

"No problem. You are family now! This will be a regular thing, you know. Claire, you and Lucas are always welcome wherever we are!"

"Wait, family? Do you know something I don't?"

"No, I just mean because Lucas is a new team member with Team Ashcraft. That makes you family! Always and forever!"

"Well, I do not know what to say, Parker." Claire is shocked at the generosity of the Ashcrafts.

"Just say yes!"

"Oh, wow, what are we just sayin' yes to over here?" Greyson blurts out.

"That Claire and Lucas are part of the family! What do you think I was sayin' Greyson?" Parker laughs.

"Well, I am not sure what I was walkin' up on. I just know catchin' the tail end of a conversation is never good with an open-ended comment like that!" Greyson has a look of relief on his face as he starts to chuckle.

"Greyson, man, you crack me up! Your mind is always off in some far-out left field somewhere. Your imagination has its own mind!" Parker rolls his eyes and winks as he gives a chuckle.

Everyone makes their way back to the table and starts to eat.

"So I do not know if y'all will be allowed to come into my class tomorrow or not, but I will be givin' my history project presentation. If you are able to, I would love for you to be there. This is a big deal for me. You all mean the world to me, and without y'all, I would never have been able to pull this off. Especially with Sophie and Obee, my two biggest fans."

"Wait! Obee, you knew about this all this time?" Parker asks like he was betrayed.

"Yes, sir, but I was sworn by the oath of secrets to keep it on the down low. I am sorry, boss. I did not see any real harm in it, so that's why I didn't say anything. I would never have allowed it if I thought it was too dangerous. I kept an eye on her, as if she were my own child. I love her like my own!"

"I love you too, Obee! Dad, please don't be upset with him. It's all on me!"

"I'm not, and I completely understand, I just feel left out, is all."

"I'm sorry, Dad. It had to be this way. But I am so glad you know now. Also, I am glad 'cause I don't have to hide it anymore! It went so much better than I had planned!"

"I am glad for you, Sydney. I hope your teacher gives you a great grade!"

"So does Syd! She hasn't turned in any of the assignments leadin' up to the final project."

Parker looks at Sydney with a "You're grounded" look when Syd says, "Thanks for the tire marks, bestie! You just threw me right out under the bus! Dad, please let me explain. So I already talked with Ms. Dixon and explained to her that if I did the small assignments leadin' up to the final project, it would give it away and I felt it would hurt my end result by not makin' it 100 percent pure. I also told her that if she didn't agree that it was an amazin' project with awesome results, she could fail me. But I think she will be just as amazed as everyone else. My grade will be fine, Dad."

"Well, Sydney, you definitely had this all planned out. I have to say, I am more than impressed with your accomplishment. And your mom was right!"

"She was? About what?"

"Well, now is as good a time as any to let all of you know that when we reopen Ivy's shop, Sydney will be in charge of mostly everything."

"Wow, Dad, thanks, but when did Mom say this?"

"To be honest, and for those of you who think I am nuts and are skeptical about what I am about to tell you, well, please be assured that I thought I was losin' my mind, so just bear with me," Parker says. "So Ivy came to me in my dreams one night and told me that Sydney had something absolutely amazin' in the works. She also told me that I would see just how great you are and that she wanted us

231

to reopen the shop, and she gave specific instructions that you are to run the shop, Syd."

Sydney sits there with tears starting in her eyes as she thinks about her visit from her grandad and her mom as well. "Dad, she visited me too! She said she was so proud of me! I will accept and make you both proud!"

"Syd, you couldn't make me prouder than I am right now! I love you, sweetheart!"

"I love you too, Dad! But I need a co-helper. Well, maybe two? By chance, would either of my two besties be interested in applyin' for the position?"

"Syd, you know I am down!" Sophie starts to kind of whisper, but at a tone that mostly everyone can still hear. "But Syd, it's a shop for mostly women. Do you think that Lucas is even gonna wanna be in there?"

"I accept, Sydney! When do I start?" Lucas proudly accepts.

"Well, then, I stand corrected! Welcome to the team, Lucas! We are glad to have ya!"

"Most definitely! Dad, when were you thinkin' of openin'?"

"I was leavin' that up to you! It's mostly in your hands. I will help with the orderin' and that end of the business if you can handle the rest?"

"Sure thing, Dad. I got this!"

They all finish up eating and head home for the night.

Lucas texts Sydney when he gets home.

Lucas
Thank you!

Sydney
For?

Lucas
Everything today! You are way too kind to me.

Sydney
Nah! You deserve it! It's not your fault that your dad passed and you didn't know how to express

*your feelins. I completely understand that, and
I won't ever hold it against you. I am just glad
you finally told me, and now we can work on
the new you together!*

Lucas
Together?

Sydney
Yes, silly, together!

Lucas
Sydney?

Sydney
Yes, Lucas?

Lucas
Can I ask you something?

Sydney
Sure thing. Shoot!

Lucas
Umm, do you have a boyfriend?

Sydney
*Nope. No, I do not. Why? Are you askin' me to
go out with you?*

Lucas
*No, never mind. I was just curious. I am just
glad to be friends and didn't want to upset your
boyfriend if you had one.*

Wow that was a close one! Lucas thinks to himself as he finishes
his text before heading to bed.

Sydney
*Well, we are good in that department! So
no worries, okay? I will see you in school
tomorrow.*

Lucas
Okay, no problem. Have a nice sleep.

Have a nice sleep? What is wrong with me? he thinks to himself.

Sydney
U2! 😊 *Good night!*

Sydney lays her phone down and closes her eyes. It's only been, like, twenty minutes and she hears *buzz buzz*. She opens her phone to another text. *Hmm, wonder who this is*, she thinks to herself.

Lucas
Sydney? I hope I am not waking you. But I was wonderin' if you had an offer for the dance on Friday night? You can just let me know in the mornin'. Good night. Sweet dreams.

"Wow, I am glad he can't see that I have received and read his message! Wow, what do I do? I'll text Sophie. Hopefully, she's still awake."

Sydney
Sophie, you awake?

A few minutes pass, then *buzz buzz*.

Sophie
Yeah, I am up. What's up, bestie?

Sydney
Umm, I do not know how to say this, but I was just asked to the dance Friday night!

Sophie
I am afraid to ask. But by who?

Sydney
Well...

Sophie
That's a very deep subject, so come on, spill it. Who asked you?

Sydney
Lucas!

There's a few minutes of silence before Sydney gets a reply.

Sophie
*Well, I was not expectin' that! Umm, you
should! I would be so grateful to help you get
ready too!*

Sydney
*Talk about not expectin' things. LOL.
Are you sure? I mean, it's Lucas!*

Sophie
*I am goin' with my gut on this one, bestie!
Yes, you need to go!*

Sydney
Your gut? What, are you hungry again?

Sophie
*Nope. Just call it bestie intuition. You are
goin' to be so beautiful! Besides, I will let you
in on a li'l secret that I seriously doubt you
picked up on. But I think Lucas likes you!*

Sydney
Lucas? Likes me? Nah, you are dead wrong!

Sophie
*Not the way I see it. Like I said before, he has
a thing for you. You just wait and see. But
that doesn't matter right now. Besides, it's just
a dance. You should go! You will go! Okay,
good night. We will talk more in the mornin'!
Love you!*

Sydney
Okay, good night. Love you too!

Sydney closes her eyes and tries to go back to sleep again.

*****

The radio announcer says, "Good mornin', Lexington! What a beautiful mornin' it is! So in the news this mornin', wow! What a shocker, folks! If you didn't already know, our beloved Chase Payne is actually Sydney Ashcraft! And Wyatt Gentry is Sophie Abbott? Who knew? Well, they did, apparently, and now all of the rest of us! What an amazin' journey those girls must have been on! Go, girls!

"In another news today…"

Sydney hits the Snooze and smiles uncontrollably at her achievement. "I made the news! We made the news! Whoo-hoo! We made the news! Now we are small-town famous!" she shouts.

"Hey, newsmaker, I take it you are up by the sounds of it?" Sydney hears from downstairs.

"Yes, Em, I am up and vertical! I will be down in a few minutes!" Sydney yells back. She quickly gets herself together and makes her way downstairs to the kitchen.

"Good mornin', bright eyes! Wow, you look amazin' this mornin'! What did you do differently?"

"Nothing, Em. Same ole same routine. But I did get asked to the dance for Friday!"

"Yep, there it is! That's what I am talkin' about! So who's the lucky boy?"

Parker comes into the kitchen just in time to hear Emma say about a lucky boy. "Lucky boy? Who's a lucky boy? What's he so lucky for?"

"A young boy has asked Syd to the dance on Friday night. I was just askin' who he was."

"Oh, any boy takin' my li'l filly to a dance is way lucky! I have a feelin' I already know who, though."

"Dad, you don't have a clue. But you do know him."

"Syd, I am your dad. I am smarter than you think! I can respectfully say 100 percent without a doubt that it is Lucas! Tell me I am wrong and I will drop it!"

Sydney looks at him with a confused look, like, "How did he know?" "Actually, you are right. But he had to have asked you first! That's how you know."

"Nope, he didn't, and I told you I knew! Syd, it's so obvious that he likes you. So what are you gonna say?"

"Wow, I must be so super distracted with my project that I never even saw it! Sophie said that she had seen it too! I told her she was crazy! Ah now it makes sense why he asked me last night if I had a boyfriend. Now I know why. I bet he's buildin' up to ask me out. Oh, I think I am goin' to be sick."

"Syd, he is a great boy, and I approve, if that's what got you all uptight."

"No, I just am not ready for a relationship! But if he asks me, I don't want to be mean and turn him down. Dad, what do I do?"

"Syd, let's not jump to conclusions just yet! Let's just get you through the dance and go from there. Maybe I can sit and talk to him. But for now, you have to get off to school! I will try to make it in today to see your presentation. What time should we try to make it in?"

"My class is after lunch. So I would say be there by 1:00 p.m. Em, can you drive me to school today?"

"Okay, I will try to be there!"

"Thanks, Dad!"

"Yes, sure thing! Let me grab my purse and keys."

"Dad, check to see if Obee can come too! I love you! See you later!" Sydney says as she heads out the door.

Emma follows Sydney out the door. They get into Emma's car and head out the driveway.

"I will do my best to come to school later today. If for any reason I can't make it, I wish you all the luck! You are so amazin', Sydney! Your mother would be so proud! Do you wanna stop and get anything from the mini market before school?"

"Actually, yes, please, I would."

"Okay, I will buy you whatever you want, and can you please get me a gallon of milk, please?"

"Sure thing, Em!"

Emma pulls in and stops and gives her card to Sydney to go get what she needs. After a few minutes, she returns with two coffees, a gallon of milk, and a bag draped on her arm.

"Thanks, Em! I got some cappuccinos for Sophie and me and a snack! Here's your milk. Oh, and your card. Sorry, my hands were full."

"It's okay. I knew you would give it to me, if not now, then when we got to your school. Does Sophie need to be picked up?"

"Let me ask."

Sydney
Hey, bestie, you need a ride?

Sophie
Umm, sure, if you can!

Sydney
Cool, no problem! Be there in a few.

Sophie
👍

"Can we please pick her up? Thanks!"

"Sure! Let's go get her."

"Thanks, Em. You are the greatest!" Sydney can't wait to see her bestie. As they pull up, Sydney sees Sophie waiting for them, so she gets ready to open the door and jump out so they can sit in the back together.

"Hey, bestie! Did you hear? We made local news! Also, I got us a cappuccino and a snack courtesy of Em!"

"Wow, cool. Thanks, Emma! You are the best! Seriously, Sydney, that's way cool!"

"No problem, girls. It's my pleasure. Okay, now, off to school. I hope you girls have a good day at school."

"Em, I may need your help after school lookin' for a dress. Do you think you can help me?"

"A dress? Wow, sure, I would love to!"

"Cool, Em. But I need to make sure that it's still a go before I ask you to commit to helpin' me. I just wanted to make sure if I needed you that you would be able to help me out."

"Oh well, so far I do not have any other plans at the moment. So I sure can help. Okay, girls, here we are. I can pick y'all up later this afternoon if you need me to."

"Yes, could you, Em?"

"Sure thing. See you girls later."

"Bye, Em! Love you!"

"Bye-bye, Emma. See you later on. Thanks again for the cappuccino and snack."

"No problem, Sophie. Okay, girls, goodbye!" Emma says as she puts the car back into drive and pulls away.

"So, Syd, how do you think school will be today?"

"Well, I do not know. But I have a feelin' we are gonna be busy."

"Why do you say that?"

"Well, look at that mob of students headed this way."

"Oh boy, hopefully they are headed somewhere else," Sophie says wth a chuckle.

What seems to be the leader of this mob of students steps up and says, "Sydney, Sophie, we have come to you today to get your autographs! You are so famous, and we want to show that you can be any plain-Jane person and do amazin' things. So would you please do us the honor and sign these pics we printed out?"

"Ummm, okay, sure. But we are still just plain Janes."

"It's okay, you have given us regular plain Janes something to look forward to."

"Yes, I would love to sign your prints."

"Thanks! It means a lot."

Sydney and Sophie sign a few pictures for the group, and then they go about their day as normal.

At lunch, Sydney is waiting for Sophie in the cafeteria.

"Hey, Sophie, over here!" Sydney is waving her arms and hands around back and forth to get Sophie's attention.

"Ah, there you are! Ooo, I'm so excited! I can't wait for your presentation."

"I know. Me either. I'm so nervous! I wonder if anyone from outside of school will show up."

"Syd, we can go to the office and see if anyone has called in sayin' that they are considering comin'."

"Yeah, okay. After lunch?"

"Sounds good to me, Syd! Hey, look, there's Lucas! Should I try to get his attention so he can sit with us?"

"Sure! Lucas! Over here."

"So much for me tryin' to get his attention, Syd!" Sophie says with a tad bit of jealousy in her voice.

"Sorry, bestie, but you mentioned it and I agreed, so I thought I could shout out for him."

"Hey, guys! I didn't know you had lunch at the same time as me. May I sit with y'all?"

"Yes, Lucas, we would love for you to sit with us," Sophie says with a smile on her face.

"Thanks, Sophie. I very much appreciate your kindness. If you had asked me if I thought we would be in this friendship situation a few weeks ago, I would have laughed and said no way! But I am truly grateful that we have moved into this status of friendship. It means a lot to me. Thanks, guys. Is it okay I call y'all *guys*?"

"Yes, it's fine, and we agree, don't we, Sophie? That we would not have guessed that we ever be friends to this level a few weeks ago either."

"True, bestie, very true! We are glad we have gotten past all the immaturity."

"Cool, awesome, 'cause I have to ask you guys something important. Sydney, I sent you a message last night. Did you get it? If so, what is your opinion on the matter?"

"Yes, Lucas, I did get your message, and I would be glad to accompany you to the dance on Friday night."

"Cool, 'cause this may be a li'l weird, but, Sophie, I did not know your number, so I couldn't ask you, but how would you like to accompany Sydney and me to the dance on Friday?"

"Wait, seriously? You want me to tag along like a third-wheel kind of situation?"

"No, as three good friends just out to have a good time."

"Syd, how do you feel about this? Are you okay with it?"

"Yes, ma'am, I think it's a great idea! Please join us?"

"Okay, I will go with you guys! Thank you, Lucas, for the invite. It means a lot!"

Ring…ring…

"And that, my peeps, is the end of lunch! Sophie, please come with me to the office. See ya later, Lucas."

"Do you think I would be able to get a pass to your class to watch your presentation? Or would you not want me to come watch?"

"I'm cool with it if you can get a pass. I just don't know where or how you would get one. I bet if you just ask Ms. Dixon, she would just write you one out after I was finished to get you back into your regular class. Stop up and ask her. Okay, hopefully, we will see you up there." Sydney grabs Sophie by the arm and pulls her to follow her to the office.

"Okay, Sydney, I will go ask. Talk to you later!" Lucas shouts out as the girls walk away.

When the girls get to the office, the secretary asks, "What can I do for you girls?"

"Are there any messages for Sydney Ashcraft?"

"Not at the moment," she says apologetically.

"I may have some family comin' to see my presentation for my project. Can you please send them to Ms. Dixon's room if and when they show up?"

"I can do that. Can I help you with anything else?"

"Yes. Is Mrs. Gossett available?"

"Yes, just a minute. Let me call her office." She picks up the phone and dials a number. "Mrs. Gossett, do you have a moment? There is a student here who would like to talk with you. Okay, I will send her back." The secretary hangs up the phone and turns toward Sydney and Sophie. "She said that you may go back."

"Thanks!" Sydney whispers to Sophie, "I will be right back."

"Okay, I will be right here." Sophie laughs.

Sydney gets to Mrs. Gossett's door and softly knocks. "Mrs. Gossett, it's me, Sydney."

"Yes, please come in, Sydney. How are you doing today?"

"I am good! I was just checkin' to see if you will able to make it up to Ms. Dixon's room?"

"Sure, I can come up for a li'l bit to see your presentation."

"Cool! Thanks! Well, I hope some of my family can make it!"

"I tell you what? I have an idea," Cora says as she has an aha moment.

"Really? What's that?"

"So it just so happens that I do some photography work on the side when I'm not here watchin' over all of you wonderful students."

"Oh, that's cool! But how is that supposed to help me?" Sydney asks in confusion.

"Well, let me show you." Cora reaches down under her desk and pulls out what looks like a black camera bag. "In here I have a piece of equipment that I can make you a special gift that you can share with your family and cherish forever."

"I'm listenin'."

"I can video it for you! So if you like, I can definitely do that. It will be my gift to you for bein' such an amazin' student with a very bright future!"

"Wow! Really? Oh, Mrs. Gossett, I do not know what to say right now!" Sydney starts to tear up.

Cora comes around the desk and gives Sydney a hug and pats her on the back. She lets go of Sydney, looks her in the eye and says, "It's okay! You did an amazin' thing. It took a lot of guts to do what you did, and you deserve to have that documented to share with your li'l ones someday. So what do you say? Do you wanna hire me?"

"I don't know if I can afford you," Sydney says, laughing and smiling again.

"I tell you what? I will make this very affordable! All I ask is that you be a good student like I saw at your party and we will call it even. What do you say?"

"Well, that is definitely doable! Hey, can I let you in on a li'l secret?"

"Sure can."

"So you know that Lucas, Sophie, and I are all talkin' and gettin' along like three peas in a pod now?" Cora nods as Sydney continues, "Well, last night, after the party, he sent me a text. He asked me to the dance on Friday night. But that's not the real fire starter! When we got to school, he asked Sophie too!"

"Wow, that's super amazin'! Most boys can't find one date, and he's got one for each arm! I am so glad for you guys. It should be a fun night for you all. Okay, well, let's get you up to class so you can do your presentation."

"Okay, cool!"

As they walk out in the front of the office, she hears some familiar voices. Then she sees her dad, Emma, and Obee. "Hey, guys, I am so glad you made it! We were just headed up to the classroom."

"Syd? What did you do?"

"Oh, she didn't do anything, Mr. Ashcraft."

"Please call me Parker. Then what's she doin' in your office?"

"She was comin' to see if I could make it to her presentation. I gladly accepted, and I also volunteered to record it for her as a keepsake so she could share this very important day with her li'l ones someday."

"Oh well, that's a relief," Parker says, sighing and laughing.

Emma places her hand on his shoulder and says, "Parker, Sydney is a good kid."

"I know, Emma. I was just hopin' that she didn't beat someone up again," Parker says, laughing.

"Okay, come on, everyone, let's get up to my class." Sydney directs her family to follow her as they file out of the office and out into the hall.

Cora directs the secretary to hold all her calls till she returns. Just as she exits the office, she sees Henry. "Afternoon, love. I wasn't sure if you would be able to make it."

"Well, this is *big* history, and I wouldn't want to miss it for anything! I am so glad to be a part of it."

"Okay, here is my class. Let me make sure it's okay for you all to come in now." Sydney goes into the classroom. A few minutes later, she returns to let everyone in.

"Good afternoon, everyone. I am Ms. Julia Dixon. Welcome to History 201. I will just have everyone come to the back of the room, and you can sit at an empty desk or stand, whatever suits you best. Sydney, you are just in time. You are up next."

"Oh, okay, thanks." Sydney makes her way to the front of the classroom. "Well, everyone, hello. I am Sydney Ashcraft. Or more recently known as Chase Payne." Sydney clears her throat, and as she continues, some of her classmates start whispering softly among themselves.

"Class, let's show some respect, and please be quiet for Sydney."

As the room quiets, Sydney begins again, "So I did a very bold project, and I had to keep it quiet till the absolute very end. Well, almost quiet. My bestie, Sophie, and my friend Obee—he's there in the back of the room," Obee waves to her classmates as they turn to see who Obee is. Sydney continues, "Well, if I had to tell anyone, these were my two."

Parker starts to look around like "What about me? I'm Dad?

"Sorry, Dad, you could have thrown a monkey wrench in my plan. If it would have been any other situation, you would have been up there with Sophie." He smiles and nods in understanding.

"But for my change, I wanted to prove that females were just as good a horse rider as males. I noticed that not many women were jockeys, so I decided to see if it was even possible to win a race. It turns out I won many races."

Her classmates start clapping.

"So not only am I a female and did as well, for this season at least, or better than most experienced males, but I am also the youngest female to win at least one race. And I took it to the next level and won seven races. I also had my bestie, Sophie, join me in the excitement. She was Wyatt Gentry!"

Her classmates start whistling and cheering. Sydney has a smile from ear to ear.

"Thank you, thank you so very much! I truly appreciate the support! But I just want to let my motto be that anything is possible with God's love and your determination! I am livin' proof!"

A classmate yells out, "Hey, Sydney, wanna be my date for the dance Friday?"

"I am sorry, I have to decline. I already have a date for the dance Friday. But thank you for the offer."

"Aww, man, well, how about your bestie? Can she be my date?"

Sophie stands up from her desk and says, "Sorry, I'm spoken for as well," then she sits back down, grinning bigger than ever before.

"Bummer!" says the classmate. The rest of the classmates start softly laughing.

"The hardest part was not knowin' if I was able to pull it off. If anyone other than my go-to two were to find out too early, I wasn't sure how it would have ended up. But the horse community was very invitin' and acceptin'. So I have hopefully changed something for the better by my li'l experiment. If anything, maybe more females and young ones will decide to take up an interest in horse racin'. I know the adrenaline rush it gave me was so excitin'. I lived for it every race day."

"Sydney, will you consider continuing this adventure in the future?" Julia asks.

"Oh, definitely, Ms. Dixon. We will be back this fall and rarin' to take more trophies! By *we* I mean Sophie, Lucas, and I. Sorry, Lucas. You are an amazin' young rider, and I am so proud to have you on our team. Hope I didn't embarrass you any."

Lucas waves his hands and says, "Nah, they were bound to find out eventually. It's all good."

"Wow, what a story and adventure, Sydney. If you have to decide again to do this project over, would you change your topic or choose this one again? And why?" Julia asks.

"Well, to be honest, I would definitely do it again. Like I said, there's nothing more freein' than the rush of adrenaline you get when ridin' in a race. Not to mention all the awesomeness that comes with winnin' a trophy. Now my name is on the board permanently at the track, not only as the youngest rider—but the youngest female rider, I might add—also for taking the most first-place wins in a season. That also lands my name on the board for most wins in any given season. I wouldn't change that for anything."

"Well, Sydney, it definitely sounds like you're going down in the history books, at least at the track, anyways. Good job and good luck with your next season. I will be cheering for you."

"Thanks! That concludes my presentation. I want to thank my family and my bestie for all the love and support that they have shown me. It truly makes a difference! Thank you, everyone, for your attention and thoughtfulness."

The class claps and cheers as Sydney takes her seat.

"If our guest would exit back out as from which they came, that would be great. Thank you all for coming."

When they get out in the hall, Cora states, "I will get you down to the front doors. Parker, I will send a copy of the video home with Sydney."

"Thanks, Cora. That was very nice of you."

As the day goes on and the school day ends, Sophie and Sydney meet up to get a ride home with Emma. As they wait, Lucas catches up with them.

"Hey, girls, just a quick question. Are we tryin' to match for the dance, or what color scheme would you like to go as? Any ideas? This is my first dance, and I am so nervous. I do not know what I am supposed to do."

"Lucas, it's our first dance too! We can pick a color so that we don't all clash. Let us do a li'l shoppin' tonight and get back to ya on all that."

"Okay, Sydney, sounds great! Well, I gotta get home. I have a few chores to get done. Hey, can I come over later to ride?"

"Sure, I will be there, and Dad should be too. But if not, I can give ya a hand. So see ya later?"

"You betcha! Bye, Sydney. Bye, Sophie." Lucas takes off running off into the crowd of students.

"Oh, there's Emma. Come on, let's go!" Sydney tugs at Sophie and starts to run toward Emma's car.

Emma starts talking to the girls through the window as they open the doors to get in. "So, girls, where are we off to?"

"Well, Em, we need to find some dresses. Not only did Lucas ask me to the dance, but he asked Sophie too!"

"Wow, that's awesome and strange at the same time!"

"Yeah, he wanted us to all go as friends. So we gratefully accepted. So we need dresses. Also, if we could stop by the shop and get a few other li'l supplies, that would be great!"

"Sure, I do not see an issue with that. So let's go to the shop first, then we can go dress shoppin'. How does that sound?"

"Good to me!" Sophie exclaims.

"Yep, definitely a great plan!" Sydney chimes in.

When they get to the shop, Emma and the girls go in and pick up some fresh, new makeup, and Emma allows them to each pick a new piece of jewelry to go with their ensemble.

"Just think, Sydney. We are just days away from our grand reopenin'. What do you think about that?" Emma asks.

"I am so excited, Em. And to think I will be in charge. That's a *huge* responsibility. I think I may need a special team associate to help me keep everything straight and on track. I know just the person to fill those shoes."

Sophie looks at Sydney and says, "Oh yeah, just who would that be? 'Cause I am already helpin' out."

"Silly goose, it's you! Will you be my special team associate? I think you would be a great partner. You have amazin' fashion sense, and I definitely need someone with good fashion sense! Lord knows I don't have a lick of it in me." The girls laugh.

"I accept, Sydney! Now I hate to rain on your li'l parade, but, bestie, we are gonna be goin' to the dance in our birthday suits if we don't get somewhere and try to find some dresses."

"So true, girls. If you have everything you need from here, let's get y'all to a dress shop," Emma states, trying to get them to finish up so they can move on to a dress shop.

They finish up collecting supplies from the shop and head to a local dress shop. They spend about an hour in the dress shop looking through and trying on all styles and colors of dresses till they finally find the ones that suit them each best and go well together.

CHAPTER 26

Grand Reopening

The rest of the week flies by in the blink of an eye. The girls have been getting things ready in the afternoons at the shop for Saturday's grand reopening. It's Friday and the day of their first dance. It's the launch from Groundhog Day.

"Seriously, if this day goes any slower, I bet we could run really fast and jump into another dimension. Why is it days fly by when you don't have anything planned or excitin' to do, and the days you do it's like the day has Chinese disease or something?"

"Syd, I am almost afraid to ask. What is that?"

"Oh, its dragon ass. Oh, wow, okay, yeah, I can see it." Sophie laughs. "So you wanna meet at my house or yours to get ready?"

"Either. It doesn't matter to me. My room is bigger."

"Well, that's not fair. I can't help it that I have to share mine with my sister."

"I know. I was just pickin'. I'm sorry."

"It's okay. I forgive you, bestie. But you are right, your room is bigger, so let's go to your house."

"Sophie! What am I gonna do with you?"

"Love me, like always?" Sophie says, trying to be funny.

"Okay, do you want Em to come get us? We can go to your house and get your things and go back to my place to get ready."

"Sure, that works."

"Okay, I will message Em and have her pick us up here after school."

Just then, Lucas walks over and startles the girls. "Boo!"

The girls scream, then turn and lightly start beating on Lucas. "You are so lucky! You were just about dateless for tonight—you almost scared us to death!"

"Hey, hey, sorry, ladies. So are you gals ready for tonight? I can't wait to show off some of the most beautiful ladies in this school right here tonight!"

"Lucas? Really, there's no need to butter us up. We aren't toast."

"Well, speak for yourself, Sophie. I am actually flattered that Lucas thinks we are the most beautiful ladies in school."

"Yuck, get a room, you two! So, Lucas, we are goin' to Sydney's after school to get ready. Are we comin' to come get you, or are you comin' to get us?"

"Well, ladies, I will have Mom bring me to you. But her car is not big enough for all of us. So I was wonderin' if maybe you have another idea?"

"I can ask Em if she can help. As long as she doesn't have anything goin' on, she will be more than happy to bring us."

"Awesome! Okay, well, let's just pray she doesn't have anything goin' on, then." Lucas laughs.

"I am textin' her as we speak. So now we wait to hear if she is available or not."

"Okay, well, lunch is just about over, and I can't be late for my next class. I will see you beautiful ladies later this evenin'.""

"Okay, bye!" Sydney and Sophie say simultaneously.

"Wow, if you told me a few weeks ago that we would be friends with Lucas like we are and that he was takin' us both to the dance, I would have told you that you were crazy! He's made a complete 360 from who he was."

"I know, it's almost scary and unreal. I am waitin' for his nasty side to come back. I sure hope it doesn't. I really like this new Lucas."

"Syd, you can't be serious? You have gone and done lost your mind, bestie."

"No, I didn't mean I like him like that. I just mean it's nice to have another friend. We can help each other through hard times 'cause we've both lost someone very close to us."

"Yeah, I remember bein' there for my bestie, but I guess that's just a thing of the past."

"Aww, stop it! You are ridiculous, and all I am hearin' is blah blah blah." The bell rings, and they both laugh and head to their next class. "Love you, Sophie!"

"Love you too, Syd. See you after school!"

They split ways and head to their next class. Sydney gets a text on her way to her next class.

> Emma
> *Sure thing, Sydney. I can take you kids to the dance. While you are there, I can do some shoppin' and then pick y'all back up afterward. How does that sound?*
>
> Sydney
> *Sounds sweet, Em. Thanks!*

The rest of the school day continues to drag on, but the day has finally come to an end after what seems like an endless day. As Sydney waits for Sophie, she sees Claire pull up. Just then, she hears, "Heads up!"

"Lucas! I hear you but don't see you, so don't you dare!" Sydney screams.

"Behind you! Sorry, I was tryin' to catch this ball and thought it was gonna hit ya. Thank God it didn't!"

"Ha! You can be grateful it didn't. Hey, your mom just pulled up."

"Oh, hey, Mom!" Lucas yells to her. "Give me one minute and I will be right back." Lucas takes off running in the complete opposite direction, back into the crowd of students standing outside, waiting for buses and rides. As fast as Lucas disappears, Sophie appears through the crowd.

"Hey, Syd!"

"Sophie! Hey, I am so excited for tonight! I didn't think this day was ever gonna end!" Sydney hugs Sophie as she nears. "Em still isn't here. But she should be here very soon."

"I agree! Hey, is that her way in the back of the pickup line?"

"Yep, but we should just wait here. I don't want her upset at us for bein' impatient."

All of a sudden, out of nowhere Lucas runs by and shouts to the girls, "See you beautiful ladies later!"

"Okay, see ya soon!" Sydney says as she looks at Sophie's disgusted look on her face. "What's up with you? Why the sour face?"

"Why must he keep sayin' that to us?"

"Sophie, he is just bein' nice. Plus, he's super excited, just like us! So let's just let it slide till tomorrow, then after the dance, if he keeps it up, then I will say something, okay?"

"Yeah, sure, I guess so."

"Well, here's Em. Let's get you to your house so we can get your things and get to mine to get ready. Or next thing you know, Lucas will be there to get us and we won't even be ready." Sydney and Sophie start laughing as they get in Emma's car.

"What's so funny, girls?"

"Ah, nothing. We were just sayin' how we needed to get movin' before Lucas gets to our place and we aren't even ready," Sydney says, laughing.

"Yeah, I do not think Lucas, or anyone else, for that matter, wants to see us in our birthday suits!" Sophie chimes in.

"That would be a huge issue, wouldn't it? He asks you two to go to the dance with him, and he arrives only to find out that y'all aren't even ready. Nope, that would not be so good." Emma starts to laugh too. "So let's get Sophie's things and get a scootin' on home."

They get to Sophie's, get her dress and accessories, then head for the Ashcraft ranch. As they arrive, Emma says, "Be careful when gettin' out of the car. We don't wanna mess up Sophie's dress this late in the game. And I wanted to offer you girls, if you need any more jewelry, that you can look through Ivy's. Parker said it would be okay. Just please be very careful not to lose whatever you take."

"Oh, okay, thanks! And we will be careful," they say as Emma parks the car and they jump out and run as quickly as they can into the house and up to Sydney's room and they shut the bedroom door so quickly it slams.

"Whoops! Sorry, Syd. I wasn't tryin' to take out your door."

"It's okay. It happens all the time. No biggie."

The girls work together to get ready in time for Lucas to come over. They do each other's hair and makeup.

"This is so fun! I really hope to let loose a li'l and have a great time tonight with you and Lucas!"

"Yes, Syd, I think we will have a bunch of fun tonight! I am so glad he asked us both. To be honest, I was a li'l jealous that he asked you and sad that I possibly was not goin'."

"Well, it's all good, 'cause he thought of that and invited us both!"

"You do not think it's too weird, do you? I mean, that he is takin' two girls instead of one?"

"Nah, hopefully we can start a new trend," Syd says as she starts to laugh.

Just then, Emma yells up the stairs to the girls, "How's everything goin', ladies? Lucas should be here soon."

Sydney yells back down the stairs, "We are doin' good! We are almost ready."

Emma notices a car coming in the driveway. She doesn't recognize it at first, then she realizes it's Lucas and his mom.

"Sydney! Lucas and his mom are comin' in the lane!" Emma shouts up the stairs.

"Ah, okay. Thanks, Em!"

"Syd, we gotta hurry and finish up!"

"It's okay. We got this. Just calm down. Let's just finish up and get downstairs. Em is gonna wanna get pics of us. Especially since this is my first dance. I wish my mom were here for this." Sydney gets a tear in her eye, and she tries to hide it from Sophie.

"Hey, girl, I love you, and I completely understand, but now is not the time to be so emotional. You are goin' to mess up your makeup," Sophie says, trying to comfort Sydney. "Come on, breathe with me. Take a deep breath in and out again." They both inhale and then exhale.

Sophie reaches for Sydney to give her a hug. "You got this, bestie. This will be a great night, I promise you."

"I'm sorry. I know. It's just this is another one of many firsts my mom will miss."

"Syd, she's not missin' anything. She is always with you even if you can't see her I can promise you that! Now, are we complete and ready to go see how nice Lucas looks?"

"Yes, I think so." Sydney smiles and dabs away the few tears that did manage to expose themselves. "Okay, all good," she says as she takes another deep breath and releases it.

They hear the doorbell. "Girls!" Emma shouts out as she answers the door. "Oh, hello, Lucas. You look so handsome, young man! The girls will be down in just a minute."

"Thank you, Ms. Emma. Umm, may I please have a glass of water? I am so nervous, and it's makin' me a li'l thirsty."

"Yes, sir, Lucas, follow me into the kitchen and I can get you some. Would you like a glass or bottle of water?"

"Either is fine. I am not picky. Thanks."

"Okay, I will give you a bottle. It will be colder and more quenching."

"Thank you so much. Have you seen the girls yet?" Lucas asks.

"No, not yet. So is this your first dance, Lucas?"

"Actually, yes, it is. I have always been too shy to ask anyone to the dances."

"Well, I must say that you seem to have gotten over that fear."

"What makes you say that?" Lucas wonders out loud.

"Well, you asked two, Sydney and Sophie. Seems like a step up from none. Seems like a great pair to ask, too, if I must say so myself."

"Oh yeah, true. Sorry. Apparently, I can't even think straight when I am nervous either!" he says as he starts to laugh.

"There you go. Laughin' helps to ease your tension. Don't worry, everything will be great! I hope you have a great time this evenin'," Emma says to try to loosen up Lucas before he makes himself sick from nerves.

Meanwhile, back upstairs, the girls are picking out some jewelry to finish off their look. "Okay, I think that's just about it. Oh, bestie, you look so beautiful!"

"Yes, so do you, Syd. How do you think Lucas will look?"

"Well, we are about to find out. Are you ready to make our way downstairs?"

"Well, I guess I am as ready as I'll ever be. I just wish my stomach would quit. I thought this team-date thing would be easier, but oh, not even close!" Sophie says as she rubs her stomach.

"Follow me." Sydney goes back to her room and gets Sophie a chewable Tums. "See if this helps."

"Okay, let's hope so. Can I take some in case they do and it happens again?"

"Sure. Here, you can even carry them. Now, let's get goin', before Lucas thinks we've backed out."

"Girls, are you almost done?" Emma shouts up the stairs.

"Yes, comin', Em!"

Lucas walks around the corner to the bottom of the stairs and waits to see his dates. Just then, the girls appear at the top of the stairs. They stop and lock stares with Lucas like they are frozen in time.

Emma sees this and tries to hurry them along. "Girls, are you okay? Come on down so we can get some pictures."

Sydney whispers to Sophie, "Now I need one. Can you please give me a Tums?"

"Sure, here ya go."

"Sorry, we are comin', Em," Sydney says as they start to descend the stairs.

Lucas just stands there in awe of his beautiful dates for the evening. Sydney has on a floor-length baby-blue dress with wide straps and sequins all evenly placed over the entire dress. Sophie has a floor-length yellow dress as well. Her dress has very similar straps and sequins over the breast area and along the bottom, with a small satin ribbon that goes around her waist to form a bow in the back with long tails.

He can't believe that they both said yes and how he is so lucky to have two very beautiful ladies by his side on such a special night. The closer they get, the more intense his feelings become. He takes a few steps back as they get to the bottom.

"Wow, ladies, you are…I am…speechless. I have to be…oh, umm, one of the luckiest guys on earth tonight! Umm, I am sorry, I have something for each of you. I wasn't sure what color you chose for your dresses, so I just got you each a white lily corsage."

"Oh, thank you. It's gorgeous, Lucas! And you look very handsome. Would you like to put mine on my wrist?"

"Ah, sure." He takes Sydney's corsage and tries to carefully remove it from the packaging so as not to damage it. His hand trembles as he finally gets it open.

Sydney notices how bad he is shaking and reaches for his hand and places it between her hands and says calmly, "It's okay, Lucas. You do not need to be so nervous. It's just a dance. Here, take one of these." She looks toward Sophie and winks.

"Ah, sorry, Syd. At first I was wonderin' what you were doin'." Sophie reaches into her purse and pulls out the Tums and gives one to Sydney. "Sorry, I was spacin' and just hopin' that tonight's going to be a lot of fun."

"Sophie, it will be! Lucas, here, for your nerves, or the very least, the butterflies in your stomach."

"Thanks, Sydney." He takes one and chews it up as he places the corsage on her wrist. He chuckles and says, "Honestly, when I saw Sophie give you something earlier, I thought it was gum for your breath or something like that. Not that I think your breath smells or anything. Or I mean that you thought your breath…I am sorry, I will just shut up now."

Sydney laughs. "Sorry, not laughin' at you but at the fact that we are all so nervous about this. We are just three friends goin' to a dance together! Come on, guys, it's just another day, except we are dressed a lot nicer than normal."

"Yeah, you are right, Syd. Lucas, you want to put my corsage on for me, please?"

"Sure thing, Sophie. I must say, though, that you ladies are absolutely beautiful tonight. Thank you again for acceptin' my invite to join me."

"I have a feelin' that we will be glad we did and we won't forget tonight."

"Okay, kiddos, let's get some pictures so we can getcha outta here and off to the dance." Emma turns for her camera while they stand beside one another and prepare for the camera session. "I must admit, when Sydney mentioned that you asked both her and Sophie to the dance together, I was confused as to why you asked them both, and I thought it was a bit odd, but you are a great kid. I think you are doin' a great thing. Just a few more. Would you like any of each of you separate, the girls together, and Lucas with each of you alone?"

"Yes, ma'am. Could we please do that?" Lucas asks.

"Oh, okay, I am down. If that's what Lucas wants, I see no harm in it."

"Okay, if Syd is chill with it, then I am too!"

Emma keeps shooting away as the kids change places and they get all the shots in.

"Thanks, Em. That should be great! Are you guys ready to go? The dance starts in less than an hour."

"Yes, I am sorry, Sydney, but this is your first dance. I guess I just got carried away. Okay, let's get you guys to school. Let me grab my purse, keys, and I will bring the camera along as well for one last shot before you all head in for the dance."

The girls grab their purses, and Lucas takes them by the hand and walks them to the car.

"Lucas, you are makin' me feel like a princess."

"Well, isn't that how a lady should be treated?"

"I guess so. I'm just not used to bein' so spoiled. I hope I don't get too used to it." Sydney laughs.

As they near the car, Lucas lets go of the girls hands and rushes up to the car to open the passenger-side back door. "Would you ladies like to sit in the back?"

"Yes, sir, that would be fabulous," Sydney says in an English accent.

"And for the other lady, madam, would you also like to sit in the back?"

"Why, certainly, sir, that would be just delightful." Sophie tries to mock Sydney, but it's not quite on par, but she doesn't care because they are just having the time of their lives.

Lucas says to Sophie, "Right this way, madam." He holds out his hand for hers. He walks her around to the driver's-side back door and says, "Let me get this door here for you and you have a great evenin'." As she sits and swings her legs in, Lucas shuts the door once she's all seated. Then he runs back over to Sydney's side and closes her door, and he sees Emma making her way to the car, so he rushes over to her door and opens hers as well.

"Ma'am, I shall get your door. Please have a seat, and thank you for your services this lovely evenin'." He shuts her door and quickly gets in, and they take off for the school.

"Lucas, where did you get such amazin' manners?" Emma asks in amazement.

"Well, you see, my mother wanted me to be more proper due to my dad bein' in the military and all. She didn't want me to embarrass him, so she had me take some classes on proper etiquette. At that time, I thought, what a waste, but it kinda made me feel more genuine, and I think it added a bit of charm to the evenin' already by makin' the ladies feel more special."

"Oh, it made me feel special, but also spoiled!" Sydney laughs.

They all laugh and smile too as Lucas says, "I promise not to make it a habit, but most definitely on special occasions like this."

"Oh, that's wonderful, Lucas, 'cause I just don't know how much of it I could take if you decided to do that regularly," Sophie says. "Sorry, didn't mean that in a bad way. It's just not what we are used to, but it definitely is different."

"Okay, kids, we are here. Can I get one last picture of all of you before you go in?"

They all agree, and as the girls go get out of the car, Lucas quickly says, "No, let me get your doors, please?" He gets out and quickly gets the girls' doors.

The girls wait till he lets them each out. He opens their door and gives them his hand to pull themselves out.

"Thank you, Lucas," Sydney says as she notices people starting to look their way.

Lucas shuts her door and walks over to get Sophie's door. "Madam, could I please assist you?" He leans in and offers Sophie his hand. She accepts and pulls herself out. He walks her over to Sydney and goes to let Emma out.

Once Emma is out, Lucas goes to stand with the girls. He positions himself between them. Emma gets the picture and says, "I will return later. Have fun kids."

"We will!" They turn to walk inside. Lucas has Sydney on one arm, and Sophie on the other, as they walk into the dance.

Other students are looking and whispering about them. But they keep walking like they don't even see or hear them.

They are dancing and having a great time, with no major issues. As the night goes on and it nears the end of the dance, Lucas dances one slow dance with each of the girls to thank them for a great evening. When the dance is over, they go out and wait for Emma.

When she pulls up, Lucas gets the doors for the girls and they head home.

"Lucas, will your mom be comin' to get you?" Emma asks. "Or would you rather I take you home?"

"Ah, well, I hate to impose, but could you take me home, if that's not too much to ask?"

"No, not a problem at all. I would be happy to take you home."

"Yeah, I would be happy to get rid of me too!" Lucas says, laughing.

"Why would you say that, Lucas? Do you think I am tryin' to get rid of you?"

"No, I was tryin to make a joke. Sorry. I guess it wasn't a good one."

"No apology needed. I understand," Emma says, chuckling.

Emma pulls up to Lucas's home and asks, "You will be comin' to the grand reopenin' tomorrow?"

"Yes, ma'am. Wouldn't miss it for anything. See you beautiful ladies tomorrow."

They both wave as Emma backs out and they pull away.

"Sophie, are you stayin' over tonight? You are more than welcome to."

"Ah, yes, but can we get Eliza too? So she will be with us for tomorrow mornin'."

"Sure. Text your mom, letting her know that we will be stopping to get her, please."

"Okay, consider it done."

Emma gets to Sophie's home in a short few minutes. Eliza is waiting outside for them. When Emma parks, Sophie opens the door and Eliza jumps in.

"Thanks for letting me stay, Em."

"No problem, sweetheart. We just need to get our rest for tomorrow, 'cause it is a big day, and we don't wanna be too sleepy."

"Got it!" She gives Emma a thumbs-up.

When they get to the ranch, they all jump out and go in and get ready for bed.

*****

Buzz buzz. The radio announcer says, "Good mornin', Lexington! What a great mornin' it is! Be sure to stop by Ivy's Boutique. It is a grand reopenin' for them today. So let's get out there and show our support for the Ashcraft family. For those of you who either don't know or are new to our area, Ivy Ashcraft was a pillar in our community. She unfortunately died a tragic death when a drunk driver killed her in a hit-and-run. It was a shock to not only her family but the community as well, and she will be sadly missed, but we can show our support by visitin' her boutique today. In other news, gas..."

Sydney hits the Snooze button and gets teary eyed as she thinks about all that has happened recently, especially since her mom's passing. Today is another huge event that she never planned for this early. It was always stated that she would take over later, when her mom was too old to keep it going. She wipes her eyes and takes in a deep breath as she turns to wake Sophie up.

"Come on, bestie, we have a huge day ahead of us! Let's go get some breakfast." Just as Sydney mentions breakfast, she can smell it. "Speakin' of breakfast..."

"You don't have to tell me twice—I can smell it! Eliza? Eliza! Come on, get up!" Sophie looks over to where Eliza was sleeping, and she's not there. "Where's Eliza?"

"I can bet you that she's already downstairs, eatin' breakfast."

"I bet you are right!" So the girls hurry and get dressed so they can get some breakfast before they have to go to the store all day.

Downstairs, Emma prepares a big breakfast. Eliza is enjoying some French toast when they hear the girls heading down to the kitchen.

"Slow down, girls. One of these days someone is goin' to get hurt, the way you girls come down those stairs."

"Sorry, Em, but we are hungry, and we have a huge day ahead of us, so we don't want to waste any more time."

"Well, I hope you keep that enthusiasm, 'cause it's a lot of work runnin' a business. You have, in my opinion, one of the easiest jobs. Waitin' on customers, stockin' shelves, keeping the place neat and organized. The paperwork end is a bit more challengin'."

"I agree with, Em, but workin' with customers is not always as easy as it sounds. But I think between Sophie, Lucas, Eliza, and I, we should do just fine. We just have to remember that everyone has an opinion and it's not always goin' to be ours. So we just have to listen to their needs and accommodate them to the best of our abilities."

"Well, if you keep up that way of thinkin', I know that you will be just fine. I will always be there in the back office, though, if you need me for anything, and if I can't, your dad should be. Okay, are we almost done and ready to head over to the shop?"

"Yes, ma'am, we are ready. I will message Lucas and just have him meet us there." Sydney messages Lucas while Emma finishes up breakfast.

"I thought I smelled breakfast out here," Parker says as he enters the kitchen.

"Yes, sir. I have a plate fixed for you and Obee. The girls and I are headed to the shop to prepare for the openin'."

"Okay, I will be over a li'l later. Good luck, girls. Make Ivy proud. I love you, Sydney!"

"Thanks! We will do our best, Dad, and I love you too!" Sydney goes to her dad to get a hug before leaving to head to the shop.

As Emma and the girls head out the door, Parker continues to eat and finish his breakfast. Parker looks over on the counter at a picture of Ivy and says out loud to her, "I love you, Ivy! I miss you so much! I wish you could have been here to see Sydney last night. I pray you are with her today as she reopens your shop. I sure hope she makes you proud. I know she will, 'cause she's not just sittin' on her bum, she's out tryin' to make a go at it. I know that always made you proud. I remember you always sayin', 'Well, gettin' out there and tryin' and failin' is better than sittin' on your bum and doin' nothing at all.' I am so glad that Sydney learned that from you. I love you, Ivy Ashcraft!"

Just then, Parker hears something that startles him, and when he turns around, he gets spooked when he sees Obee standing there behind him. "Obee, how long have you been standin' there, listenin' to me?"

"Not long, sir. I just came in."

"Oh, okay. Well, I will be heading to the shop later. You are welcome to ride along if you want."

"Actually, I have a bunch of things to do here, but this is a one-time grand reopenin', so yeah, I will ride along, if I'm not too much of a bother."

"Obee, you are no bother. I would like to go in about an hour or so. Does that work for ya?"

"That's great. I will be ready. Thanks, Parker."

"Yeah, no problem. Emma has a plate of food for ya. Okay, I have a few things to get done too, so see ya in about an hour or so."

"Good deal, Parker!"

In town at Ivy's Boutique, it's almost time to open the doors, and people are already starting to line up outside. The back door buzzer goes off.

"Sophie, that should be Lucas. Can you please go let him in? Thanks!"

"Ten-four, bestie!" Sophie heads for the back door to let Lucas in. "Hey, Lucas, come in. You got here just in time for us to unlock the doors."

"That's great! I was hopin' I would make it in time. Where's Sydney?"

"She's up front."

"Lucas, awesome, you made it in time!" Sydney runs over and gives him a hug. "Okay, so for today I was wonderin' if you would mind handing out these discount flyers as people come in? And then just over here, there is a snack table. Can you just keep an eye out and keep it filled up, please?"

"Sure. Anything you need, I can do. Thanks for letting me join you, ladies."

"Thank you, Lucas, Sophie, and Eliza, for your help. It is very much appreciated. Now, are you all ready for this big, grand openin'?"

They all agree, so Sydney does a countdown to unlocking the doors. "Okay, here we go, in three…two…one, and we are open for business!" As she opens the doors, she makes an announcement to the customers just outside the doors. "Excuse me, please, if I may have your attention. When you come inside, there will be a discount flyer available for today only and one per person, please. So with that said, we would love to welcome you to Ivy's Boutique! Enjoy and thank you for your business!" Sydney steps out of the way and lets the customers in.

"Sophie, can you please cover anyone who needs help, especially out front here? And I will try to get the ones in the back, closer to the register. Good luck, guys!" Sydney walks to the back of the store to the register and watches for anyone who looks as though they may need help, until she gets her first customer.

The day goes so well, and they stay super busy for most of the day. There is about thirty minutes left till they close down for the day. The customers have slowed, and Lucas and Sophie are straightening up the products on the shelves and walls. Sydney prepares the register for the final count of the evening. They hear the bell on the front door. When Sydney looks up, it is her dad. She puts the money in a bank envelope and lays it in on the desk and pulls the door closed. She runs up to her dad and gives him a huge hug.

"Oh, Dad, this was the best day ever! We were so busy." She quietly tries to scream, then she whispers, "We made a lot of money, Dad!"

"Really, my li'l filly? That is amazin'! So how was your team? Did you find any flaws that we can work on to make the customers' experience any better?"

"Parker, I believe it went fairly well for the first day, and I feel we can find more weak spots on a more normal day, once we get open more regularly and we see how things work. If you want, I would be happy to make a suggestion box so customers can express how they feel. Maybe we can, say, like, once a week, we will pull from the box and each person we pull gets a gift certificate to spend right here in our store. Not only do they think that they are gettin' somethin', but we get ideas, whether it is new products or better customer service. Which, to be honest, I feel Sydney did a spectacular job on." Lucas feels eyes searing through him again. "Sophie and Eliza did very well too!"

"Well, Lucas, you did well too! Don't forget yourself," Sophie kindly states.

"Nah, I didn't do anything. You gals put in most of the work and customer service."

"Excuse me, to anyone left in the store, we will be closin' in about five more minutes. Thank you! Please don't rush. I was just lettin' you know that's when we will lock the doors."

"See? She's so amazin'!"

"Lucas, she is your boss. Careful, you don't want to get fired for harassment!" Sophie says as she laughs.

Lucas laughs as he looks away and blushes.

"Oh, Lucas, I wouldn't fire you," Sydney says as she smiles at him.

Sydney sees a customer making their way to the register. "Are you ready to check out?" she asks.

"Yes, ma'am, I am," the elderly lady says.

"I can take you over here on this register. Did you find everything okay?"

"Well, I believe so. I am sorry, I got here a little late, so I didn't get to look around as much as I wanted to, but I will be back another day. Thank you," the elderly lady says.

"Okay, well, till school lets out this summer, we will be open in the late afternoons till the midevenin'. And then we will be open mostly all day on Saturday and Sunday. So we sure hope to see you again soon, ma'am."

"Oh, sweetheart, I will be back. Thank you again. Your store is beautiful." The elderly lady grabs her bag and turns to head for the door.

"Follow me, ma'am. I will let you out the front door. Thank you. Please come again. Have a great evenin'!" Sydney says as she lets the lady out and locks back up. "Okay, can I ask you guys to straighten up and restock while I finish the register's end of the day?"

"Yes, ma'am, I am on it," Lucas says.

"Right behind you, Lucas," Sophie happily responds.

"Can I help too?" Eliza asks.

"Sure, Lizzy. Come help Lucas and me," Sophie tells her.

Once Sydney has the register counted and set up for the next day, she helps finish restocking and taking a small inventory to see if anything needs reordered right away. "Okay, I think we are good! So how about we go out for a celebration dinner again? You all game?"

"Sydney, we can just have a cookout back at the house, if that's okay with you?" Emma suggests.

"Well, I mean, it's okay with me. How about everyone else? What do y'all think?"

"Yep, sounds great!" Lucas says.

"Same for Lizzy and me!"

"Yeah, I think it will be good," Parker says.

As everyone goes to the back door to leave, Lucas lingers back a little bit. Sydney notices and walks over to him. "Hey, you okay?"

"Yeah, I just had something I wanted to talk to you about."

"Oh, okay. Well, let's chat. We got a few minutes."

"Not here, Sydney. Maybe back at the ranch?"

"Oh, okay, no problem. That sounds like a deal. Okay, but for now, we need to hurry and get back to the ranch, because I am famished!" She gets Lucas and everyone out of the shop and locks up. They get in the cars and head off for the ranch.

Acknowledgments

Many thanks to the following:

I had always wanted to write a book but just could not get it done. Well, here is my first novel, and writing this was like words falling like a waterfall from my brain to my fingertips. There were people who stood beside me for the whole process that I would love to thank. Because with them it made the whole process much better. (My list of names is in no particular order. I also hope I do not miss anyone, and if I do, I am totally sorry.)

I would like to thank my hubby and better half, Allen, for putting up with the few weeks of complete silence because I was so dedicated to writing and getting my words written down—any chance I could get, I was on it! In some ways, I am so sure that he secretly loved the silence from my motor mouth, but he knew it was for a chance of a lifetime to get my first novel written and ready for print. I love you so much for all the understanding and sacrifices you made for the time I was with you but was silent. I really wasn't ignoring you, sweetheart. You are the best thing that has ever happened to me!

Next, I would like to thank my best friend, Darlene! She has been the greatest best friend anyone could ever ask for! She was the first to read my book, and she has helped me throughout my thought process. When I needed some suggestions on certain parts in the book, she gave her input and helped me work through it. So thank you from the bottom of my heart, bestie!

I would also like to thank my family, who gave me confidence to push on and keep motivated. So thank you, Brittany, Kristina, Marsha, Lily, Mark, Tesa, Mark, Brandon, and Amber!

I would also like to thank my other friends who either read my book, made editing suggestions, or just gave me good vibes to push on. Thank you to Stephani and Dave, Gigi, Linda, Kelly and Zach, Monica, Mike, Patty, Todd, and many more from Facebook!

I would also love to thank my friend and author Sabrina Burkins! Because if it waeren't for her writing her first book of three in her series Her Secret Is His Desire and me supporting her by reading hers, I might not have written mine as soon as I did. Also, thank you for the information that got me to, in my opinion, the best publishing company out there!

Thank you to Lisa, my LDA, for hanging in there with me while I messed around, trying to come up with a title and to get through my life issues in order to get my story to where I deemed it good enough for publishing. She seemed as excited as I was when I finally got it turned in for approval. So thank you! You are the best! Can't wait to do more books with you!

Thank you to Liz, my publication assistant, and to my publishing team for all the great work you did! I appreciate everything you did for me, because even if I wrote the story, without you all, I wouldn't have this amazing novel to share with the world! Thank you so very much!

Last but not the least, I would love to thank Tonda, my mother-in-law in heaven, for her words of encouragement and enthusiasm. She read as much of my book, as I was writing it, as she could before she passed away from angiosarcoma on June 11, 2021. Thank you again, Mom! You will be dearly missed.

About the Author

Susie Wright has been married twenty-four years to her wonderful husband, Allen. Brandon, Amber, Kristina, and Brittany are their bright and amazing adult children, who they love very much. They love doing things as a family whenever possible. They love the outdoors, crabbing and fishing, boating and kayaking, beaching and looking for unique and beautiful shells and shark teeth, and riding trails at ATV parks to see how far they can push their luck on steep hills and mud bogs. Susie and Allen enjoy doing everything all the time they can together and with family. She also loves photography and has been known to take way more pictures than needed just to get the right one.

Susie's current hometown is Brogue, Pennsylvania, but she grew up in Gettysburg, Pennsylvania. She attended Biglerville High School of the Upper Adams School District. Marsha is her only living parent. Her father passed away when she was thirty-five. She has one younger brother, Ronnie.

Susie is an animal lover. Her family had a Shetland pony that was given to them in the early eighties, when she was in elementary school. She loved Rusty till the day he passed during spring her seventh-grade school year. She currently has a chihuahua named Jake. With Allen's help, they have had many fish aquariums over the years. Her favorite is saltwater. It's so relaxing watching all the little critters you can find in the rocks, especially at night. Her favorite are the brittle stars.

Susie's hobbies include crafting with leather, wood, shells, and other miscellaneous items. She loves metal detecting, painting, dabbling in new things, and she takes pride in everything she does.

Susie and Allen also love to just drive around and see the sights God has given us all. Recently, they have decided to put all their faith in God to work and made a major life change. They quit their careers, where they worked at together, to team-drive a truck together. Why not see the country and get paid to do it?

Military has been on her mother's side of the family. Now it is being continued within her immediate family as well. Her youngest, Brittany, is part of the US Navy. Susie is very proud of her family and all their accomplishments.

She thanks God every day for all she has because "with God's love, anything is possible" (Matthew 19:26).

Please follow along on Facebook for Susies other outstanding books: Author page for all my books: https://www.facebook.com/SusieWrightAuthor/ My group page for the Sydney's Passion series: https://www.facebook.com/groups/4474219465968140/?ref=share_group_link

CPSIA information can be obtained
at www.ICGtesting.com
Printed in the USA
BVHW050525160922
646950BV00001B/4